To Emily, who started our family's rescue dog journey

To Ryan, for always, always believing

A NEW LEASH ON LOVE

❧ A RESCUE ME NOVEL ❧

DEBBIE BURNS

sourcebooks
casablanca

Published by Sourcebooks Casablanca, an imprint of Sourcebooks, Inc.
P.O. Box 4410, Naperville, Illinois 60567-4410
(630) 961-3900
Fax: (630) 961-2168
www.sourcebooks.com

Printed and bound in Canada.
MBP 10 9 8 7 6 5 4 3 2 1

Chapter 1

THERE WERE A DOZEN REASONS NOT TO PICK UP BERNIE'S call. He only called for one thing. And try as she might, she'd never been able to tell him no.

Today of all days, Megan didn't have the time for him. When his call came, she was pulling into the parking lot at the High Grove Animal Shelter, ready to start a cram-packed day that would likely be cut short by the massive front of freezing rain passing overhead. Saying yes to Bernie would cost her.

She berated herself for answering, for agreeing, for jotting down his location and heading off to meet him instead of taking charge of her own day. He was a good twenty minutes away, and icy patches were beginning to form on the heavily salted roads.

This morning, Bernie was in a part of St. Louis where Megan had never been, a residential area north of downtown. Imposingly tall but narrow redbrick houses spanned several blocks. They were old homes—she was willing to bet a century, at least—and some were in better shape than others. The one Bernie's truck was parked in front of showed obvious signs of neglect in patches of crumbling brick, broken concrete steps, and a mangled metal fence that had collapsed along one side of the house.

The street was practically empty. Megan pulled in behind the city animal control van where Bernie was holed up. She stepped out and reached into the back of her car for her coat. The rain was coming down heavier. If predictions were correct, there'd be nearly an inch of ice covering everything tomorrow.

Bernie joined her, hitching up a pair of cargo pants that sagged under the weight of his belly. "It's those eyes that are going to melt you," he said. "Warm, brown, and super smart. Like you've never seen."

Megan shook her head, unable to suppress a smile. "I should turn on my voice recorder app," she teased. "Then next time you call, I'll prove you say the same thing every time."

"I'm not denying I've said it before. But this guy is different. You'll see." He threw an arm over her shoulder and pulled her in for a hug. "How've you been, kid?"

"Pretty good. Money-wise, things are really tight at the shelter. There's been one big expense after another with the heat going out and that problem with the circuit breaker. We've had some great adoption matchups though. Remember that Yorkie? The one the Macy's employee found when he heard her barking in one of the purses in a mound of other purses?"

"Yeah," Bernie said, chuckling.

"Well, she went to an awesome home. You won't believe this, but her new owner makes her own line of designer purses. The woman saw her on Facebook and drove in from Ohio to get her. The Yorkie is going to be her company mascot. That little face is already all over the designer's Facebook and website. It's so cute. Oh, and remember the Rhodesian ridgeback no one had the energy for? Last Saturday, he went to a marathon runner who was looking for a running companion."

"That's nice. I'm guessing those'll make your newsletter? It's the one newsletter I always open, since I know the only stories you publish are ones with happy endings." From the pocket of his coat, Bernie's phone rang out. He glanced at the screen, silenced the phone, and frowned. "You aren't going to like this, but I'm going to have to run. Not ten minutes after I called you, I got a call from my boss. Looks like his mother-in-law has a family of raccoons holing up in her chimney, probably to weather out this storm. You know I could use getting in good with him, considering how things have been lately. But you'll be able to handle this guy, no problem. Like I said, he's as smart as they come."

"Where is he?" She scanned the front porch and windows. No dogs were in sight.

"Around back. Chained up. I'd have saved you the trouble of unchaining him, but I phoned in that he was already taken away by a friend of the owner. Can't risk someone seeing me with him and then not bringing him in. You understand, don't you, kid?"

"Yeah, I do." Bernie worked for the city animal control department. He was old enough to retire, but a few years ago, his daughter had moved back in, along with her rambunctious triplets. He needed the salary, benefits' package, and pension that came with his position, even if his big heart left him better suited for a job at an adoption shelter like hers whose mission was finding forever homes for four-legged friends.

"The woman's inside." He ran a hand, freckled with age spots, down the length of his coat zipper. "She's terrified of dogs, and she's, uh, not in the space to keep him. The shepherd was her son's. He was called back for active duty. Some neighbors complained about the dog's living conditions. The woman was served a notice ten days ago. She's been looking for someone to take him but hasn't had any luck."

"How…" She started to ask how bad off the dog was, but stopped. She'd see soon enough.

"He doesn't look mistreated," Bernie replied, picking up on her thoughts. "She's been feeding him. Just can't do more than that. From what the neighbors shared, he's got no history of aggression."

"You have an extra leash?" she asked.

"Always." He popped open the van's back door. It was cluttered with cages, nets, cheap nylon leashes, and long metal poles with corded nooses at the end. There was a large, fat possum in one cage. It blinked its small eyes, unaccustomed to the light.

Megan took the leash Bernie handed her and tucked a strand of hair behind her ear. "She's good with me coming onto her property, right?"

"Yeah. I told her you were taking him, and she said you were a blessed angel. She's good with it."

"Okay. Hey, I'd better get moving." She stepped in for a hug, his belly pressing against her. "Be good, kid. We'll catch up soon. I'll swing by and take you to lunch. Shoot, I said that last time and I haven't yet. But I'm good for it. Promise."

He hopped into his van, and Megan headed for the side yard. The gate was so crooked it was stuck in the ground, and a thin glaze of ice was forming over it. Rather than mess with it, she walked alongside the neighboring yard to the spot where the fence had collapsed and crossed over the slippery chain link.

The backyard was long and rectangular. A tired privacy fence blocked the view of the alley behind the house. The dog, a German shepherd, was in the far corner, chained to a pole. She knew exactly how far the chain reached, because inside that distance, the grass had died off and there was only mud. Near where he was lying were four overturned bowls, and the ground was pocked with small patches of water ringed by ice.

There was a dilapidated doghouse within his reach. But it would be a snug fit for a dog his size, and Megan suspected it hadn't kept the rain out for a long time. The most inviting thing in the area was a massive old tree that would shade the whole yard in summer.

Surveying the scene from fifty feet away, she could feel the judgment sliding in. She did her best to shake it off. The dog was dirty and wet and chained up, but he looked healthy enough. And German shepherds were bred to handle the cold. *Only, looking at all that fur, could you really tell if he wasn't being fed?*

Her fingers were starting to shake, and her chest was tight. She wasn't meant for this sort of thing. She took these cases too personally.

Plus Wes, the founder of the shelter, was always reading her the riot act over helping Bernie. But there was no use deceiving herself. She'd always take Bernie's call. Wes never got that mad, and as rough as these experiences were, they'd also made a big difference in the animals' lives.

The dog was awake and watching her but not barking. When she closed the distance to twenty feet, just a few feet beyond the reach of his chain, he lifted his head off the ground to stare at her intently.

She could tell from the footprints Bernie had left that he'd only made it a step or two farther. He'd made his assessment about the watchful shepherd from this distance.

Megan paused to study the dog at the outer reach of the chain. He wasn't barking or growling or acting territorial in the slightest. He simply watched her. Bernie was right. His eyes were big and brown and intelligent. And, judging by the way his eyebrows drew up into peaks as he stared, sad looking.

"How long have you been here, buddy?"

She walked forward purposefully. Showing fear or hesitation could be a mistake around a dog that hadn't been socialized in a while. Rather than stare, she kept her gaze locked on the ground halfway between them. The only visible footprints in the mud belonged to him. How long had it been since anyone had handled him?

She talked, keeping her voice low and steady. He rose to his feet and lowered his head when she was a body length away. "It's all right, boy."

She said the words over and over. Her heart was thumping, and her palms were sweating. He was a big male with powerful features. She'd put money down he wasn't neutered.

"How'd you like to get out of here?" She fished into her jacket pocket for the treats she always had with her. Keeping her movements slow and deliberate, she offered one in his direction.

He didn't move.

The suspense wearing on her, she made eye contact. He was watching her intently, his tail neither tucked nor erect. His lips weren't curled back in warning, but his mouth wasn't relaxed either.

He was waiting for something. He was watching her and waiting for something. But what? What would a chained-up, neglected dog be waiting for?

For permission, she realized, a chill rushing over her.

She made a kissing sound and sank into a squat, balancing on the balls of her feet. Obediently, he walked her way. He smelled awful—wet dog at its worst. He sniffed her face, her hair, and the fingers of her open hand. Then, with a quick lick, the treat disappeared from her palm.

Megan felt tears sting her eyes. Someone, either the soldier or someone before him, had put a great deal of care and training into this animal. Still in a squat, she reached out to touch him, attempting to keep her knees off the ground so her jeans wouldn't get saturated in the same winter mud that was trying to soak into her shoes.

His fur was wet and partially frozen at the tips. Lower down, closer to the base, it was warm and dry. She burrowed her fingers into the mane-like mass at his neck and spoke to him. Then in the time it took her to blink, there was a flash of pointy white, and his mouth was wrapped around her wrist.

She gasped and waited for the sinking of those massive teeth into her flesh, but it didn't come. His tongue pulsed rhythmically against the inside of her wrist. Affectionately. A wave of relief swept over her. It was the way some dogs expressed trust.

"Attaboy." She extracted her arm and moved his collar around so she could see the chain. The clip was rusted shut. Maybe it'd be easier to unhook the opposite end at the pole and take the whole chain.

Or she could get him out of that mud-encrusted collar. She brushed away some mud, inspecting it. It was thick, weathered leather. There was writing carved into the side at sharp angles. She wiped mud away until she could read it. Sledge.

"Sledge. Is that your name?"

There was a flash of pink, and his tongue brushed her nose. She laughed, and he wagged his tail.

"Sledge. You're such a tank that it fits you. Let's get you out of here. The shelter's no Hyatt hotel, but I don't think you'll complain."

It took her fingertips growing numb, but she was able to unhook the cold, wet collar and drape Bernie's nylon slipknot leash over the shepherd's head. She broke the final treat into two pieces and gave him one when he started following her.

He was hesitant to cross over the fallen chain link, but relented after a bit of cajoling. The front door opened as they walked into view. A woman crossed the covered porch, holding out a brown-paper sack in offering. She was wearing a purple jogging suit that complemented her mocha skin. The pink scarf wrapped around her head was all it took for Megan to let go of the anger sliding up her throat. This woman had sent a son off to active duty and was battling cancer.

"You aren't the first angel I've come across, but you're an angel all the same. I've been praying on this something fierce. And here you are, taking him before the worst of the storm."

Megan ran her tongue over suddenly dry lips. What on earth was she supposed to say to her? "Thank you." The only other thing racing to her mind was business. "I was wondering if your son had any of the dog's paperwork? Any record of shots or registration?"

"I'd be surprised if he had gotten any. Antonne brought the dog home because he didn't think he was being treated well."

"Do you, um, know where your son got him?"

"Lord only knows. He just came home with him one morning. That was back in June, a few months after Antonne came home from his first tour." She shook her head, eyeing Sledge like he might jump up onto the porch. "It don't make sense, but I'm more afraid of dogs than anything."

Megan was at a loss for words. Beside her, Sledge stood patiently, studying the world around him.

The woman leaned over the porch railing and waved the paper bag in Megan's direction. "So hopefully you'll forgive me for not coming down. I made muffins this morning. Banana nut. My specialty. Once you get where you're going, why don't you make yourself a cup of coffee and have one?"

Megan reached up for the bag, and her frozen fingers locked over the top. Her chin was starting to wobble, and she knew it was from more than the bitter temperature and soaking rain.

The best thing she could do for this woman tugging at her heartstrings was thank her and take the dog off her hands. "I'll, uh, I'll make sure we find him a good home."

"I thank you, honey." The woman reached up to adjust her head scarf. "It'll be one less thing to pray over."

With nothing else to say, Megan led Sledge to the car.

Craig Williams had few memories of his grandfather that didn't involve the front porch of his modest, well-kept home and the stiff rocking chair where he sat in the evenings and mornings, and a bit of the afternoons too. Back when Craig was a kid, his grandfather's ability to sit and reflect was unfathomable. As was his dad's random comment one summer evening as they headed to the car and then back to the bustle of life that somehow didn't pervade his grandparent's quarter acre of ground. "The older I get, the more appealing it is to know someday that'll be me," Craig's dad had said. "One day, all my big decisions will have been made. And all the wrong ones will be water under the bridge."

His dad might as well have been speaking Latin. Back then, sitting still was Craig's biggest torture. Reflection was for dreaming and when your mind stripped the important from the not-so-important and sent them off to different places like a sorting machine. Perhaps because he'd been so full of silent disagreement, Craig had committed those words to memory and mulled them over every so often, remembering but never understanding.

Now, at thirty-five, those words came to mind again. For the first time, Craig felt a tired wistfulness from deep in his gut rise up in agreement. Someday, he'd be finished making mistakes. Someday, he'd embrace more reflection than action.

Just not today.

He punched in the door code to the sprawling home that had been his the last eight years but was now about to be listed for sale. The door swung open. Instead of going in, Craig studied the outside entryway. The tall columns and imposing portico didn't suit a rocking chair. The massive urns and topiaries looked like watchmen at the column's sides, standing guard over a wide lawn that had been more formal than playground these last few years.

This was never intended to be a home for quiet reflection. It was meant to provide all the spaces a bustling family of five would ever need—and arguably a few spaces they didn't. Who needed dedicated spots for crafts, gaming, movies, exercise, and meditation? Whatever happened to simple finished basements and all-purpose rooms?

Well, there was no need to argue over what constituted a waste of space any longer. No need to argue over anything. Jillian, Sophie, and Reese would live here until the house sold. Jillian had her eye on half a dozen smaller homes nearby. He'd stay holed up in the corporate apartment he'd rented until at least something in life made sense again.

Inside, the house was unnaturally quiet. He couldn't remember the last time he'd been alone here. It was silent and expansive and reminded him of a cave. No wonder Jillian always had something calming from Pandora playing over the speakers.

Sophie's and Reese's schedules required them to be out all afternoon, which was why he'd been asked to come to do it today. Though with the storm blowing in, if Jillian had any say-so, she'd cut the day short before the roads got messy. She hated driving in bad weather.

From across the room, there was a jostling and an almost inaudible yawn. His gaze flicked to the crate and the brown, silky ball curled in its corner.

"Give me a few minutes before you get antsy, little guy. There are a few things I need to grab."

The puppy dragged one paw against the crate door

but allowed his head to sink back to the fuzzy bed he was curled up on. The little guy kept one eye open, focused on Craig in a way he couldn't help but feel was suspicious. As if he knew why Craig had come today.

Craig headed to the study, his gaze landing on the impressive wall of refurbished walnut bookshelves that flanked the far side. They were imported from Florence, from a mid-nineteenth-century hotel that had been torn down on Via del Parione. They were adorned with impressive hand-carved appliqués and were the thing he'd miss most about the house.

He was surprised how many framed pictures still adorned the shelves. He almost never even glanced at them anymore, but today he allowed himself to take them in, to feel the wild mix of pleasure and pain they stirred awake. Sophie and the twins. Always smiling. Always laughing. Always playing. Pumpkin patches, Christmas tree lots, school plays, sandy beaches, snow-covered mountains. The real estate agent had asked Jillian to take them down before the house went on the market. Buyers needed to notice those shelves, he'd said, not be distracted by their beautiful family.

Family. The word reverberated through Craig's head. Sophie and Reese hardly resembled the happy, carefree kids in those photos. He hadn't thought of it until now, but they'd all but stopped taking pictures during the last three years. Who wanted to sit for photos now? They'd gone from a family of five to a family of four to not even a family at all.

Releasing a deep breath, Craig headed over to his desk. The puppy's paperwork was on top as promised. Just as he was picking it up, the sound of a door opening and shutting broke the silence. It came from the direction of the kitchen and was followed by a familiar shuffling.

Inez, their housekeeper. He'd know the sound of her walk anywhere.

Back before their world fell apart, he used to like listening to her move about, shuffling as she went. She was short, under five feet, but not overweight enough to warrant all that shuffling.

Taking the paperwork, he headed for the kitchen. She was slipping out of her coat, and an overnight bag was on the floor beside her. He didn't need clarification of why she'd come on a Sunday afternoon. She'd driven in now to avoid the worst of the storm. Jillian would happily give her a day or two off, but that wasn't Inez's way. She'd stay over in bad weather rather than risk not being able to drive in. She simply wouldn't miss work unless there was no way she could avoid it.

"Inez, good to see you." He nodded and slipped his hands into his pockets after dropping the paperwork on the counter.

"I heard you were coming today, Mr. Williams. It's been an awful go with the puppy the last few weeks."

"So I've heard. Soph's called me in tears a few times."

Inez hung up her coat and tucked her bag in the mud-room closet before joining him in the kitchen. "In the long run, it'll be for the best."

"So Jillian assures me."

"Can I fix you something to eat, Mr. Williams? Something warm before you head out into this weather."

"No. Thanks though. I should be out of here before they get back. Jillian thinks it'll be easiest on Soph not to see him leave."

"How about something simple? It doesn't look as if you've been eating well."

He sank against the granite countertop and wrapped his hands around the beveled edge. "I won't starve."

"No, but not eating and not sleeping takes its toll," Inez said, pulling out a frying pan from one of the bottom drawers. "I haven't seen you looking so poorly since..."

As her words trailed off, she stood straight and smoothed out the front of her crisp blouse. "I will make you some eggs, Mr. Williams. You always like them. And some coffee too."

"Thank you, Inez." He knew better than to argue with her over a meal. He crossed to the island and splayed his palms on the cool granite, wishing it was cold enough to sink in and quiet his insides.

Inez's unfinished sentence rang in his ears, burning them, and making his throat and neck feel as if they were on fire. *Since Andrew died.* Three little words that were never spoken. They were tucked up and put away alongside feelings that were never felt.

"If you are changing your mind, it is never too late to try again."

He pressed his thumb and forefinger over the bridge of his nose. "It's been too late for a few years now, Inez." When she stayed silent, he added, "It's just going to be rough during the transition. It'll be better on the kids in the long run."

Who was he reassuring, Inez or himself?

Inez pursed her lips but remained quiet as she cracked an egg over the frying pan. He'd expected her to disapprove of the divorce. She was a devout Catholic, and she loved Reese and Sophie like her own.

"Have you decided where to take the puppy?" she asked when she broke the silence.

The anxiety curdling in his stomach seemed to bubble. Try as he might to stop it, their wake of destruction was still growing. "No. Jillian gave me a list of acceptable shelters. Any preference?"

"When my son had to get rid of his Rottweiler," Inez continued, "he took him to a nice shelter in Webster Groves. He said it was a happy place. My heart tells me you should take the puppy there."

"All right." He sighed. It seemed the puppy was just one more thing getting trampled in this divorce.

As if on cue, the puppy began to whine from the adjacent room.

Inez cracked a second egg as the smell of frying butter filled the room. "It's been a few hours since he's been out of his cage. He might have to make water."

"From what I've heard, he does that *in* the cage, doesn't he?" Craig said, even though he stood up to take the dog out.

Inez nodded approvingly as he turned to go. "I'll keep your eggs hot for you, Mr. Williams."

Craig walked into the family room, unhooked the cage door, and caught the mass of silky brown fur bounding out like he was catching a pass in football. It wiggled and squirmed, whipping its head back and forth in an attempt to latch its razor-sharp baby teeth into anything it could grasp.

The puppy caught his shirtsleeve and began gnawing away. Craig extracted his sleeve as he headed outside. He was surprised by a blast of freezing rain stinging his face. So the storm was picking up.

Lowering the puppy to the ground, he watched it squirm down the slippery steps and tear around the yard as if it were a lit firecracker, yapping and bounding all the way. The pup's unbridled joy brought forth a rush of memories.

How many times had he stood here over the years, watching his kids play in the yard, pulling wagons, tossing balls, blowing bubbles? How many times had he chased them around, roaring as they screamed in delight?

The puppy continued to run back and forth and chase its tail. It was a shame they couldn't have gotten him years ago when his joy and wildness would've blended right in.

Craig turned his face toward the blanket of leaden clouds and sucked a breath deep into his lungs. It numbed his insides a bit, but not as much as he'd hoped. The bitter-cold rain pricked his cheeks, ran down his neck, and soaked into his shirt.

"Sorry, pup, you're a day late and a dollar short for this family."

Chapter 2

IT WOULD TAKE MORE THAN ONE BATH TO RID SLEDGE OF HIS smell. Megan could only hope it wouldn't linger in her car. By the time they reached the shelter, she was fairly certain it had seeped through the blanket she'd tossed over the backseat and into the fabric. It wasn't the first time since buying her RAV4 that she wished she'd gone for the leather package. But the shelter operated on a shoestring budget. With her salary, leather was too much of a luxury.

It took close to an hour and what felt like a game of musical chairs to get Sledge set up. He'd be in quarantine a few days, and tomorrow, a Monday, she'd call Dr. Washington to schedule an exam and Sledge's neutering. It was the shelter's policy, ensuring that all animals they adopted out were spayed or neutered.

Images from the morning flashed through Megan's mind as she worked, cleaning the other kennels in quarantine. She was bending over a bucket of bleach water when Patrick tapped on her back.

"I just made five dollars, Megan. Five dollars off old Marv."

She stood, wiping her hands on the back of her jeans. "How?" She moved to the side a foot as she turned, knowing he'd be right behind her. He stood close to everyone he trusted, and avoided people he didn't like the plague.

Patrick had Asperger's and was hands-down the shelter's most unusual employee. With things that piqued his interest, his memory was infallible. This included the shelter animals that came and went, baseball stats, and all things chess. He also understood the unspoken language of animals better than anyone Megan had ever met.

"We're getting our first Christmas puppy," he answered. "Marv thought we wouldn't get one until next week. But a mean-looking fellow just came in with one."

Her heart sank. She'd almost forgotten it was the time of year—nearly the middle of February—that was notorious for failed-Christmas-puppy surrenders. But they barely had room for Sledge. They couldn't make room for another dog today. It was a reality they faced as a no-kill shelter. They'd fill up and stagnate until adoptions picked up.

"It's that kind of day, isn't it?" She squeezed Patrick on the shoulder.

"It's a Lab too. A chocolate one. Last year, the first three Christmas puppies were Labs. But the first two were yellow…"

"Patrick," she interrupted. He'd go on and on unless she stopped him. "Did you send him on? Did you tell him we don't have any room?"

"Yes."

"Good." She reached into the bucket for the rag and started to wring it out. But Patrick didn't leave. He hovered expectantly. Twisting the rag, she stood back up. "Is there anything else?"

"Marv called every place on our list, and the only

other shelter that's open in the storm is in North County. Marv whispered that he doesn't think the man will drive that far. He thinks he's a dumper."

She dropped the rag into the bucket and let out a sigh. "Marv worries that everyone we send away might be a dumper. Let me guess. Since we're out of kennels, he thinks we should use one of the big travel crates for a few days." It wasn't ideal, but they'd done it before in a pinch.

"We have four that could work. If you don't take height into account, the large crates are only six square inches smaller than the small kennels."

It wasn't something they could make a habit of, but there was a terrible storm raging outside. And with any luck, they'd get the puppy adopted or into a foster home in the next few days. In case Marv was right, they should take the puppy. If the man was in fact a dumper, the poor thing could freeze to death in this storm before anyone found it.

Megan wished Kelsey hadn't called in sick and was here to do the required paperwork. She felt like hiding out in back and avoiding anyone else today. Her nerves were just plain frayed. She'd nearly wiped out on the slick roads on the way back from picking up Sledge. Then she'd opened the mail from yesterday and discovered the electrician's repair bill was twice as much as they'd been expecting.

But if someone was here with an animal, she couldn't just hide out. Kelsey was out, Marv was a volunteer, and Patrick didn't have the people skills to get all the information they needed.

Patrick was still talking about crate dimensions as

they headed through the glass doors into the main building. The man was standing near the front by the gift shop, holding the puppy. She lost a beat in her stride as she took him in. Patrick had said mean-looking, not trip-on-your-tongue striking.

Her best friend, Ashley, was always telling Megan that lingering fears from her former failed engagement had stripped her of her ability to find men attractive. But not him. He was undeniably gorgeous. And well dressed, though she knew very little about high-end men's clothing. And fit. Very fit. Clearly. Even underneath a long, tailored coat.

And tucked in his ogle-worthy arms was a round and fuzzy—perfect—chocolate Lab puppy.

She glanced out the wide front windows. There, parked in front of the door, was a large silver Bimmer. Of course he was rich. What else would someone who looked like him be?

The judgmental side of herself—her abiding sin—reared its ugly head with full force. She wondered if he was here on behalf of a child who'd decided Christmas puppies chewed too much on other Christmas toys or a wife who'd decided Christmas puppies pooped and peed too many times where they shouldn't.

She sucked in a breath, attempting to rein in her feelings. Whatever the reason, it didn't matter. There was a storm raging overhead, and this puppy needed shelter. It was so cute that they'd no doubt find it a home quickly and easily. A forever home.

She reminded herself that for every bad news story, there was a good one. A plus for every minus. It was something she repeated over and over in moments like this. Moments when she knew she'd have to reach deep to keep her composure.

Seconds passed, and no one said anything. Even Patrick stopped talking. In the ominous silence, Megan reminded herself she was the boss. The onus was on her to talk, to welcome this man, this holder of the first Christmas puppy.

But she couldn't make herself do it.

Maybe if it'd been someone else. Someone not struggling with so much perfection.

The one to break the silence was Marv, good old Marv, who was puttering in the gift shop. "Think we can squeeze the puppy in, Megan?"

The puppy was squirming in the stranger's arms, full of energy and wanting to play.

Finally, Megan found her voice. "I think we can make it work." She motioned toward one of the tattered adoption-and-surrender desks in the middle of the room. "Have a seat over there. I'll be with you in a minute."

———∿∿∿———

Craig sank into the worn plastic chair where he'd been directed and tried, but failed, to calm the brown wiggling ball on his lap. He watched the girl walk into a cramped office and sift through a filing cabinet.

Her faded jeans were soaked from the knee down, and she smelled of bleach when she passed by. She had chestnut-brown hair knotted into a messy ball at the back of her head. Wisps had fallen loose in places, clinging to her face and neck like a silken frame for an exceptionally pretty face. She had it all. Smoky-green eyes, full lips, good skin, and a body he had to force his gaze not to linger on.

Although she'd caught him off guard, he wasn't in the space to be looking at a woman. Not now. Besides, he hadn't missed the disdainful way she'd dissected him. And he'd overheard that strange guy's comment through the closed doors. The old man thought he was a dog dumper.

The thought had ruffled his pride enough that he'd considered walking out with the little menace in his arms. But the only other open shelter would be an agonizing drive in this mess. And Sophie had prepared herself for the puppy being gone when she got home today. Waiting another few days would only make it harder for her.

The girl—Megan Anderson was her name, Marv had told him—returned and sat down at the desk opposite him, offering a smile that didn't reach her eyes.

"You'll have to excuse me," she said, scooting her chair in. "Our adoption coordinator is out for the day. I don't usually work with surrenders."

Surrenders. The word came out sounding very much like *lepers.*

"Or adopters either," she added, perhaps realizing how harsh she'd sounded.

He said nothing in return and tried not to wince as the puppy's sharp milk teeth sank into his hand. She noticed, pursed her lips in thought, then disappeared into the office another second.

"This might help." She passed a worn rope over the desk. "Puppies have an insatiable need to chew."

Amiable, Craig. Be amiable and get through this. "I've noticed that with this one."

"It's because he's teething. They tend to be over the worst of it by the time they're six months."

Craig clamped his jaw tight. He could feel the inevitable sales pitch coming on. Damn it for not trying harder to get Inez to do this. Whether she was pretty or not, he couldn't handle this girl's attitude. Not today. Not when everything in his world had closed in so tightly.

The girl glanced up and made genuine eye contact with him for the first time. She did an obvious double take, then shifted in her seat and cleared her throat. "We have some forms and a short questionnaire. And there's a seventy-five-dollar surrender fee."

"Fine."

She fidgeted with her papers and chewed on her lower lip—a particularly full lower lip—before speaking. "We pride ourselves on being a very special shelter. We do our best to offer every animal we house exceptional care. Because of this, we have to limit the number of animals we take in. And we like to start by asking if you've tried everything possible to make your relationship with this puppy work. There are dozens of skilled trainers out there that we could refer you to. There are even places where you can board him or her while—"

"Please," Craig said, holding up a hand to stop her. "There's nothing you can say or do to convince me to keep him. There are extenuating circumstances, and this is my only option, so let's cut to the chase. Will you take him or not?"

He watched her mouth fall open an inch or two. The smooth skin of her cheeks blushed pink. Her fingers drummed on the desktop. She started to speak, stopped, and started again.

"Our recommended legal care limit is seventy-five animals. Yesterday when I left, we had fifty-three dogs, eighteen cats, and six rabbits. This meant we were over the limit by two. With your puppy and the dog I brought in this morning, we're—" She stopped abruptly and gave a little shake of her head. "It's not like you care."

Who was she to presume what he cared about? Craig felt the adrenaline surging through his veins, readying him for a fight. And he could fight with the best of them. Just not right now. And not with this pretty, impassioned girl who reminded him of a someday Sophie. Whether he liked it or not, his daughter was going to grow up to be all heart, just like this Megan woman was.

Gathering the puppy in his arms, he stood up from the desk. "This is unbelievable." He'd sneak the little devil into his no-pets apartment tonight and find another shelter in the morning.

Feeling the frustration knotting her belly switch to worry, Megan jogged after him. In case Marv was right, she couldn't let him leave.

She caught up with him as he reached the door. "Listen, sir, we'll take your puppy provided you fill out the questionnaire and pay the required fees."

The man's shoulders dropped, and he turned to face her. She noticed his clenched jaw by the defined muscles highlighting his cheekbones.

He turned to Marv, who was standing at the nearest clothing rack pretending to organize the T-shirts while he eavesdropped. "Is there someone else I could work with?"

It felt like a slap in the face. Had she really been that offensive? Marv looked at her and offered a helpless shrug.

"Not today, unfortunately," Megan said. Then realizing how much it sounded like a slam, she spurted out something about the lead adoption coordinator being sick.

With a shake of his head, Craig followed her to the desk. "What questions do you have?"

Suspecting she was treading on thin ice, Megan sank into her seat and rolled her pen between two fingers. "Just a few to help us find him a new home."

He readjusted the puppy as he sat down. It rested its head in his elbow, its small blue-brown eyes watching her from across the desk.

Looking up from the puppy and directly at the man, Megan felt heat flash up her neck. She couldn't remember the last time she'd felt this unsettled. If only he wasn't so good-looking. Or if he had a blemish she could focus on. A large, hairy wart. An exceptionally weak chin. A long, black hair sliding out of his nose. Something—anything—besides eyes as deep blue as the seas off the Maldives and features chiseled to perfection.

His hair was dark blond. That was something. She preferred men with darker hair.

She did her best to pay attention to the questions in the paperwork in front of her. But on top of his looks, there was his anger. Those remarkable eyes were shooting venom-crusted daggers at her.

"His or her name to start with," she said. Her voice sounded smaller than she wanted it to. She sat straighter and arched her back, then wished she hadn't because he'd probably think she was trying to draw attention to her boobs. With looks like his, those clothes, and that car, she bet women were always throwing themselves at him.

He blinked and glanced down at the dog. "His. They were having a hard time deciding on one. I can't remember what they finally decided. And I can't see how that matters."

Try as she might, Megan couldn't not respond. "Dogs are intelligent, social animals. And they're quick to learn their names. His might be of some comfort if he hears it in this unfamiliar place. Names also help our customers identify with these animals as individuals."

"Hershey," he said after a delayed silence. "I'm pretty sure they'd decided on Hershey."

"Okay, Hershey it is. Do you have any idea how old he is?"

"They got him about ten days before Christmas. I think he was six weeks old at the time. I left his papers in the car."

"He's registered then?"

"Yes."

Megan nodded. Hershey would be adopted way before Sledge, no question. Unlike full-grown German shepherds with unknown histories, purebred Labs a few months old were always in demand. She could tell the man this to ease his conscience—something she pretty much doubted he had—but opted not to.

"Has he had regular veterinary exams?"

"Yes. I have those records in the car as well."

"Good." Why couldn't Kelsey be here? She did such a better job at this. Megan's notes looked like chicken scratches dotting the page. *Cut it short and get him out of here.*

"Is there anything you'd like us to know about his personality?"

The man shrugged nonchalantly. "He's your typical insane little puppy."

Another retort tumbled out before she could pull it back. "Fortunately for many dog owners, insane little puppies grow up to make pretty incredible pets."

His jaw clenched, and he shifted in the chair. "Look. I can see this is a disappointment for you. But I'd think, in the position you're in, that you would be accustomed—"

"To disappointment?" she finished. What was wrong with her? Why couldn't she just shut up? Showing this man that he was wrong wasn't the answer to anything. Still, she pressed on, letting her emotions take the lead. "I'm accustomed to disappointment. I could take you back to the kennels and introduce you to some disappointments that would probably keep you awake tonight. What I've forgotten how to handle is when I see people rise to the occasion. When they do their personal best."

The room fell remarkably silent. In the gift shop, Marv stopped shuffling. As if he'd picked up on the tension rippling through the air, Patrick stopped mumbling and the water hose in back flipped off. The only thing to break the silence, as the seconds tumbled on, was a single yawn from the puppy.

Megan held her breath. She didn't know what she wanted the man to say, but she wanted a response. More than anything else she could think of right now, she wanted his response. She had no idea why. But she did.

He searched her face for what felt like forever, then stood up.

"If you're going to take him, take him. I'm done with this." He plopped the dog on the desk, pulled a hundred-dollar bill from his wallet, and tossed it next to the dog.

Megan popped up, scooping the puppy into her arms before he could wander over the edge of the desk.

The man started to turn away, then changed his mind and stared at her for several seconds. He looked as if he was about to lecture her, but then he gave a small shake of his head. He stormed through the lobby and out the door.

Patrick, astute as ever, stepped in from the kennels and joined her at the desk. "He didn't stay to get his change. Why didn't he stay to get his change?"

"Something tells me he doesn't need it, Patrick," Marv said, closing the distance between them. "You okay, honey?"

She was glad there was a desk between her and Marv. She didn't want comfort right now, or she'd start crying. In almost four years here, she'd seen a lot of surrenders and had always managed to hold her tongue, however ridiculous or inhumane the owners seemed. This puppy was fat and healthy and had clearly been given the basic necessities. She'd seen worse. No question. It wasn't fair of her to have lost it with that man.

But she hadn't been able to stop herself. It had to be because of the monster overload of emotions still pressing against her chest from this morning.

Resting in her hands, the puppy had watched the man walk out the door and was beginning to whine.

"Don't cry for him, little guy. He isn't worth it."

—◆◆◆—

Megan's body was humming with unspent adrenaline ten minutes later as she stood outside her RAV4. Stinging-cold drops of rain pelted her face. She wanted to scream at the top of her lungs or start kicking the side of her frozen-shut door until the ball of tension inside her receded.

Instead, she pressed her forehead against the edge of the roof and let the glaze of ice sting her skin. It was stupid to try to drive now anyway. The roads were getting worse, and she was wired. But she wanted to get away. *Needed* to get away. Gritting her teeth, she yanked on the door again. It was no use. The freezing rain had sealed it shut.

She lifted her foot against the slippery frame as a brace and tugged the handle as hard as she could. The door wouldn't budge. Ready to give up and skate-walk her energy off out in the cold, she heard a car come to an abrupt halt not far behind her. She looked over and let go of her hold on the car. It was *him*.

A wave of disbelief rushed over her as he stepped out and crossed in front of his car. He was still angry. She could tell by his walk and the set of his shoulders. Maybe even angrier than when he'd walked out. Without so much as glancing her way, he yanked open the passenger door of his car and leaned inside.

She stood frozen in place, waiting for whatever retaliation he intended to dish out. She'd acted inappropriately. Now that she had a few minutes' distance from it, she saw it. If he intended to call her on it, so what?

He stood upright, slammed the door, and turned her way. She saw a flash of white in his hand. *Papers*. It was only the papers.

"Here," he said, holding them out.

With shaky fingers, she slipped them inside her coat to keep them dry. "Marv can still give you your change if you want it," she offered, not able to summon the apology hiding down in her throat. It wasn't the right thing to say. She could tell by the fresh flash of anger that shot through his eyes.

He turned away, shaking his head and heading back to his car. Just as she let out a sigh of relief, he whipped around and stalked toward her again. He stopped close, so close she could count the dark-blond stubble covering his cheeks and chin if she wanted to. Since leaving, he'd taken off his overcoat and was standing in a dress shirt that gaped open at the collar, exposing a vulnerability she hadn't seen inside.

"Do you know what pisses me off?" he asked, leaning closer. So close that his breath—minty fresh—brushed against her nostrils.

He didn't wait for her answer. "It's bleeding-heart romantics like you who can't possibly bend to see something from someone else's side, not even for a second. It wasn't easy for me to bring that damned dog here. It's going to break my daughter's heart to lose him. And that heart of hers has already been crushed to pieces."

He backed off an inch or two and ran his fingers through his hair, spraying raindrops. "And you...you can't even bring yourself to understand that circumstances change. Things *happen* we don't plan for. Six months ago when we started looking for a dog, I had no idea what would be happening in my life right now. And you with your contempt for those of us who lack your passion for *this*." He waved his hand toward the shelter. "You had to show up today of all days. Well, it certainly wouldn't kill you to swallow some of that contempt the next time someone humbles themselves to bring in an animal that isn't working out for one reason or another."

She kept her arms locked across her chest as she listened. The rain was coming down harder, soaking her, and she was starting to shake.

But fresh, hot anger burned her lips. He didn't see it. He didn't see how special this place was. "I'm sorry if I failed to notice how you were *humbling* yourself this afternoon. My job is to care for these animals, not to care about the people who fail to care for them."

He pointed a finger toward her chest. "You are employed at an *animal shelter*, lady. Like it or not, you need people like me to keep your business going. Otherwise, you'd run out of animals and have to shut your doors. But let's not hope for that, because then you'd have to let go of the grudge you're carrying."

"Ha," she spat out, angry but also very close to crying. "There's a fat chance in hell something like that'll happen. *Ever*. You wouldn't believe the battles we face every day. And it's the same all over the country. Only you've no idea because people like you have their heads in the sand."

"I've got my head in the sand, huh? Maybe that's why everything looks so shitty."

She swallowed hard and swiped at a single escaped tear. "What you don't understand is that bringing that puppy through our doors means one less chance of someone adopting one of our long shots. And when we can't take any more animals in, they may not have the same chance elsewhere."

He held up his hands, splaying his fingers. "That's not my problem, lady."

Another stupid, rebellious tear slid out, and she saw his gaze get drawn to it, which made her angrier. "That's right. You paid your dues. You can sleep soundly tonight."

He held up a hand as if to stop her, then let out a low, dry laugh that sounded raked with pain. "Just back up a minute, will you?" He sidestepped around her and reached for her door handle.

She slid out of his way, stunned, trying to erase the smell of cedar and sage from her nostrils.

Jaw clenched, he braced one hand against the body of her car and pulled hard on the handle with the other. At first, nothing happened as he strained against it. Then there was a loud sucking sound, and the door popped open. The interior light flipped on, illuminating his eyes and highlighting the water droplets on his face and shoulders.

"There you go. Though if you ask me, you shouldn't drive until you calm down." He stared at her hard as he brushed the rain from his forehead. A silence passed between them heavier than the ice layer causing nearby branches to creak.

There was a *thanks* somewhere in the back of her throat, but Megan knew if she said it, she'd start crying for real.

With a brisk nod, he stepped back. "With any luck, we'll never cross paths again."

Chapter 3

WITH RAGE RACING THROUGH HIS VEINS—AND SHUSHING the regret attempting to push to the surface—Craig navigated semi-hazardous roads a full twenty minutes before noticing his surroundings. The place he'd driven to while on autopilot didn't surprise him. He didn't come here often. In fact, he rarely made the conscious decision to do so. Yet he'd find himself here at times when he had somewhere else to be but had allowed his mind to wander while driving.

He'd blink in surprise at the imposing wrought-iron gates and the rolling fields pocked with cold marble headstones and dotted with sprawling oaks. The quiet roads that led here weren't on the way to anywhere in particular. Yet this place beckoned him when he needed it most.

Craig turned in cautiously, doubting the narrow cemetery roads had been salted. Not many people would be out visiting the deceased today. He'd never forget choosing this place amid the numbing chaos in the days—or was it hours—after Andrew's death. His final resting place. Craig had wanted to smash the funeral director's face in when he spoke those simple but devastating words. Now it was nearly three years later, three impossibly long and at the same time short years.

He stepped from his car still coatless and worked his way up the slippery hillside to Andrew's grave.

Reaching it, he shoved his hands in his pants' pockets and passed the first several minutes in silence. Gradually, he became aware of the gentle tapping of the rain and sleet soaking his clothes and the melting ice beginning to soak through his leather shoes.

Craig closed his eyes and was surprised at the image of a pair of tightly drawn but rosy lips that still resided behind his lids. The girl from the shelter was an intruder, flashing into his mind in this private world of Andrew's. Here he thought and spoke only of family and of all things Andrew. Of Reese and Sophie growing up while their brother didn't. Of Jillian slipping away from him. Or had he slipped away from her? Of her distinctive signature—crisp and bold—sprawled over the divorce papers tucked in an envelope on his passenger seat.

When the image burning his lids abruptly switched to a quivering chin and wispy strands of hair that were starting to freeze, he opened his eyes and scanned the marble headstones nearest Andrew's. No one new had joined his son's silent world.

"I was an ass today. You'd have been disappointed." A bitter laugh worked its way out as he thought of the shambles of Andrew's family. "Who am I kidding? When wouldn't you have been disappointed lately?"

Craig swallowed and pulled his right hand from his pocket, rubbing his thumb and forefinger together. Even in the heat of the moment outside the shelter when he was pissed as all hell and not even sure what he was saying, he'd been shocked how he wanted to run his thumb over her lips and brush the half-frozen wisps of hair back from her face.

And here she was again, invading this sanctuary. He

owed her an apology, yet he'd never give it to her. He knew when it was best to let something lie. Everyone had their own battles. And hers were too different from his to tangle with. By tomorrow, the long-slumbering hollow in his core that she'd stirred awake would be numb again. If he still felt the urge to apologize, he'd do something rational, like have his assistant send a note and a small donation for the shelter. The puppy would be adopted out, and the girl would go on to face her next battle. There was no fathomable reason ever to see her again.

The wind picked up, and a chill rushed over him. Sighing, Craig stepped up to the headstone and squatted to pull free the teddy bear, which was half-frozen to the earth. He righted the sorry, bedraggled thing and rested it against the stone. A folded piece of paper that had been underneath was now visible. It had been thoroughly soaked before it froze, causing the ink to run. He recognized Reese's irregular handwriting bleeding through the paper. On a different day, he might've been tempted to read it in hope of getting some sense that Reese was healing. Today, he left it frozen to the earth, comforted enough that Reese had finally found some words to share with his brother.

Still squatting, Craig pressed his palm on the ice-cold marble, letting it sting his skin like fire. "I'd have traded places with you, buddy. I know it doesn't change anything. I just hope you knew that."

With no answer but the gentle pelting of rain onto already heavy branches and freezing earth, Craig headed for his car.

A half hour of hiding out at the back of Panera, sipping her favorite mango tea, wasn't enough to erase the evidence of Megan's tears. A glance in the restroom mirror assured her of this. Her green eyes shone brighter and were rimmed by puffy lids, and her cheeks were splotchy.

She needed to get back to the shelter though. Hopefully Marv, who'd grown increasingly worried about road conditions, had gone home and she'd only have to face Patrick. He'd notice, of course. Nothing got by Patrick. He noticed everything, especially about his friends. He commented when she tried a new shade of eyeliner, when Fidel trimmed his moustache, or when Kelsey forgot and wore one of her T-shirts out of rainbow color order, something she typically strictly adhered to. He'd certainly notice Megan's I've-had-a-breakdown eyes.

But Patrick wasn't one to press things. So if she didn't want to rehash what had happened outside in the freezing rain, she didn't have to. She didn't want to replay the scene—how that man told her off and then played hero opening her frozen door, somehow making his words sting worse.

When she got back, she found Patrick in the kennels, taking the bigger and more active dogs out to the gravel lot behind the shelter one at a time.

"Hey." She pulled on one of the parkas hanging by the service door. "Who'd you take out so far? I'll help so we can get home before it gets worse. Though I'm really hoping that iffy second wave they're talking about doesn't hit."

Patrick scanned the cages. "Bella, Ice Man, and

Henry. I'm taking Kaldi now. I saved Sledge for you since you like him so much."

Megan glanced toward Sledge's kennel. He was standing up, watching her expectantly from the back.

"Hey, Sledge," she said, sinking to her knees after opening his door. It took him three full minutes to approach her, minutes she spent talking to him quietly and keeping her gaze on the floor.

Finally, he came over and licked the tip of her nose. She hooked him up gingerly and joined Patrick out back where the stinging rain was coming down a bit softer— for the time being, at least.

"That man made you cry." Patrick's voice turned up a bit at the end, but his comment was a statement as much as it was a question.

"Yeah."

Sledge headed to the wide gravel island they'd nick-named the Island of Many Smells and started urinating over other dogs' scents. Patrick kept Kaldi, a soft-coated wheaten terrier and Lab mix, at a distance, since Sledge was in quarantine and couldn't be socialized yet.

"Was it because he was standing so close?"

Her throat tightened as the raindrops that'd been run-ning down the stranger's face and neck flashed to mind. Right along with the smooth skin disappearing into his shirt collar.

"No." Her cheeks warmed, and she tilted her head to the leaden skies, letting the rain cool them. "Today's just been a hard day."

"How so?" It wasn't Patrick who asked, but a new voice interrupting them.

She turned to see her best friend, Ashley, standing

in the back doorway and waving a Tupperware dish her direction.

"And maybe you just need to look at things from the other side of a bowl of my spaghetti marinara," she added.

Megan laughed for the first time all day. "Ash, what are you doing out on these roads when you could be home chilling with the boys?"

"Jakey's down for a nap, and Mike's parked in front of ESPN. Remember I told you my uncle broke his hip? I made a triple batch to share with his family and thought I'd drop some off for my Meggers along the way. Patrick, there's enough for you too."

Patrick squinched his face. "I don't eat tomatoes."

"Even in sauce?"

"He doesn't like savory fruits," Megan said. "When he learned they're fruits, he stopped eating them."

Ashley pursed her lips. "You know, that has some merit."

"Can you stay awhile?" Megan asked. "I'll be in soon. Sledge needs a bit longer out here."

"So this is Sledge. I should've known." Pulling her hood up and hunching her shoulders, Ashley crossed the slushy, de-iced ground to join them.

Megan had called her friend this morning and told her all about the dog. The same way she did just about everything.

"God, he's beautiful." Ashley held out her hand as Sledge dove as far away as the leash allowed, eyeing both her and her Tupperware.

"He's a bit stranger shy, it seems."

"Well, you can't blame him." Her gaze flicked in Megan's direction. "Hey, have you been crying?"

Patrick answered for her as he pulled out a bag to pick up Kaldi's poop. "It was the man who surrendered the first Christmas puppy. He was angry, and he stood too close."

"Is that so?" Ashley huffed. "You know I'm going to want the full story."

Megan's mouth watered as she anticipated a savory blend of tomatoes, basil, oregano, and garlic. "Heat that up, and it'll be my truth serum."

Ashley laughed. "Does the microwave still work?"

"So far, so good," Megan said as she coaxed Sledge across the lot. He eyed the door as if it were a large set of jaws but trusted her enough to follow her through.

The microwave was in a small, cram-packed multi-purpose room at the far end of the kennels. Tall metal cabinets, boasting an extensive refrigerator magnet collection, lined two of the walls. The collection had been started by the shelter's founder, Wes, but had been expanded by numerous volunteers and staff. The cabinets were the one spot in the shelter where animals weren't featured. Instead, hundreds of cities, parks, monuments, and countries were displayed. There was a multitude of little star magnets too. Over the years, people had rated would-be destination spots, lining star magnets alongside dream destinations. Some of them— like Venice, Yellowstone, Hawaii, and Cancun—were obvious favorites. Nepal and Budapest also had an impressive collection of stars, as did Cape Horn and Mount Vesuvius.

The third wall of the busy room was dedicated to an old washer and dryer set that had paid for itself a hundred times over. Megan sometimes shuddered at the

condition of some of the items that were run through
them. Thank heavens for bleach.

Along the fourth wall was a makeshift kitchen. There
was the microwave in question, a commercial blender,
and a stove, along with a hodgepodge of dishes and
silverware brought in by dozens of volunteers over
the years.

The stove was used for the animals more than it was
for people. Diarrhea-ridden dogs needed a diet of rice
and ground beef to settle their systems. Hardly a few
days went by without at least one of them needing the
simple, healing diet.

Sledge stood hesitantly by the door while Ashley
popped the spaghetti marinara in the microwave. Sixty
seconds later, Megan heard a loud meow simultaneous
with the oven's ding. Sure enough, Trina, the shelter's
longtime resident three-legged cat, was headed their
way. Since Sledge hadn't been introduced to any cats
yet, Megan kept the leash short and spoke reassuringly
as Trina passed by without so much as glancing in
Sledge's direction. She hopped onto the counter with a
grace that surprised people seeing her for the first time.
She butted in front of Ashley and sniffed the air as if
debating whether or not to lay claim to the aromatic dish.

Ashley laughed and scratched the top of Trina's head.
The cat had lost most of one front leg while she was a
young kitten but never let it slow her down. She was
creamy silver-gray and had bright-green eyes. She
could've been adopted a dozen times over, but Wes
made the decision years ago to keep her as an ambas-
sador for the shelter.

He was debuting a sponsorship program, and Trina's

story was compelling. She, her mother, and four other kittens had been pulled off floating debris in the flood-waters following Hurricane Katrina. The litter was only a few weeks old, and her young mother had to have gone to considerable trouble to rescue them. As for Trina's missing leg, no one knew how it had happened, but it was severed before the family of cats was rescued by emergency workers in boats. Wes credited Trina and her upbeat personality with helping secure enough funds for a much-needed kennel remodel that had been completed nearly a decade ago.

Sledge did nothing more than pump his tail while studying Trina. "Attaboy." Megan gave his chest an enthusiastic rub. "What do you say we head up front and watch the storm? Hopefully the roads won't get any worse over the next half hour."

"Sounds great."

Rather than put Sledge in his kennel, Megan decided to keep him with them. Lit only by lamps this after-noon, the front room felt especially cozy. She stopped at a credenza and pulled out two clean blankets, one for her, one for Ashley. Although no "Closed" sign had been put on the door, she doubted anyone else would come by today.

The rain continued to tap against the windows. It was freezing as it dripped down the panes. The parking lot and surrounding trees and dimly lit buildings looked magical behind the ice haze.

Megan sank to a seat at one of the front desks, tucked her feet under her thighs, and cuddled into the blanket before taking the first forkful of delicious pasta. "Spectacular as usual," she mumbled, remembering she'd been too upset to eat anything more than a few bites of that woman's amazing banana-nut muffin earlier. "Want some?"

"I ate before I left. I'm about to pop."

Megan broke off a piece of garlic bread and swiped it into the sauce at the side of the bowl. She could actually feel her tension draining away. But now that her anger was gone, remorse was sliding into its place. She could think of a dozen things she could have said or done differently to prevent that confrontation outside.

"I was a bitch," she said, starting the inevitable conversation, "but I'm pretty sure he's an asshole, so I guess we were both wrong."

Sledge, who'd been sitting attentively at her side, sank down and flopped sideways, letting out a yawn.

"You mean the Christmas puppy guy?"

"Yeah. You know how we're never supposed to get mad at people when they're surrendering animals? Well, I did. I know it wasn't right. Especially considering how healthy the puppy is. But I don't know; I couldn't help it. I think it was because of what I saw earlier with Sledge. That lady seemed to have little more in life than a deployed son and cancer. And she still wanted to do what's right, even if she didn't have the means to do it."

"And how does that connect to Mr. Christmas Puppy Guy?" Ashley asked, scratching Trina under the chin. The cat had followed them and was sprawled on top of the desk.

Chance, a blind cairn terrier and the shelter's only other free-roaming animal, was curled in his cozy bed over in the gift shop, snoring and seemingly oblivious to the storm.

Megan shrugged, contemplating the question. "You know how you say I haven't been attracted to anyone since Paul, and you think I should have my hormones checked?"

Ashley laughed. "Uh, yes, but hearing you put it like that, I sound like the bitch."

Megan waved off her friend's comment. "Well, believe it or not, I actually found someone attractive today. And not just *sort of* attractive. He was drop-dead gorgeous. Only he brought in the first failed Christmas puppy of the year. And he clearly wasn't needy. He drove a Bimmer, and he was dressed like James Bond. Even his puppy is exceptionally cute. I'll show him to you when I'm finished eating."

She paused to swallow another bite. Ashley waited semi-patiently with her head tilted forward and her eyebrow cocked. "And?"

"There was something else too," Megan said finally. "Something in his eyes. Like he knew he wasn't this person, this dumper of the first Christmas puppy. And I *wanted* him to be more, only I went about helping him realize that all wrong."

"How wrong?"

"Really wrong. I've never made a customer mad before. He stormed out. Afterward, I was upset and needed to get away. Then he came back with the puppy's papers, and we met in the parking lot. We argued again, and I've never argued with anyone like that before. Not even with Paul. It was weird. Kind of intimate even. Like we'd known each other for years, but we were finally cutting through the crap and getting to the important stuff.

"And then…" Megan sighed, her shoulders sinking. The marinara couldn't ease this part. "Then he went out of his way to open my frozen-shut car door and said something about how I shouldn't be driving, as upset as I was. It made me feel about two feet tall."

"Sounds…I don't know, interesting. Weird, but interesting. And that last bit was romantic. How many guys would do that for someone they were arguing with? Was he wearing a ring?"

Megan blinked. "I don't think so. I didn't think about it till now, but I noticed his hands. He has nice hands. I think I'd have noticed a ring."

"You've got his number, right? Call him tomorrow and apologize. Or at least give him an update on his dog. See if you can smooth things over. If nothing else, it'll ease your conscience."

Ashley was right. That's what she needed to do. Apologize. Give him an update on the puppy. Thank him for opening her door.

Megan buried her face in her hands. The weird and unexpected truth popping up in her chest was something she wanted to deny.

Giving Craig Williams a call was exactly what she wanted to do.

Chapter 4

IT DIDN'T MATTER THAT HALF THE CITY WAS SHUT DOWN in the wake of the second wave of the ice storm. In Clayton, St. Louis's largest business district, the streets were clean, the power was on, and it was business as usual.

On a typical day, Craig's mind never wandered. It was his company, after all. If he wasn't one hundred percent engaged, how could he hope anyone else would be? His thoughts wandered more than they kept on track today though. Yesterday's encounter with the girl from the shelter kept forcing its way to the surface, as did his daughter's emotional call late last night.

Though Craig had done the dirty work, the decision to surrender Hershey was between Sophie and her mom—as the original decision to get him had been. The reality they'd faced was that Hershey was a bundle of unstoppable energy and would be for a very long time. Sophie hardly made it through a day without breaking into tears, regardless of all the books and videos she'd read on puppy training. And Jillian, who'd never been a fan of dogs, was regretting the decision to bring a puppy into a house about to go on the market.

After a lot of indecision, and one very trying day in which Hershey chewed a hole in Sophie's new bedspread while she was doing homework, Sophie agreed to her mom's repeated proposition. Sophie could try again—with a calmer breed—in summer when they were in a new house and she was out of school.

But when Sophie had gotten home last night and Hershey's cage was empty, reality had sunk in. Hershey, spastic but lovable Hershey, wouldn't be there to greet her ever again. She fell apart. Completely apart. Her sobs kept coming to mind while he was reviewing final drafts of client ads.

His lead graphic designer was in his office when Craig's cell lit up, showing Sophie's number. He excused himself and took the call.

"Dad?" She sounded almost as nasal as she had last night. "Mom said I could try again. She said we could get him back."

Craig pressed his eyes shut. This had always been between her and Jillian. "Good," he said, forcing himself to sound hopeful and upbeat.

He headed into an empty conference room and over to the wall of windows. His office was on the eleventh floor. An ambulance was parked on the street below, lights flashing. A man sat on the sidewalk, favoring his right leg. Two emergency personnel knelt beside him. So Clayton sidewalks weren't as cleared of ice as they seemed at first glance.

A feeling, more than a thought, washed over him. He'd experienced enough days like that. Days with a calendar full of appointments and a lulled sense of control that vanished when chance—or was it fate— slammed in.

"You won't go it alone, Soph," he said, meaning it. "I'll help you. We'll take him for long walks. And we'll get a trainer this time. He may never be the cuddler you were hoping for, but that doesn't mean you can't enjoy a different sort of relationship with him." He thought of the girl—Megan—and wondered how she'd react to this news. Somehow, he was certain she wouldn't be haughty about it. That run-in of theirs had been an icy-sidewalk moment, a collision of the unplanned. How long its effects would reverberate, he didn't know. "Has your mom called the shelter to tell them?"

"She did, but we don't think their phone is working. It rings and rings. I asked if we could drive over, but she doesn't want to go anywhere today because of the roads."

"That makes sense. Half the city is without power, and the roads are still a mess. Besides, they may very well be closed today."

"What if someone adopts him before they know we want him back?"

"I wouldn't worry, Soph. I'd drive you over there myself, but I've got meeting after meeting until after dinner. How about I pick you up from school tomorrow, if they don't call it off again, and we head straight there?"

She sniffed, but Craig suspected her tears were those of relief rather than sorrow. "Thanks, Dad."

When he hung up, he lingered by the window, watching the man half step, half be lifted into the back of the ambulance. The lights stayed on after the driver took off, but the sirens weren't turned on. There were degrees of emergencies, and thankfully this one wasn't life-threatening. The guy may have sprained—or even broken—something, but clearly he was going to be all right.

Rather than let memory—and the ache of loss—take over, Craig turned from the window and headed back to a soothing pile of unremarkable advertisements that he was willing to bet wouldn't turn into an icy-sidewalk moment for anyone.

———∿∿∿———

It didn't seem possible that something so pristine and fairy tale–like could wreak so much havoc, but Webster Groves was a beautiful mess. The thick glaze of ice coating the area was causing a record number of homes and businesses to be without power. And the shelter was one of them.

"At least it isn't summer," Kelsey said so nasally that she sounded as if she should be in bed under the covers. "If it were, we'd have to worry about the animals over-heating. It might get cold in here today, but no one's in any real danger."

Kelsey was tall, naturally blond, and almost never wore makeup. She reminded Megan of Gaia, the Greek earth goddess, and seemed to own the role even more by having no clue how inherently beautiful she was.

This morning, Kelsey was wearing a faded orange T-shirt that read *Make a Friend for Life, Adopt* over a long thermal undershirt. For the last year or two, she'd dressed for work by the colors of the rainbow— ROYGBIV—starting on Sunday. If Megan ever forgot what day it was, she could figure it out based on Kelsey's attire. It was a fad that Kelsey suggested for all shelter volunteers and employees. Only Patrick, being extremely fond of routine, had taken her up on it, though he was a stickler for single-pocket polos.

"True," Megan answered. She worked to catch her

breath. She and Patrick had just hauled the generator up from the basement.

It seemed today would be a day of triage. They'd take the dogs out in groups and keep the exterior doors shut as much as possible. Once the storm had finally passed, the temperature had plummeted. The winds were ferocious, and the windchill was near zero. With the generator, they'd keep the refrigerators, deep freeze, microwave, and stove working, but they could do without computers for a day. Phones too, for that matter. In addition to the simple notes alongside each kennel, they kept hard copies of all the animals' special needs, so no one would go without meds.

"Did you get a count of all our clean blankets?" Megan asked.

"Thirty-three," Kelsey said.

"Patrick, I know you'll know this. How many dogs do we have that are under a year right now? And how many are seniors?"

Patrick tucked his thumbs in the loops of his cargo pants and looked toward the ceiling. "Thirteen under one. And seniors…thirty-two."

Fidel, who had just come in from de-icing the lot, cocked an eyebrow appreciatively. Megan knew what he was thinking. Who needed a computer when Patrick was around?

"Well, let's cut some of the bigger blankets in half."

She wasn't worried about the cats keeping warm. Trina had a warm box on top of the fridge where she loved to hide out. The cats up for adoption were nearly all double-kenneled. They could cuddle if they wanted to. Fortunately, the temperature in the front of the building was hovering near sixty, and the kennels, packed with body heat, were a touch warmer.

A wave of apprehension passed over her. Her degree was in social work, not business management. At times like this, she felt underqualified to be in charge of Wes's shelter while he was recuperating from his heart attack and triple bypass back in November.

Thankfully everyone she worked with was more than competent. Patrick was quirky but more dependable than anyone she'd ever met. Kelsey had been here three years longer than Megan and knew operations inside and out.

Fidel was not only a hard worker, but also the best dog trainer Megan ever met. He had a newly pregnant wife, three kids under four, and a second job as a night chef that paid better. He was hourly rather than full time, and Megan knew they were lucky to have him as often as they did.

Knowing the work that was ahead of them, they all got busy in the quiet shelter. Chance, who seemed uneasy with the high winds whipping around the building, followed Megan everywhere she went.

"I could see these winds being scarier to a blind animal," she said before realizing Kelsey, who'd been in the gift shop moments ago, must have headed to the back. She scooped Chance into her arms and pressed a kiss onto his forehead. He had a sandy-colored coat and a dirty-gray muzzle. His pupils were waxy gray, his ears were raised and alert whenever he was awake, and his expression conveyed a unique comprehension. His litter had been infected with parvovirus, and Chance was the only one to survive. He'd been adopted once but returned and had become the shelter mascot. Now he was nearing nine.

Still holding him, Megan headed to the front by the large display window. Although he'd been declared officially blind, he was sensitive to light and on calmer days always knew just where sun was streaming in the windows. Even if it was smack-dab in the middle of the front room, that's where he'd take his nap. He never flinched when the staff stepped over him.

"It's just wind."

He let out a whine but stopped when she scratched his chin. She was admiring the sunlight reflecting on the ice-coated branches when she spotted a tall, lithe woman wearing a full-length hooded parka heading toward the entrance.

"Angela Milburn," she called, opening the door, "don't tell me you walked here."

Angela turned down her hood as she neared. "Okay, I won't tell you. But you remember I only live a half mile up the road."

"I do, but that had to have been a treacherous half mile."

Angela Milburn was seventy-two and one of the shelter's most active volunteers. She'd come every Monday, Thursday, and Friday for the last two or so years. Megan couldn't remember her missing a day, but even so, having her show up today in this mess was a surprise.

"That could've been bad." Megan made an effort not to sound motherly but suspected she did anyway. "They're saying to watch out for black ice. You could've hit a patch and fallen."

Angela shrugged sheepishly as she unbuttoned her

coat. "I considered that when I slipped and nearly lost my skater's balance. But I was over halfway here so I kept walking. I figure one of you can drive me home tonight. Though if the power doesn't come on, I'm in no hurry to get there. My house is darker, quieter, and colder than it is in here."

Seeing Angela fold her long, brown parka over her arm caused Angela's old dog Cocoa to pop into Megan's mind. Angela had come to the shelter to inquire about volunteering a month after he died. She'd had him nearly sixteen years and was lost without him. She still spoke about him almost as often as she did her late husband.

Cocoa had been the last gift her husband had given her before being diagnosed with lung cancer. Now that the pain of losing Cocoa wasn't as acute, Angela had considered adopting a few different shelter dogs, but she'd always found a reason not to. None of them, she always decided, could live up to him.

Cocoa. Megan had never met him but had seen a few dozen pictures of him. He was a purebred chocolate Lab that her husband had purchased from a reputable breeder. And as much as Angela enjoyed the motley crew of animals who passed through here, she was a lover of Labs. And not just any Labs. *Chocolate Labs*.

A surge of hope rushed through Megan. She couldn't believe she hadn't thought of it sooner. Their new addition, the chocolate Lab puppy, needed a new home. Angela needed the love connection. If Angela reacted the way Megan hoped, that little puppy would be in the best of hands.

And when things got back to normal, she could call

Craig Williams and not only apologize—she could, with luck, give him really good news.

"Angela," Megan said, setting Chance back on the floor and giving him an encouraging pat. "We brought someone in yesterday that I'd really like you to meet."

Chapter 5

MEGAN WAS EXHAUSTED AND STILL CHILLED TO THE CORE, even though the power had finally clicked on shortly after six that morning. Twenty-eight hours after going out. Now she sat with her legs curled under her in her office—Wes's office actually; she had to believe he'd eventually recover enough to come back and run things—and stared vacantly at the stack of papers in front of her. There was so much to do, and she was even further behind than she'd been at the end of last week when she'd made a commitment to get caught up under any circumstances. *Total fail.*

She was debating using the paperwork pile as a temporary pillow when Kelsey popped her head around the doorframe. "Hey, Megs, you never said he was hot."

"Who's hot?"

"The Christmas puppy guy. He's outside in the parking lot on a phone call. Patrick noticed him. From what he said, it sounds like you two were shooting off some sparks."

Megan's stomach leaped into her throat. Craig Williams. He was back. Only what for? Maybe he'd found more paperwork. Maybe he wanted to know how Hershey was doing. Wouldn't he be surprised to learn the happy news?

She almost asked how she looked, but realized it was a pointless question. This morning, she hadn't had time to wait for her water heater to warm up so she skipped a shower, which was why she felt so out of sorts. A day didn't really begin until she'd savored ten or fifteen minutes in the shower.

Sweat blossomed on her palms. "Should I wait for him to come inside?"

Kelsey shrugged as she headed back out. "Are you looking for customer advice or man advice? Because I can dish out the first all you need."

"Funny." Megan rubbed her lips together and raked her fingers through her hair as she followed Kelsey into the main room.

Sure enough, Craig Williams was in the parking lot. Heat warmed Megan's cheeks, and for the first time all day, she didn't feel cold.

A few other customers had come in while Megan was in her office. She was glad for the distraction they offered. She recognized a regular who came in every week to buy their healthy, volunteer-baked dog treats for her Dalmatian. Also in the gift shop area was the miserly woman who came in once or twice a month to complain about their selection of miniature dog collars. She never quite seemed to get that it wasn't their goal to have the same selection as Petco.

And Ms. Sherman was here too, inspecting this week's selection of cats. Usually she came on Monday morning shortly after nine. The storm must have her off schedule, because here it was, nearly eleven on Tuesday.

And more surprising than that, she seemed to have brought along a guest, a girl that Megan guessed to be around thirteen.

She made eye contact with the girl and smiled. When

the girl seemed to be eyeing her curiously, Megan crossed the floor to join them. Trina was sprawled atop the counter that separated the cat kennels from the rest of the front room, and the girl was petting her. Megan wondered why she wasn't in school before remembering that half the schools were still called off.

"Ms. Sherman, how did you and your cats make it through the storm? Did your power stay on?"

Ms. Sherman turned, eyeing her over top of her rectangular glasses. "Megan, hello. I didn't see you when I came in."

"I was in my office watching my stack of paperwork grow."

She pursed her lips at Megan's attempt at small talk. "We lost power, but thankfully one of my neighbor's children got a roaring fire going in the fireplace and I was able to keep it up."

Megan smiled at the girl. "Oh, how nice."

The girl's eyes widened, and she gave a light shake of her head. "I'm just waiting for my dad." She raised her finger and gave a little point toward the parking lot.

Oh no. The girl wasn't with Ms. Sherman. She was with Craig Williams. Megan's heart skipped a beat. *Please, God, don't let her have overheard Kelsey saying her dad was hot.* And then there was that bit said about sparks. Kelsey clearly had not seen the girl come in.

"The yellow tabby," Ms. Sherman said, oblivious to Megan's turmoil. "Is he as friendly as he looks?"

"Um, yes. Friendlier, actually. And he's declawed in front. His owner moved in with her dad, and he's allergic."

Ms. Sherman pulled off her right glove and touched the tip of her pointer finger to the wire door. The tabby pressed his nose against it and meowed. She lingered a second or two, then stepped back and gave a stiff nod.

"Worth considering," she said. "Mortimer didn't have a good week at all." She slipped her glove back on and gave Megan a quick nod. "I'll see you next Monday, if not before."

"Of course," Megan said. "I hope…I hope it all works out."

When Ms. Sherman pushed out the door, bells jingling, the girl looked at her curiously. "Is she an inspector?"

Megan shook her head and smiled. "Only for her own purposes. It sounds a bit, well, weird, but she keeps ten cats: five girls, five boys, no more, no less. And three—I think it's three—of those ten are, like, eighteen years old, which is really old for a cat. When one passes away, she adopts a new one from here. It's a lot of cats, but she takes fabulous care of them."

The girl shook her head and laughed. "That does sound weird. Are any of the ones she adopted on your wall?" She had brown hair and hazel eyes and was a bit heavyset. At first glance she looked nothing like her dad, but Megan saw a faint resemblance now that they were talking. It was somewhere in the eyebrows and nose. Maybe in the face shape.

"I think I remember Kelsey convincing Ms. Sherman to take a picture with one of the cats she adopted once. She's not big on pictures, or small talk, which you probably noticed. Kels," Megan called in Kelsey's direction, "is Ms. Sherman up there?"

Kelsey pressed her lips together a second. "Yes, actually she is. Toward the left, about a third of the way over."

"Want to see if we can find her?" Megan asked. The

wall the girl was referring to was the Wall of Flame, which was a pun playing on the love connections they made here. Anyone who adopted a forever pet was encouraged to send in a picture or drawing. It had grown so crowded over the years that they'd had to expand it. Now it took up most of the east wall of the building. It proved to be a bit of fun for repeat customers to come in and find their picture.

Ms. Sherman's lack of smile stood out to Megan right away, but she gave it a minute as the girl scanned the wall. The cat in the picture was a pale Siamese Megan didn't remember.

"Oh, here," Sophie said, pointing to her. "The cat's pretty."

"She is. I can't remember anything about her though."

The front door jangled open, and Megan's stomach flipped. He'd said that bit about never crossing paths again, yet here he was walking into the shelter. He was in a dark suit with a white shirt and a blue-gray tie. Megan clamped her fingertips over the edges of the sleeves of the cozy Henley she'd slipped on this morning.

His gaze dropped to her hips a split second before connecting with her eyes. *Are eyes ever really that blue?*

"Ms. Anderson," he said, a smile pulling at the corners of his mouth. "And here I worried we'd never meet again."

Megan's heart slammed against her rib cage as she took his extended hand. An electric current raced up her arm at the skin-to-skin contact. "It is sooner than I'd have thought. But I have great news about your puppy."

"I hope it's that you potty-trained him. Wouldn't that be nice?" He gave his daughter a playful wink.

An alarm went off at his words. That was definitely hopeful-for-the-future talk. "I'm sorry, Mr. Williams. Are you... Were you... Are you here because you're hoping to get him back?"

He looked from her to his daughter, then back to her. His smile fell. "Are you saying he's been adopted?"

The girl's hands flew to her mouth.

This isn't happening. Megan racked her brain for the right words, but her mouth went dry.

"Are you telling me half the city was closed down, your phones were out, and someone still came in and adopted Sophie's puppy? All that talk about how hard it is to get an animal adopted, and he didn't even last a day?"

Megan's pulse tapped an erratic beat in her neck. She forced herself not to crumple under his direct gaze. She'd thought she'd done a good thing adopting out his dog. Until now.

"What I said is true. We have at least a dozen dogs that have been here over a year waiting to be adopted. Only there's this woman..." she began. "I didn't make the connection until she came in yesterday. She lost a chocolate Lab a couple years ago, and for the last several months, she's been considering a lot of dogs. Yesterday, she, uh, she really fell in love with Hershey. He went home with her last night."

An earsplitting silence carved a canyon between them. Up front, in her peripheral vision, she could see Kelsey folding and refolding the gift shop sweatshirts as she undoubtedly hung on every word.

"This is unbelievable."

"Dad, you said nobody would take him!" The girl

covered her face in her hands and let out a single heart-wrenching sob before turning her back to them.

"I'm so sorry. It's just that I can't remember the last time someone's come back to reclaim a dog. Not with an owner surrender."

"I shouldn't have said okay," the girl said, her back still turned as she wiped tears from her cheeks.

"Soph," Craig said, "it's going to be okay. Just hang tight a minute. Let me see what I can do." He looked pleadingly at Megan. "Is there somewhere we can talk? Privately?"

A place to talk in private? There were the dog kennels, separated by thick glass doors, but the dogs were wound up from not having any real walks due to the storm. It'd be impossible to hear in there. There were the bathrooms, the mini kitchen area, and the storage closets. And there was her office. Her small, cramped office. With one chair, a desk, and a hodgepodge of file cabinets. If she tucked in her chair, they could stand comfortably.

She nodded as if on auto response and headed that way.

"Can I ask who's in charge here?"

The answer clung to Megan's tongue like cough syrup. "I am. Our director's on extended leave. And as for my office, it's tight in here, but please," she said, motioning to the desk-high file cabinet that lined the far wall as he walked in, "feel free to lean."

A shadow of a smile passed over his face as he pulled the door shut behind him. "Inviting."

She hadn't envisioned the door being shut. There was less than ten square feet not taken up by furniture. She crossed her arms as he scanned the small room. His gaze lingered on the bulletin board full of her personal items, which included handwritten thank-you cards, pictures of her and Ashley, and a few shelter articles she'd been quoted in. "Isn't it?" She tried to sound confident even though she wanted to squirm.

"This woman… You said she'd been coming in a while. How well do you know her?"

"Well enough." She didn't intend to reveal that Angela was a volunteer.

"Are you willing to call her, to explain the situation?"

"I am, but you should know that she called this morning. I've never heard her sound so happy. She says he has the same personality as her dog that passed away. She said it was a match made in heaven."

He rested against the low file cabinet, splaying his hands along the cabinet edge, drawing her attention to them and his bare fingers. So he wasn't wearing a ring. Somehow, this entire affair would be easier if he were.

"Can you think of anything to persuade her?" he asked, his tone nonaccusing. "Money, a sad story, some place she's always wanted to go but never been."

"She isn't like that. She's just a kind lady who lost her husband and her dog, and she thinks Hershey may fill a void that's been haunting her."

He tucked his hands into his pants pockets. "I can relate to that. Unfortunately, so can Sophie. She's a good kid. A phenomenal kid who's had a hell of a lot thrown at her. We surrendered the dog. I know that. And after the way I talked to you Sunday, you probably don't want that dog anywhere near me. But Sophie…" He paused and shook his head. "She could really use a second chance."

Megan tucked a lock of hair behind her ear. She'd wanted to call him and apologize. Instead, she'd adopted out his dog, a dog he'd come back for. "If you give me a few minutes, I'll call her. I'll do what I can."

He stood up, his hand closing over the knob. "I'd appreciate that."

As uncomfortable as it was to be closed up in the tight space with him, she felt a rush of disappointment that he was leaving. His scent—clean and masculine and reminding her of cedar—was prevalent now. She wondered how many minutes it would linger.

Megan shut the door behind him and skimmed through her contacts for Angela's number. Adopting out that little chocolate Lab to her felt like such a win. The best one she'd had in a while. Now, at most, it was a win-lose situation, something she always hoped to avoid. Whatever she did now, someone was going to be heartbroken. A kind and lonely volunteer or a cute, in-need-of-a-pick-me-up young teen.

Dread filling her, she picked up the phone and dialed.

———∿∿∿———

Megan poked at the now-cold veggies and pasta she'd tossed together. Even though she should be hungry, she wasn't. Her stomach was in a knot. She'd barely touched her lunch, and it was nearly eight o'clock. The temperature had plummeted again, and the cold was seeping through the windows and door seams of her normally cozy condo. The only thing she was in the mood for was her soothing cup of chamomile and lemongrass tea.

She kept seeing the girl—Sophie—heading to the car, head down, shoulders sunk. She needed a win, and

Megan was giving her just the opposite. When she'd explained the situation, Angela had asked for the afternoon to think it over, but her initial answer was that she would exercise her right to keep the dog. The papers had been signed. By both parties. She'd paid the adoption fee. And even in such a short time, they'd bonded.

So Megan sent Craig and Sophie on their way, promising to call when she had a definitive answer. Just as she was leaving for the night, she'd gotten that answer but still hadn't placed the call. Sophie might be expecting a no, but that didn't make it easier to give it to her. What kid her age wanted to be told there were countless other fish in the sea?

Abandoning her pasta, Megan carried her steaming tea to the living room and curled into her favorite cozy chair. Her two cats jumped up beside her, demanding the attention they'd gone all day without.

Moxie, a girl, was the younger. She was small and dainty and a long-haired Himalayan-Siamese mix. Max was older and bigger and a temperamental gray tabby. Megan had imagined adopting a dog after splitting with her ex-fiancé a year ago, but this condo had fit her budget and dogs weren't allowed.

Shortly after she moved in, Moxie and Max were surrendered together. They were healthy but FIV positive. People were hesitant to adopt a cat that would likely become sick in later life, let alone two. Not wanting to split them up, Megan had brought them home to foster them and later decided to adopt them.

Moxie, a snuggler, curled into Megan, while Max sprawled out on the ottoman.

Megan sipped her tea and reminded herself what

she needed to do. Her cell lay abandoned on the side table, Craig's business card tucked underneath it. She picked up her phone. The only new emails were shelter-related, and she was too tired to focus on them tonight. Summoning courage she didn't feel, she dialed the crisp, clear cell numbers written along the top of Craig's card.

It'd be easier if he didn't answer. She'd leave a message, and it would be over. They'd probably start searching for another breeder right away.

He answered on the third ring, his low, easy tone tickling her ear. "Ms. Anderson. I was just thinking about you."

Her hand froze around the mug. He was thinking about her. *Get it together, Megs.* "I'd ask if it was good or bad, but if it wasn't bad, it's probably about to be."

"So she's keeping him." He let out a breath that was somewhere between an exhale and a sigh. "I suspected as much."

"I'm sorry. I feel terrible for your daughter. I'm not sure if it'll help, but he's in a great home."

"I don't doubt that."

"Please tell your daughter I'm really sorry."

"I will, but you did nothing wrong. It's been my experience that apologies don't change things. We wrap them in colorful bows and pass them out like Christmas gifts, but nothing ever changes."

Megan blinked. It was his tone as much as his words that caught her off guard. She could almost swear he was wanting to make a connection. But after the way they'd clashed and then this fiasco, how could he be? She wanted her reply to be witty and compassionate, but the thought of the conversation becoming a personal one locked up her throat.

"I couldn't be in this business if I didn't believe in the possibility of change," she managed. "Which brings me to your daughter. I'd love to make it up to her. She might not be interested now, but when she's ready, we have some spectacular dogs—old and young alike—that I could introduce her to. And if she ever wants to adopt one, I'd waive all the fees."

"That's a kind offer. I'll pass it along to both her and her mother. The decision is between them, and my ex-wife is days away from listing our—her—house. I suspect she'll ask Sophie to wait until they've completed the move."

"That makes sense."

"In the meantime, that dog-walking program of yours... Do you have to be sixteen? Sophie picked up a flyer before she found out about Hershey. When she feels better, she may still be interested, and I think it could be good for her."

Megan's jaw fell open. She'd only been able to picture him hanging up and having nothing more to do with the shelter after hearing this news. "Um, how old is she?"

"Almost thirteen."

"She could become a junior protector." Megan's voice rose almost into question form before she managed to find her confidence by thinking of what the shelter had to offer. "It's a mentoring program we have for kids over twelve. They don't have the full freedom the adult volunteers do. But she could participate in the Saturday morning walking program and join us at off-site adoption events or even do service projects at the shelter."

She turned her mug in a circle on top of her knee, holding her breath. It made absolutely no sense, but she wanted to see him again. And she wanted him to know what an awesome place the shelter was.

"It sounds like something that would be up Sophie's alley."

"Great. We'd love to have her."

"Well then, Ms. Anderson, where do we go from here?"

His tone was playful, engaging. She could envision those blue eyes and that spectacular mouth like he was right in front of her. Her pulse quickened. "There's an application and a fifty-dollar joining fee. Considering what happened, I'll happily waive it. Usually there's a formal tour too."

"Tell you what. I'll pay the fee—double it even—if you're the one to give us that tour and we get through it without either of us laying into each other like we did Sunday. Sound okay?"

Megan laughed. "That sounds nice."

"I take it this is your cell? Or are those cats purring into the receiver at the shelter rather than your house?"

She laughed again. "You're observant. I'm home and about to crawl into bed. It's been a long few days. Call me when you're ready for your tour. I'm there every day except Monday, unless it's a Monday after an ice storm that shuts down the city and keeps would-be pet owners from reclaiming their dogs. I'm there those days too."

They said their good-byes, and Megan sat in her

chair with her knees tucked into her chest and her mug perched precariously on top. She was smiling and biting her lip and wondering how she'd gone from never wanting to see him again to feeling as if the next time couldn't come soon enough.

Chapter 6

A LIGHT DUSTING OF SNOW WAS FALLING FROM THE steel-wool blanket that was the sky as Craig parked in front of the shelter. Maybe it was worse because it was winter and the pots and landscaping were bare, but the building had seen better days. The sign above the entrance was faded, and paint was peeling in the corners. At least the red brick of the single-story building was nicely intact and the roof seemed to be in decent shape.

It wouldn't cost much to give the exterior a facelift, the interior either. But if the shelter was operating on a bare-bones budget, as he suspected, he doubted they'd be able to scrape up the money to do so.

But he could make it happen. His company had the money. Just last week, his CFO had tried to pin him down. "Name a place," he said. "We've got money to dump." There were thousands of causes. Dozens Craig had been able to think of off the top of his head. But he'd walked away, saying he needed time.

Looking at the shelter, he thought maybe he knew why. For the first time in a long time, something felt right.

Beside him, Sophie grinned like it was cutest building she'd ever seen. It was Sunday afternoon and a week since he'd brought Hershey here. She wasn't exactly over losing her dog, but she was resilient and always found a way to look at the bright side. She was ecstatic to start the program, and she'd been reading up on shelter facts this last week. After the move with her mom was finished, she was determined to get a shelter dog.

She wanted him to get one too, once he settled wherever he was going to settle. Right now, the idea of life outside his sterile corporate apartment was impossible to imagine. All he could tell her was the elusive maybe.

He shut off the ignition, and Sophie clicked loose her buckle. He spotted Megan through the large window, laughing at something the tall blond was saying. He told himself not to stare. Sophie might notice. But he couldn't look away. Megan's hair was swept back, and loose tendrils framed her face. Even from this far away, he could envision running his thumb along her smooth, delicate jawbone. He felt a pull in his chest that was both familiar and foreign.

He'd been faithfully married for thirteen years before they divorced. Jillian had been six months pregnant with Sophie when they married. He was twenty-two. She was twenty-five. Starting his career at the same time he started a family wasn't something he'd imagined, but he'd done his best. It was miraculous and stress-ridden at the same time.

After Andrew died, everything had unraveled at the seams. Craig hadn't known grief could do that, make a stranger out of a lover. But it had for both of them. And even the last couple years, when they'd become more business partners than spouses, he'd never allowed himself to look at another woman.

Whether he was ready for it or not, someone had caught his attention. Eyeing her through the dancing snowflakes, it was as if a set of long-frozen cogs in his

chest was rumbling to life, sending a forgotten heat pulsing along his limbs and into his extremities.

He wanted to shake it off, to slide back into the dull
numbness he'd grown comfortable with. But he knew
from experience the feelings that budded out from deep
inside, whether ripping you apart or helping you rise
from the abyss of loss, couldn't simply be shut down.
They either blossomed or waned.

And the only thing that could rule them was time.

"Ready?" He couldn't help but wonder if he was talking to Sophie or himself. When she didn't answer, Craig
looked over to find she was already headed for the door.
"I guess so," he said. "I guess so."

***

Snow was tumbling out of the sky as Sophie headed
toward the shelter. The thick, round flakes framed
the building, and soft, yellow light streamed from the
windows, reminding her of a snow globe. It was weird
coming back here and actually being excited about it,
considering this was the place that had separated her
from Hershey for good.

But her mom was always telling Sophie to trust her
instincts. Even though she was referring to making
friends in middle school, Sophie figured the same thing
applied to this place. The first time she stepped inside,
a wave of happiness had washed over her, one that
reminded her of life before Andrew was gone.

She was a bit surprised how much she liked the place.
The desks and chairs were old, and the counters were
chipped. And it smelled like a weird mixture of bleach,
poop, and puppies. But it was bright and colorful, and an

entire wall was covered with photos of happy people and their adopted pets. There was a friendly three-legged cat and a gift shop full of shirts and sweatshirts with cool sayings. And of course, the shelter was full of animals— cats and dogs and a few rabbits. And at first glance, each and every one seemed cuddle-worthy.

The shelter was the opposite of her house, Sophie realized. Her house was enormous and quiet, and if she or Reese ever tracked in more than a speck of dirt, Inez took care of it right away. Sophie's house had no clutter and no smell at all, unless you counted when Hershey pooped on the floor.

She was stamping her boots on the mat when the director—Megan Anderson—spotted her. Her dad, who'd been slow to get out of the car, was closing the door behind her.

The way Megan looked at her dad and then *didn't* look at him made Sophie think of the other worker's comment last week about her dad being hot. That girl, a pretty blond, was here again too. Even though she'd been the one to make the comment, the conversation that followed made Sophie think of the way her friends commented encouragingly if someone else pointed out a boy they liked.

Whether or not the director liked her dad, Sophie was pretty sure her dad wouldn't like her back. He had once married her mom, after all. Her mom was a living version of their house. She was beautiful and perfectly put together. Nothing was missing, nothing was extra, and nothing was out of place.

Sophie couldn't imagine her dad falling for someone who wore faded jeans and her hair in a messy ponytail and spent her life helping animals, no matter how pretty she was. Not when the woman he'd married had such an aversion to animals.

Suddenly, Sophie wondered if it was possible that Megan would stand out to her dad the way the shelter stood out to her. A refreshing opposite that promised a balance he didn't know he was missing until he saw it.

Unlikely, she thought. Her dad was a grown-up after all. They didn't think the same way as kids.

She also wondered how she'd feel if for some reason he did. She wouldn't know for sure unless it happened, but at first thought, the idea didn't make her stomach curl the same way the thought of moving into a new house did.

Megan seemed nice enough, not fake and trying to hide it like some adults Sophie knew. The whole way over, she had been worried she might not be accepted into the junior protector program. But right away, Megan talked like Sophie was officially in, which made her feel better.

Megan took their coats, then introduced them to the blond who'd made the *hot guy* comment. Her name was Kelsey, and she was the lead adoption coordinator. She was wearing a bright-red T-shirt that read *Proud Parent of a Rescue Dog*, and she seemed as friendly as Megan. They were also introduced to one of the regular Sunday volunteers named Marv. He wasn't quite as friendly, especially toward her dad.

"The front half of the building is fairly basic," Megan said after introductions. "It's where we carry out adoptions, and there's a pretty nice gift shop, thanks to Kelsey and a couple of volunteers like Marv. The cats and rabbits are at the back of this room. They're separated from the dogs to help reduce their stress levels. Oh, and since we're passing it, Sophie, you've seen our Wall of Flame. If you'd like to tell your dad about it, feel free."

Sophie hoped her dad thought it was as cool as she did. "There are a ton of pictures, aren't there, Dad? When you adopt one of the animals, you can get your picture taken and put up on the wall." She pointed to Ms. Sherman. "I met this lady here while you were on the phone. She has ten cats and comes in every week in case one of her cats dies so she can be ready to adopt another."

Her dad raised an eyebrow. "Is that so?"

"It sounds a bit *crazy cat lady*," Megan said, making air quotes, "but her cats are really well cared for."

"Is it just me, or do you find that cat people tend to be stranger than dog people?" he asked.

"No, I don't," Megan said, laughing. "I've been here long enough to see some strangeness on both sides of the fence. Though the vast majority of pet owners we encounter are your everyday run of normal."

"What do weird dog people do?" Sophie couldn't help but ask.

"Hmm, let me think." Megan swiped a loose lock of hair behind her ear. She had pretty green eyes and perfect lips, and Sophie desperately wished to be as pretty one day. "A few weeks ago, we had a man get down on all fours as he toured the kennels to better commune with the dogs. Only it drove them nuts. And there was once a woman who said she pre-chewed all her bichon frise's food so he didn't get a stomachache."

"Eww," Sophie said as her dad chuckled. "And what about cat people?"

"Ms. Sherman is probably one of the most unusual, though we did have a woman pass away and leave us her entire estate because of her cat."

"What do you mean?" her dad asked.

"She had this beautiful, feisty Maine coon that she adopted from us a while back. She lived alone, and the idea of her cat going to a strange home really bothered her. She bequeathed her house and just about everything in it to us with the understanding that we'd maintain it until her cat passes away. Kelsey stops by every day to feed him since it's on her way home. He's not very friendly, but he has a cat door, and he comes and goes as he pleases. In the meantime, we have to pay the tax bill and some necessary upkeep like mowing."

"And the house is definitely haunted," Kelsey added as she stepped behind the counter to grab a piece of paper.

"Cool!"

"So tell me," her dad said, "have any of these quirks caused you not to adopt to someone?"

"We do turn people down, but not because they're odd," Megan said.

"Did you adopt a dog to the guy who got down on all fours?"

"No, actually we didn't, but not just because of that. His behavior set off obvious radar, so we got Chance's opinion and it wasn't good. After that, we asked to do a home visit, and the man has never called back to arrange it."

"Who's Chance?" Sophie asked.

"I forgot that I didn't introduce you to him, Sophie. He's a resident here, a Cairn terrier. He was asleep behind the counter last I saw him."

"I don't get it. How does Chance help?"

"He's blind but extremely intuitive. We've found he's an amazing judge of character. It's not something we advertise, but if someone sets him on edge, we find a polite way to put the adoption on hold until we can do a home visit."

"Can we see what he thinks of my dad?" Sophie asked.

"Sure," Megan said, looking her dad in the eye and blushing. "Chance, boy, come here." She whistled, and everyone fell quiet.

Sophie heard a collar jingling and ears flopping as a dog shook its head, and a couple seconds later the cutest little dog jogged around the corner. Megan turned her back to them and squatted as Chance headed over. Sophie couldn't help notice how at first her dad was staring at Megan rather than the dog. But then again, the Victoria's Secret underwear that hugged her hips above her jeans would probably get most boys' attention.

Megan gave the dog an encouraging scratch behind the ear. "Hey, boy, how'd you like to meet our new junior protector and her dad?" She stood and stepped to the side. "Sophie, you can call him first."

Sophie squatted down and made a kissing sound. "He's so cute." Chance trotted her way. He sniffed and licked her outstretched hand while wagging his tail.

"That is what we call a clear pass," Megan said. "Mr. Williams, how about you?"

Her dad shook his head but squatted down and reached out his hand. "Hey, boy."

Chance zoomed his way, tail wagging. He licked his hand vigorously before diving into the vee her father's legs made. He smelled his crotch, then jumped up to lick his chin. Sophie burst into a fit of laughter.

"Easy, boy." Her dad gave him a gentle pat.

"I think you passed too, Dad."

Megan gave Sophie a playful look. "Well, I guess we can't expect Chance to be right *all* the time."

Her dad laughed. It was a deep, happy chuckle Sophie hadn't heard in forever and made her think of the lesson they'd just had in science on magnets. Maybe her dad would make the same connection she'd made after all. Only by the way he kept looking at Megan, Sophie figured it would be with Megan and not the shelter.

After Chance trotted back over to his bed, Megan introduced them to the cats. Knowing there would only be one pet in her immediate future and that she wanted it to be a dog, Sophie made a conscious effort not to fall in love with any of them too much.

A lot of them had interesting stories, including one little female that a family had found hiding out in the basement of their hundred-year-old home. She was young and really people shy. Before they discovered her, she had been surviving on a box of saltine crackers she'd ripped open with her claws and possibly a few mice. They called her Tina because of the saltines.

Sophie's favorite cat was the shelter cat, Trina. She moved about just fine considering she was missing a leg, and she was the friendliest cat Sophie had ever met. She also thought it was funny how Trina liked to sleep on the counter right in front of the cat cages like she was showing off that she was free and they weren't. The fact that her entire family was rescued off a floating door seemed just about impossible.

Next came the dogs. Sophie was hoping one would

stand out to her as *the one*, but so many looked like they needed cuddling that it was overwhelming. A lot of them were like Hershey, owner surrenders, and the only thing really wrong with them were the bad habits they'd picked up. Several others had come from animal control or other shelters, and their histories were unknown.

When Sophie asked, Megan admitted to participating in a few rescues herself, even though the shelter wasn't licensed for her to do so. One of them was a beautiful German shepherd named Sledge who Megan seemed to really like, even though he hadn't been there long. Sledge was also the first dog her dad commented on as being a really good-looking animal. Sophie was a bit surprised to learn her dad's dog type. She'd figured he was a Lab lover like her.

The other animal Megan had helped rescue was a brindled pit-bull mix named Sol who'd been left in a car at the zoo on a ninety-degree day. Someone from zoo security lived near the shelter and had called the shelter instead of animal control. The guards ended up breaking the window to free the dog since she was showing signs of heat exhaustion. Megan brought her to the shelter and she recovered just fine, but her owner never came to claim her. The fact that she'd been here since August and nobody had adopted her made Sophie want to cry.

When the tour was over and they got back in the car, her dad gave her a little wink. "So what do you think, Soph? Think the junior protector program is for you?"

"Are you kidding? It's awesome. Only I wish I could adopt them all. The cats too."

"Those were some moving stories Megan told, I'll

give you that. She and those volunteers are making a difference. I'm sorry how we found the place and that you lost Hershey, but I think the shelter's going to be a good experience for you."

"I know." Sophie thought about how she'd heard her dad belly laugh for the first time in forever. "I bet for you too, Dad."

Chapter 7

MEGAN HADN'T BEEN WEARING RAINBOW-COLORED GLASSES when she accepted the job four years ago. She knew it wouldn't be all snuggly kittens and playful puppies. She'd need to wrap barbed wire around her heart to survive some of what she'd see. Wes said it best when he told her there'd be days she would question humanity and days she'd praise it.

She'd already seen that in the job she'd left to go to work at the shelter. She hadn't been out of college long and had come to understand that social work wasn't the best fit for her. Ever since she lost her dad, she'd wanted to help people. But the reality of the work had been too much.

After a particularly hard day, she'd taken a walk in Forest Park and met up with Wes and the gang from the shelter as they walked dogs. Kelsey had been walking a cute little Jack Russell that Megan had fallen in love with. She took a card and showed up at the shelter a few days later. It was an odd turn of events that the spunky little Russell had been adopted and the welcoming staff drew Megan in. Wes hired her on the spot, and she'd never looked back.

He told her early on to never forget what had drawn her to the shelter, even if she didn't know it at the time. It took a few weeks to understand what he meant, but eventually Megan did. What drew her, what drew all of them, was the compassion—the humanity, he'd called it—of the animals they rescued. Their willingness to trust again, to love, to accept a new partner no matter how badly their first one—or sometimes several—had failed them.

That compassion swept over her in the quiet of the morning as the dogs and cats yawned and stretched and rose to accept another day of whatever lay in store for them. She felt it in the tentative licks of animals whose wounds—whether physical or emotional—were healing. She saw how other people experienced it in the happy photos and artwork that came in the mail and in the meaningful donations from the longtime shelter supporters.

This was what kept her here, what got her through days like this one. Days when the barbed wire just didn't work.

The puppies, two little beagle mixes, had come in a few minutes before she arrived. If she hadn't snoozed past her alarm, she would have had a face and voice to go with the words circling in her head. The puppies were brought in a half-collapsed, soiled cardboard box. Fidel was getting out of his car when the woman walked up with it sagging between her arms. He said she seemed apologetic. The puppies had been a gift from a relative to her husband, but he was down on his luck and not in the space to care for them.

Not in the space to care for them. The words circled on auto replay as Megan dialed the vet. Sometimes there was a difference between abuse and neglect, and sometimes neglect *was* abuse. The puppies were skin and bone. Their coats were dull, and their eyes were glazed. The stools saturating the box were severely loose. They were probably ridden with worms. There was a science to hydrating and fattening up puppies this thin, which was why Megan had made the emergency appointment with the vet. They were old enough to be on solid food at least. She guessed they were somewhere between eight and ten weeks old, but it was hard to tell in their condition.

The worst part was discovering the damage their collars had done. Even underfed as they were, they'd grown and their collars hadn't been loosened. How had they even swallowed? Thank God for Patrick. Megan had lost it when she realized how scabbed and sore the skin underneath the collars was. Patrick might often miss everyday social cues, like when someone was being sarcastic or making a joke. But he always knew how to read animals.

And this morning when Megan's vision was too filled with tears to get those stupid collars off the terrified puppies, Patrick knew just how to calm them. He turned down the lights and let the puppies hide under a loose blanket with a slit cut in it wide enough to allow him to snip through each collar, bit by bit, until they were off.

They gave the puppies a quick but desperately needed bath to wash away the matted stool. Then Megan gave them a few tablespoons of canned puppy food—which they devoured after a bit of sniffing and licking—and a few licks of water. They wanted more, which was a good sign, but offering them too much too soon could be dangerous with puppies this underfed.

She wrapped them in a soft blanket and put a heating pad under only half the crate in case they got too warm and wanted a cooler spot. Since it was the quietest part of the building, she tucked the crate into a corner in her office and shut the door to block out whatever noise she could. Dr. Washington was in surgery and would swing by after lunch to examine them. He was only a few years from retirement, and Megan worried who'd they find to replace him when the time came. He was a wonderful advocate for the shelter and never charged for his time, only for use of equipment, surgical supplies, and shots.

Not wanting to leave the puppies alone, Megan sat down and forced herself to go through her neglected pile of paperwork. Staying in the room with them was silly because they had each other and didn't seem to find much comfort in human company. But she was overdue for some dedicated desk time anyway.

What a crazy whirlwind of a week it had been in the wake of the storm! Today felt like Friday rather than Monday. Mondays were usually her day off, but she hadn't taken one in a few weeks because things had been so crazy. It wasn't until yesterday that they'd been fully operational again with the thawing of the ice in the play yards. And thank goodness for that. All last week, the sidewalks had been too messy to walk the dogs properly. The best the staff and volunteers could do was get them to the small gravel lot behind the building. As a result, the dogs still reminded her of shaken-up soda bottles with so much pent-up energy.

She was just getting in the groove, knocking out replies to overdue emails and signing off on inventory sheets, when awareness of what had slipped her mind slammed in full force. Her heart plummeted to her stomach. It wasn't possible. She couldn't have missed something this important. She clicked to last week's calendar and saw the warning reminders she hadn't been able to access without power.

She'd missed the deadline for the most important grant they received each year. The one from Maclind Pharmaceutical that paid for a full year's supply of food for all the dogs that came through the doors. They'd gotten it nine years in a row, and she'd missed the deadline. *She'd missed the deadline.* What would happen in October when the new funding season began? How on earth were they going to pay for food when they were barely scraping by as it was?

She found the application at the middle of her stack of paperwork. She flipped through and read the small-print details. No late entries would be accepted. With shaky fingers, she picked up the phone and dialed. Surely they'd make an exception. Especially considering how the storm had shut down half the city. She explained the situation twice to sympathetic employees who would gladly extend the deadline if it were in their power, but it wasn't. Finally, she was transferred to a monotone, high-up accountant who wouldn't have cared if there'd been a 9.0 earthquake last week. Deadlines, he said, were deadlines, and thirty-two other worthy candidates had made it. With no inflection, he invited her to try again next year.

Megan didn't know if she was going to throw up or cry. Or maybe both. This had been her responsibility — and her responsibility alone. She'd been writing all the grants for the last few years. It was everything else she'd taken on in Wes's absence that had been causing her to feel as if she was slipping. This proved it. She'd more than slipped. She'd crashed headfirst.

And what would happen to the shelter? Her vision went blurry. She wanted to find Kelsey and cry on her shoulder, but Kelsey probably wouldn't react any better.

This could shut our doors. The wave washing over her was nothing short of horror. Only somehow she wouldn't let it happen. She couldn't.

Megan dragged her hands through her hair and leaned back in her chair. If she told Wes—after he got over the shock and disappointment—would he have the connections to secure funds elsewhere? He was the founder. He'd gotten the shelter off the ground and saved it from more than a few crashes. But post–heart attack, Wes wasn't the same person who'd founded this place.

Her mind began to race as other possibilities came to her. Maybe she wouldn't have to turn to him. Surely there were volunteers who were well-connected, some who'd know of other grants or funding sources. She could do a press release. Channel 3 came out every month to feature a dog or cat. Maybe they'd run a story.

The idea of *why* the shelter was going to be in such a funding crunch was sickening. She could envision Tom Lanford interviewing her and having to admit she'd let a ball—no, a boulder—drop.

Knowing that if she sat still any longer she'd go berserk, Megan stood and flung open her door. Standing on the opposite side of the threshold, raising his hand to knock and looking just as striking as ever, was Craig Williams.

Craig Williams.

Because of course.

Just last night she'd gone to bed hoping she'd redeemed herself a bit with a successful tour. He'd laughed. He'd been fully engaged. More than a few times, he'd shaken his head in sympathy. Before he left, he'd shaken her hand. And maybe sent chills down her spine.

"Hi." Her voice sounded small and broken and tearful, she realized as she smoothed back the mess she'd made of her hair. She'd been crying and didn't know it.

His smile fell, and a crease formed in his forehead. "What happened?"

She swiped away the tears clinging to her cheeks. Kelsey and Fidel were around the corner talking. She wasn't ready to tell them. Not until she had a definitive plan of action. "It's just not been a good day."

"I'm sorry to hear that." He pulled back his sleeve to look at his watch. "Fortunately, it's not even ten o'clock. There's still time to turn it around."

If he only knew. "I wouldn't have pegged you for an optimist."

"That's because I'm not. However, when I see an eternal romantic such as yourself sinking like this, I'm usually spurred to action. You in the mood for a cup of coffee?"

She put a hand on her stomach. "I don't think I could handle coffee right now."

"Tea then?" One eyebrow raised slightly, playfully.

She would've bet it impossible, but somehow he was helping her feel better. "Maybe if it comes with a scone."

His laugh was soft and low. "Then it'll come with a scone. I have about an hour. How about you?"

She glanced back at the crate in the corner. She could see the tips of the puppies' noses poking out of the blanket. They were sleeping peacefully, and Dr. Washington wouldn't be here for a while yet.

Wes had told her a hundred times to pay attention to what he called *the flow*. He said life sent you what you needed when you most needed it. Sometimes she agreed with him; other times she absolutely didn't.

She said a little prayer that this could end up being one of the times she did. She stepped in for her purse and frowned at her reflection in the glass of a framed picture. It was no use. He'd seen her pink, splotchy cheeks already.

"Do you have some place in mind?" she asked as she checked the floor of the crate to make certain it wasn't too warm over the heating pad.

"I know of one or two, but I'll happily defer to you since this is your stomping ground."

"With animals, I try not to play favorites, but that doesn't apply to coffeehouses. I know exactly where we should go."

—m—

Craig had to admit the Sipperie was more to his liking than he might've guessed. Its clean, modern look was warmed by an impressive stone fireplace and cozy leather couches. He and Megan shared a small sofa that was paired with an antique wooden coffee table.

As soon as they sat down, Megan slipped off her shoes and curled up, facing him. It was hard to tell she'd been crying, though a part of him still wanted to brush his thumb over her cheek to make certain it was dry.

"Any chance you're British by heritage?" Unlike her, he'd ordered a coffee. The tea she'd chosen was something mixed with mango. She'd added a bit of milk and honey.

"A bit, actually. From what I've been told, representatives from most European countries stepped up at one point or another to contribute to the Anderson bloodline. I guess that makes me a run-of-the-mill mutt like most of the dogs we take in. I'm just a foodie, and scones have it all."

She was right about the scones. He hadn't had one in forever. He remembered them as dry and wanting. They'd ordered Megan's two favorites, and she'd asked for them to be cut into halves. One was a triple berry; the other, orange. They were rich, dense, and buttery. "They are really good. And this place is nice. Though I've never had a steak drawn in the foam of my coffee."

She laughed as she balanced her mug on her thigh. "I'm pretty sure that was a heart, not a steak."

"Wouldn't that be overkill paired with those chocolate heart candies they're giving out?"

"That sort of thing happens on Valentine's Day."

"Just to set expectations, I'd not made that connection when I asked you to coffee."

She laughed again, warm and inviting. She was wearing jeans and a soft, green sweater that complemented her eyes. "If you haven't noticed, it happens every fourteenth of February."

"I tend to ignore things that don't pertain to me. It's a coping mechanism, but a fault, I know. So about your morning. Would you like to talk about it, or just put it behind you?"

"Unfortunately, it's not something I can put behind me. I haven't told Kelsey or Fidel yet, but I messed up really bad last week. Catastrophically bad." Her voice pitched at the last few words. She focused on her mug, running her thumb along the rim.

"Want to tell me?" His need to make whatever happened right again was surprisingly strong.

She gave a one-shoulder shrug. He sensed it wasn't because she didn't care, but because she cared immensely. "We survive on donations and grants—obviously—and there are some we tend to get every year that we count on to keep the doors open. I'm the grant writer…" She paused and tucked her free hand under her knee. "Last week was the deadline for a really important grant, and I missed it."

"I can see why you were upset. Who was it with? And how much?"

"Maclind Pharmaceutical. Just over a hundred thousand. We've gotten it the last nine years. It's paid for our dog food all that time."

"You said the deadline was just last week? Right in the wake of that ice storm. Have you contacted them? I'm betting they'd understand."

She swallowed hard and set her cup on the table. "That's the first thing I did. I got through to one of the head accountants. He invited me to try again next year."

"But it wasn't John Benchley?"

A hint of a smile crossed her lips. "He's the CFO, and it's a billion-dollar company. I don't think there's anything I could say to get a call through to John Benchley."

Craig considered consoling her before pulling out his phone, but he'd lived so long using sarcasm and indifference to get by that the idea felt foreign. He flipped through his contacts and hit Send. "Is John busy?" he asked when John Benchley's assistant answered his personal line. She must have read the caller ID because she explained he was in a conference most of the day and promised to leave a message. "That's fine. Just have him call me when he's free."

He slipped his phone into his pocket and broke off a bite of scone. "Do you have a favorite? I'd have guessed berry myself, but the orange is surprisingly good."

The bewildered look Megan had gotten during his call remained. Little peaks formed over her eyebrows. "It depends on the day." She sounded mystified. He fought back the smile tugging at his mouth. "It was just a coincidence that you called someone named John immediately after bringing up John Benchley, right?"

"Like most people, when I know someone well enough, I never use their last name. So back to that grant. Did you finish it? Is it sent?"

"No, I remembered it minutes before you came in. Why?" She bit her lip, drawing his attention to her mouth before he noticed the tension suddenly making her rigid.

"How quickly can you wrap it up? Can you FedEx it this afternoon?"

She blinked. "Did you seriously just call *the* John Benchley?"

"The John Benchley? As names go, Benchley's not altogether uncommon, and there's a John everywhere you turn. I'm betting there are a few at least." Craig took a sip of coffee to keep from laughing.

"You're not funny."

"I kind of think I am. But yes," he relented, chuckling, "I did. We belong to the same country club. We golf together sometimes. Though he takes the sport a bit more seriously than I do."

Megan sat up straight. Her eyes brimmed with fresh tears. "Do you seriously think we still have a chance?"

A wave of guilt washed over him for messing with her in the first place. "I do. John owes me a favor, but he's a softie for dogs anyway. Get it wrapped up today if at all possible, and regardless of what the guidelines say, send it to his attention. I'll let his assistant know to look for it."

She crumpled over and buried her face in her hands. Before he realized it, Craig's hand was halfway to her shoulder. Silky waves of chestnut hair spilled over it, calling him. The desire to comfort her was a whole-body one, deep and nearly overpowering. So of course there was nothing else to do but pull his hand away. He made a fist and forced his attention to one of the baristas passing out roses to the customers.

He wouldn't touch her. He didn't touch anyone anymore. Sophie was the only one who proved an easy exception to that rule. Reese was too much like him to accept affection in this world after Andrew.

Megan sat upright and brushed away a few tears. She cleared her throat and took a sip of tea. "Why did you come today?" Her words were lined with tension.

He hadn't expected her to be defensive, but it appealed to him. If she'd been overly thankful and gushing, it wouldn't have felt sincere. "Not," he said, "for one of those." He let his gaze settle on the barista who'd just reached them with a smile and an extended rose before she eyed Megan's tears.

His comment brought a hint of a smile back to

Megan's face. She shook her head politely at the barista who walked away faster than she'd come over.

"Is sarcasm your armor?" she asked, somehow cutting through everything all at once.

"We had a bargain," he said when he recovered, returning to her earlier, safer question. "Only I forgot to leave you a check yesterday after that successful tour in which neither of us got heated in the slightest. I told you I'd double Sophie's program fee."

"Then she's decided?" Megan's voice turned up hopefully. "She wants to be in the program?"

"Sophie? Are you kidding? You had her at *woof*. She's all set for the Saturday walk. I'm sorry I can't join her this weekend. I have a previous commitment."

"That's great! I'm glad. She's sweet."

"She is sweet. As sweet as they come."

"Do you have other kids?"

He looked away and at the flower-bearing barista who was giving the last two roses to two women seated by the door. They accepted them with smiles and words of appreciation he couldn't hear over the solo guitar music coming out of the speakers.

Did he have other kids? Andrew always felt impossibly far away and close at the same time at moments like this. Like he'd never existed and had also somehow never left. Sometimes Craig could say it, say he'd had two identical twin boys, but one was living and one wasn't. Other times he couldn't.

"I have a son. Reese. He's nine and not the lover of animals that his sister is." He just couldn't go there. Not with her. She was already tearing down his defenses.

"There's still time for that, though he's too young for

our program for a few more years." Megan paused and pulled in a deep breath. "I wish I'd gotten to this sooner so it doesn't seem insincere with you making that call, but I'm sorry for the way I treated you the day you came in with Hershey."

"There's nothing you should be sorry for."

She held up a finger. "We see worse all the time. Hershey was healthy and loved and fed. I shouldn't have treated you the way I did. This morning, some woman dropped off two puppies who were severely neglected. There are two of them, little beagle mixes. Boys. Maybe they'll live, and maybe they won't. We'll do our absolute best. And I guess I'm telling you this because this won't be the first or last time we bring dogs through our doors in this kind of shape. I'll try to keep Sophie from seeing it though. We do with all the junior protectors."

"I thank you for that. She's, ah…she's dealt with enough." Andrew and his story were on the tip of Craig's tongue, but his tongue turned to cement at the thought. "It goes back before the divorce" was all he could make himself say.

Megan nodded, her bright-green eyes searching his, waiting for more. Waiting for what he wasn't able to give.

"We should probably get you back." He set his mug on the table and stood up. "You have a grant to finish and puppies to save."

He dropped a tip on the table and headed for their coats. He helped her with hers, and her delicate scent filled his nostrils, then his lungs, calming him better than aromatherapy.

Megan was exceptionally quiet in the car. He pulled into the shelter lot, noticing the faded sign and thinking how it would be nice to help them—help her—develop a new logo and a new sign. He could do it easily. He owned his own marketing company after all.

It wasn't until she unbuckled that she finally spoke. "The suits you wear. This car. I guess it should've been easier for me to believe that it was Maclind's John Benchley you called. Only why'd you ask me out for coffee?"

Craig slipped his car into Park. "Careful. It almost sounds like you're saying people with connections don't drink coffee."

She shook her head, cutting through his bullshit once again. "I suspect you wouldn't give me an honest answer anyway. But thank you all the same for giving me this second chance with the grant. You have no idea what it means to me. What it'll mean for the shelter."

He was pretty sure what it would mean for the shelter. And for her not to carry the guilt of forgetting, of not following up. Guilt of any kind was hard to carry. He could tell her that, tell her something real. It was clearly what she wanted from him. "It's my pleasure. You have my cell. Call me if you need anything."

She looked from him to the shelter and back again. She studied him openly, not blushing or looking away this time. "You have mine too," she said finally. "If you need anything." Then she got out and headed into the shelter without looking back.

Chapter 8

MEGAN PULLED HER RAV4 INTO THE EMPTY SHELTER parking lot and was reminded of the way it felt when a wild roller coaster rumbled to a stop at the end of the ride. If there'd been a day with as many ups and downs as this one in recent months, she couldn't remember it.

She grabbed the FedEx receipt off the passenger seat and headed inside the empty building. It was a quarter to six, and the sun was sinking low on the horizon. Inside, the fading light shone through the west windows, casting a soft yellow glow around the front room.

Chance trotted over, wagging his tail. It still amazed her how he knew her by the everyday sounds she made or by her smell. He didn't greet visitors or volunteers this way. He saved his warmest hellos for the small group of people who cared for him daily. She dropped her things on the counter and sank to the floor. "Hey, boy." She scratched behind his left ear where he seemed to like it most. "Well, I can't promise you everything's going to be just fine, but at least we're not ending this day in certain disaster."

Just after lunch, Dr. Washington had examined the puppies and put them on a special diet for the next week. He'd been hesitant to commit to their odds, which bothered her, but she could swear they were already more alert. To help get their strength up, they'd need to be fed every four hours. Tonight they were going home with Megan, which her no-dogs landlord wasn't going to be happy about. They'd hardly be out of their crate though.

After Dr. Washington left, she'd locked herself in her office to finish the grant, which was a feat. She made it to the nearest FedEx just before closing, sending it off as directed.

Chance rolled onto his back. She rubbed his belly, happy to pass a few minutes simply relaxing. Now that she wasn't inundated by the grant, her thoughts kept returning to Craig. Was it crazy to have felt a connection with him? Crazy to think he felt it too? They were different in so many ways.

And even though Ashley kept telling her enough time had passed, Megan hadn't thought twice about a guy since she and her ex-fiancé had broken off their engagement. Their breakup had happened so close to Wes's heart attack that it had been easy to immerse herself in work and forget about men entirely.

But something about Craig—and not just his looks—got her blood pulsing. It was a whole-body feeling, the way she wanted to break through the obvious barriers and get to know him. Intimately. When he made jokes but his eyes said something else entirely, the desire to know what he was thinking felt primal.

She found Chance's favorite spot and was scratching away, his back leg thumping on the floor like a rabbit, when her cell chirped. She rose to her knees and dug it from her purse just before it went to voice mail. She said hello without looking at the number.

"What exactly did you mean by *need anything*?"

It was Craig. She'd know his voice anywhere. Her

palms started to sweat. So the point she'd made to him as she was leaving must've gotten through.

She sank to the floor, and Chance crawled onto her lap. She was almost certain Craig's greeting was his typical sarcasm, not fishing for any real depth of conversation.

Two could play that game.

"Tit for tat, of course," she replied playfully. "Like by offering to connect you to notable innovators in conservation and animal welfare."

A low, easy laugh rumbled out of him.

"Only something tells me you have all the connections you need."

"You're good on the fly. I'm impressed."

"Thank you, but you should know it's my nature to downplay compliments."

"Noted."

"Are you calling to tell me not to bother with the grant? Because if you are, it's too late. I made it to FedEx just before closing."

"How do you like your news, good or bad first?"

Her heart sank. "Poop. He said no, didn't he?"

"So bad first. Well, that stuck-in-his-ways accountant you reached was right. They're too big, and they're publicly traded. They can't risk favoritism. Even to multiple-year recipients like you."

Megan pressed her eyes shut. Dear God. All that for nothing. What would happen now?

"But," Craig said, his voice turning up, "the bad news ends there. I told you he was a dog lover, didn't I? I spat out some of those facts you shared on the tour. Let him know what that money meant for your shelter. You may not have known this, but they make ten or fifteen

donations a year in addition to the grants. John has sway
there. Your grant last year was for a hundred and eleven
thousand, right?"

"Yeah."

"I hope you don't mind, but I gave him your cell
number. He's going to call tomorrow with a verbal commitment. He suspects it'll be close to a hundred and fifty
thousand, but he guaranteed at least one twenty-five."

A hundred and twenty-five thousand dollars.
Guaranteed. "Are you kidding?"

"It would be bad form to kid about something like
this."

She put her hand over her mouth. John Benchley
was going to call her. They weren't going to be short
on money. She'd messed up, but things were going to
be okay.

"Look at that. The woman with all the quips and
comebacks is speechless. There is one caveat though."

Her mind was processing slowly. The animals were
so quiet she could hear one of the cats purring. The
sun was sinking below the horizon, and the room was
taking on a golden glow as darkness filled in the corners.
"What is it?" she managed.

"The money won't be disbursed until next January.
Didn't you say the grant funding started in October?"

"It did. But we'll be able to make it two or three
months. I'll work something out with our vendors if I
have to."

"Then your crisis has been averted."

She let out a heavy breath. "I don't know what to say.
I mean I do, but I have a feeling if I say it, you're going
to dismiss it."

"That's probably true. You're good. I'm betting you were at the top of your class. How long have you been running the shelter?"

She strained her ear to hear something on his end—music, a TV, someone else in the room, anything. There was just his voice, low and quiet and prickling her ear. "A little less than a year. Our director had a heart attack. There are just four of us on the payroll. The rest are volunteers. It's a bit chaotic without him."

"Throw in an epic storm, and deadlines get lost. It's understandable."

"Not to the animals we take in, which is why I owe you immensely."

"What was that?" he asked, his tone playful. "You say you're taking me to lunch next week? Thursday? Hold on, let me check my schedule. I'll see if I can make it work."

Megan laughed.

"You're in luck," he said as he came back on. "Can you come to Clayton? Noon works for Wes."

Megan blinked. "Wes is coming?"

"Yes. I just got off the phone with him before I called. And sorry, that date you were hoping to ask me on will have to be postponed. It's business before pleasure. Or, as is often the case with me, it's just business."

She was too stunned by the mention of Wes to fully process the date comment. "You talked to Wes? How do you even know about him?"

"I couldn't recommend the High Grove Animal Shelter to *the* John Benchley without doing a little research first. So pick your favorite Clayton restaurant. I'll meet you two there. Wes said to leave it up to you."

Megan shook her head. She had no idea what to say. What did it mean, him asking her and Wes to lunch?

"Is this really twice in one conversation that you're speechless?"

"No, just speech delayed."

A soft chuckle tickled her ear. "You're a pleasure, Megan."

She ran her hand down the length of Chance's tail. She kept imagining Craig's mouth up against his cell phone. He had good lips. Really good lips. And his lips were definitely not what she should be thinking about. She wanted to ask what this was all about, but if he wanted her to know beforehand, he'd tell her.

"In the meantime it seems you have a puppy or two to save."

"That we do." She thanked him again and hung up, thinking this was hands-down the most unusual Valentine's Day she'd ever spent.

The moss-topped pavilion on the side of the trail was a great stopping place, Megan decided. This was a first-time walk for both Sophie and Sledge, and at three and a half miles, it was a decent length. Plus, it would allow Patrick a chance to catch up. He'd paired up with Minnie, an older volunteer who walked at a shadow of Patrick's normal speedy pace. The two other women on the walk were in their thirties and now far ahead, out of sight. They came almost every week and chose active dogs. They called it their weekly power walk with a purpose.

"What do you say we take a break to practice some

training behaviors with Sledge and Dolly?" Megan asked. "Practicing their training in a busy park with loads of distractions is often challenging, but it's also good for them."

"Sure." Sophie wiped a bead of sweat from her brow, even though it was only in the high forties. They'd gone about halfway, and from her smiles and laughter, it looked like she was enjoying it. Dolly, the middle-aged Boston terrier and Lab mix Sophie had chosen to walk, pulled her toward a trash can alongside the pavilion. She giggled as Dolly sniffed the sides of it with sudden vigor.

Sledge glanced back at Megan and wagged his tail. She couldn't remember the last time she'd met a dog like him, one who was so willing to be in sync with his owner, if that's what he thought she was. He knew to ask permission for certain things, and he did it through eye connection. She gave him a bit of praise and loosened his leash. With a wag of his tail, he leaped toward the can and began sniffing alongside Dolly.

He trusted Megan now, and it had been easy to gain his trust, which was promising for his adoption. He still didn't trust strangers that easily, especially men. During the first half mile of the walk, he'd been so hesitant about walkers approaching from the opposite direction that she'd almost second-guessed her decision that he was ready to come along today. After a handful of people passed by uneventfully, he relaxed. Once or twice, he'd even gotten so lost in the scent-filled path that he'd forgotten his well-instilled manners and tugged her off it for a better sniff of whatever drew his attention.

"I heard dogs have a really good sense of smell,"

Sophie said. "Wouldn't it be cool if Dolly was smelling a dog she knew before she came to the shelter?"

Dolly let out a muffled yip as she sniffed. She was a mellow, good-natured canine who walked with a mild limp.

The fact that Sophie asked to take a dog who'd been there awhile instead of choosing one of the more personable dogs who'd likely have a shorter shelter stay made Megan admire her even more. She was a good kid. A really good kid.

"That would be cool," Megan agreed. "One time we adopted out a dog, and his new owners ended up tracing back his ID implant and finding out his littermates were just down the street. And what you've heard is true. Dogs have an amazing sense of smell. There's research to suggest a dog's sense of smell is anywhere between a thousand to a million times stronger than ours. Which is a big reason why more and more dogs are being brought into different fields of work."

"I know they can find bombs, but is it true they can smell cancer?"

She nodded. "They can be trained to. Last year we had an Irish spaniel who was adopted by an oncologist. He's in a training program with her now. The goal is to teach dogs to detect diseases even before tests can."

"That's so cool. When I grow up, I want to work with dogs."

Megan smiled. "Really? Well, there are lots of opportunities out there. And you're great with dogs."

"I'm not sure what my parents will think. Before my mom stayed home, they both worked in marketing. My dad even started his own company. It's cool to see some of the stuff his team comes up with, but I don't think I could be happy if I wasn't working with animals."

"I don't know your parents that well, but most of the time grown-ups come to realize their kids will be happier if they follow their hearts in terms of a career, even if they have different opinions on the subject."

Sophie gnawed her lip. She had full, round cheeks but her dad's nose and eye shape. The darker hair and eye color must have come from her mother. "It's just, after what happened to my brother, if I think about doing something that'll disappoint them, it makes me want to throw up."

Megan blinked back her surprise. Craig had told her he had a son, but he hadn't said anything about him that hinted at the heaviness suddenly lining Sophie's face. She also wasn't sure if Sophie knew she and Craig had gone for coffee and talked at length like they had. Megan needed to watch what she said.

As it was, Sophie didn't give her time to reply. "I don't mean Reese. He was the one in the car when my dad dropped me off."

"I didn't know you had another brother."

Sophie ran her hand down the length of Sledge's tail. Her eyes grew big in the same way they'd done at the shelter when she was trying to keep from crying. "I knew he didn't tell you. He never tells anyone."

Didn't tell her what? She thought of Craig in the coffee shop, pausing before answering how many children he had. She felt the muscles in her throat close up. Somehow she knew before Sophie confirmed it.

"I had another brother. His name was Andrew. He died three years ago. He was Reese's identical twin."

Megan hugged Sophie tight before she had the time to worry about whether she'd want her to. "I'm so sorry."

Sophie hugged her back. When they pulled apart, she worked her lower lip back and forth under her top teeth and swiped away a single tear. "He had congenital heart disease. He was born with it."

Things happen that we don't plan for. Craig had said that when they were arguing out in the cold. Megan pressed her eyes shut, remembering the drops of rain running down his neck. She'd been so frustrated at the time. But she'd seen something in him as he said those words, a crater of vulnerability he hid from the world. She'd ignored it and argued with him some more. Now she knew this was it. This was what she'd glimpsed. The scar that's left when you lose one of the people closest to you in the world.

She shifted Sledge's leash from hand to hand as a gust of wind pressed against them. She shivered. It wasn't just Sophie she wanted to hug. She didn't think she'd be able to see Craig again without wanting to wrap her arms around him and not let go. No wonder he hid behind sarcasm. "The world isn't always a fair place. I wish it was, but it isn't."

"He wasn't supposed to die." Sophie headed into the pavilion and sank onto the bench, pulling her knees in to her chest. Dolly wandered underneath. Megan noticed her leash getting tangled up but ignored that for the moment. Sophie was carrying around an enormously heavy weight. She wanted to talk, and Megan didn't want to interrupt her for anything. "He was in school and sports, and it was being managed with medicine and stuff by a bunch of doctors. But he got pneumonia and…"

Seeing that Sophie was collecting herself, Megan stayed silent.

Eventually, Sophie shrugged and let out a long breath. "It happened really fast. Nobody was ready for it."

"I don't think you can ever be ready for something like that."

"That's why Reese is the way he is. He always used to be happy and a goof, and he could never sit still. Then Andrew died, and he just…I don't know…changed."

Megan shook her head. Even in the full winter sun, she felt raw and cold and exposed in a way that only the comfort of a steaming-hot bath could cure. "I'm so, so sorry."

"My therapist says there's a difference between being sad and being sorry. She says we can want things not to have happened without feeling guilty because they did."

"That's very true." Megan sank beside Sophie. Under the shade of the pavilion, it was considerably colder. She zipped her cozy fleece. Sledge plopped down onto the concrete, content to relax while Dolly sniffed and wound her leash tighter around the legs of the bench.

"It's not the same thing as losing a brother, but when I was a kid, I lost someone very important to me too."

"Who?"

"My dad." Megan's throat tightened reflexively as his face flashed into her mind. She told herself she wasn't changing the subject away from him because she couldn't handle talking about him even after all these years. "So I've got an idea of how incredibly hard it is, but what you said earlier…about wanting to throw up when you thought you might be about to disappoint your parents?"

"Yeah?" Sophie dropped the leash so Dolly could

extract herself. Once she did, Dolly plopped down a few feet from Sledge and panted.

"Is this something you've told your therapist? Because I have a feeling she or he would want to hear it."

"She," Sophie said, shrugging. "Yeah, I guess. All things in time, she says."

"Well, just keep in mind, it's never easy to disappoint your parents. But especially after what your parents have been through, what you've all been through, I'm sure they want you to be able to be yourself. I don't know your mom, but I can see that in your dad. He definitely understands how much you love dogs. And they're both letting you volunteer. And adopt another dog someday. So just take it a step at a time and know they love you."

Sophie nodded. "Thanks. I'll try. I'm sorry about your dad. What happened?"

It was the question that always came up. The same one she always wanted to avoid. Commotion on the path twenty feet away saved her from having to go there. It was Patrick and Minnie and their dogs.

"Trouble?" he asked, eyeing them quizzically. He looked coordinated in his cargo pants—the more pockets for him, the better—his hiking boots, and his army surplus jacket.

Megan stood up and headed out to meet them. Sledge studied Patrick a second, then relaxed, his tail dropping. Dolly gave a yip at the sight of the short-legged corgi paired with Minnie. They'd become friends in the play yard.

"No. We thought we'd hang here a few minutes and practice some training behaviors that we'd worked on back at the shelter before leaving."

"Want us to stay with you?" Patrick asked, pulling out his phone, probably to confirm a travel distance that he already knew instinctually. "Minnie and I should take another forty-five minutes to finish up."

"No, go ahead. We're good, aren't we, Soph?"

Sophie, who was letting Dolly and the corgi sniff each other, agreed.

After confirming that Minnie was doing fine, Megan waved them off. Sophie watched them leave with a quizzical look in her eye.

Megan pulled a handful of treats from her jacket and offered them Sophie's way. "Dog treats for your thoughts?" she asked playfully. "Since pennies aren't that exciting anymore."

Dolly and Sledge sat at attention when they got whiffs of the peanut-butter-flavored treats.

Sophie giggled, pointing out how much younger the dogs looked with their ears pricked forward. "I was just wondering about Patrick," she asked afterward.

Megan prepared for her to ask why he was so unusual. After a short time with him, most people picked up on his uniqueness, though not many realized he had Asperger's until they really got to know him.

"Are you two dating?"

"Dating?" Megan swallowed back her surprise. "No, we're not dating. Don't get me wrong. I love Patrick, just more like a brother. I think he'd drive me up a wall if we dated. He's much more particular about things than I ever could be, down to the number of slices of salami on his sandwich and the precise order in which he goes about his day. He's great though," she added, "especially with the animals."

Sophie nodded and shifted the treats she'd taken into the palm of her left hand. Holding one up, she told Dolly to sit, then giggled as she realized both dogs were already sitting at attention. "I think they've mastered the sit part already." She gave them several treats and added, "I think Patrick's kind of cute, but I see what you mean about the way he acts. So are you dating anybody?"

Megan wondered about the interest in her personal life, but attributed it to a curious teenage girl. "Most days I feel married to the shelter, but no, I'm single."

Sophie nodded and instructed Dolly in too many words to lie down. Sledge sank to the ground immediately, but Dolly just wagged her tail. "I guess whoever you date would have to like animals, right?"

"Like animals, yes, but you know what they say—opposites attract. The guy I almost married a while back liked dogs, but he had an entirely different career path. He was a chef."

Sophie's eyebrows rose considerably. "But you're not together anymore?"

"No," Megan said, working not to read into the conversation. "We're not. Not for a while now."

Sophie turned back toward the dogs. She sank into a squat and let Dolly lick her empty palm. "My parents are divorced. I used to want them to get back together, but not anymore. My therapist says people always keep changing, and I kind of think they grew into different people."

This training session had gone off the rails, Megan realized. Sophie still needed pointers on how best to communicate with the dogs, but now didn't feel like the right time. Today, she decided, just needed to be about Sophie and whatever she wanted to talk about.

"That happens," she replied, "even if it isn't easy for kids to experience. My mom remarried after my dad died—kind of quickly, to be honest—but they have a different relationship than the one my parents had. And it works for her."

"That's good," Sophie said, scratching Sledge on his stomach as he rolled onto his back and wiggled. "I won't be mad if my parents date other people. Not anymore."

It was Megan's turn to nod. For a reason she couldn't explain, her cheeks were growing warm. She looked at the line of naked trees in the distance and watched a group of crows flutter their wings and hop between the branches.

"My dad likes dogs more than my mom does," Sophie added.

Megan's cheeks went from warm to burning hot. *What do you say to that?* There was no need to feel guilty, she assured herself. No need to feel as if Sophie had been reading her thoughts. Not that she had any to hide. She wasn't crushing on Sophie's dad. No way. It wasn't as if she'd just been thinking minutes ago about wanting to wrap Craig in her arms and not let him go.

Nope. Not even close.

Thankfully, Sledge rolled over and stood up, shaking loose pieces of grass and dirt off his back. He looked toward the path and whined softly. *Bless you, Sledge.*

"I don't know, Soph, but I think that's Sledge's way of telling us he's ready to head back. What do you think?"

"Sure." Sophie stood up and wiped her hands on the front of her jeans.

"So it's your first walk, and we're just over halfway. How are you liking it?"

"Are you kidding? This is the coolest thing ever. It's like my dad says, you had me at *woof*."

Megan laughed as they started down the trail. Sophie's words brought to mind her and Craig's intimate experience on the couch in the coffee shop and the moment he'd shared the same thought with her. Brought to mind the way those remarkable eyes had seemed to be taking in things about her no one else noticed, and making her heart flutter. She'd had the crazy urge to kiss him in the car while he was taking her back to work, but she'd fought it off. And she hadn't even known about Andrew then. If she had, she'd probably have crawled onto his lap and done her best to kiss away the hurt and not gotten off until he made her.

What a crazy mess this was, she thought, wrapping the nylon leash in circles around her palm.

She remembered something her dad had told her just months before he died. He'd been in the garage all day working on an old car. When she came home from a friend's and joined him, he was a mess of oil and grease.

Sometimes, little Megs, to get something to work again, you've got to make a mess of things. That's just the way it is.

If she could go back, she'd tell him he was right instead of just rolling her eyes as she tossed him a rag. But you couldn't go back. Sophie seemed to understand that. You could only go forward.

Chapter 9

SOPHIE SANK INTO THE FRONT PASSENGER SEAT OF HER DAD'S car, kicked off her shoes, and flexed her sore feet. Reese slunk into the back and pulled out his Nintendo DS. He never fought for the front seat anymore.

"So how was it?" her dad asked, pressing on the ignition. "Think it's something you'll want to do again?"

It was the direction of his eyes—through the shelter window to right where Megan stood talking to a customer—more than his words that caught Sophie's attention. A week ago, they'd been on the tour together and she'd watched her dad stare at Megan in an I-can't-see-anything-but-you way.

Well, a week hadn't made her dad forget Megan, and the walk this morning was proof that she was absolutely worth whatever attention her dad was thinking of giving her.

The fact that her dad's crush ran an animal shelter just made the idea of helping with matchmaking so much cooler.

"It was fun but hard. I love the dog I had. She's kind of old though."

"You know that path you took this morning was almost four miles. I'm proud of you."

"Proud enough for a favor?" She wiggled her eyebrows in a way that always made him smile.

"What sort of favor?" He slipped the car into reverse.

"Megan told me there was a rescue this week. Two little beagle puppies so underfed at first that the staff wasn't sure if they'd make it. Now one is doing great, but the other's just okay. I really, really want to see them."

Her dad put his foot on the brake. "We're just headed to lunch. If you want to go back inside for a bit, we're not in any hurry."

"They're not here today because Saturdays are so busy and the dogs end up barking so much it might have caused them extra stress. Megan has them at her house. She's going home to feed them at one o'clock. She gave me her address and said she was fine if we met her there. It's only a couple miles from here."

Her dad frowned. "Soph, that sounds awfully invasive to me. What about waiting till a day that they're back at the shelter?"

She clamped her hands together. "Please, Dad. Please, please, please. They're so little. I saw a picture on her phone. She wouldn't have given me her address if she didn't want me to come."

Her dad's jaw grew tight in consideration. "Reese, what about it? How about eating lunch around here today?"

"Can we get boiled hot dogs?" He didn't miss a beat with his game. "For some reason, I'm starving for one."

"Funny, Reese," Sophie interjected.

Her dad just shook his head. "And you're sure this was Megan's idea? You didn't press her?"

"I'm almost thirteen, Dad. I think I've got the etiquette thing down pat."

He chuckled as he drove out of the lot. "Then boiled hot dogs and emaciated puppies it is."

—*w*—

With the taste of Korean barbecue still on his tongue, Craig pulled into the driveway of the address Megan had given Sophie. It was on a street lined with big trees and old, well-kept homes in north Webster Groves. She lived in a house that had been converted into condos. Even with the modifications involved in converting one residence into two, the house still retained its fairy-tale gingerbreadishness. Seeing it stirred awake a surprise longing in the frozen tundra filling Craig's chest.

Megan pulled in two minutes after them, offering a faultless smile as she stepped from her car. "I hope you weren't waiting long. We had a last-minute adoption."

"No, not at all." He told himself to look away, but he couldn't force his eyes off those lips. And if he did, they'd probably just drop to the hips he'd envisioned closing his hands over more than once.

She was nervous and working to contain it. He could tell by the way she shifted her feet and tucked her hands into her back pockets. With the hint of a blush coloring her cheeks, she was quick to focus her attention on Sophie, who asked who'd been adopted.

"Two rabbits, actually. To a guy who lives a few blocks down from here." With a conspiratorial grin, Megan dropped her voice to a whisper. "Thankfully, the puppies are doing a lot better. Even the little one. Ms. Calbert, my landlord who lives next door to me, is ready to call in the Webster Groves cavalry if I bring them home another day."

She led them down the drive and onto a sidewalk

that wound around a large evergreen with a half-melted mound of ice and snow.

"Oh, I should warn you in advance. Even if they've had an accident in their crate, the first thing we do when getting them out is to take them outside. It helps with eventual potty-training."

"We did that with Hershey," Sophie said, following Megan through the doorway.

Motioning for Reese to go ahead in front of him, Craig trailed in last. He studied the foyer and living room with a touch of surprise. Everything about Megan's place was inviting. Classy even. The floors were a rich hardwood; the ceilings were high and trimmed with antique molding. There was a fireplace with a mahogany mantel on the far wall—wood-burning, not gas—and the sofa and accompanying chairs seemed to call out an invitation to relax, have a seat, and stay a while.

He watched his daughter let out a coo at the sight of the puppies whine-yawning and stretching in the crate at the side of the room. A quiet hiss resounded from the adjoining kitchen. Craig spotted a gray-striped cat atop the fridge, staring at the caged puppies.

"Really, Moxie." Megan said, hanging up her fleece and heading over to the crate. "You'd think that girl would have started getting over them by now. She's been around dogs before."

Megan squatted down to open the cage door and try as he might to look elsewhere, Craig's gaze was drawn like a magnet to her backside. She wore low-rise jeans that hugged her hips and a tight, gray shirt that rose as she knelt, giving him a view of the smooth skin of her back. It had to be instinctual, the stirring that stretched from his chest to his groin. It'd been such a long time since looking at a woman woke him up from the inside out like this that it seemed foreign, like trying to say something in Spanish all these years after college.

"First things first," Megan said, catching one of the wriggling puppies in her arms. "Ready, Soph? You can bring one out with me. They don't need leashes yet."

She stood up and met Craig's gaze for the first time since she'd gotten out of the car. "Have a seat. Or whatever. We won't be long."

Sophie followed Megan out the front door, leaving him and Reese alone to scan their surroundings. Reese beelined for the kitchen and stood underneath the cat, meowing up at it softly.

"I didn't know you liked cats," Craig said. He headed for the frames lining the mantel. A younger version of Megan was in a few, hugging or leaning against friends or family, happy and bright-eyed.

"I don't," Reese said when he abandoned the meowing. "It has nice eyes though."

"There's supposed to be a second one around here somewhere."

Reese turned toward him, squaring his shoulders the way Jillian unconsciously did when something threatened her. "How come you know so much about her?"

"I know very little about her. But I do know she has two cats." Craig considered saying more but decided against it. He turned back to studying the room. On a side table, a marketing book he'd read a dozen times sat on top of a worn copy of *Wuthering Heights*.

"There it is, the other one," Reese said, pointing toward the coffee table.

Craig stepped back a foot and saw a larger cat with gray and white patches of fur eyeing him with careful regard.

"Maybe I *will* get a cat someday. I like how indifferent they look," Reese said.

Craig huffed. "Couldn't you find something more inviting to like about them?"

"I don't like needy things."

"No, you don't, do you?"

He walked toward the kitchen and Reese, who was still planted in front of the fridge. As he passed, he noticed Megan's bedroom off to the side. He took in as much as he could without pausing. The sight of her bed, with its fluffy accent pillows and coordinating cream-colored duvet, stimulated something inside him again.

"Do you think I can hold it?" Reese asked, meowing up at the cat once more.

"I don't know. It looked pretty irritated by the dogs."

"They're outside."

Craig stepped beside Reese and held up one hand. The cat rubbed its chin along his fingers, switching its tail back and forth.

"It seems friendly," Reese said hopefully.

Swallowing back his reservation, Craig reached for the cat. Reese almost never showed an interest in anything outside his DS and iPad anymore. When he did, Craig tried to encourage him at all costs.

The cat showed no objection as he cupped his thumbs underneath its arms, so he lifted it in the air. As he was lowering it, Sophie threw open the front door and he heard a puppy's nails start to dance across the tile entry. The cat's sharp claws slashed across Craig's cheek before it lunged off him and hit the floor with a thump, dashing out of sight.

Craig brushed his fingertips over the wet drops of blood bubbling from the angry scratch along his cheekbone. Beside him, Reese inhaled sharply.

"I'm sorry, Dad." A seldom-seen look of compassion and fear filled his eyes. "It was stupid to want to hold it."

Craig felt an all-too-familiar feeling locking up his chest and weighing down his shoulders. As if he were trying to superglue together a ceramic vase that's been broken into a thousand pieces. "It's just a scratch, Reese. And it isn't your fault. We'll try it again sometime when there aren't dogs around."

"You should keep antibiotic ointment on it the next several days," Megan said, shutting the door of her medicine cabinet after grabbing a tube of the ointment. "Cat scratches can get infected."

Craig was standing two feet away in the threshold of her bathroom, leaning against the doorframe. He had the wet paper towel she'd given him pressed against his cheek and was watching her in a way that stirred up a slew of unsettled emotions. It was as if he was taking in *everything* about her.

Having him block the door wasn't helping calm her either. *But thank God for that cleaning binge the other day.* At the very least, he wouldn't leave with the impression she was a slob.

Leaning one hip against the counter, she uncapped the medicine and swallowed back a stomach full of reservation. "So can I have another look?"

He lifted the paper towel without taking his eyes off her, and her pulse started to sprint. She stepped closer, drawn in by a magnet-like pull as a siren went off in her head. She bit her lip, calling his gaze straight to her mouth.

"Tell me, doctor, will I live?" His tone was lighter than the look in his eyes.

She racked her mind for something to say. He'd lost a child, and he hadn't told her. She understood not wanting to talk about a loved one's death, not wanting sympathy, not wanting to have to comfort someone else because they didn't know how to comfort you.

With words evading her, she focused on his scratch. There were two lines running along his cheek, but only one was deep. She could hand him the tube, and he could use the mirror to treat himself.

But he wasn't moving and she wasn't handing.

His kids had busied themselves with other things when they saw that he was okay. Sophie was planted on the floor, cooing over the squiggling puppies. Reese was trying to call Moxie out of hiding.

With her ears burning, Megan squeezed ointment onto one fingertip and stepped closer. She froze with her finger an inch from his face. He was still focused on her lips, and her ears were going from burning to ringing. *It's okay. He's just Sophie's dad. This is nothing.*

Only it was something, this expanding electric field she felt whenever she was around him. It was the same as when she caved and baked her grandma's triple-chocolate Bundt cake. One bite was never enough. Neither was an entire slice.

Finally, a few words rose to the surface. "Tell me if

it hurts." She closed the last inch between her finger and his skin.

She could smell the clean scent of sage again and something else she couldn't discern. Cedar or pine maybe. She wanted to lean in and breathe until she could commit the smell of him to memory forever. Re-create it and stick it in a sachet by her pillow.

And then there was the feel of him. At the top of the scratch, his skin was smooth. As her finger moved downward, she ran into stubble. She ached to run her fingertips along the rest of his face—the bridges of his eyebrows, his temples, his jawbone.

She was impossibly close to letting herself do it when he shifted abruptly, stepping away from her and clearing his throat.

"I take it you have a trash can in your kitchen," he said, holding up the folded paper towel. He walked off without waiting for an answer.

With shaky hands and a pounding heart, feeling more alive than she had since she didn't know when, Megan turned on the faucet and drew in a long, deep breath.

Chapter 10

MEGAN WAS USING AN X-ACTO KNIFE TO OPEN THE BOX that had just arrived. It was the new T-shirts she'd ordered, heather gray with a dog silhouette on front. It read *Until there are none, rescue one*. For the last year, she'd been letting Kelsey place all the orders. Last month, she had noticed that the gift shop had become a rainbow of brightly colored T-shirts, sweatshirts, and hoodies. In Kelsey's world, there was no place for black, gray, or white. But not all their customers felt that way, and sales were showing it.

It might dampen her afternoon, but Kelsey would have to find a place for gray.

The front door jangled open, and Megan looked over to see Wes striding in, accompanied by McTavish, the very senior golden retriever Wes had adopted forever ago. Although he was moving slower than the last time Megan saw him, McTavish lost no time smelling all the nooks and crannies in the front room.

"My beautiful, beautiful Megan," Wes said. "How are you today?" He draped an arm over her shoulder and pulled her close, filling her nostrils with the scent of a robust pasta sauce mixed with his trademark Old Spice.

"As good as you!" She planted a kiss on his salt-and-pepper-stubbled cheek. Seeing the crinkles around his eyes curled in their own sort of smile, she held up a finger. "Wait, let me guess." She paused for effect. "It was a chess club morning, wasn't it? And by the look on your face, I'd venture to say one of those games that drags on over months is finally over and you won."

His mouth fell open in mock hurt. As if he wasn't aware that chess had become his all-consuming passion ever since his wife passed away. Megan suspected the gusto he'd put into his matches lately was his way of coping with her loss more than anything else. "Has my life become so mundane that you only see me excited about my chess successes?"

She made a face. "Am I supposed to answer truthfully?"

He laughed and ran his hand down the back of her hair, pulling her into a second hug. "If I find this news better than any game of chess, I know you're going to too."

McTavish had made his way over to her. He nudged her dangling hand with a practiced roll so that it landed squarely atop his head, leaving her little choice but to scratch.

She sank to her knees and gave him a two-handed rubdown behind the ears. He panted happily, and she tried not to breathe in old-dog breath. "What's your daddy so happy about, McTavish? Huh, boy?"

"Who's here today? It's only fair to tell you all at once."

"Kelsey and Fidel. They're in back. It's Patrick's day off."

"Shame he's not here. Maybe I'll drive by his place on the way home. Stay put. I'll get Kelsey and Fidel."

Megan shook her head as he walked away, wondering what Wes would find better than chess. She was running her hand soothingly down McTavish's arthritic leg when Craig popped into mind. Not that he hadn't popped into her mind at all sorts of times lately, but this was different. It was ridiculous to think there was any connection, but she had the oddest feeling there might be. She realized this was her opportunity to ask Wes what their phone call had been about. Their upcoming secretive lunch date was all she'd been thinking about.

Fidel was the first to step through the kennel doors, followed by Wes, then Kelsey. "¿*Qué pasa*, old man?" Fidel asked, grinning. "You have a look that says Christmas has come early."

Megan stood up, and McTavish shuffled over to the cat kennels, his ears pricked forward in a way that made the years seemingly fall away from him.

"As a matter of fact, it has." Wes squeezed Fidel on the shoulder as they joined her. "The truth is, my friends, we're getting an unexpected donation." He splayed his fingers in front of his chest and tapped his fingertips together. "A big one. In fact, it's more than half our annual budget."

A shock wave rocketed through Megan's system. Their annual budget was just under eight hundred thousand dollars. Beside her, Kelsey jumped up and down, then cartwheeled across the center of the room, screaming with joy. Megan's knees went weak. It felt as if she'd been struggling to tread water forever and suddenly her feet had touched ground.

"You aren't talking about Maclind's verbal pledge?" John Benchley's impending donation had been confirmed a week ago, but it was for one hundred and thirty-eight thousand.

Wes shook his head and gave her a wink.

She had a flash of what it could feel like to pull up QuickBooks and not have to hold her breath in hopes that they wouldn't be in the red. Her eyes watered, and her mouth went dry. Though they were just feet away, Fidel and Wes faded out of focus.

Craig Williams. There was no reason in the world to continue with this assumption, but she did anyway. She was standing in the rain again, and he was prying open her door. She was in a cozy coffee shop and he was taking her coat, his fingers accidentally brushing against her skin and sending a shock wave of yearning through her. He was placing a call that might literally have saved animals' lives and pretending it was nothing.

Unlikely as the correlation seemed, it was him. It had to be. Craig had told her he owned his own company, and from the look of his clothes, connections, and car, it was doing exceedingly well. But did he have access to that much overflow money? And even if he did, would he really give it to the shelter?

Her knees grew too weak to hold her. Fidel and Wes were coming out of a bear hug when she pushed a pile of red long-sleeved tees aside and sank onto a rickety gift shop table.

Fidel crossed himself, smiling wide enough to show every tooth in his mouth. "How did you manage that, old man?"

Wes jutted his thumb in Megan's direction. "I didn't. Megan did."

With three sets of eyes staring her down, Megan shook her head. "I didn't… I didn't do anything."

"Intentionally," Wes said, smirking.

"*Oh my God.*" Kelsey lunged forward and grabbed Megan's shoulders. "It's the rich hottie, isn't it? I *knew* he was into you. I could see it the other day when he was here. How could you sit there all morning and act like you didn't know?"

Megan shook her head, shocked, amazed, not quite knowing how she felt. Could Craig have done this for her? Impossible. Wasn't it? "Kels, I swear, until a second ago, I didn't know anything either."

Fidel held up a hand. "¿Qué es? What did I miss?"

"Have you met Craig Williams, Fidel? He was the one who came back with his daughter to reclaim her puppy, only to find the dog had been adopted already." Wes paused for a nod from Fidel, then continued. "Turns out, Megan turned this unhappy event into a happy one. She gave them a tour and brought his daughter into the volunteer program. The girl's head over heels for this place. And lucky for us, Williams's company needs to unload some cash before the end of the quarter. When you put it all together, it's what they call serendipity."

"How much?" Fidel yanked off his ball cap and worked it in a circle with his fingers.

"Four hundred and twenty-three thousand, give or take a thousand or so. The numbers won't be finalized until the end of the week. But I want you all to know," he continued, "that when this money comes through, there will finally be the raises you've been hoping for. We're going to reenergize our mostly defunct board of directors. I'm officially declaring retirement and taking a seat on it. Mr. Williams, our generous benefactor, will become president."

"Wait. What? He's joining the board?" Megan felt like the last of the blood was draining from her cheeks.

Wes squeezed her arm. "I wouldn't be surprised if someone of his professional stature loses interest quickly. But hopefully not before he makes a difference." He gave a modest shrug. "Who knows? Before this is over, there's talk of a decent benefits package."

Fidel patted his chest and whistled. "You'd better slow down, old man. I'm having chest pain."

"What if he changes his mind?" It was out there before she could pull it back. Everyone was so happy. Why couldn't that be her only emotion too? She could feel the relief, but she was also terrified. And confused. Very, very confused.

"He won't, Megan. He'd still like the three of us to meet for lunch on Thursday to go over the details."

She nodded, but her mind was far away. It was as if she was standing in the rain with him again. Only instead of arguing, she was touching him this time, running one finger down his cheek, and her skin was burning from the feel of him. *Things happen that we don't plan for*.

Shaking it off, she refocused on Wes. Seeing his glee, she couldn't help but smile.

He glanced at his watch. "I'd stay, but I have an appointment with my cardiologist, and I want to swing by Patrick's place. But needless to say, I'm feeling lucky today. When I'm finished, I'm heading home to contemplate my next move with the match I have going with that haughty librarian over in England. This very well may be checkmate."

~~~

Sinking to the floor in a wide circle of moms, one dad, and a dozen toddlers, Megan crossed her legs and did her best to ignore the stickiness of the gym mat pressing into the backs of her legs. Beside her, Ashley adjusted

Jake in her lap, took his chubby hands in hers, and started clapping them together. He was getting antsy, waiting for the music to begin and the teacher to start the toddler gym class.

Megan managed to carve out a couple of hours every other week to attend Jake's exercise class and join Ashley and him for a quick, early lunch—no matter how busy things were at the shelter.

Arching his back, Jake wiggled out and dove for Megan's lap. Her heart turned to mush at the big, drooly smile he gave her. He dragged his moist hand across her cheek and slipped one finger into her mouth and under her tongue, then broke out into a hearty giggle.

"You love your Auntie Megan, don't you, Jakers?" Ashley said, tugging on the back of his shirt.

"Auntie Megan loves him right back," she said, brushing aside his fine baby locks to press a kiss on his forehead. "Lots and lots and lots and lots."

Ashley shoved out her lower lip. "Have I told you lately how much I wish we were going through this together?"

Wrinkling her forehead in mock concentration, Megan said, "Um, let's see. A few hundred times maybe."

"It's just, you know—" A guilty look passed across Ashley's face.

"I do," Megan finished. "I know."

They'd been best friends since third grade. Ashley moved that year to West Plains, the small Missouri town on the outskirts of Springfield where Megan was born. They hung out with different kids until the day henceforth referred to as the Day That Changed Everything, or the day they'd become indisputable best friends.

Ashley was hanging out with two girls Megan couldn't

stand. Snobby, spoiled girls who thought they were the best in school. One day at recess they turned on Ashley, telling the other kids she was crushing on the most awkward, backward boy in their class—the one who couldn't keep his finger out of his nose to save himself. All because she'd spoken out in his defense when the girls were teasing him.

She'd been crying behind the gym set when Megan found her and took her hand. "Don't let them see you cry," she'd said. "They'll never let go of it. Cartwheels are way better. How many can you do?"

Ashley had looked at her like she was crazy, but then started to laugh. "Three without stopping."

"Let's see if you can get it to four."

They'd been inseparable ever since, crossing the boundaries into a near-sisterhood. At one time, there'd even been a list of all the first things they experienced together. Ten consecutive cartwheels. Successful backsprings. First kisses—the same night—at a middle school dance. C's on a test they'd forgotten to study for when Ashley's first boyfriend broke up with her. First jobs at a roadside ice-cream stand. First time having sex, the very same month. Moving away from home. Dorm rooms at Webster University. It went on and on. Of course, Megan couldn't imagine having survived her dad's death without Ashley's help.

Marriage and babies had been placed preemptively on that list the night they kissed Don Halverson playing spin the bottle. As had a bunch of other things. Some had come to fruition. Others hadn't.

The list was still around somewhere, tucked in a drawer in Ashley's house. Maybe they weren't adding to it anymore, but it didn't change that we're-in-it-together feeling they shared.

Beside her, Ashley nudged Megan's elbow as the instructor sank to the floor, picked up a tambourine, and started singing. She whispered, "I'll love your babies whenever you have them, you know. Even if you're fifty."

Megan waved her off. "Fifty? Who are you kidding? I'm waiting till sixty now."

Drawn by the tune, Jake waddled across the mat and sank in front of the instructor, pumping his fists to the rhythm along with a dozen other toddlers.

Ashley clapped and pretended to sing along. "So, what happened last night after we talked? Did he call?"

Megan looked away reflexively. It was safer to keep her eyes locked on Jake if they were going to talk about Craig in person rather than over the phone.

"Nope."

They'd hung up last night with Ashley absolutely sure Craig had donated the money to get in Megan's pants, and Megan insisting her friend was crazy. No one in their right mind would do that. Would they?

"Hmm."

It was quiet enough but caught Megan's attention all the same. "*Hmm* what?"

Ashley dropped her voice as the other parents sang along with the instructor. "Just thinking. I might've been wrong about the pants thing."

"What do you mean?"

"Wouldn't he have at least called you? Maybe you're right. Maybe he just did it for his daughter."

The instructor motioned everyone to their feet and started them running in a circle, waving at the babies to join them. Jake squealed and ran to Megan. He giggled continuously and held her hand as they ran around, switching directions every few circles.

It was ridiculous to feel disappointed that Craig hadn't called her. They'd had a few moments. Really, really good moments. At least in her mind. He didn't owe her an explanation for making a donation.

She supported Jake to keep him from face-planting on the mat as he ran on his toes and reminded herself that she hadn't picked up the phone to call Craig either. It wasn't that she hadn't wanted to. The whole thing was just too big to wrap her head around.

"So you're saying to show up at lunch tomorrow and be all business?" Megan said over her shoulder.

"I'm saying to act natural and do your best to read him. Then drive straight to my house, and we'll discuss."

"What is it you think we're going to be discussing?"

Ashley gave her a malicious grin as they switched directions. "It depends on how he acts. Wedding plans or shelter plans. I'm hoping for the first. *Obviously*."

"You're funny, Ash. Besides, knowing you, I could tell you something that'd change your mind about him."

"What do you mean? Have you been holding out on me?"

The music changed, and everyone was instructed to gallop around the circle. *When in Rome*, Megan thought, giving Jake a little neigh. "Not purposely." Her words were broken by her body's rhythm. "You and I had bigger things to discuss last night. But Sophie's mom dropped her at the shelter yesterday after school. Sophie comes out as often as someone will bring her. It's cute. She's even fostering those two beagle puppies tonight since they're doing so well. I'm dropping them off at her house on my way home. But anyway, yesterday I went with her on a walk since she can't take dogs out by herself."

"And?"

"And she mentioned offhandedly that she wished her parents had had another kid after her brother died, but her dad had already had a vasectomy."

The song ended a second before she finished, and *vasectomy* rang out across the room. Megan and Ashley sank back to their invisible circle on the floor amid more than a few curious glances.

"Well, that puts a damper on things," Ashley said when the other parents' attention turned back to the instructor. "Megs, I can see it on your face. You're crushing on him. Big time. And I'm not saying this for me, but whoever you end up with has got to be baby-crazy. You love babies too much to be a good match with anyone who isn't."

The fact that a dozen tiny arguments rose in Megan's throat—from adoption to vasectomy reversals to throwing thought to the wind and worrying about it later— showed how right her friend was.

Megan was seriously crushing on Craig Williams, and the odds were the only thing it would lead to would be a broken heart.

—ⵗ—

Megan let the car idle in the circular driveway as she double-checked the address she had with the one on the brass plate by the door. It had been obvious from the get-go that Craig had money. From his car, his suits, even the way he carried himself. Yet none of those things had prepared her for this. His home. His used-to-be home anyway.

It was immense. It stood at the top of a circular driveway in the heart of Ladue—a fusion of stone, brick, gables, and pillars. At the base of the drive, a Realtor's sign announced the house as *Coming soon*.

Unable to move, Megan gawked at the house that was really a mansion. Ashley was right. Someone with this much money wouldn't make a big donation in hopes of getting in her pants.

The truth was that if he ever looked twice at her pants, it would probably be to confirm they weren't the right brand.

All that flirting that wasn't flirting that made her skin crackle with anticipation was probably something he did with everyone. Or she'd misread it. Most likely, she'd misread it.

In the backseat of her car, one of the puppies yawned and started to stir. Thank goodness, they were still mostly kept in their crate. She wouldn't want to be responsible for one of them pooping on one of these floors just as the house was going up for sale.

She was debating pulling out her phone to snap a picture for Ashley when the front door flew open and Sophie stepped out, smiling a big, awkward smile.

Killing the ignition, Megan climbed out of the car and reached into the back for the traveling crate and the bag of supplies she'd brought for Sophie.

"Thanks so much for coming," Sophie called as she jogged down to meet her.

"The puppies will be thanking you for having

someone to play with tonight. And by the way, they're just waking up, so we should give them a few minutes on your beautiful lawn."

Sophie squatted to open the crate door after Megan set it down. "I wonder if they'll be able to smell where Hershey used to pee."

"I suspect some of those smells are still around. To a dog's nose, at least."

"Look at that," Sophie said before praising the small one who immediately squatted to pee after being placed on the ground. The larger beagle trotted in a circle, his nose to the ground. After a bit of sniffing, he lifted his head to howl.

Megan and Sophie laughed as he broke into a lop-sided run, veering in odd figure eights around the lawn.

"Have you guys come up with names?" Sophie asked.

"Actually, we have. We're sending out a press release Friday, but you can be the first to know. Patrick came up with them. He's good at coming up with practical but suitable names. Since he recovered so quickly, Mister Running Legs here will be named Turbo. We're going to call his brother Tyson since he had to fight so much harder to survive those first several days after he came to us. What do you think?"

"Turbo and Tyson. They're great names. I love them."

Although Sophie hadn't committed, she seemed to be leaning toward adopting Tyson, the smaller of the two beagles, if her house sold quickly and he was still at the shelter. If she became serious enough about him, Megan would remove him from adoption for her. She suspected Sophie was hesitant to make a decision after the struggle she'd had with Hershey. She hoped the adoption success stories Sophie overheard at the shelter would boost her confidence.

At least her mom was open to fostering. And tonight would be good. It would help Sophie if she could bond with the dog she ended up choosing before making such a big commitment.

Within a few minutes, both puppies had peed and pooped. Sophie scooped them into her arms, while Megan grabbed the crate. The wide stairs leading to the house required two full steps each. They would've made a regal setting for Sophie and her first homecoming.

"So tonight, when they're awake, I'd keep them in your kitchen since you said it's tile. And they're used to spending most of the day in their crate, so when they get tired, don't feel bad when you crate them. They're still gaining strength too."

"Thanks so much for trusting me to do this. Especially after the way I failed with Hershey."

"Oh, Sophie, you didn't fail. Puppyhood's never easy. It's hard work even for the best trainers out there. I'm no expert, but when the time is right and you make your decision, hopefully I can teach you a few tricks to make it easier. I brought you a few books to read."

"Maybe my mom will read them too." Sophie headed through the open door as they reached the top. "She's pretty tense because the house is going for sale Friday." She rolled her eyes and motioned Megan in. "Everything has to be perfect. But at least she's still okay with me trying again after we move."

Megan managed to keep her mouth shut as she walked in behind Sophie. Though she was expecting impressive, her jaw still went slack.

The foyer's marble floors gave way to a massive great room that could belong in a governor's mansion or something similar. It was decorated to the nines. Megan couldn't imagine anyone actually sitting on the perfectly appointed furniture. The room was remarkable, to say the least. But she couldn't help but wonder where the *living* in the house was done.

Without pausing, Sophie headed straight for what looked like a dream kitchen through the passageway to the right. It was dimly lit, and classical music was playing through a set of Bose-quality speakers.

Although Sophie hadn't asked, Megan slipped off her shoes and tucked them by the door before following her. She didn't want to leave the only shoe prints this place had ever seen.

She didn't see Jillian anywhere and wondered if it was too much to hope she'd get out of here without running into her. She'd seen her at the shelter a few times but had a feeling Jillian wouldn't recognize her if they ran into each other in public. She was beautiful and severe and intimidating. It was hard to match Sophie—with her sweet, friendly expression, stocky build, and the freckles speckling the bridge of her nose—with her mother.

At least to Megan, Jillian seemed anything but welcoming.

Turning her attention to the work at hand, Megan scanned the kitchen. The passageway to the great room—or whatever that room was called—was very wide, and there didn't seem to be a way to partition off the massive kitchen. Instead of a training session, it would be puppy pandemonium.

"This kitchen is the prettiest kitchen I've ever seen, but

it's also enormous, and I don't see a way to easily block off a training area. I don't suppose you have a smaller spot where they'll have minimal distractions while we practice a few things before I leave you to them?"

Sophie nodded enthusiastically. "Follow me. I know just the place."

Chapter 11

"SOPHIE? SOPH, WHERE ARE YOU?" JILLIAN'S VOICE PIERCED the closed door from down the hall.

Megan silently admonished herself for allowing Sophie to talk her into doing the puppy training in this room, of all the rooms in this massive house. When she'd agree to it, she'd envisioned it totally empty, but it wasn't. Some of Craig's things were still in here, and seeing them felt a bit stalkerish.

Oblivious to Megan's turmoil, Sophie reached up and threw the door open. "In here, Mom."

Megan listened to heels click on tile, then fall mute along the carpet, then click again as Sophie's mother reached the bathroom tile that butted up against Craig's clothes closet.

"Sophie," Jillian said, "why do you insist on playing in your father's closet?" She rounded the corner, and her eyes widened at the sight of Megan sitting crossed-legged on the floor across from Sophie. "Oh. I forgot you were coming tonight."

"I reminded you after school, Mom."

Jillian pulled a curtain of hair over her shoulder and rolled one foot around the axis of her three-inch heel. "That's right, you did, but you know I've got a lot on my mind right now. Why are you working with those puppies in here?"

"The kitchen was too open. This is the only place where the floor is tile and they can't crawl under something or start chewing something up. Besides, whatever Dad didn't take is hanging up or in drawers. And since it's still here, I doubt he wants it anyway." Sophie reached out and stroked Tyson's silky ear. Content for the moment, he was sprawled on his back, chewing on a rope while his bigger brother nipped at his tail.

"They are cute. I'll give you that." Jillian released a long breath as she looked them over. "Well, I guess your father doesn't live here to object, so use the closet if you'd like. However, I'm grimy and sweaty from all the packing I've been doing, and I was hoping for a relaxing shower before dinner and I don't want to block you in. If you're working in here, I'll use the one in the guest bedroom." Her gaze flicked back to Megan. "Did Sophie offer you something to drink?"

"Yes, thanks. I'm fine. I just finished showing her a few pointers."

Feeling like an idiot sitting crossed-legged on the closet floor, Megan resisted the urge to stand up. It would only make her feel more confined, holed up like they were. She did her best not to stare at Jillian. In addition to the heels that showed off perfectly polished red toenails, she was tall. Impressively so. At the shelter, Megan hadn't realized it. And she held herself with such confidence. She towered over them in matching lululemon yoga pants and a halter that exposed a bronze and beautifully toned midsection.

Because who doesn't wear three-inch heels and lululemon to pack?

"I appreciate you dropping them off and for helping

Sophie so much. Was I supposed to have a check ready for you?"

Did she know about her ex-husband's donation yet? Would she care? Megan felt her cheeks grow warm as she closed the treat bag. "There's no fee for fostering, and I was just giving Sophie some pointers. I'm not a professional trainer."

"She's *really* good, Mom," Sophie said, crawling over to wiggly Turbo and pulling him onto her lap. "A lot of things make so much more sense now."

"That's great, sweetie."

Feeling like the newest addition in a terrarium, Megan tried not to notice Jillian's gaze sliding over her body as she stood. Her hands closed automatically over her outer thighs—thighs that suddenly seemed to have doubled in size. "Sophie, did you want me to show you how to fix their food before I leave?"

"Yeah, that'd be great." Sophie pushed up and draped Turbo and Tyson over her shoulders, then burst into giggles as Tyson licked her neck.

Jillian laughed, showing a tenderness for her daughter that softened Megan toward her. She might be the ex-wife of Megan's crush, but she was Sophie's mom and, from everything Megan had heard, a good one. "If you two don't need me, I'm going to hop in the shower. Megan, I'm sure I'll be seeing you. I've come to accept that this puppy business isn't going to go away."

"Well, I'm happy to help however I can. Any of us at the shelter are. And sorry about the intrusion."

"Like Sophie said, he isn't here to object, is he?"

—∿∿—

The awkwardness Megan had felt at the beginning of the lunch returned when Wes wiped his mouth with his napkin and scanned the room. He excused himself, saying he'd be just a minute, then headed toward the restrooms.

Don't leave me here alone, Megan wanted to plead. Instead she folded her napkin, then refolded it once more because she was one hundred percent sure Craig was staring at her.

She'd spent the better part of last night debating a hundred ways to say it—to thank him for the game-changing donation he'd made. She'd had a few different lines on the tip of her tongue and figured she'd go with whatever came out. But when the time came, nothing did. She'd managed to smile and nod along with Wesley, who was congenial enough for both of them. The two guys did all the talking early in the hour. When it got down to particulars, to how the money could be spent, she unfroze and added her input.

If Craig noticed, which she figured he did, he didn't show any offense. She might not yet understand the motivation behind his donation, but she knew it wasn't because he was looking to be praised. She was certain of that.

About halfway through the meal, it had occurred to her that the reason he hadn't called her was because she wasn't that important in his life. They hardly knew each other, after all.

Whatever his reason, it shouldn't matter, Megan told herself. The donation was incredible. Its potential effects were still popping into her mind at different times. On top of that, Craig was a truly admirable person. But the stirrings, the crush, the connection she thought she felt…

they must have been one-sided. She needed to accept this—and fast. He was the shelter's biggest donor ever, and he'd be stepping in as president of the board.

So what to the rest of it. So what that he'd been in her house. That she'd been in his car. Heard the intimacy in his voice late in the day over the phone. Or that they'd argued in the rain.

The server came while Megan was finishing folding her napkin into a square for a second time. Craig handed over his card, then leaned back against his chair. "So which is it? Are you angry with me, or are you just afraid?"

Her mouth went dry. Abandoning her napkin, she locked her hands under her thighs. She looked his way, startled by the blueness of eyes she'd already committed to memory. "You could have told me."

It came out before she'd even contemplated it. She reminded herself that he had no obligation to her. No reason to tell her anything.

Craig ran his thumb over the edge of the tablecloth. "Yes, I expect I should have."

Somehow the fact that he'd agreed so easily stung. "So why the shelter?" Even though she hadn't meant it to, she realized the question probably sounded like an accusation. To soften it, she added, "Because Sophie loves it so much?"

He was studying her so intently that it took her a bit to realize he wasn't responding. His gaze slid over her face, dropped to her jawline, and lingered on her sternum before flitting back to her eyes.

"That cemented it, yes. And because of the shelter itself. It's a remarkable place you've all built." Craig reached for his glass, swirling ice around the bottom. Tension suddenly lined his shoulders. "But, as you seem to have guessed, there *is* one reason I didn't share with Wesley. If you two hadn't ridden together, I'd ask you to stick around. I think the sooner I make my intentions known, the better."

Intentions? Ashley's words rang in her ears. "Whatever they are, I think you should know I don't sleep around." It took three full seconds to realize the declaration had come from her. Her cheeks flamed burning hot. *Bravo, Megan, bravo*. She was fairly certain that she'd never said anything dumber in her entire life.

He didn't seem offended in the slightest. His laugh was low and playful. "Megan Anderson, you're a pleasure."

The server returned, and Craig signed the check. Megan swallowed her humiliation and scoped the hallway to the bathrooms in hopes of Wes's return.

"Step outside with me?" Craig asked. Then, when she didn't respond, he added, "Please."

With no sign of Wes, she was forced to make eye contact again. There was a softness pouring off him that she'd never glimpsed before.

She felt herself nodding. "Okay."

Craig motioned her forward first. She crossed the restaurant and headed outside into a blustery wind, puffy blue-gray clouds, and no sign of the sun. The door fell shut, and Megan was suddenly acutely aware of a lack of other people.

It didn't help that he looked good enough in his suit for it to serve as a further distraction. His broad shoulders and trim waist drew her attention when she should only be thinking about donations and how to recover from the embarrassment of that comment she'd let slip inside.

"Megan, I..." Craig went quiet and shifted in place. Then he turned away and began to pace the sidewalk.

His tie was gray with bits of purple and black, which matched the small purple-and-black paisleys in her cream-colored blouse. Like they'd coordinated. Instead of jeans, she'd worn her nicest black pants and dress boots. It seemed appropriate, dressing up to meet your best donor and incoming board president. *You look nice*, he'd said when he saw her, as if their relationship warranted the special notice.

He stopped pacing and faced her, dragging his fingers through his hair. "So you're worried I donated that money to get you into bed." It was a statement, not a question.

"I know you didn't. What I said inside was stupid. I'm sorry."

He swallowed and looked from her eyes to her lips, then back to her eyes. After a dozen erratic thumps of her heart, he said, "The truth is, that other reason, the one I didn't share with Wes... Well, it's pretty much just the opposite, actually."

She shook her head. "I don't understand."

He reached out and came close to brushing his hand against her hair. Just before touching her, he pulled back and shoved both hands in his pockets. "I'm not going to lie. I'd like very much to get you into bed. And I know I've done a pretty poor job of hiding it."

Megan's heart pounded in her chest. She wasn't crazy. She hadn't been picking up on something that wasn't there. She pressed her lips into a line as he leaned in to speak into her ear.

Could two people stand closer without touching?

"I want you, Megan. More than you know. I haven't stopped thinking about you since the first day we met. I thought I would just get past it. And I'm not. But Sophie's involved now. Reese too. And I'll do anything in the world not to hurt them again after all they've been through."

It was too much. His body mirroring hers. His breath brushing against her ear. His words that healed and cut at the same time. She backed up until she bumped into the brick wall of the restaurant. She began to breathe normally again when he didn't close in against her.

"So now," he continued. "That move you were worried I was going to make? I can promise I'll never attempt it."

She blinked at his change of direction. She took a few seconds to process his comment, then said, "That doesn't make sense. You donated the money, and that prevents you from making a move somehow?"

"I donated the money to the shelter because it was the right thing to do. Now that I have though, I can promise you're safe from any move I might've made."

Damn it anyway. Why was she so close to crying? What was he doing, giving her such a clear yes and no at the same time?

And damn Wes and his digestive problems. What was taking him so long? She wanted him here. She wanted to leave. She wanted to run. Wanted to scream or cry, whichever came first. Maybe even stamp her feet.

"It still doesn't make sense. How does it prevent you from…from—"

"Sleeping with you?" He closed the distance between

them once more and splayed his hand on the cold brick by her side. "It's one of my cardinal rules. I don't believe in mixing business with pleasure."

She shoved away from him. "Then I'm sorry for you. If you liked what you do for a living, you'd find pleasure in it. And maybe then you wouldn't have to make giant donations just to disconnect yourself from your feelings."

The hurt in his eyes made her want to scream. It was her turn to pace the sidewalk. She'd done that. She put that pain there.

"If I recall, you were the first to say you weren't going to sleep with me."

She opened her mouth to speak, then stopped and swallowed hard. He was right. He watched her, waiting for her to say more. But she couldn't bring herself to utter a word.

The door of the restaurant opened, and Wes walked out, rubbing his stomach and offering a sheepish smile. He was followed by two women who were chattering like birds. "Sorry about that. I didn't mean to keep you waiting."

Craig returned Wes's smile with one that didn't come close to reaching his eyes. "It's all right. I'll be in touch. And like I said, I'm happy to offer advice…but how you move forward from here is up to you."

With the first rebellious tear sliding down her cheek, Megan turned abruptly and headed for Wes's car, hoping beyond hope Craig had parked somewhere else.

Chapter 12

STARING AT THE REGISTER SCREEN IN THE CHECKOUT LINE, Megan frowned. Eighty-six dollars. And most of it was feel-better-quickly, bad-for-you food she didn't need. Maybe eating to comfort her emotions wasn't the answer, but she couldn't think of anything else at the moment.

Deflated, she swiped her card and did her best to keep up with the small talk of the cashier. He was sweet and older, and she always chose his line. Today, it would've been better to be checked out by someone else. But she'd caught his eye and hadn't wanted to be rude.

Maybe there's a time for being rude. She tried the idea on like she was stepping into a costume. She could start today. Tell the cashier she didn't care about this year's squash crop. Or how the price of pork should start to drop next year. From there, she'd work on no longer seeing the good in people. Learn to take people like Craig Williams, dog dumper, and never let them become more than a harshly formed first impression.

Circumstances could never be extenuating. And things could never happen that weren't planned for.

This didn't make her feel any better. She said good-bye to the checker whose line she'd choose again next time and pushed her rickety cart outside. She was loading her bags into her trunk when her phone rang.

It was her ex-fiancé, Paul.

He'd called twice last week, and she hadn't picked up. He hadn't left a message either.

So he was thinking about her now, when for months she'd been thinking about him. Only she wasn't any longer.

Megan sank into the driver's seat and released a tired breath. Her body ached from the unexpected hurt of this afternoon. She'd only known Craig a few weeks. How could his words have wounded her so much?

She drove home through the streets of Webster Groves, trying to sort out a tangled mess of feelings that wouldn't unravel. When it came to Craig Williams, everything was too knotted together to decipher.

Pulling onto her cul-de-sac, she felt her heart thump erratically when she spotted a BMW 7 Series parked in her driveway. She hit the brakes, then the gas a bit too hard. The engine revved, and heat rushed all the way into her fingers and toes.

Please don't let him have seen that. She parked in her driveway alongside his car and attempted to step out as gracefully as possible. He was still in his seat, talking on the phone. She headed around and leaned against her passenger door. Meeting her gaze, he held up a finger and offered a secretive smile that lightened her mood more than a whole bag of comfort food could've.

She heard a handful of words through his closed window. They were boring ones that had to do with sales and reports and projections. Then he said he had to go.

With a wave of insecurity washing over her, Megan pulled her jacket closed. The sun was setting, and the temperature was dropping.

Craig stepped from his car wearing a dress shirt that

was open at the collar and no coat. Keeping one arm draped over his door, he stared at her without saying anything. Just three feet, maybe four, separated them.

"Hey," she said. Why was the onus on her to talk first? He was standing in *her* driveway.

"I wanted to give you something. If you have a few minutes."

She rocked back on her heels. "I think I have a few."

With a hint of a smile curling his lips, he reached into his car and pulled out a brown-paper gift bag. "It isn't another donation, so I'm hopeful it won't piss you off."

A laugh bubbled out of her. "Based on our history, I'd have to say you never know." She took it, admiring the gold tissue paper poking out the top. "Did you bag this yourself?"

"I feel compelled to say I'm not that good at domesticity."

She separated the folds of tissue, then paused. "Let me guess... You bronzed my pooper scooper?" She said it in hope of easing the tension still hanging in the air. He'd commented at lunch that with the new employee they were going to add, her poop-scraping days might well be over.

Whatever he'd given her was flat, wide, and rectangular. Pursing her lips, she pulled it out and held it up in the dim light. "Um, is it a little chalkboard?"

He laughed in the low, quiet way that made her tingle down to her toes. "It's more of a metaphorical gift."

Megan tilted her head, looking from him to the chalkboard. "If you're saying not to use your donation on new technology for the shelter, you could've given me a Hallmark card. Nothing says *I don't do technology* like Hallmark."

"Try again, Megan. This is about this afternoon. It has nothing to do with the shelter."

That word again. Her name. Only when he said it, it was like a tall stack of chocolate chip and pecan pancakes with extra syrup.

With her heart running its own marathon, she forced her attention to the shiny new chalkboard in her hand and tried to figure out how it could be metaphorical. Suddenly she got it. Unable to keep the grin from spreading across her face, she held it up. "Are you offering me a clean slate?"

He smiled wide enough to show a set of very white, straight teeth. "Yes, as a matter of fact I am." Pulling one hand from his pocket, he held up a finger. "And hopefully a better explanation than the one I gave you this afternoon, if you'll allow me."

Her heart plummeted into her stomach, then leaped into her throat. "I will."

"That's good. Really good." He moved a step closer, returning his free hand to his pants' pocket. Megan suddenly wondered if he wanted to touch her as much as she wanted him to. "Look, you haven't had kids so you may not understand this, but the thing is, right now my life is about my kids. My ex-wife and I didn't divorce for the chance to be with other people. Not now. Not at this stage in the game."

Why did it suddenly feel like he was dumping her? With a chalkboard? Swallowing hard, she nodded. "I get it, Craig."

"Please let me finish. I hardly ever say things. But

I have to say this. To you. Because you're real and because you matter."

She swept a lock of hair behind her ear and nodded him on. "Okay."

"You see, a few years ago, something happened and the kids—" His voice cracked, and he cleared his throat.

Her own throat was so damn tight, but she had to spare him from continuing. "Sophie told me. She told me what happened."

Craig stared at her for a mile of heartbeats before starting again. "Then you know that I can't hurt them. Not now. Not more than the divorce already has."

Her insides turned to mush. "I know, and I get it. Like I said, I'm sorry for the accusation I made earlier."

With a bitter laugh, he walked away from her, pacing again. "I deserved it. And more. You caught me off guard right from the start. With what you said to me the first time I met you. About rising to the occasion. And just about everything else from then on. But I'm not making decisions for me. I *can't* move forward with you in that way. And let's face it, it's obvious to the world you aren't one-night-stand material. I probably wouldn't be half as attracted to you if you were." He sighed and dragged his fingers through his hair. "This is a terrible apology. I've never been good at them, but now I'm really out of practice."

"It's all right. I'm okay with your faults, numerous as they are." Megan grinned and held up the bag she'd slipped the chalkboard into. "Besides, we're starting over, remember?"

Shoving his hands back in his pockets, Craig walked close, stopping just a foot in front of her. "That's the thing I wanted to ask you. I don't have room for a lover. Not now and not for a long time. Nor am I asking you to wait. But right now I do have room for a friend. A genuine one."

He was laying his feelings out there without even questioning whether she returned them. Was it that obvious? Who was she kidding? *You don't insult someone, then start to cry because they're donating money to your work.* He knew her feelings.

Hardly daring it, Megan brushed the tip of one finger over the ridge of his collar. She wanted to brush her fingers over his smooth, muscular neck but knew it wasn't okay. Pulling her hand away, she nodded.

She forced a playful tone into her voice. "Do you want to know one thing friends do for friends in need?"

He shook his head. "What?"

She jutted her thumb toward her trunk. "They make them dinner. Calorie-laden but very tasty and wounded-soul-healing dinner. Grab a bag, will you? As long as you're here, I'm putting you to work."

This feeling twisting up his core wasn't new. The first time he'd experienced it, he was still a teen. He'd wanted the Yamaha street bike for sale in the cycle shop so badly his muscles ached. So he'd saved up and, against his parents' wishes, bought one shortly before turning eighteen. He'd ridden it every day of his senior year and loved that little bike all through college too.

Later, after college, interning at the marketing company where Jillian supervised him and a few other wet-behind-the-ears newbies, the feeling rocketed through him when she bent over his desk, letting her hair drape over his shoulder, always chewing on her lip and smelling of upscale perfume. Three months later, she was pregnant with Sophie, and they were both scared as hell.

He'd felt it when Andrew was born sick, a desire so deep-rooted he was certain he'd be able to move mountains to save his son. And he thought he had. The best doctors. The best facilities. The best treatments. He'd watched his son grow, lagging behind Reese but not so far he couldn't keep up, and that feeling had faded as a false and wicked sense of security crept into its place.

Now he stood in Megan's kitchen, watching her twist a mass of wavy hair up into a knot, leaving lone strands clinging to her neck, and he felt it again. His world was full of women who would be less complicated. Women who wouldn't tie up his core and make him ache until his lungs seemed to scrape against his ribs.

What was he doing? He'd sworn to himself he'd stay away, but he'd driven here as if on autopilot rather than waiting for another time to give her the silly little present. Being with her was a mistake, even under the pretense of friendship, when he knew she wanted him as much as he wanted her. He'd make a bigger mess of a disaster.

She was unpacking groceries and making small talk he couldn't process. Pulling out a colander, she filled it with fruit and washed it in the sink. When she turned off the water, she looked his way for the first time since he'd followed her inside carrying her packed-full reusable shopping bags.

"You okay?" She wiped her wet hands on her hips. "You look, I don't know, confused." She grinned suddenly and made air quotes as she continued. "Is it your *lack of domesticity*? Did I blunder by bringing you into my kitchen?"

Craig shook his head, surprised by the laugh that erupted from his chest. "No, you didn't blunder."

"Good, because I'm going to let you put together a plate of cheese and fruit while I take a shower. And don't think that's anything special because I always shower after I work in the kennels. I hate smelling like bleach and God knows what else."

He felt his tension easing away as she spoke. He could do this. He could handle being with her. Tonight at least. A salve for wounds so raw he couldn't ignore them any longer.

Megan pointed to one of the bags. "There's fresh bread in that one. And crackers in the cupboard if you prefer." She walked over to a cabinet beside the fridge and made a *ta-da* gesture as she opened it to reveal a latticed assortment of wines. "You can choose the wine, if there's any you can stomach. I'm sure you don't know any of the brands because they're all under eight bucks a bottle."

"Funny," he said, "but most likely true."

She shrugged, clearly unoffended. "Make yourself at home. I won't be long."

Under the watchful gaze of the cat that had scratched him, Craig pulled the rest of the contents from the bags after she left, then searched through cabinets and drawers to find a cutting board, a plate, and a knife.

By the time he'd chosen the wine, opened it, and laid out a decent-looking arrangement of cheese, fruit, and crackers, Megan was back, filling the small room with the scent of shea and lavender. She was dressed in a long-sleeved Henley and lounge pants, her hair still dry but free again. It was full, wavy, and beautiful, and made him want to lose his hands in it.

"Impressive." She eyed his plate and cocked an eyebrow. "So there's more to Craig Williams than marketer and entrepreneur extraordinaire."

"You forgot abandoner of dogs." He leaned back against the counter, trying not to focus on the small patch of skin between the rim of her shirt and the elastic-waisted pants that would be very easy to slide off.

"I didn't forget. I'm officially forgiving you for that. And excuse the pants," she said, noticing the direction of his gaze. "But your little slate came with the call for friendship, and there's nothing like a pair of look-I've-added-ten-pounds cozy pants to meet that call, if you want my opinion. That and they're comfortable."

He passed her a glass of the wine. "As long as they're comfortable."

"Ha, are they that bad? On second thought, don't answer that."

"I won't, but for the opposite reason of what you're thinking. After asking for friendship, I don't want to come across as if I'm hitting on you."

A blush lit her cheeks as she sipped the wine. "Okay then. So, since you made the first course, I'll get busy with the pizza. I've been told I make a killer pizza. In fact, it's one of my best dishes." She gave an exaggerated toss of her hair. "All it takes is one slice to become a true believer."

Craig refilled his glass, noting the buzz washing over him. A buzz he realized he desperately wanted. Letting the halfway decent Syrah roll across his tongue, he sank to a chair at her table and watched her move about her kitchen with the confidence of someone who not only had committed everything about it to memory, but enjoyed it.

"I didn't know you liked to cook."

"You mean in my shoe filled with dogs?" Megan wrinkled her nose at him, remembering a joke he'd made about his thoughts on her home life during his and Sophie's tour. "I do actually. I love it."

"What's your favorite dish?"

"To bake or cook?"

"Is there a difference?"

"A huge one. My favorite thing to bake is an in-season pie from fruit I've actually picked. To cook… That's a hard one. I like to mix it up."

"I'm sold on the pie." He ran his fingertips over the smooth top of her table. "Let me know if I can help with anything."

"You're good for a bit. I'm going to teach you how to toss a crust. Everyone should learn to toss a crust."

Craig chuckled. "Like they do in Italian kitchens? Don't tell me some of those Europeans you mentioned at the coffee shop were Italian. You don't look it."

"I'm like an eighth or something. My dad worked his way through college in a pizzeria. I think I could toss a crust before my training wheels were off."

He sank back in his chair and shook his head. Maybe it was the wine. Maybe it was her. Most likely it was her.

The cuts and scrapes and bruises that filled his insides had fallen silent for the first time in a long while. Finishing off his wine, he savored the peace washing over him.

"*So*," Megan said, sinking onto the couch with the same, cautious, at-least-eighteen-inches-separate-us space they'd maintained before she'd gotten up to grab another bottle of wine. She twisted sideways this time, tucking her feet under her and facing him. "About this drinking thing…"

"What about it?" He sank against the back of the couch, resting his muscular, defined hands over the tops of his thighs. The pizza was almost ready, but Megan had a feeling that, like her, he'd snacked too much already.

"Would you think it was weird if I asked for your keys?"

His brows furrowed together. "Is there somewhere you need to go?"

She bit her lip, embarrassed to take this where it needed to go. Unable to think of anything more tactful, she plunged ahead. "No, but I'm worried you might have to. Or I might say something wrong and you'd want to take off. And I…" Her throat constricted into a knot. She cleared it and forced out what she could. "I was close to someone who made the wrong decision once. One of those decisions you can never take back."

He studied her face before answering, perhaps debating whether or not to ask for more. "Okay." He slipped a hand into his pocket and pulled out a set of three keys. Their hands met in the middle of the suddenly cavernous space. Megan's palm lit with electricity as their fingers brushed together. His hand lingered over hers, his thumb trailing the side of her palm.

Then he pulled away and sat forward, reaching for

the wine. "Do you have a time frame for me reaching full sobriety?"

"Nope," she said, feeling her tension start to recede. "I have another four bottles in the kitchen. There're a half a dozen bars within walking distance too. And more than one person has slept it off on this couch."

"Hmm, be careful what you offer. This couch is a thousand times more comfortable than the stiff bed I've been sleeping on." He sat back, wine in hand, and Moxie hopped to his lap for the second time, purring loudly and digging her paws into his thighs.

Ever jealous, Max found Megan's lap, adding percussion to the purring. She was glad for his company, to have the distraction from Craig. Right here on her couch. A hint of flour dotted his temple where he'd miscalculated his dough twirling. She contemplated brushing it off, but didn't. She didn't tell him either. All she could think about was that it was there because of her. A temporary, fleeting sign she'd touched his life. Stupid really, but hers to hold on to all the same.

She thought of him staying in an apartment furnished with impersonal things, sleeping on a stiff mattress, away from his kids more often than not, and a fresh twinge of sympathy filled her. "What you're all going through... It has to be hard."

"Divorce..." He pursed his lips and waved his hand through the air. "It's a bitch. When you have kids at least."

"They're okay though?"

"As far as Jillian and I and our over-consulted therapist can tell."

A smile curled on Megan's lips as she refocused her attention on Max, who was lying on his back sandwiched between her legs with his feet in the air. She loved Craig's dry and understated humor.

"Now it's your turn," he said. "And the question that's much easier to ask after three…four…glasses of wine is why the hell are you single?"

A snort-laugh escaped, and Megan shook her head. "You're definitely on the road to drunk, and you haven't even tried my pizza. Save an ounce of sobriety for one slice, will you?"

"I will, but you're evading."

"I'm not evading." She shrugged. "If you really want to know, I was engaged for two years, and now I'm not."

More silent studying. Finally, he asked, "Are you okay to tell me why?"

"I am. It's not that scandalous or anything. We worked long hours and had nearly opposite schedules. Officially, we grew apart and decided to take a break. Stay friends for life. I'm sure you've heard the drill."

"And unofficially?"

Megan pressed her lips together and smoothed Max's baby-fine stomach fur. "He came home one night and admitted his head was turned by an ambitious grad student who was working for him at the time." She shrugged again and wished it didn't hurt to say it all this time later. "He didn't have an affair or anything. He just came out and said that if we were as good together as we were supposed to be, he shouldn't want her as much as he did."

Craig's fingers tightened around his glass and his brow furrowed. She was left wondering what it meant for only a second. "Did you have anyone to kick his ass?"

Megan laughed. "No, it ended much more congenially

than that. I didn't fight to keep us together. A couple times I worried that was a mistake. But the truth is that I loved him, just not enough. Not enough to go the distance."

He emptied his glass and ran his hand over his face. "Do you know who I'd like to meet?"

"Who?"

"The woman that someone left you over."

Her heart did a flip, then a little skitter. *Don't let it go there. He asked for friendship, and now he's on his way to being too drunk to hold himself to it.* She forced herself to keep it playful. "I have a feeling there's an insult in there, but I'll let it slide."

"Trust me. That was completely insult-free."

Feeling a deep flush creep up her neck just as the oven timer buzzed, Megan dumped Max to the floor and stood up, brushing off her pants. While the pizza was cooling, she decided to brew a large pot of coffee. God knew they were both going to need it.

Working to suppress the shivers traversing her spine, Megan switched the travel mug of sweet-scented mocha to her free hand and tucked her half-frozen one into her coat pocket. She tried not to focus on how much warmer the shoulder was that was rubbing against Craig's upper arm as they meandered the darkened streets of Webster Groves.

"I wish it were still Christmas so you could see it," she said. "I always feel like I'm in a snow globe because the houses are done up so cute."

"It'd be colder if it were Christmas. It's mid-March, and I can't feel my toes."

"I told you that you needed a jacket."

"Wearing your ex-fiancé's left-behind and heavily sentimental hoodie didn't have the right energy to it."

"So now you're freezing."

"I'm still too drunk to be that cold."

"Thus the walk and the coffee." She wrinkled her nose at him, then grabbed his elbow to pull him to a stop. "We almost missed it." She pointed through the darkness to a big house with white-painted brick, tall gables, glowing lamps in the windows, and a small porch lined with black rockers and big pots of seasonal greenery. "It's one of my favorites. They decorate just right and never overdo it."

Craig said nothing as he took it in, then nodded appreciatively. "You're right. It's well done. Want to knock on the door and introduce ourselves?"

"It's almost ten o'clock, goober."

He laughed. "I can't remember being called a goober before. Ever."

"There's a first time for everything."

"So," he said, sipping his coffee as they started walking again, "did you grow up around here?"

"No. I grew up in the sticks. My house looked like a double-wide, like almost every other one in a ten-mile radius. Except that we were among the lucky ones and had a basement. And a tire swing."

From her coat pocket, her phone chirped. She pulled it out and felt unease wash over her. "It's Sophie," she said. "I'm talking to her class tomorrow about the shelter."

She stepped away to answer it, trying to sound chipper and sober and not out walking with Sophie's dad.

After assuring Sophie she wasn't in bed yet, she listed the dogs she was bringing and reviewed the highlights of what Sophie wanted her to talk about. Once she hung up, Megan pulled in a breath before turning back to Craig, who was looking at her in a way she couldn't decipher.

"When I'm with you, I keep forgetting about your relationship with her."

"It's weird. I know." Megan dropped her phone back into her pocket and fell into step beside him again. "She's a great kid. I really adore her."

Craig's arm brushed against her shoulder again. "You mean a lot to her. In fact, I'm pretty sure she idolizes you."

"Well, I'm honored to be idolized, especially by someone like her. I want you to know I'm not... Well, I haven't been...you know..."

"Leading her along to get on my good side?"

She nodded, pointing a finger his way. "Yeah, that."

"There's no need to state the obvious. But *I'm* honored you're acknowledging I have a good side."

Megan gave him her best mock-glower. "Now you've taken it too far." With her attention off the sidewalk, she tripped on an uneven slab and went sprawling forward, splashing a stream of coffee over herself and slamming her knees and palms into the rough concrete. "*Ouch.*"

"You okay?" Craig's hands closed over her sides as he helped her up. As soon as she was standing, he moved in front of her, reaching for her hands and turning them palms up. Nearby, her upturned coffee made gurgling sounds as it drained onto the sidewalk. Neither of them moved for it.

"I'm fine. And you're supposed to be the drunk one." Her hands stung like fire, but that paled in comparison to the fact he was so close, cupping them in his, the aroma of her spilled mocha heavy in the air.

What would he do if she slipped her arms around him and pressed her lips against his? Push her away? Pull her close? The urge to experience the pleasure of his mouth made her empty of everything but want.

One of his hands left hers, and he brushed a splash of coffee off her cheek. His fingertips traced the side of her face, traveling along her chin and down her neck until they were blocked by her coat collar.

He was so close. Twelve little inches separated them. That and a canyon between two different lives, one more in limbo than the other. His thumb circled the hollow of her neck, and he released a slow, controlled breath that washed against her forehead, smelling of wine and mocha. Would one kiss—one night—be enough? Why did it feel like moving on from anything with Craig would hurt more than her split with Paul had? That it'd be like being thirteen again and learning to live without the one person closest to her in all the world?

His other hand released hers and closed around her hip, claiming it and his desire for her in one fluid motion. He pulled her inward until their bodies pressed together. Megan's pulse raced from the feel of his muscles taut against her. A groan filled the small space between them, but she wasn't sure who it had come from. She knew the choice was to jump in and be engulfed, or step back and wither away from want.

Then, from inside her pocket, her phone chirped. She knew the answer before the phone chirped a second time, loud and demanding. It was Sophie, calling with something she'd forgotten to say or ask. Megan knew this even before pulling the phone out to check caller ID. Tonight wasn't going to happen. They would come to their senses and wither away.

It couldn't hurt forever though. Losing something you never had. Could it?

Chapter 13

THE *PING* OF METAL BATS CONNECTING WITH BASEBALLS greeted Craig as he stepped into the expansive warehouse of indoor batting cages. Reese trailed just behind. The building was a chorus of these *pings*, laughter, and the bursts from the pitching machines. Maybe because the scene was a throwback to his youth and the best times he'd had with his father, an unexpected calm blanketed Craig even before the door swung shut.

He'd distanced himself from this sort of energy for a while. Had almost forgotten what it felt like. Reese hadn't wanted to play any sports in the last three years. Before that, he and Andrew had been on several teams together. But then Andrew had vanished into thin air, and no one was in the mood for camaraderie or team spirit or cheering for anything.

If it were up to Reese, they wouldn't be here now. But this was a decision Craig and Jillian had made months ago. Since Reese wouldn't choose a sport, he was being forced into rejoining his old baseball team. They were happy to have him back. Craig had even agreed to be the new assistant coach.

"Do you see your team?" Craig turned to Reese, who was dragging his brand-new gear bag on its side as they headed toward the crowds. He wanted to call Reese on it, make him flip it over and roll it on the wheels, but he suppressed the urge. Reese was here against his will. If he got through tonight with this small act of defiance, it wasn't the end of the world. God knew, that was much worse.

Reese shrugged and scanned the groups hovering around the various cages. "Just look for a bunch of douche bags."

"Hey!" Craig took his arm and turned him so they were facing each other. "Come on, Reese. Enough already. If I thought you actually knew what that meant, I'd ground you for a month."

"From *what*?" It was a dare and came out with an anxious smile that showed a glimpse of the boyishness still hidden behind Reese's usual impassive exterior.

Craig knew where this was headed. They'd tried it once, grounding Reese from his DS and other devices. But Reese loved to read and retreated into his books. It hadn't changed anything. He hadn't rejoined the world. If they took the books away, he'd only retreat deeper into himself.

Sighing, Craig told himself to face the facts. He was the grown-up here, forcing his son to shake things up. He needed to be the mature one. Surely he could handle that.

"From having fun," he answered. "Oh, wait. You already grounded yourself from that three years ago, didn't you?" It came out sounding snide and bitter and far from mature. *Wonderful, Craig. Absolutely wonderful. Next time, see if you can make it all the way to the cages first.*

"Like you're any different." His son's cheeks and neck blossomed with red splotches, and Craig's mounting anger receded abruptly.

It was the truth. Undeniably. He pulled in a long, deliberate breath. "You're right. These last three years have sucked. But it doesn't mean that every day from here on out has to suck, does it?"

Reese pulled his lips into a tight circle and rocked onto the sides of his shoes. Craig could tell he was dangerously close to crying. This was new territory. Reese hadn't cried in forever. But crying meant caring. Feeling. Hope surged in Craig's chest, and he closed one hand over Reese's shoulder.

"Listen, forget it. Forget what I said. Just listen to the sounds a second. The *pings* of the balls and bats colliding. Do you hear them?"

Reese squinched up his face. "Uh, how could I not? They're everywhere."

Craig closed his other hand over Reese's other shoulder. "Really listen, Reese. When it's a wooden bat, the sound is a crack, and that's way better, but for now the ping will do. Forget your teammates this season—the douche bags, if that's what you want to call them. We're going to start with the pings. That's all we're going to focus on this year."

"Dad, you're being weird."

Craig knelt down, lowering himself to Reese's eye level. "Yeah, well, maybe it's time for weird. We've tried everything else, haven't we?"

Reese chewed his lip, but the hint of an awkward smile pushed through. "What do you mean, 'focus on pings'?"

"It boils down to physics. When a bat and a ball traveling in opposite directions and at different speeds collide, something happens. I'm going to teach you how to connect it with that ping."

"Something happens like the ball heading to the outfield?" It was sarcastic, but he was making eye contact.

"Yes, but something happens inside you too."

"I remember. Your hand hurts."

Craig laughed. "At first, but you get used to that. Something *good* happens. Look, get through this next hour without making any new enemies. I'll see if we can stay after, and I'll show you what I mean. Okay?"

"Yeah, whatever."

Craig nodded. *Yeah, whatever.* It wasn't much, but it was enough to start.

———

Nearly bounding with excitement, Craig reached for his phone for the third time in a handful of minutes. How he was so certain he wasn't sure, but he was on the verge of a breakthrough. He'd swear to it. The truth of it was there, deep down, rolling around his gut. This was going to work. And he had an itch to tell someone.

And not just anyone.

His phone was locked, but his fingers danced over the screen, longing to enter his code and scroll through his call log for Megan's number. But every time he considered it, his stomach would lurch in a different way and he'd put his phone away.

She'd care, of course. She'd listen. The same way she had when he'd told her how he'd gone to bed the night his world began to collapse. Told her how he'd ignored the warning signs screaming at him to fix things. To make things right. To never, ever let the boys go to bed angry.

The story had poured out of him on the walk the other night, after he came to his senses and remembered that sleeping with her was the worst of all ideas. She'd listened perfectly, as he knew she would. She took his hand and listened as they walked. The release he'd felt was indescribable. He'd been thinking about it ever since. He'd held his feelings in for too long. Way too long.

It was late that night—the night that was the beginning of an end no one could conceive was coming—and the boys were fighting over something stupid and inconsequential. Whose turn it had been to kick the last ball at recess, if he remembered correctly. They'd both been undeniably right, and Craig had been too tired to deal with it.

They'd been at school late for Sophie's class play, and Craig had to pack for an early flight to Portland. Jillian was busy dealing with Sophie and some drama going on with her friends. No one had the time or energy for Reese and Andrew to fight about a dumb ball. They'd gone to bed angry, using words like *idiot* and *hate* that weren't allowed in their seven-year-old vocabularies.

Craig had drifted off wondering if the boys were still awake, lying in their beds, holding on to their anger. He'd been close to getting up to check on them. To make them talk. Make them apologize. Remember that they loved each other best. More than a ball. More than a game. More than anything.

But he'd fallen asleep, and just before his alarm went off, Andrew woke everyone with his coughing. From what Jillian said later, the boys either made up that morning or had forgotten about it. They'd parted ways friends. Reese to school. Andrew to the doctor. Craig had left for the airport hours earlier, not thinking about the fight and only mildly worried about the cough.

He'd turned on his phone as soon as he landed and

heard a panic so deep in the message Jillian had left that he boarded the next flight home without setting foot outside PDX.

Nine surreal days later, he was sitting in disbelief at a funeral parlor, unconsciously glancing around for Andrew, uncomfortable that he was out of sight while Sophie and Reese sat together in a corner not moving and not smiling.

He'd confided all this to Megan on the walk back to her place. She'd listened without interruption, rubbing her thumb over the back of his hand. Afterward, they stood around her driveway, and he directed the conversation toward more inconsequential things. Things that didn't split him in half to think about. Then, having proven his sobriety, he headed home. She'd asked him to come back inside, but he'd refused, unable to tell her that if he followed her through that door, he'd never want to leave.

Every hour of every day since, Craig had wanted to call or stop by the shelter or drive by her house. But this... This was different. He was on the verge of a breakthrough with his son. She'd want to hear. Hell, she was still young enough and optimistic enough to believe him. Or believe *in* him. Something he hadn't felt for a long time.

He'd given her a stupid slate and asked for friendship but knew he couldn't maintain it. It was all or nothing, and both scared the hell out of him. Since he kept putting his phone away and *not* driving by her house or the shelter, he figured *all* scared him more than *nothing*.

Keeping his phone in his pocket and forcing away the urge to hear her voice, he watched Reese endure the next hour. He seemed comfortable in his peculiar world of not fitting in with the other kids, not having a good time, and not hitting the majority of the balls that came his way. How long would he stay like this if someone couldn't reach him?

It's okay. This too shall pass. Maybe he was too old, too agnostic, to be silently quoting the Bible, but Craig believed it anyway. He was inspired. And he was about to have a breakthrough with his son.

———

"So," Craig said, brushing the salt from the pretzel off his fingertips. "Ready? Our cage is open now."

Reese rolled his eyes as he sucked on his slushie. "Can't we just *ping it* another time?"

"We can, but we can ping it now too."

Craig grabbed his bat and headed over without looking to see if Reese was following. By the time he had the pitching machine loaded, Reese was hovering near the plate, tossing his bat into the air and catching it.

"Have you learned about kinetic energy yet?" Finished filling the machine, Craig joined him at the plate.

Reese huffed. "I'm still in fourth grade, Dad."

"Maybe, but you watch all those science shows."

Catching his bat, his son shrugged. "It has something to do with motion, doesn't it?"

Craig bounced a ball on the end of his bat a few times before it fell to the ground. "That's it exactly. It's the energy an object has *because* of its motion. When the ball's flying your way, it's full of kinetic energy. And obviously you get that it takes energy not only to stop it from heading past you, but to send it sailing in a new direction."

"Yeah," Reese said, missing his bat midcatch and letting it clank to the floor. "Obviously."

"Good. That's the energy in your swing. When you don't do it right, you feel it in your hands as you said, which is why your stance is so important. But more than that," Craig said, tapping his son's chest, "is what's happening in here."

"I don't feel anything there."

Craig watched Reese fumble for his fallen bat. "No, but you will. We're going to start with release and work our way up to satisfaction."

Reese screwed up his face. "Oh, come on. *Seriously?*"

"Pretty darn." Craig tapped his own bat on the rubber plate. "Tell you what. I'll go first and show you what I mean." He jogged down, flipped the switch on the pitching machine, and headed back as the first ball sailed past. "No matter. There are plenty more where that came from."

Reese stood to the side, plastering on his best look of skepticism and rolling his bat in circles between his hands.

"You've heard the expression 'getting something off your chest,' haven't you?" Without waiting for an answer, Craig pressed on. "Well, you and I, Reese, we hold things in. Everything. And I'm sorry about that. We can't choose the genes we pass to our kids. Your mom and I, your therapist, we can tell you how important it is to talk your feelings through, but that doesn't mean it's easy to let them go."

"This sounds lame." Reese's shoulders slumped, and he tossed his bat to the floor.

Craig pointed his finger Reese's way as a third ball

sailed past. "Then that's a good starting place." He sucked in an exaggerated breath and sank into batting position over the plate. "Lame exercises that your dumb-ass dad makes you do. That's the next ball headed our way."

He fell silent as he waited, feeling the anticipation setting up inside him. He heard the burst of air as the ball rushed toward him, too slow and too low for his liking, but he swung anyway. The bat and ball connected with a satisfying *ping*, sending the ball sailing toward the end of the cage where it caught in the netting.

"There," he said. "That felt good, and it wasn't even my frustration. It was yours. So I'm calling the next one. Let's see. What's weighing me down? I know. That boy two cages over earlier. Did you see him? He was totally bald, and his face was puffy."

Reese was staring at Craig, really staring at him. He nodded lightly, almost imperceptibly.

"I figured you did. And I figured you knew he was sick, just not how. To look like that it had to be chemo. Which means he has cancer. I hate seeing kids with cancer. That's my next ball. Not the kid. But the way seeing him made me feel. Helpless and sad."

Reese stared but said nothing.

Craig settled into position, and the comforting sounds coming from the other cages fell silent. The next ball left the machine with a declaring *whoosh*, and he sent it flying, savoring the release that washed over him. He didn't look directly at Reese, but knew he had his rapt attention. Craig could see him in his peripheral vision, standing still, watching intently, mouth lightly agape.

"Next, I'm going for divorce. Because not seeing

your kids every day *sucks*. And it makes you feel like a selfish, rotten bastard."

He could have sent that one out of Busch Stadium and wished it hadn't been trapped by the confines of the net.

"I guess you know it's coming, but this next one's for Andrew. For the way it feels having to let him go. For the guilt that comes with moving on." Craig swallowed hard. His eyelids felt like a floodgate suddenly. Behind them was an endless river of tears that'd never been shed. Doing his best to shove them away, he pressed on. "For leaving him behind when he should be here."

He missed this one, and missing it made him want to scream. Swiping at the wetness that felt so foreign sliding down his cheeks, he returned to batting position. He'd crack the next ball in half. But movement distracted him. He glanced up to see Reese pounding toward him. He stood upright as his son barreled into him, throwing his arms around Craig's waist and burying his head in his chest. Reese was sobbing. Wild, wicked sobs that rattled his thin frame and sounded as if they were choking him.

Craig dropped his bat and engulfed him in the embrace Reese had deprived himself of for too long. Far, far too long.

"It's okay, Reese." He brushed back his son's hair and pressed his lips into the wet tangle his own tears were creating. "Everything's going to be okay."

Chapter 14

IT WAS DECIDEDLY FANGIRLISH, GOOGLING IMAGES OF CRAIG Williams. Admitting it was a new low, Megan closed her browser and slumped over her desk. Her forehead pressed into the keyboard, causing the speakers to emit a series of angry protests.

There were dozens of pictures of Craig online from interviews and websites he'd been featured on, which she'd discovered when she first Googled him after he made the donation. But just because she hadn't seen him in the eleven days since he'd been at her house didn't give her the right to stalk him online. Or fantasize about him. Or experience the little rush his picture sent through her.

Since that night at her place, she and Craig had exchanged a few emails about the long-range planning in progress for the shelter. But that had been it. She knew from Sophie he'd been out of town twice and they'd had a lot going on. Unfortunately, that hadn't stopped her from holding her breath as she pulled onto her street at night, hoping to find his car in her driveway again.

The truth was plain and simple. And she needed to face it. Not only was he nearly a decade older, but he was also in an entirely different place in life. He was fresh out of a divorce and needed to focus on his kids. Thoughts of him should not—definitely not—bring rushes of electricity comparable to grabbing the big electrostatic ball on her trips to the children's museum with Ashley and little Jake. They shouldn't remind her of the ball's wild, ever-changing current inundating her, making her feel small and insignificant and part of something immense and very much alive at the same time.

Irritated by the incessant bleeping of her computer, Megan sat upright and forced her thoughts back to reality. Sophie's party started in half an hour. Like it or not, she'd be dealing with Craig and his entire family at once.

This made her feel like she was about to perform in a play but had forgotten to study her lines. Maybe it wouldn't be so bad if she'd seen him since he showed up at her house. Since that amazing evening that had left her place a bit too quiet and empty and lacking. Or if afterward they'd had some we-really-can-make-it-as-friends exchange.

But they hadn't. He'd poured his heart out on the walk, and she'd taken his hand and invited him back inside. But rather than accepting her invitation, he'd closed up entirely. It'd been like watching a curtain shut. Only it hurt.

Megan stood up from her desk, thinking of something her dad had said when she was seven or eight. A bird had flown into their family room window and gotten stunned. She'd wanted to keep it after it recovered. *You can't hold on to something that isn't yours*, her dad had said.

If she knew what was good for her, she needed to get through tonight and put Craig out of her mind. Romantically anyway. With his commitment to shelter planning and Sophie's love of the place, he wasn't just going to disappear.

She scooped Trina, who was purring as loud as a dragon, off her tall filing cabinet and carried her to the main room. The shelter was quiet and empty, having closed a half hour ago. Since they didn't have a dedicated area big enough to accommodate party guests, parties were held in the main room after closing. Kelsey had been the last to leave after triple-checking that Megan was all set for the party. Kelsey loved working birthday parties and would've joined her, but her brother needed an emergency babysitter this evening. The only people working the party would be Megan and Samantha, one of their college-age volunteers.

She plopped Trina on the counter and flitted through the front room, checking things that had already been checked. Even though they only began hosting parties for older kids this year, the few they'd hosted were hits. Girls Sophie's age typically enjoyed crafts, so Megan needed to stop worrying the party could be a flop. It's just that Sophie was so excited. She was head over heels in love with the shelter and had no doubt her friends would feel the same way.

Megan shook the tension from her shoulders. The girls were going to have a blast. Sophie and her friends would paint ceramic pet dishes to take home, make homemade enrichment toys to leave with the dogs, and watch a short training session. Parties ended with the guests getting some cuddle time with a couple of the friendliest dogs and cats, which was always a favorite activity. More than once, these parties had resulted in adoptions, and they helped generate money for the shelter, so this one was going to be a success all around.

Megan's stomach roiled as Jillian's black Escalade

pulled into the lot. What if Jillian picked up on her crazy, mixed-up feelings for Craig? She could think of few places she'd rather be than in the same room with both of them at the same time.

Enough, Megs. Just because Jillian was a gorgeous exercise goddess with spectacular hair and stellar pedicures and wore heels with yoga pants… Well, there was no reason to be intimidated by her.

Megan took one calming breath and headed for the door.

It was surreal, having his kids, his ex-wife, and the woman he was falling for all in the same crowded room. Sophie was having a blast, and thankfully so were her friends. They laughed and cooed over everything, which was a relief because for the first time, Sophie was having problems with friends in school. Craig had heard it was a common middle-school thing, but hopefully this would help.

Megan was phenomenal with the kids. Not that he'd had any doubt. She largely avoided Jillian and made eye contact with him only once. She'd been giving the girls painting instructions and faltered, having lost her train of thought. Sympathy swirled through his chest. Clearly, this was as hard for her as it was for him. He should've called her today before the party. The only reason he hadn't was because of how much he wanted to. Anything he wanted that much would never be simple.

Halfway through it, Craig knew he could call the party a success. Reese was the only kid here not enjoying himself. He'd spent the first hour off to the side, unengaged, absorbed in a game. Painting pet dishes was gay, he'd told Jillian when she pressed him to participate. Her jaw had tightened, and she'd reminded him to watch his language. As if controlling his words was the most important battle.

But she didn't really think that. She just had a difficult time relating to the vast complexity of Reese. Not for lack of trying. Jillian exercised or cleaned her way out of the abyss of grief. It worked for her. Reese withdrew from a world he'd become highly perceptive of. It wasn't working for him.

Craig attempted to engage his son when he wasn't flanked by the dads who'd chosen to stay at the party. Tonight, Reese wasn't having it. After a bit of debate, Craig decided to leave it alone. The party was only two hours, and Sophie clearly wasn't bothered by her brother's disenchantment. She and her friends were having too much fun.

Then, to Craig's surprise, Megan used the downtime while the kids were eating pizza to sit by Reese, who was cramming in large bites of pepperoni pizza and playing his DS at the same time.

Unfortunately, Bob Sullivan, one of the girl's dads who'd stayed for the party, seemed to be only about halfway through a monotonous story about the moles that were invading his lawn. It was all Craig could do not to shush him so he could overhear Megan and Reese's conversation. A few minutes into it, Reese actually stopped his game. He nodded a few times and even smiled a half smile. They got up and walked over to the cat cages at the back of the room, staying there until the girls were nearly finished eating, then disappeared into the dog kennels for a few minutes. When they came back into the main room, Reese was actually laughing.

Megan headed to the front and announced they were ready to begin the dog-training demo. Everyone headed to the training platform at the back edge of the gift shop. Turbo and Tyson were up first. They looked drastically different from the afternoon Craig saw them at Megan's. Then, they had looked like white, tan, and black spotted rats. Now, they looked like healthy puppies. Even their necks had healed from the too-tight collars.

Megan's helper passed them to Megan while she finished strapping a treat-filled training pouch just above her hips, hips that Craig could easily envision closing his hands around.

"Turbo and Tyson are three months old and a really good age for training," she said to the small crowd filing into seats around the stage. She took the smaller of the two beagles from her helper. "This is Tyson. Tyson and Turbo were in pretty bad shape a month ago when they were brought in. Turbo perked up superfast with the care he got here, thus his name. For a week or so, we weren't sure Tyson was going to make it because his appetite didn't increase and he wasn't gaining weight. But he's a fighter.

"The last several weeks, he's been doing great and even gaining on his brother. In fact, the vet was here yesterday and cleared both these guys for adoption. So now that the hard part of their care is over—getting them healthy—we'll be focusing on training them until they find forever homes. And I'm crossing my fingers that these minimally trained puppies will be good subjects for you today."

The girls, who'd been cooing as Megan spoke, went into an uproar of oohs and aahs and begging the parents who'd stayed to adopt one.

"The trick to training," Megan said after the commotion died down, "is knowing that not only do dogs and puppies love getting praise from their owners, but they also can be ruled by their stomachs. If you have a ready supply of delicious treats, they'll perform little miracles for you. And from there, it's just a matter of habit forming."

She called Sophie up to the training platform. To Craig's surprise, in just a matter of minutes, with some guidance from Megan, Sophie had the two beagles sitting at attention, awkwardly sinking to the floor to lie down, and following her around the stage. Craig bet this would go into the books as Sophie's favorite birthday ever.

"I know you all want some time to pet and play with animals," Megan said after Sophie sat down, "but I thought it would be fun to show you a couple of tricks from a dog who's had a bit more training. I heard you girls all saying how much you love dogs and cats, so I know you're believers. Now—and no blaming him, girls—I may have overheard one person here say that animals were stupid... I know, I know, but I'm pretty sure it was just a figure of speech. And even better, this young man agreed to let me prove him wrong. Reese, how about it?"

Reese nodded and disappeared toward the kennels as Megan handed the beagles off to her helper. She stayed on the small stage and started placing toys from a basket randomly around the floor.

Craig blinked in surprise as Reese headed back into

the room, trailed by the impressive-looking German shepherd he'd seen on the tour. The dog followed Reese up to the stage, ignoring the girls as he passed them. Sledge—if Craig remembered correctly—sat at attention as Reese produced a treat from his pocket and offered it to him. While the shepherd was munching it, Reese produced a second treat and held his hand at mid-chest level. As soon as Sledge finished chomping, he lifted his paw and let Reese shake it. A wide grin spread across his son's face as the dog gobbled a second treat. *Way to go, Megan.*

"Now, the average trained dog understands over a hundred and fifty words," Megan said, unclipping the treat pouch and passing it to Reese. "Sledge certainly does. He's about five years old, and like the beagles, he's only been here about a month. Keep in mind as Reese works with Sledge that they just met today and neither of them are used to each other. Reese is going to show you how Sledge can pick up his toys using a series of three commands: take it, bring it, and drop it. I've talked to Reese about how to do this, but he hasn't tried it."

She gave Reese an encouraging smile. "Reese, I've scattered nine toys around our stage. So that we know Sledge is listening to you, before he starts, why don't you point out a couple that you don't want him to pick up?"

Reese shrugged and pointed to a purple bone and a blue rope. "He should leave those two."

Megan nodded him on. "Great. Just remember what I told you. Sledge will listen to you. You've got bacon-flavored treats after all."

She set the basket at the edge of the training stage,

closest to the girls. As soon as Reese said, "Sledge, come," the shepherd was on his feet, attentive to Reese. Sledge picked the first toy up, a white cotton rope, after Reese pointed and said, "Take it." The dog carried it over to the basket and dropped it at Reese's commands. The audience roared with approval. By the time the seventh toy was in the basket and only the two Reese had chosen to leave out were left, ignored by the dog, Reese's lopsided grin was as big as ever.

Megan high-fived him and Reese said that maybe just birthday parties—and not animals—were stupid.

For the second time that night, Megan's gaze locked on Craig's. She held it just a second or two, then looked away, biting her lip.

He thought of the walk they'd taken at her place and how close he'd been to kissing her. How the only reason he didn't was because he knew he wouldn't be able to stop. Until tonight, it had been impossible to believe that he could be ready to hold on to someone this soon.

But whether or not he was ready for her, Megan was here. And he didn't want to let her go.

If his kids weren't going home with him tonight, he would have committed to making right the idiot decision to avoid her that he'd somehow managed to keep this last week and a half.

───~~~───

With the saltiness of leftover cheese pizza and the clingy sweetness of root beer still on her tongue, Megan sank to her seat and shut the driver's side door. In front of her, the shelter was dark and quiet, lit by the emergency-exit lighting. Letting out a tired breath, she glanced at the clock on her dashboard. It was almost nine o'clock. Friday night or not, as soon as she gathered the strength to start driving, she was headed home to curl up in bed. On top of a full working day, Sophie's party had exhausted her physically and emotionally.

Sophie had had a blast. That was the most important thing; it was her thirteenth birthday after all. And Sledge had rocked. Halfway through the party, Megan had thrown caution to the wind and done her best to help Reese make a connection with something other than a video game. She was fingers-crossed hopeful that it had worked. Her heart went out to the kid. When she was just a few years older than him, she hadn't thought anything could be worse than losing her father. But Reese had lost his identical twin brother. She could only imagine how long the aftershocks of that would shake the Williams family.

Jillian seemed as put together as a woman could be, but Megan had glimpsed the vulnerability that had to have come with loving her two surviving kids in the aftermath of losing the third. It had happened when Reese was leading Sledge back to the kennels. Sledge was following him for another treat, and Reese was still forgetting to hide that spectacular smile of his. Jillian's composure faltered for a second or two, and her mask fell away. She'd been near tears. Tears, Megan suspected, of relief or hope. How scary it had to be for her to march forward, promising her children things would be okay, when she knew such promises can never really be made.

Then there was Craig. Everything about him called to Megan's soul. He also had put on an amazing front, but it was one Megan could see beneath. Maybe he hadn't called in eleven days, but in just a few exchanged looks, she knew it wasn't because he didn't want to.

He was afraid. And why shouldn't he be? What would bringing her into his world do to his kids when they were already adjusting to new lives?

She certainly wouldn't be the one to press him into anything before he was ready. She'd made it through tonight. She could make it through anything. Right now, it had to be about Reese and Sophie. She got that in a way she hadn't before. They'd been through enough. They were still going through it. Losing someone you loved wasn't something that happened over one day. Like water carving away at rock, it would continue to shape them for years.

Fishing through her purse, Megan pulled out her phone and unlocked the screen. She didn't do it to make a call or to check her email. Instead, she stared at her background picture. She'd taken the photo when she was twelve. It was film originally; she'd had it converted to digital when she was seventeen.

She brushed a fingertip over her dad's image. It wasn't the best picture, but she'd been the one to take it, and it had been a really good day. It was taken outside, late fall when the leaves were a golden yellow-brown. He was wearing his favorite plaid fleece and blue vest. He'd been working in the garage, restoring an old Camaro. She'd been hanging out with him, laughing and listening to his stories. She ran in the house for a camera when she noticed a dark smudge of oil on his cheek. Instead of telling him, she took his picture. Most likely he'd figured out something was amiss, but he grinned a cheesy grin and let her take it.

It captured his playfulness, and even though it wasn't perfectly focused, she loved it. Less than six months later, he was gone. How long had it taken, she wondered, for the pain over his death to stop carving away at her? Not knowing the answer, she flipped her ignition and started for home.

Chapter 15

Standing at the sink, Craig stared out the window into the darkness. A single streetlight glowed yellow in the distance, illuminating a redbud that was beginning to bloom, and making a halo of the rain falling in horizontal sheets across the parking lot. A flash of lightning danced across the sky. A crack of thunder shook the walls.

Pressed against his ear, his cell ceased to ring and Megan's voice mail picked up. He hung up without leaving a message, frowning, wishing he'd been able to call earlier. Tossing his phone on the counter, he paced his darkened apartment. But the sterile and confining kitchenette and adjoining living room weren't big enough to work off his energy.

Not only was there tension lining every muscle, but his skin was tight, uncomfortable. The compact apartment had never been so stifling. If it wasn't storming, he would go outside for a run, despite the fact that it was nearly midnight. Long runs always took the edge off. Sophie and Reese were old enough now. And they were both sound asleep in their cramped, shared bedroom. He could leave them long enough to run himself to an exhausted calm.

When the storm passed, that's what he'd do. Until then, he needed to think of something. He shoved aside the coffee table and sank to the middle of the living room floor in push-up position. His chest and shoulders started to burn when he reached seventy, but he pressed on, not willing to stop until the burn turned to fire and the fire to acid.

From the counter, his cell began to ring. Rising to his knees, he wiped the sweat off his brow and forced his breathing under control. He answered after the third ring, just before the call was lost to voice mail.

"Hey," he said without looking at the screen. "Thanks for calling back."

"That's okay. Is everything all right?" Megan cleared her throat. Her voice was heavy with sleep, which made him visualize her smooth neck and how much time he wanted to spend kissing it.

"Yeah, everything's fine. Sorry if I woke you."

"It's okay."

He took a breath, his heart still beating rapid-fire in his chest. "I wanted to call earlier, but I have the kids. They were up late. I think it was all that cake and caffeine."

"Sophie's with you? She's okay?" Megan sounded tired, confused. And there was something else in her voice he couldn't place.

"She's fine. Why?"

"I don't know… It was a dream, I guess. It was terrible." Afraid, Craig realized. She sounded afraid.

"She's asleep in the next room." He stood up and headed for the kitchen, leaning over the sink to look at the rain. "Snoring even."

"Thank God. Nightmares, you know? They suck. But when I woke up, my phone was beeping with a missed call from you, and it seemed like too much of a coincidence."

"Would it help to tell me what it was about?"

The line fell silent. A bolt of lightning flashed across

the sky. "Not really," she said finally. "I just have night-mares sometimes."

"Megan…" Her name was all that would come out. What could he say to her? Ask if there was something he could do to take her fears away? Hell, he hadn't been able to do that with his own kids.

"Will you promise me something?" Her voice was soft, innocent.

"If it's in my power, yes."

"It sounds stupid saying it, Budweiser commercial stupid, but Sophie… I don't know… I was her age when it happened. A few days from turning thirteen. She's always talking about how alike we are, but I never did tell her the whole truth. I wanted to, but I couldn't. I don't know why. I never tell people."

Craig watched the rain racing nearly sideways toward the ground as everything fell into place. Suddenly he knew what she was going to say. He'd heard her allude to it in small snippets of conversation that were never pursued. He'd seen it in the photos at her place of a father who wasn't aging. Felt it when she reached out to take his keys.

He could tell she was fighting the unevenness in her voice. Trying to keep strong. "My dad, he wasn't a drunk. He just made a mistake one night. My parents were fighting over something stupid. They'd have these rows, but then they'd make up. One night, they had one and he stormed out. I guess he met up with some friends at a bar." He heard her swallow. Could tell there were tears sliding down her cheeks. If he was with her, he'd kiss them away, one at a time. She paused, swallowing hard. "I guess you know where this is headed."

"Yeah, I do. I'm so sorry, Megan."

"It's okay. I survived. Those of us who are left behind survive, don't we?"

"We do, but surviving isn't everything, is it? We have to learn to do more than survive. It's taken me a long time to realize that. But I get it now. How can I expect Reese and Sophie to heal when I'm not?"

"What you're doing for your kids, I respect that. Believe me. My dad was only gone a year when my mom got serious about someone new. Six months after that, she remarried. Some guy they both went to high school with." Megan laughed, but the sound was mingled with tears. "Want to talk about grudges? I'm still holding one. It's probably why I never tell anyone. In the long run, my mom remarrying turned out for the best. I have a brother and sister now. They're a lot younger than me, but they're amazing kids. I'm crazy about them."

Craig turned away from the rain and pressed his eyes shut, picturing her face. From the first time they met, he'd been drawn to everything about her. Her skin, her mouth, the shape of her nose. Hair he wanted to sweep back so he could lose himself in that neck of hers. Eyes that seemed to read him in a way no one else's ever had. And that…that was above the neckline. The rest of her stirred him to life, making him feel as if his sluggish body was waking from a hundred-year slumber.

He felt it sliding in with these thoughts, the fear that came with wanting someone as much as he wanted her. Exposing himself to something else that could be taken away. Diving into something that could cause his kids more pain. The fear was so strong that he was almost surprised by his next words.

"I have to see you."

Her laugh was subdued, painful, and muffled like she was wiping away tears. "We saw each other tonight."

"That…that was torture."

"I haven't gotten to that promise," she said. "About you and never driving drunk."

"Okay." He paced his apartment, itching to grab his keys and take off for her place. "That's an easy promise. I haven't done that since college. If losing Andrew and then watching my kids as I went through the divorce didn't push me into it, I can promise nothing will."

She let out a slow, even breath. "Thank you."

"Megan." He stopped pacing and sank to his couch. "Christ, Megan. What am I going to do with you?" He closed his eyes, waiting for her to respond, wishing he could reach the pair of lips on the other side of the line.

"Nothing," she said finally. "Because right now, nothing is the right thing to do. When it isn't storming and the middle of the night, you'll remember it too."

"Would you care to guess how many times I've reached for the phone to call you this last week and a half? How many times I've nearly had to tie myself down to keep from driving to your place? And then tonight you were so phenomenal with Sophie. And Reese… That was nothing short of a miracle. It made me realize this doesn't have to be something else to tear the kids apart. It doesn't have to be wrong."

"It's wrong if you jump into something. If *we* jump into something."

"Then how about we don't jump? How about we walk or crawl or, hell, we can slither."

She laughed, low and quiet and in a way that called

to his soul. "Oh yes, please. Let's slither. I've always dreamed of that."

He chuckled, and the line fell quiet. The part of him that'd been waking up was humming with wild tension. "I'll never regret a minute with my kids, but I have them through Sunday. Otherwise…" He stopped pacing and brushed his fingers down the ridge of the front door-frame. "I think you know the otherwise."

"Craig, I… This scares the hell out of me."

Unlocking the door, he stepped onto the threshold and soaked in the crisp, clean scent of the spring storm as the rain battered the ground. "They always do, you know. Those things we want the most."

A blue-white flash of lightning and simultaneous boom of thunder exploded over the parking lot as if in agree-ment. He felt the energy surge through the air, matching the tension inside him. If there was any other way than to face this fear head-on, he certainly didn't know it.

―――

Megan was in the kennels squatting—*did she have to be squatting?*—in front of a slobbery mastiff mix when Craig walked through the glass doors and into the noisy room, stopping not far behind her. Rather than turning to acknowledge him, she stood up and handed the mas-tiff's leash to the new volunteer who had a hankering to take him today.

"He's been walked a few times," she continued. "No complaints so far, except that it's best to stand off to the side when other dogs are going to pass. He's a bit skittish around other males, but he hasn't shown any hint of aggression."

Megan heard Sophie and Reese in the background, squabbling over something as the volunteer leaned over to let the mastiff lick her cheek. Though she had her back to the three of them, she could hear the kids moving from kennel to kennel, looking at the whimpering and pleading dogs.

Keeping her attention on the woman, Megan said, "Would you like to walk him around outside while I get the rest of the dogs ready?"

The new volunteer agreed, only half acknowledging Megan as she cooed to the dog and headed toward the back doors.

Facing the new arrivals, Megan self-consciously wiped her hands on the backs of her pants. She was fairly certain her cheeks had reached a deeper shade of red than they had been since grade school as Craig, who was now standing behind his kids, winked at her. In blue jeans, a fitted V-neck, and a light jacket, he exuded a meet-me-at-the-park male model aura.

Because she felt as if she'd have less chance of falling apart, Megan forced her attention to Sophie. "Hey there, thirteen-year-old. We're walking in Forest Park this morning. Trees are starting to blossom, so it'll be a beautiful one."

"Great. And in case I forget later, last night was the best birthday party ever." Sophie bit her lip and motioned toward her dad. "Would it be okay if they walked some dogs too?"

An entire morning with Craig. Somehow Megan managed to shrug as she turned her attention to Reese, who was mock-whimpering at a Great Dane nearly his height. "Sure. Reese, was this your idea?"

He scoffed loudly enough to be heard over the dogs. She wasn't sure why it surprised her to see his guard up again. "Walking's gay."

"Reese," Craig interjected, "enough."

Joining Reese in front of the showstopping Great Dane, Megan pulled out her keys to unlock the cage door. "I'll let that slide since you're a kid, but there are better adjectives out there for your lack of enthusiasm in activities."

One corner of Reese's mouth pulled up in a shadow of a smile. "Maybe. But walking in a park to smell the spring flowers is definitely gay."

Stepping into the Dane's cage, Megan motioned Reese to follow her, then directed her next words Sophie's way. "I don't know, Soph, but I'm pretty sure drastic grudges call for drastic measures. Think Peanut can win him over?"

Sophie giggled. "If any of these dogs can, it'll be Peanut."

Thirty minutes later, Reese's dog stopped in his tracks as the group rounded a bend in the trail overlooking a gurgling stream. "I'm *so* not picking that up." He gagged as Peanut pulled in his massive haunches to take a dump the size of Reese's head.

Megan fanned her nose. "His poops are always huge and stinky. It's Peanut's only downfall. That and the Great Dane's short life expectancy, I guess." She pulled one of the bags from her jacket pocket. "We have a strict rule here, but I'll give you this one-time exception since we're trying to win you over. Otherwise, it's each walker to his own crap."

Closing off her breath, Megan bagged the poop and jogged back with Sledge to the nearest trash can. When she returned, Reese was still holding his throat.

"It was *so* big. How's that possible?"

Craig, who was farthest away, motioned to the Chihuahua-dachshund he'd been given. "I told you we should trade."

"I wouldn't walk that dog if you paid me," Reese replied. "That shows you shouldn't say you don't care what kind of dog you get next time."

"At least his crap will only be the size of my pinky."

"I'm just glad you're open to a *next time*," Megan said, cocking an eyebrow at Reese.

He turned away with a shrug, but not before she caught the hint of a smile that belied his indifferent expression.

Sophie groaned. "Can you two *not* ruin this for me? I look forward to this all week."

"Sure thing, sweets," Craig said, resuming his place beside Sophie. "How long a walk is it today?"

"About the same as Sophie's last park walk, three and a half, maybe four miles," Megan said from behind them.

"Do you honestly think this little dog can make that distance?"

She smiled mischievously as he turned to give her a private wink. "If she starts pawing at your legs, that means she wants you to carry her. That's why I picked her for you. I thought that casual look of yours today would be well-paired with a purse puppy."

Bringing up the rear, Reese belly laughed. "Maybe my dog can give yours a ride, Dad."

Chapter 16

ONE WORD TICKLED MEGAN'S EARS TWO DAYS AFTER HER late-night call with Craig, making her stomach flip and her heartbeat flutter. It kept popping into consciousness at different times, sending a rush of warmth over her skin and making her palms sweat.

Otherwise.

Otherwise what? He didn't clarify because he didn't need to. She understood the answer as well as he did. And it scared the hell out of her.

Pacing her living room wasn't helping as the sun inched toward the horizon Sunday evening. Over the last two days, she'd cleaned every square inch of her place. Even organized a few drawers and her bedroom closet. She'd bathed, shaved, flossed, and perfumed. In case. Slipped into her sexiest matching bra and panties, then—after a half hour of debate—covered them up with a pair of worn lounge pants and a cozy sweater. She didn't want to look ready for the *otherwise*.

Glancing at the microwave clock—6:16—Megan felt her stomach flip again. Had he taken the kids back yet? Maybe he wouldn't even call. Maybe he'd changed his mind. He hadn't said anything yesterday at the shelter or on the walk. There hadn't been an opportunity.

Still, there'd been the way he looked at her when his kids weren't watching. Like he was aching for the *otherwise*.

Clenching and unclenching her fists, Megan headed

out the sliding glass door onto her back patio. The cool evening air that filled her lungs helped relax her a bit. Moxie followed her, twitching her tail as she meowed at the birds hopping from branch to branch in the thin strip of woods a few dozen feet away.

Leaning down, Megan scratched the base of the cat's tail. "You'd know what to do, wouldn't you? What am I saying? You're a love sponge. You'd jump his bones the first chance you got. However, you're spayed so you'd just want a good rubdown or something."

You've reached a new low, Megs. Soliciting relationship advice from your cat. Sinking to the concrete slab, she pulled a potted plant—frozen in its wintry death— toward her. She plucked off the brittle leaves one at time like she was plucking daisy petals.

She'd talked to Ashley ten times since Friday night. If she called her friend again, she'd not only interrupt their dinner, but she'd hear the same advice. *Have fun. Lock your heart away. Call me in the morning.*

Ashley didn't get it though, and Megan hadn't been able to explain it to her. Make her understand the immensity of the *otherwise*. It'd be like trying to explain the vastness of the Grand Canyon to someone who'd never been there.

Through the still-open sliding door she heard the thin, high ring of her doorbell. This far away, it seemed like a trick of the imagination. Moxie made it clear it wasn't, tucking her tail and flying inside and under the couch where she always hid when the bell rang.

Megan's stomach lurched as she stood up. What if she puked before he kissed her? While he was kissing her? Attempting to shake the tension from her shoulders, she made her way to the front door on shaky legs. *Pretend you aren't here. Don't open it. If you do, everything's going to fall apart.*

The little voice was still screaming as she turned the lock and pulled the handle. Craig was standing on the other side of the threshold, staring at her with eyes as blue and clear as any she'd seen.

He wasn't smiling. Or maybe he was smiling a hint of a smile. Megan opened her mouth, but nothing would come out. Her pulse was pounding so intensely behind her ears that she couldn't hear a thing.

She backed up a half foot and stared as he pressed her door open the rest of the way. *Oh God, say something. Stop this. Because he won't. You know he won't.*

He closed strong fingers over her wrist, keeping her from backing up farther and sending a wild shiver racing up her arm.

"This isn't..." Nothing else would come out. She wasn't strong enough to stop him. Or maybe she needed him too much.

He let out a breath as his other hand slipped into her mass of hair. The smile that wasn't a smile disappeared as he leaned in. Their lips met, softly at first. Then harder. Then urgently. Something akin to a laugh welled in her throat and froze. How could he have denied her this for so long? His lips and tongue were perfection. It was like a dance, kissing him.

He pulled away long enough to look at her, then pressed her against the foyer wall. The second kiss zapped the breath from her lungs. His hands abandoned her hair to tug up her sweater. He let out a groan when they came into contact with her skin.

How many times had she appreciated just looking at him? Allowed herself to imagine what he'd feel like? Now her body melted into his, and she struggled to commit the sensation to memory.

His lips traveled over her neck, and she seemed to be slipping away from her body. *Don't blow this by fainting, Megs.* She needed to focus. Focus on something besides the wetness of his mouth on her skin and the strength of his hands on her body. His strong, muscular hands. A moan filled the narrow space between them as his lips traveled over the hollow of her neck. Had it come from her? She wasn't sure.

She felt him tugging at her sweater and raised her arms to let him pull it off. Their eyes met for the first time since the kissing started. He grinned, a lopsided one she'd never seen, before the distance between them disappeared again and her shoulder took a turn experiencing the pleasure of his mouth.

The rattling engine of a car speeding down the street pierced through the sound of the blood pulsing behind her ears. The door. It was wide open, and she was in her foyer—in her bra—making out with the hottest guy in the world. Craig swung the door shut with one hand, not looking, his mouth not budging from her skin.

And then he was dragging her to the floor.

The floor. *Holy crap.* This wasn't just kissing. This was happening here. Now. Her shoulder was pressed against the wall, and the cold tile of the entryway seeped up through her pants as he lowered on top of her. She grasped for some sort of protest, but words evaded her. She'd never done anything this spontaneous before. Ever.

And damn the decision to wear lounge pants. They

offered no resistance. The feel of his hands on her hips—sliding down the underwear that matched the bra he wasn't even paying attention to—was brain-numbing. Reservation melted, and words leaped further away as his hands raked her skin. Any last hint of reasoning abandoned her.

Lacking his fluid precision, she tugged at his clothes, yearning to connect with flesh. Ignoring his shirt, she went for his pants as he found her neck again, distracting her. He had a belt, a button, a zipper. When this was over, she'd burn them.

As she tugged down his zipper, an alarm blared in her mind. "Wait. Hold on." She struggled to keep hold of the words. Of the warning she'd felt. His hands weren't ceasing their exploration. "Birth control may not be an issue, but there are diseases." Thoughts were melting into sensation. "Are you sure…"

"I'm sure." He pulled back enough to look her in the eye. "I'm clean."

She felt herself making a small nod. "Aren't you going to ask me?"

"You're too damn honorable not to tell me if you weren't."

Then he was kissing her again, and her case for protection felt like a small item at the bottom of a long-forgotten to-do list.

The moment he was free, he entered her. One second they were two people; the next, they were one. The cry of pleasure that echoed through the hallway didn't sound like hers, but she knew it was.

His thrusts were desperate, pressing her tighter against the wall and matching the urgency welling inside her. She clamped a hand around his hip, wanting him closer. Her free hand groped his body, hungry to experience taut muscles covered by smooth skin.

It was so much to handle, wanting him the way she did. She wanted more. Knew she'd never have enough. Not of him.

Afterward, he brushed back her hair and laughed while still inside her, heightening the intimacy of their connection. His laugh, deep and low, rolled on like a clap of thunder, muffling once he buried his head in the crook of her neck.

"I'm sorry." He rose so his face was even with hers, his eyes shining, and he laughed again. "I'd ask if I can come in, but I'm not sure you'd find it funny."

She watched his gaze land on the trail of a tear that had slipped from the well beneath the surface. He dried it with his thumb, then traced her jaw. She racked her brain for something to say, but everything paled in comparison to the one thing she couldn't find the strength to say. *I'm afraid. More than afraid. Terrified.*

"I had plans," he continued, letting his fingers trail to the hollow of her neck. "Romantic ones, believe it or not. They just fell by the wayside when I saw you. It's been like a jail sentence, wanting you like this and having to hold back."

She swallowed hard, trying to swallow away the fear with it. The adrenaline was waning, and she was coming to her senses, realizing what they'd done. It had happened so fast. Her pants and underwear were knotted around one ankle. Her bra hadn't been touched.

What would happen now? Where could they possibly go from here? Panic was building inside her. Had they blown this, this thing they could be together? Undefined sex. Was there anywhere to go now but apart?

"Hey," he said, splaying his fingers against the side of her face and forcing her to look at him. "It's okay, Megan. It's going to be okay. As a matter of fact, it's going to be more than okay." He closed the distance between them with a kiss, a gentle one. Ended it by nipping at her lower lip.

"And this…" he said, chuckling again, shaking his head. "I'm going to spend the rest of the night making this up to you. Promise."

She gnawed her lip as his hand left her face and slipped her bra strap off her shoulder. His mouth danced across the swell of her breast as his thumb trailed the lace edge of her bra.

"Hey, nice bra."

With that, she started to laugh.

—⁓—

A soft thud roused Craig awake. He'd been drifting off. Glancing around the dark room from the cozy nest that was Megan's bed, he made out the shape of one of the cats on top of the dresser. Another thud. It was the cat, he realized, knocking his belongings off the counter. His watch, wallet, and phone lay in a pile on the floor.

He got the message. He wasn't supposed to be here. The cats had paced outside her closed door for the first few hours, slipping their paws underneath and rattling it. Finally, the intensity of all he and Megan were doing wore down, and she'd gotten up to let them in.

She'd been talking about making something to eat

when she drifted off, nestled in the crook of his arm. They'd missed dinner—had had sex right through it.

The dull hum of electricity, though muted, was still flowing over his skin. He was happy. Satisfied. In a way he hadn't been in a long time. He wanted to stop time, to savor it, since he knew how quickly this phase passed.

If he was lucky, he could draw it out from mere days to weeks or a month, this first bit of exploration. This little piece of heaven before the world settled in. Before they'd face the trickiness of fitting her and Reese and Sophie into a more complicated picture.

With nothing else of his to knock off the dresser, the cat pounced to the floor and batted his phone around the carpet. Refusing to be baited, he slid his hand over Megan's stomach. Her bare, silky skin roused his senses immediately. She was fit and had curves in all the right places, mouthwatering curves. There was also a softness about her that he hadn't felt in a long time. Around her smooth hips and along her thighs.

He slid his hand over Megan's hip and down her thigh. As he was hoping, that stirred her awake.

She swallowed and blinked her eyes, lifting her head just enough off his shoulder to look at him in the darkened room.

"Hey." She ran her fingers through her hair, sweeping it from her face. "Guess I fell asleep."

"I guess you did."

He closed his hand over the back of her leg and pulled their bodies close. With skin pressing onto skin, his blood pulsed wildly once more.

She bit her lip, half smiling, half groaning. "Aren't you tired? My muscles feel like wet noodles."

"No, not yet." He smoothed back her hair and kissed behind her earlobe. He felt like a schoolboy, unable to keep the smile off his face to save himself. "Not the least bit, in fact."

Pressing her to the bed, he rolled on top of her, letting his mouth stay lost in her neck. He had no idea a woman's neck could stir him to life like this. Make him forget everything.

Sucking in a breath, she ran her fingers over his cheek, then along his shoulder and down his back. "You... Wow. I didn't see sexual superpowers listed on your résumé when I was Googling you, so is there any chance you took one of those libido-inducing pills before coming over?"

He laughed and rose up on his hands to look at her. The room was so dark that he had to strain to make out the smile curling her lips, but the whiteness of her teeth was like a beacon in the night. "No, but if you'd like me to, I'd consider it. What you're seeing tonight stems from a handful of years of enjoying next to nothing."

"Ouch." She nipped at his lower lip between his words. "Sounds like that might have some side effects."

He wrapped one hand around her hip and rolled over, pulling her on top of him. "Mmm, it's like secondhand smoke. It's going to keep you up all night as well."

She sat back and ran her hand along his stomach, waking individual muscles as if stroking keys on a keyboard. "I could think of worse things." Her voice was low and husky, heightening his desire.

He cupped a hand around each side of her face. An unlikely mix of feelings slid over him—desire keeping time with anxiety. "I can't let you fall asleep." He tried to keep it playful, but he could hear the desperation slipping into his words, calling him a liar. "'Cause if you do, I will too. And what happens if I wake up and find you're just a dream?"

It was such a fluid movement—their bodies becoming one again—that he wasn't sure who led it. Like waves sliding over the shore and carrying away the sand when they left. Her mouth opened in a gasp, and she bit down on the thumb he brushed across her lips.

"I don't know about you," she said, "but my dreams are almost never this good."

Chapter 17

A RADIO FLICKING ON AT FIVE A.M. LULLED CRAIG FROM an unsettling dream. He blinked, taking a second or two to familiarize himself with his surroundings. The silky sheets and cozy mattress made it clear he wasn't in his sterile apartment. He rolled onto his back, rubbing sleep from his eyes. Maybe the disorientation would lessen if he and Megan each settled on a side of her bed, but he'd intentionally tried to keep that from happening these last three and a half weeks. Tried to keep the habitual from announcing itself and setting in.

Not that he'd mind the habitual with her. Of her being there for him both physically and emotionally as much as he needed her to be. He'd been thawing with her, coming back to life. But with life came fear. Fear of losing things that sucked out your soul when they left.

She hadn't pressed for more than the simple present that he'd confessed was all he could give her that first night they were together. She was in complete agreement that Sophie and Reese should discover nothing. It wasn't the time, she'd said. Not yet. And their future together—whatever it might be—was never discussed.

Shutting off the alarm before the music swelled loud enough to wake her, he slid out of bed, causing as little disruption as possible. He used the bathroom without turning on a light, then returned to the bedroom for his things. He could just make out her silhouette; she was sitting upright, head resting on her knees and arms draped around them. He sank next to her automatically, pulled as much by need as want.

It was a simple morning gift he allowed himself, letting his fingers get lost in her hair. But doing so set his morning on a different path, started happiness pressing in. With it came an unsettling anxiety. Uncertainty.

This wasn't the way he liked to start his day. He preferred to leave while she was asleep. To keep his guard intact. It was easier to go about his routine this way. At night, once everything was done, it was easier to let that armor down.

"Hey," he said, "sorry to wake you. That was my alarm. You've got another hour and a half to sleep."

She groaned and leaned in to him. "I know. I was thinking I should force myself awake and go in early. There's always so much to do."

"Hmm, let me guess. Your boss has really been riding you, huh?"

Something between a snort and a giggle slipped out of her. She pulled away and mock-pushed him sideways. "You're not my boss, idiot."

It was a second small gift, allowing his lips to brush her temple. The intensity that swept over him as he experienced her soft skin was almost painful. It was like acting: keeping it light, keeping it playful. "Maybe so, but 'board president' didn't sound as good. Go back to sleep. Work will wait."

"You get up at this ungodly hour every day."

"Yeah, and I've been doing it for years. I'm used to it."

"A hot shower does wonders. I'll be fine."

"Suit yourself," he said, letting his fingers trail over

her shoulder as he stood up. "I'd better get moving. If I don't make it by the gym, I'll regret it later. I have the kids from after school until about eight or so tonight. Do you have any plans later?"

"Mmm," she said, stretching and arching her back. "I think my boss may stop by. Other than that, I'm free."

He laughed as he slipped into yesterday's pants. In hopes of keeping it undefined, keeping the complicated at bay as long as he could, he never brought along anything aside from the clothes on his back. His gym clothes were in a bag in the car. After his workout, he'd head to his lifeless apartment to get ready for the day.

She started the shower while he was buttoning his shirt. He could feel the steam pouring into the room from the open door, beckoning him. Still dressed in the T-shirt she'd fallen asleep in, she returned for a good-bye.

"I haven't brushed my teeth yet," she warned, kissing his neck. "See you later."

He made it to the front door before he pulled out his phone to check his schedule. He had nothing till eight-thirty. How much could it hurt, starting his day with letting her in? With dropping his guard? Just this once.

She was already in the water when he returned. "Forget something?" she said, her voice hollow behind the glass doors.

"No. The opposite actually." He stripped off his clothes, tossed them on the bed, and slid open the door farthest from the shower head. "Mind if I join you?"

She melted into him, burying her head in the crook of his neck and resting her cheek against his chest. "Never. I was wondering how you do this so well."

His hands closed over the soft skin of her back. "Do what?"

"Get up. Go into work when you've had so little sleep."

"Something tells me it won't be so easy if you waking up with me becomes a habit."

The feel of her warm, wet body against his in the dark quiet of the morning was comforting in a way he hadn't expected. Disarmingly so. *Just this once. Then back to the routine you know you can handle.*

Trying to escape the feeling that he was somehow cheating, he draped his arms around her and closed his eyes as the water fell over their bodies, seeming to weld them together into one.

"What?" Megan said after the hot water tank emptied and freezing water had forced them out. She'd wrapped her hair and torso in overwashed towels and was in front of her sink applying the little makeup she tended to bother with before work.

"What do you mean?" Craig had gotten dressed again and was leaning against the doorframe watching her.

"You're staring. Something tells me you're not new to women putting on makeup. Am I doing something wrong?" Megan flashed him a smile in the half-foggy mirror.

"No." He said it without smiling back. "I don't know."

It was his tone that alerted her. Cautious. Guarded. She screwed the cap onto her mascara and turned to face him as he reached in to hang up his towel.

"What don't you know?"

"Much of anything it seems, but most especially this."

Most especially this. Doing her best to lock on a poker face, Megan slipped the towel off her head and brushed back her damp hair. So he finally wanted to talk about it, this thing they were becoming that they'd both spent the better part of a month ignoring. "I never said you had to," she finally replied.

Craig wrapped one hand over the doorframe, pressing his thumbnail into one of the ridges. "You said you believe in commitment."

"Yep, I said that," she said, nodding slowly. "And that's true. And if I remember correctly, I also told you I'm okay with keeping this undefined right now. You come and go as you please. You don't have any obligations to me. And I haven't asked you to make any. So I don't see what's gotten under your skin."

She could feel the heat zinging her cheeks. He'd been staring at a spot on the doorframe, picking at a bubble of dried paint. His jaw was tight, the muscles lining it rippling with definition.

Releasing a breath like a hiss of steam, he bolted forward, kissing her hard on the lips. Too hard. She pulled away before her mounting anger abated.

He cupped her face in his hands, brushing a drip of water from her temple with the tip of a finger. "What happens if I get hooked? What good's that going to be to you? What would you get from becoming wrapped up in my life?" There was a desperate look in his eyes. "Not much, if you ask me."

Fear dumped into her chest, competing with her anger, masking it. What *would* happen when it was over? So what if he came here every night with nothing. He was still leaving little memories—beautiful ones—over every square inch of her place. She'd look at nothing the same when this was over. Ever.

She wanted to flee the confining, steamy room, but he stood in front of her, blocking the narrow path to the doorway. She backed up, jamming the small of her back into the vanity and pulling his hands off her face.

"I think you're picking at something that's too fresh and undefined to be picked at. I think this is complicated, and I think it's very early in the morning." She closed her hands over the edge of her vanity and clamped it hard. "I think you should go to work."

She hadn't turned off the shower faucet tightly enough. It dripped three times while he watched her, not seeming to breathe. His piercing gaze softened, then lowered to her lips. He leaned forward, letting his mouth trail over hers in a whisper. His hands wrapped around her shoulders as he stepped closer, pressing his body against hers. She shook her head and pulled away, but his lips found her neck and her knees went weak.

Still gripping the vanity like a vise, she attempted to lock in her resolution. She needed to send him away. Away so she could think. But his mouth on her neck and his hands on her skin melted her resolve.

One of his hands left her shoulders to travel up her thigh and underneath her towel. Her skin was damp from the shower, adding friction to impede him. She could call on that sticky wetness—that and her will—to tell him no. It wasn't a good idea. Not right out of the shower. Not while a fight was brewing.

But he lifted her onto the vanity top with the ease of water pouring from a glass and unbuttoned his pants for the second time in twenty minutes. Instead of resisting, she lifted his shirt and closed her hands over his still squeaky-from-showering hips.

What were they doing, taking this to a place they were both too terrified to define?

Once dressed—skin still firing from his touch—Megan found Craig in the darkened kitchen, leaning over the sink and looking out the window. The sky was beginning to lighten on the horizon.

"Did I tell you I'm going on a trip this weekend?" he asked without turning.

"No, but Sophie mentioned it when we were walking the dogs on Tuesday." She felt a heaviness in the room akin to the wet, heavy St. Louis air before a storm rolled in. Making what was probably a futile attempt to ignore it, she reached for the coffeepot. "But the next several days are going to be crazy for me too. I think I told you about the parade this weekend. The volunteers organize it mostly, but it's still pretty consuming of our time."

Craig turned to face her, leaning against the sink. His lips pursed almost imperceptibly. "You told me. I'm sorry to miss it. So, Sophie told you about my trip? How come you didn't say anything?"

Megan joined him at the sink with the pot in hand, resisting the urge to rest her forehead against his shoulder as she waited for it to fill. "Because it's still a gray area, I suppose."

"How so?"

Flipping off the faucet, she let out a long breath and looked at him. Only an inch or two separated them. It felt like a mile. "If you must know, when I'm with her,

I feel about two inches tall for sleeping with her father and pretending I'm not. So I'm not about to break her trust and tell you the things she says to me."

His shoulders sank as he exhaled. "Okay. You're right. Thank you for that."

"So if there's something you want me to know about this weekend of yours, now's as good a chance as any."

She turned and dumped the water into the coffeemaker's reservoir, then pulled the lid off the shade-grown, fair-trade Colombian roast that was a morning staple. She was making enough for him without asking if he wanted any. He needed it. Needed his workout too. He was still as tense as wire. In a way she hadn't seen since that day they'd stood out in the storm arguing.

Her heart plunged into her stomach. Was he going to break it off? Screw him if he was. If he'd slept with her first and was planning to do it this morning all along.

His fingers drummed the counter. "There's nothing specific really. I just thought you might want to know."

Finished prepping the coffee, she faced him again. "Okay. I know." It was the look in his eyes—despite the tension lining his body—that calmed her. Craig Williams, marketer and entrepreneur extraordinaire, was afraid. "It's what you need, by the way—a getaway in the Bahamas with your best friend."

His jaw tensed, then relaxed, then tensed again. "That's it? Nothing else?"

She let a smile play on her lips. If he was going to be a stubborn idiot, then she could be coy. "Umm, have a good time? It's what you need, you know…to get away from everything."

His shoulders tensed again, and his drumming

reached a new crescendo. "He's looking forward to it more than I am, I believe. His divorce finalized about a year ago, and he's excited to have another bachelor to pal up with."

Resisting the urge to yank the frozen-into-a-lump bag of ice from the freezer and knock him on the head, Megan retrieved two mugs from the cabinet and the cream from the fridge. "Sounds…fun."

"That's it?" Craig asked, his voice turning up at the end.

"Um, don't forget the sunscreen?" She gnawed on her lip to keep from smiling. Or screaming. She was as angry as she was touched by his efforts to rile her. There was only one thing she could think of that could have gotten under his skin so badly to elicit this please-let's-have-a-fight behavior of his this morning. *Her*.

"Look," she said, "picking a fight with me so you don't feel guilty about your boy-bachelor weekend isn't going to work. I'm not your wife, and I'm not under the delusion you've made any promises to me. You're free to do what you want…who you want, if that's what you're hinting at."

Color raced up his neck, and his knuckles shone white. "Thanks. I'll keep that in mind."

Despite her efforts, her anger soared. Screw him. She wasn't playing this game. Whirling away, she yanked her lunch bag from the pantry and shut the door too hard.

She dove into making her lunch with rare gusto. She could feel him across the room, staring. When she was halfway done with her sandwich, he was beside her, brushing her hair from her face and pressing his lips against her temple. "I'm sorry. Did I ever tell you I can be an ass?" He hooked his hands around her hips—hands that made her insides turn to maple syrup even when she was pissed—pivoting her toward him.

"No, but some things don't have to be stated. *Ever*."

He smiled and trailed his thumb down her cheekbone. "I'm sorry. I freaked. This morning…the shower… I'd be a liar to say I was ready for you. But here you are anyway."

Rather than answering, she pulled away from his touch and dragged her fingertip along the side of her knife, coating it with jelly. She swiped it on the tip of his nose, leaving behind a sparkly dot, then two others, one on either side of his cheeks. He grabbed her hand and sucked the remaining jelly off her finger.

"Are you trying to get me in the shower again?"

"No, but I am trying to sweeten you up."

He locked her in an embrace and dragged his face back and forth on the front of her shirt, leaving smears of purple jelly over her boobs.

"No fair." She swatted his shoulder, a bubble of laughter escaping. "I haven't done laundry in a week because of you. It's this or something dirty…er," she added, glancing down at her shirt.

"Why don't you pull something off Kelsey's rainbow collection in that gift shop of yours?" As if reconsidering, he shook his head. "Or maybe not. How about I help you catch up on your laundry tonight? I'll make up for my assishness over the wash cycle."

A shiver ran down her spine as he kissed her earlobe. "Then what'll we do during the dry cycle?"

"That," he said, "I'll leave up to you."

Chapter 18

THE BLARE FROM THE MARIACHI BAND THRUMMED through her chest and tingled her lips, fingers, and sandaled toes as Megan scanned the presenter groups lining up on Lockwood Avenue for the Everything Webster Groves spring parade. Beside her, Sledge's ears perked forward as he studied the bright costumes, but he stood without darting behind her as he sometimes did when tall, big men came into the kennels to look at the dogs. The company of the other shelter dogs in the parade with him would hopefully help his confidence.

Judging by the elaborate costumes and floats lining the street in either direction, this year's parade would be bigger and more elaborate than ever. Now that she knew they'd be following immediately behind the zealous band from Agave Verde, Webster's family-friendly Mexican restaurant, Megan was a bit worried how some of the dogs would react. So far, the group seemed fairly calm. She hoped the noise-tolerance training the participating dogs had had this last week would help.

It was the parade's tenth anniversary, and according to polls, the shelter's float had been one of the top favorites ever since they began participating six years ago.

This was Megan's fifth parade, but every year, the shelter's participation grew in scale as well as importance. Preparations for the building of the float, the making of costumes for both animals and people, and the training that went into the dogs was mostly done by an all-volunteer committee of parade-crazy members.

This year, the parade was on Megan's twenty-sixth birthday. She didn't mind, although it would've been a good weekend to spend with her mom and little brother and sister. They'd been twisting her arm to make the trip out there for over a month. Megan hadn't yet told her mom about Craig, so she hadn't been entirely honest about why her schedule had become even more jam-packed than ever.

She was actually quite glad the parade coincided with Craig's trip out of town. All the planning and preparation of the last few days—and the intensive assembly that had started an hour before dawn this morning—helped keep at bay any worries about what, or who, Craig might be doing on his weekend getaway.

No matter what she said—or what she sent along in her care package for his trip, for that matter—the idea of him hooking up with another woman was nearly debilitating.

He wasn't interested in seeing anyone else. She knew that. He was with her every spare night he had. But after him riling her like that just days before leaving, all she could think was that he'd expected her to object, to worry about his fidelity. And somehow she'd made it through their confrontation seeming more elusive and indifferent than she really felt.

The night before he left, she'd been close to asking him what he would do if the opportunity presented itself. But she hadn't. And all he'd done before taking off was tell her that he'd miss her and promise to call.

The entire thing made her ache for a clarification she was too stubborn to ask for.

Grasping that her mind was circling into a scenario she'd chosen to do nothing about, she forced her attention back to the parade. It was such a big ordeal that she really needed to be on top of her game.

The shelter's participation was planned out for months by the committee. The staff and volunteer costumes got more elaborate every year. This year, the winning vote for float decorating resulted in converting their rickety eight-foot trailer into a circus-themed "Just Married" scene. A senior pair of brother and sister pugs were playing the elaborately dressed bride and groom. They'd won the starring role because they were so well trained and didn't mind being dressed up.

The hope was that they would stay seated for the duration of the parade on a bright-red sofa Patrick had found at Goodwill. Kelsey would be the only person on the float. She was playing the part of the minister, which made Megan a bit jealous since her costume would be a lot easier to walk around in.

Thanks to a volunteer with connections to a florist, they spent the early-morning hours decorating the float with beautiful arrangements left over from what had to have been an extraordinary wedding reception held at the Pageant last night.

In practice, as Fidel had hauled the trailer around the back lot while everyone ran around making as much noise and distraction as they could, the pugs had sat on the sofa remarkably well. The fact that Kelsey would have a pocket full of their favorite treat—pineapple— would hopefully seal the deal.

Everyone else who'd be participating would be walking alongside the float, with the exception of Fidel, who'd be driving the decorated-like-a-dog Volkswagen Beetle that pulled the trailer. Half of the volunteers would walk along leading their own wedding- and circus-themed costumed dogs. The other half would pass out heart-shaped shelter business cards with circus peanuts attached.

All shelter dogs who were calm enough to participate did, which accounted for twenty-two this year. It was a great way to show off dogs that were up for adoption. Last year's parade resulted in eleven adoptions. The goal was to beat that this year.

To up the ante, this year's costumes were definitely attention-getting. There were three "fake" circus poodles—since the shelter didn't have any real poodles at the moment. One of them, a stocky chow with fake pink poodle puffs on top of his head and the sides of his haunches, was the funniest. He was sure to win hearts the way he wore the poofs and poodle skirt without complaint. There was a shaggy retriever with a lion mane that couldn't have been tailored to fit him better. There were two Chihuahua flower girls, a pink-polka-dotted white lab, a terrier peacock, three clowns, and several dog ballerinas. Aside from Kelsey who was conservatively dressed as the minister, most of the other staff and volunteers, including Megan, were dressed rather loudly.

She wasn't at all crazy about the outfit she'd been asked to wear, but she'd consented because Linda, the committee chair, was so excited about it. Megan was still experiencing waves of disbelief that she was out in public dressed in a peach taffeta bridesmaid dress, complete with off-the-shoulder puffy sleeves and a large—very large—satin bow at the waist. She'd scrapped the dyed-to-match peach high-heel pumps for white sandals, or she'd likely have broken an ankle.

Another reason she'd relented was that she'd been assigned to walk with Sledge, who was dressed as a police dog keeping the other dogs in line. Megan was playing the role of a bridesmaid who'd been arrested and would be "chained" to Sledge just before the parade started. She'd wear fake handcuffs that she could get out of, if needed.

The funny thing was that when Megan had asked why she was supposed to have been arrested, no one had a solid answer. Hopefully they'd be moving too quickly for any of the parade attendees to ask.

All in all, Megan determined it was just one of those things that would go down in history as proving she was one hundred percent dedicated to the shelter.

Thankfully, the weather promised to cooperate, something that didn't always happen on parade days. Last year, it had been hot and humid, and the last hour wasn't fun for anyone, dog or person. The year before that, the parade was cut short due to a massive storm. A few years, the weather had been cold and windy. But today was forecast to be partially cloudy with a high in the low seventies and no chance of rain.

And no one would have to worry about the dogs getting overheated.

Out of view, the band at the front of the parade started to play. Megan glanced at her watch. Just five minutes till it began. She gave Sledge a pat and urged him toward the open driver's window of the Beetle.

"Hey," she said, leaning forward and tugging up her costume at the same time. "Ready?"

"*Sí*. You could have told them you wouldn't wear that," Fidel said in a fatherly tone.

"Want to switch? You can wear this, and I'll drive the car."

He chuckled. "Do you think we would get more dogs adopted?"

"If you wore it, they'd be knocking the door down in droves, and you know it."

After spotting Ashley on the other side of the road where they'd arranged to meet, Megan stopped walking to snap a picture with her phone. Fidel had kept her phone for her during the parade. After it was over and everyone was headed back, she'd barely remembered to grab it before leaving the group to meet up with her best friend. She was glad for the photo op because not only was Ashley weighted down with colorful beads and a fuzzy pom-pom headband, but she had Jake slung around one hip and was sipping a grande frozen margarita with her free hand.

Only on parade day, Megan thought. One of Jake's cheeks was painted with a football, the other a blue, big-eyed fish.

"Look at you, lovely," Ashley called as Megan neared.

Jake pumped his arms and woofed at Sledge.

"I see a dog in your future, girl."

"I see a margarita in yours." Ashley drew Megan into a hug, and Jake dove into her arms. "If you're too tired to go out tonight, I'm warning you now, I'll cry. Our once-a-month Saturday night outs are about the only 'me time' I get anymore."

Megan adjusted Jake over her hip after letting him pet Sledge and narrowly stopping him from yanking off the police hat Sledge had worn so well in the parade. "We're going out. I promise. Though it may require copious amounts of caffeine. Is Mike still picking you up from the shelter?"

"Yeah, parking was a disaster. He's getting the car."

"Good. Since I've lost everyone, I really don't want to walk the streets alone in this getup."

"I don't know why. You look great. Kudos to whoever picked the outfits this year. Mike didn't even recognize you when you guys paraded by earlier. Jakey did though. Did you hear him calling your name? Meg-nan, Meg-nan."

"I didn't hear it. The band was too loud, though you know how I love it when he says my name. I could tell how excited he was though." Megan pressed a kiss into Jake's soft cheek. "As for Mike, hopefully you didn't point me out. I'm already worried about never living this down. Sophie and Reese and their mom were out in the crowd. I saw them about halfway through. They were standing next to two guys who wolf-whistled. It was horrible. Sophie's coming by later, I think, but I really don't care to see Jillian."

Ashley took a sip of her margarita. "Speaking of guys we're sleeping with and telling no one but our absolute best friends about, has he called yet?" She wagged her eyebrows.

"Funny, but no, not yet. Give me a sip of that, will you?" She handed Sledge off to Ashley and switched Jake to her other arm, since the one that had been holding him was starting to cramp. She pressed her tongue against the rim of the cup, savoring the salt mixed with the sweet frozen concoction. It was so good that she downed some more, even though she knew it would make her thirstier than she already was. The blare of the band still resounded in her ears, and the parade had been over for fifteen minutes.

Her phone chirped as she took another swig.

"You're downing the whole thing," Ashley said.

Megan handed it over, then lifted her phone to check the number. She blinked at the extra digits.

Craig. It had to be. No one else would call her from out of the country. Her mouth flashed dry, and her throat constricted. "It's him."

"Oh my God. Answer it."

Feeling her shoulders tense up immediately, Megan passed Jake back to Ashley and accepted the call. She headed over to a landscaped island out of earshot.

"Hey there, beautiful," Craig said when she picked up right before losing the call to voice mail. "Can you hear me? I don't think the reception's very good."

She tugged at her earlobe like a schoolgirl getting a call from her first crush. "Yeah, I can hear you fine. How is everything? Are you having a good time?"

"Yeah, everything's great. We're keeping busy. It's remarkable here. I'll tell you all about it later."

"That's great."

"I was sorry to miss the parade. I wish I could have seen you handcuffed to Sledge. Did they ever tell you what crime you'd committed?"

She laughed, feeling relieved and almost a little giddy. She'd focused so much on not worrying about this trip, but here he was calling, telling her she was beautiful, and apologizing for missing the shelter's big parade moment. It didn't sound like he was putting her out of his mind at all. "No, but I'm thinking it was a misdemeanor. Toward the end, I was released for good behavior. I'm excited to show you the pictures of the dogs when you get back. I think it was our best parade yet. I'm heading back to the shelter now. I don't know if you heard, but Sophie's coming by in a bit since she wasn't old enough to walk a dog in the parade. She might even be there already."

"She called and told me all about it, and texted half a dozen photos too. If I didn't know better, I'd have thought those pugs were stuffed animals, they were sitting so well. I wish I'd been there to see it all in person. I'll make it up to you for being away on your big weekend. As a matter of fact, I keep thinking how much I'm going to enjoy making it up to you."

A dry shiver ran down her spine and circled around her hips. He was a thousand miles away, but his lips still tickled her earlobe when he spoke.

Focus, Megs. Like her, he was calling from outside. She could hear the wind blowing over the receiver. And something else. She strained to make it out and realized it was waves, large rolling waves.

"There's nothing you need to make up to me. I'd love a seashell though. And not one from a store, please. One you find on the beach."

"I would have guessed that. It's genuine or nothing with you."

She laughed and pictured his perfect blue eyes against the waves she could hear crashing into the shore.

"Hey," he said, his voice dropping, "about that care package you sent with me and asked me not to open until I arrived?"

Her cheeks flamed matchstick hot. She knew what was coming. What kind of relationship did they have, never having discussed something as important as this in person? "Yeah, what about it?"

"It was thoughtful, to say the least. But one thing threw me."

She forced playfulness into her voice that she didn't feel. "The sunscreen?"

"No, not the sunscreen."

Sucking in a breath, she went for it. "Look, I know it's weird, but it's something we've never talked about, and I didn't know how to bring it up."

"So you put a couple condoms in my care package?"

Hearing him say it, it sounded crazy. "It's just… We aren't exactly defined, and you freaked me out with that boys' weekend talk. I'm not saying I'm fine with it, but…I don't know… Diseases are rampant. Especially in tourist spots."

"So I've heard."

"And I know we both promised we're disease-free, but now that you aren't married, it doesn't mean you'll stay that way if you start…" She pressed her thumb and forefinger into her temples. "Ugh, this isn't easy."

"No, it isn't. But as long as I protect myself, you don't care if I sleep with other people. Is that what you're saying?"

Sweat blossomed on her palms and under her sandaled feet. "You aren't funny."

The speaker rang out with the din of someone else's laughter, temporarily drowning out his voice. An image of him standing barefoot at the corner of a tiki-hut bar packed with beautiful women—tan and lean and gorgeous in their skimpy swimsuits—filled her mind. *I don't care what I said. Please don't sleep with anyone.*

"I'm sorry," he said into the silence. "I'm the king of bad jokes sometimes. You don't need to worry. Condom or no condom, I never intended to sleep with anyone. Between you and me, I'm the bacon."

Her ears started to burn. The reality of how much his not sleeping with someone else meant to her crashed in with a force that nearly brought her to her knees and, inexplicably, sent a wave of nausea rolling across her stomach. The third one she'd had that day. She managed to spit something out, though she was sure it was entirely off topic to whatever he'd been trying to say at the end. "I don't eat bacon."

He laughed. "Do me a favor, will you?"

She mumbled a yes.

"Enjoy your parade celebration. Enjoy the hell out of it. When it's over, make a list of all the things you want to talk about. I promise we'll talk about them. And afterward, maybe I'll get you an outfit that goes better with those handcuffs and you can model it for me."

She joked that maybe she would in a million years, then matched the huskiness in his good-bye with a heartfelt one of her own. She hung up reluctantly and headed back to Ashley. Jake was standing beside Sledge, digging his chubby fingers into Sledge's fur.

"What does it mean when someone tells you they're the bacon?"

The skeptical face Ashley made showed that her friend didn't know either. "I think it has something to do with money growing on trees."

"That doesn't make sense."

Ashley passed Sledge's leash to Megan, then pulled out her phone and started typing. She scrolled through options, then raised one eyebrow. "It doesn't have anything to do with money growing on trees. It says here it's an expression of total commitment. It's the difference between the chicken and the pig in making breakfast. With an egg, the chicken was just involved. The pig, however, was committed."

Ashley tucked her phone into her pocket and jumped, her pom-pom headband jiggling wildly. "Oh my God! He said that to you?"

Megan's jaw went slack. Commitment. No-turning-back commitment. *That's pretty close to love, isn't it?*

Ashley bolted forward and draped Megan in a near choke hold, knocking over her nearly empty margarita and sending drips of half-frozen slush down her calf. "Holy crap. That means he's the pig, sweetie. And my best friend in the world is officially completely in over her head."

The front half of the shelter basked in early morning quiet as a fading stillness hung over the kennels. Soon the dogs would wake and stretch, and a chorus of claws pacing on concrete would blend with yips, howls, and whines, serenading everyone in earshot. But not yet. For a bit longer, Megan savored the temporary quiet. Coupled with the gray drizzle escaping from dark, heavy clouds, she was hardly able to keep her eyes open. Coffee. She needed coffee.

Abandoning her confining office, she made for the front room where a fresh pot waited. A car pulling into the lot caught her attention as she headed past the large front windows. A sleek, dark-gray BMW. Her knees threatened to buckle as she met Craig's gaze through the windshield. He winked as he opened his car door.

Forgetting the coffee that was no longer needed as adrenaline dumped into her system, she headed for the doors and flipped the lock.

"Hey." Gnawing on her lip to keep her smile from spreading to her ears, she pushed open the door and breathed in his scent as his fingers closed over her elbow. There was the familiar wet cedar and leather of his cologne, but he smelled of something else too. The beach, she realized. And sun. "Welcome back. I didn't think I'd see you till tonight."

His grin was just a bit sheepish. "Well, that *was* the plan." Still in the open doorway, he stepped closer, holding her against the frame.

Chance heard Craig's voice and came trotting over to greet him like he did all the regulars. Craig knelt down to give him a proper scratch before he stood up and turned his attention Megan's way.

She cleared her throat as he eyed her lips. "Fidel and Patrick are in the kennels." She could see the hunger in his gaze, the tension in his shoulders, the want in his slightly parted lips.

He blinked once, then backed off and followed her inside. "This is for you." He handed her a brown paper bag that sagged in the middle. "Can we talk privately a moment? About the upcoming meeting?"

Feeling herself salivate as his eyes stayed locked on her lips, she managed a nod. "There's my office."

She followed him into the cramped room, wiping her

palms on the back of her jeans. They'd kissed so many times now. How could the thought of it still make her feel like a schoolgirl?

His mouth closed over hers before the door was half-way shut. All sense of responsibility jumped ship as his hands tugged up her shirt and slid to the small of her back, drawing her against him. Being with him was like melting, or standing at the edge of a cavernous abyss. There was the taste of his skin and his mouth, clean and fresh like mint, only not the manufactured mint that reminded her of the dentist office. Swigs of the fresh mint of summer she liked to drop in her tea.

Then there was the feel of him, lean muscle under smooth skin. Touching him reminded her of Christmas and life before Dad died, of seeing all the beautifully wrapped gifts under the tree. She'd pull one of hers on her lap at night while sitting under the sparkly lights and know that it didn't matter if what was inside was something she'd asked for or not; it was hers, and it was perfect.

The spray of the hose clicking off in the kennels sent blood rushing back to her brain. She stepped back, creating a shred of space between them. "They'll know something's up." She rested her forehead against his chest, struggling to come to her senses and catch her breath. "I never close this door."

"Does it really matter?" Craig asked, tilting her chin up and running his thumb along her jawline.

"You know it does. Sophie…"

He blinked and slipped his hands out from under her shirt. Mouthing his daughter's name, he opened the door.

Megan was still holding the weighty bag in one hand. She lifted it between them in the space that suddenly felt like a canyon and shook it softly. "Did you want me to open this?"

"Go for it."

Sinking against her desk, she rested it on her thigh and unfolded it. Her jaw dropped as she pulled out a gigantic conch shell. It was the biggest she'd ever seen, bright pink and white with perfect spikes all around. "You aren't seriously going to tell me you found this on the beach?"

His mouth turned up in a half smile as he brushed back a lock of her hair. "As a matter of fact, I didn't find it on the beach."

"No fair. You said you wouldn't buy one."

After a glance toward the kennels, he let his thumb trail over her lower lip. "I didn't buy it. I found it on the ocean floor while I was scuba diving."

Laughing, she shook her head. "Wow! You're crazy, you know that?"

"Crazy enough." Pressing her into the corner where they couldn't be seen from the doorway, his lips found hers again, and his fingers tugged at the button of her jeans.

Listening to the muffled voices behind the kennel doors, she closed her eyes and savored the moment. He could have anyone, and he wanted her. They'd been together so many times now, and he wanted her as much as he had the first time. Aloud, she kept it playful. "You should become a case study, you know. So men all over the world considering a vasectomy won't worry about it harming their libidos."

Craig, who was running his lips over her sternum, released her shirt collar and pulled back to look at her, his brow wrinkling. "That'd only make sense if I'd had a vasectomy."

As his words sank in, her stomach flipped. Not a tiny flip or a somersault. An overturned-shipping-vessel-on-rough-waters sort of flip.

She was eyeing her trash can as Patrick threw open the kennel doors, calling her name. She'd been feeling tired and queasy the last several days, but she'd attributed it to long hours and a few too many sweets to console herself while Craig was away. Unaware, Craig made for the doorway, pasting on a smile and waving Patrick over.

Please God say he forgot—who the hell forgets they've had a vasectomy?—or at least let it be another one of his jokes. She did her best to fumble through a few of Patrick's questions before excusing herself. She could hear Craig answering questions about his long weekend—all politeness and small talk—as she jogged across the main floor to the bathroom. She was queasy all right, but so far no actual vomiting. Thank goodness for small favors. She moved to the sink, rinsed her mouth, and splashed water on her face and neck.

Looking in the mirror, she noticed her face was white, and there were beads of sweat clinging to her forehead. After rinsing out her mouth once more, she forced herself out the door.

Patrick was returning to the kennels, and Craig was standing in the middle of the main room with his hands shoved in his pants' pockets. As the glass doors swung shut, he moved her way. "He, uh, didn't have a clue if that's what's gotten to you. But I *am* sorry. From now on, I'll keep it to strictly business here."

Swallowing, she shrugged it off. "It's okay." *It's a dumb joke. That's all it is.* "So, um, you were kidding, right? About not having had a vasectomy?"

His eyebrows furrowed like she'd spoken Latin. "Granted my kids are older, but why would you think I'd had a vasectomy?"

She could see the sincerity in his eyes, hear it in his tone. Dear God, she was either going to puke for real or start bawling. Shoving her shaking hands into her back pockets, she pressed on. "I'd never assume that. Sophie said…she said you—"

"Oh, Christ." Craig's eyes widened and he dragged a hand through his hair. "You're a beautiful, single woman in your midtwenties, Megan. Please tell me you're on birth control. I meant to ask that first time, but then you said something about it not being a problem so I-I assumed…"

She opened her mouth, but words escaped her. With knees rebelliously weak, she sank to a nearby chair. Her pulse was pounding behind her ears, dulling all other sound. She didn't even attempt eye contact, but saw in the periphery of her vision that he'd begun to pace the floor. When she finally looked his way, she saw that his face had drained of color as well.

"Sophie told you I'd had a vasectomy?" he repeated as if he were still processing the full possibility of this unexpected predicament.

Megan nodded, but it didn't feel as if her head belonged to her body. "She said she secretly wished for a baby more than anything after Andrew died but that you'd already had a vasectomy."

"I have no idea where she got that. Wait. I went to the hospital with a kidney stone a few months before Andrew died. She was only ten then. Honestly, I doubt she knew what a vasectomy was at the time. Maybe she remembered it and came up with that idea later. I would never have even guessed that she knew what a vasectomy was yet."

"From what I've heard, kids her age are learning everything faster than we did. You won't say anything to her, will you?"

"No, of course not."

She needed him to go. She needed to think. To let the fact that she'd just spent the last month having constant unprotected sex settle. "Look, I'd, um, better get back to work."

He nodded, looking just as eager for some time to let this process. "You'll, uh, you'll take a test, right?"

She swallowed hard and closed her hands over the arms of her chair. "I'm sure it's fine, but yeah, of course. It's a bit early in my cycle, but I will. I'll let you know when I do."

"Okay, whenever you think the time's right." He dragged his hand through his hair. "Holy shit. It's a lot to absorb. Listen, I've got the kids tonight since I haven't seen them all weekend. I could swing by afterward, but it might be late. Then I'm in New York for two days."

"It's okay. We can catch up later in the week."

"For sure. I'll call you." He pressed a quick kiss against her temple before heading out. He was clearly as stunned as she was.

When he was out of the building, she curled forward in her chair, feeling the last of her energy seeping from her fingers and toes. She pressed her forehead against her knees and wrapped her hands around her shins. *If you were on a plane, you'd be in crash position.*

A laugh bubbled up her throat, dry and foreign and not seeming to belong to her. "That's good, Megs, because you may very well be about to crash."

Chapter 19

COLLAPSING TO THE SEAT OF HER CAR, MEGAN SHUT THE door and plunked her head against the headrest. The parking lot surrounding Walgreens was nearly full. Twenty feet away, a van door was remotely opened, lights blinking. The woman holding the remote was a mother with a full, swollen belly, a toddler slung over one hip, and a young boy clinging to her free hand. She was talking to her son and laughing, her movements fluid and natural. She helped the boy climb in, then buckled the toddler into a car seat without seeming to lose a beat in their conversation.

Is everyone capable of that? Am I? Megan ran her thumb along the rim of the steering wheel. Did she want to be? She let out a long breath and closed her eyes, hoping the answer would present itself in an easy-to-understand format. But no words came. Instead, a rarely felt emotion swept over her, subduing the raw shock and nausea that had carried her through the morning. It was an emotion she experienced so seldom that she needed a few minutes to understand it. But finally she did.

Peace. She felt an incredible peace washing over her.

Kids loaded and automatic van door shutting, the mother slid into the driver's seat, mindful of her swollen belly, and drove away. Megan could hear the erratic beat of a peppy children's song as they passed behind her car.

In the now-quiet lot, she sifted through her purse and

pulled out the EPT test that she'd taken in the store bathroom, needing to see it again. She stared at the plus sign and took in a slow, steady breath. A plus, of all things. It wasn't just a positive sign. A plus was for addition. For becoming part of something bigger than what you started with.

Holy crap. This was real. She was pregnant. And Craig was the father.

She drummed her fingers on her knees a few seconds, then pulled out her cell phone, thinking she should call him. When her fingers didn't seem to want to dial, she dropped it back in her purse. She needed to savor this feeling of peace for a little while longer, and talking to Craig about this momentous news was going to introduce a whole new level of—what? The uncertainty alone made her feel queasy.

The plain truth was, she had no idea how he'd take this news.

Megan dabbed at the broken faucet that had become her nose. She wasn't crying. Not anymore. Her nose just hadn't gotten the memo.

For the first time in over a year, she took part of a sick day. Stomach flu, she'd told Patrick, which hadn't felt like a lie since she'd puked three times since leaving, most likely a combination of morning sickness and terror.

She cried it out, then meandered a few miles through Forest Park in solitude, noticing moms and babies and little kids she never would have spotted on a normal day. Afterward, she showed up unannounced on Ashley's doorstep while Jake was napping. She spilled the news before the front door was shut behind her and cried it out all over again. After her well of tears ran dry and Jake woke up, they'd headed to a neighborhood playground three blocks from Ashley's house.

Now Megan sat on the grass, watching Jake bury his toys in a sand pit a few feet away. Surreal thoughts swept over her in waves, like how she'd never really gotten what a tiny miracle Jake was. Miniscule fingers and toes, pouty mouth and plump cheeks, chubby thighs and smooth-as-silk hair.

"I blame you, you know that," she said. Her throat was raw, and her words were thick in a way that only happens after a lot of crying.

"Mmm, *that's* fair." Ashley flicked a mangled dandelion at her. "After all, I was an integral part of the completely unprotected sex you were having, wasn't I?"

The first smile since Patrick had butted into her office what felt like an eternity ago curled the corners of Megan's mouth. "You were always saying I should hurry up and get pregnant."

"Well, I didn't mean like this." Ashley wrapped her in a one-armed hug. "But you're not alone, you know, whatever he decides."

"He doesn't want to have a baby with me, Ash."

"Not being ready and not owning up to your responsibilities are two different things. And everything you've said about him makes me think he'll do the right thing."

"What's the right thing? His kids are ten and thirteen. He's recently divorced, and he warned right at the start that he wasn't ready for complicated. And I don't know if I told you, but his ex-wife got pregnant *while* they were dating. What about this screams 'Come on, let's have a baby together'? Nothing, that's what."

Ashley shook her head. "That still doesn't mean it can't work for you two. It's been obvious you're crazy about him. And he said that bit about being the bacon or the pork chop or whatever. And besides, for some people, things just fall into place the second time around."

Ashley's words struck a chord. Memory slammed in so fast that Megan had to steady herself by wrapping her hand around a clump of grass. There she was, sixteen, walking the aisles of the grocery store alongside her heavily pregnant mom a few days before she went into labor with her sister from her mom's second marriage. Tyler, her half brother, a toddler at the time, was tucked in the cart irritably munching Cheerios. Her mother was pushing him along at a snail's pace, her enormous, swollen belly pressed against the handle. They were in the canned goods aisle, a list of things to buy a mile long, when her mom started singing. Not humming, and not mumbling, but full-scale singing. Megan ignored her at first, though her ears grew warm in embarrassment.

Maybe it was the song—Aretha Franklin's "You Make Me Feel Like a Natural Woman"—that made it worse, but it struck Megan so hard that she stopped in her tracks halfway down one aisle. When her mom noticed Megan had fallen behind, she stopped and asked what was wrong.

She could have told the truth—probably should have—but she didn't. That first time she put two and two together had been enough. Her mom never sang when she was married to her dad.

"Hey, Jakey, no!" Ashley said, jumping up and

pulling Megan from her reverie. Jake had found a pacifier buried in the sand and was about to put it in his mouth. "Yucky, baby."

Megan sucked in a deep breath, hoping to ease her nerves. Watching Ashley attempt to pry the sand-encrusted pacifier away from her determined toddler helped more than the breathing. She loved Jake. She loved all babies. She always had.

"Is it me, or did you just see a ghost? Because all of a sudden you look as pale as one," Ashley said after successfully swapping the pacifier for a new plastic shovel she'd kept hidden in the diaper bag for such an occasion.

"I was thinking about my mom."

Ashley pursed her lips. "Which explains that look of yours. Did you tell her yet?"

"No," Megan said. "God no."

"Being three hours away and having a demanding family to care for doesn't make her not your mom, you know."

"Ugh. Spare me the lecture please." Megan collapsed back against the ground. Itchy blades of grass pressed against her neck and shoulders, and she'd cried so much that lying on her back made her words even more nasal.

A new, blue-whale-sized fear was suddenly weighing down on her. *What if she never loved my dad?*

It was a stupid thought and pointless besides. Her dad had died half her life ago, and her mom had been remarried nearly as long as she'd been married to him. And right now, Megan had bigger issues to deal with than worrying about the relationship her parents had.

But somehow this thought seemed to take precedence over everything else.

"Do you think my parents loved each other, Ash?"

Ashley went from gazing down at her to looking away. "I'm sure they did. I never really thought about it."

"They weren't affectionate like her and Rick though, were they?"

"We were kids, Megan. I never paid attention. I honestly can't even remember them being in the same room enough to know how affectionate they were. What I do know is that they were great to you. Great to me too."

"I'm still so angry at her sometimes, you know. For getting over him."

"I know." Ashley had the pacifier and was turning it in circles with the tips of her fingers. "I just don't think your dad would want you to be, whatever kind of relationship they had."

A second whale-sized fear rushed in behind the first. "What if this baby ends up feeling the same way about me?"

Ashley dropped the pacifier and loomed over her. "So you think your mom's not a good mother? Because she loves her second husband and the rest of her kids? Have you forgotten how she was always there whenever you needed her? Even in the dorm, her care packages were the best around. She even remembered me. Every time."

Megan shook her head, smashing grass against her hair. When she didn't answer, Ashley continued.

"And did you think I couldn't be a good mother because my mom spent so much of my childhood dealing with her addiction to painkillers after her accident? What I'm saying is that we've all got our crap to deal with, Megs, but it doesn't mean we can't be good parents and we can't experience meaningful love."

Megan took in her friend's words and slowly pushed up to a sitting position again. She leaned into Ashley and rested her head against her shoulder.

"I want to believe you. I really do."

Chapter 20

WHEN PATRICK LEANED INTO HER OFFICE FRIDAY EVENING to say he was leaving and to ask if he should lock the door behind him, Megan shook her head. "Nope. I'm out of here in a few minutes myself. I'll see you tomorrow."

"Maybe next week will be better for you," he said as he turned away.

Megan frowned as he headed out, mumbling to himself about her spirits being down during the shelter's best week in seven months. He'd clearly picked up on her inner turmoil.

Shoulders slumping, she sighed and answered the empty room. "Well, it can't be any worse." A memory of her father and the last day she saw him flashed through her mind. "Never mind that. I hope so too."

Patrick was right about the shelter. Things were looking up. At least she had that to console her. Craig's donation was the defibrillator this place needed. The marketing plan that had sat abandoned in her desk drawer for so long was in full swing, and results were already visible. Donations were coming in, not pouring in but not trickling either. Not counting Craig's donation, they were on track for this to be the strongest year in over a decade. Added to that, a few Girl Scout troops had dropped off an impressive number of supplies from their wish list. When you put it all together, it was as if Santa had been very good to them.

There'd also been a slew of adoptions after the parade. Turbo was adopted by a family with two boys. Sol, the pit bull mix rescued from the hot car at the zoo, finally found a home too. Her new owner was a young, single guy in his twenties who'd just moved to St. Louis and wanted a companion, especially for walking, which Sol loved. Peanut, the Great Dane, was adopted to a very short, fine-boned woman in her forties. The two were an unlikely match, but the woman had emailed several pictures proving they were hitting it off just fine.

Tyson would've been adopted three times over, but he was officially on hold. Sophie's house sold quickly, and she'd be moving into her new home in the next couple of weeks. Ever since she'd made the decision that Tyson was the dog for her, she'd been glowing from head to foot. She came in at least twice a week, and after Tyson conked out from playing with her, she'd walk dogs until her mom or dad picked her up.

Watching it all happen felt like a small miracle. No doors were going to close this year. Never, if Megan could help it. She was certain it'd be easier moving forward. She was a few years older now. And wiser. Seasoned to the realities of running a nonprofit. This place had the air of a business that'd been turned around, and she'd make sure it stayed that way.

At least this part of her life had some clarity. If she wasn't pregnant, she could relax and enjoy watching the shelter grow. If she wasn't pregnant.

But she was.

Not ready to head home where she was sure her thoughts would spiral into a mess of self-doubt, Megan walked into the kennels and paused in front of Sledge.

The last she'd heard, a few different people were considering adopting him. Megan was both hopeful and hesitant about this. At the very least, she wouldn't let him go to anyone who she didn't think was a perfect match.

At the sight of her, Sledge stood up, stretched, and relaxed enough to give a hopeful wag of his tail.

"Attaboy," she said, lifting a leash off a nearby hook. "I bet a walk will do us both some good."

Outside, the temperature was dropping, but it was still a beautiful late-April evening. Hoping her mind would be carried away by something else, she allowed Sledge to set the pace, a medium trot, and headed into the neighboring residential section of town. But even with Sledge and a pretty row of historic homes to keep her mind occupied, it took less than a minute for her thoughts to turn to the baby she was carrying. This time, what did it were the chirping birds and the landscapes bursting with bright flowers—signs of spring and rebirth. Like it or not, life was renewing both outside and in.

And try as she might, all week it had been impossible to separate thoughts of pregnancy from thoughts of Craig. They were too entwined. They didn't have to be though, and they might not always be. But right now, the baby and Craig were chicken-and-egg thoughts. Megan couldn't think about what to do with the baby until after she'd told Craig. But she wasn't going to tell Craig until she was positive what she wanted to do with the baby. She couldn't help laughing—she sure was the bacon this time.

Getting pregnant and having kids had always been something she wanted. If things had worked out with Paul, she would have wanted to start trying in a few years. But she wasn't with Paul. She was alone. Or at most in a very new and uncertain relationship with a guy who'd probably be as excited about the idea of bringing a child into this world with her as he would be about having a kidney removed.

What she needed to do was get thoughts of Craig out of her head so she could start giving serious thought to what to do with this child they'd created. Abortion wasn't a possibility. Maybe for other people. But not for her. So it was raising this child on her own or giving it up for adoption. But every time she formed the word *adoption* in her head, it was followed by a sharp inner scream of *No!*

She'd only known she was pregnant for five days, and each day that *no* grew louder and clearer. The truth was, there was no denying it any longer. She knew the answer. She was just afraid to voice it.

"I'm going to have a baby, Sledge," she said aloud.

Sledge slowed his step and turned his head to look her way, then seemingly satisfied, beelined for a light pole to mark it.

"And I'm going to keep it. And just like with the shelter, I'm going to give this baby everything I have. I can do it. I *want* to do it. No matter what Craig decides."

Relief washed over her from saying the words aloud. *There. Give your confidence a day or two to build, and you'll be ready to face him.*

On the walk back, it felt like a truckload of bricks had been lifted. For the first time all week, stirrings of happiness overrode the unease in her stomach. There were plenty of single moms successfully raising children. She could join a support group and call on the aid of friends or a hired nanny when she needed to. Confidence rising, she knew just what to do with her Friday night. She'd swing by the grocery store and pick up the makings of a healthy meal, then dive in to one of the half-dozen pregnancy books Ashley had loaned her.

When she rounded the corner of the parking lot, her heart skipped a beat. Craig was parked out front, leaning against the side of his car and scrolling through his phone. Next to him, on the hood of his Bimmer, was a bouquet of bright-yellow daffodils.

Most likely, he'd tried the door and realized it was locked but had seen her car and figured she was out with a dog. He knew it was one of her favorite ways to end her work day.

She took a second to collect herself before he noticed her. He'd had a crazy week, and she hadn't seen him since Monday morning when everything changed. That seemed like a year ago.

Her body responded on autopilot just looking at him. Her chest lit with the stirrings of lust mixed with something subtler that she was a bit terrified might be the beginning of love. Fear and a ferocious hope swirled inside her too.

Looking at him, she realized what she wanted more than anything was for him to be okay when she told him. Not to sweep her off her feet and rush her to the altar. She wasn't looking for fairy tale here. Just to be okay and not reveal some ugly, mean side he'd kept hidden so far. To respect her decision and not run for the hills. To be supportive and understanding once he had time to digest everything.

But she wasn't ready to face the reality that she had

no real idea how he'd react. Before clearing her throat to get his attention, she abandoned the idea of telling him. Not yet. What could it hurt, letting it go another day or two?

"I'm sorry, sir, but we're closed. You're going to have to take your business elsewhere."

He turned at the sound of her voice, smiling and slipping his phone into his pocket. He nodded in Sledge's direction. "With that bodyguard, I'm obliged to listen to you."

As they neared, Sledge tucked his tail and dropped behind Megan, showing that he was still hesitant to trust men he didn't know.

"I guess he's still a bit of a mess. I forget sometimes, considering how obedient he is."

"I can see that," he said as Sledge hovered behind her. "He's a spectacular-looking dog though. He was awesome at the party too."

Craig sank to a squat and held out his hand, speaking Sledge's name gently and taking Megan by surprise. She held her breath and waited, hopeful. It took a full minute, but Sledge tentatively slipped around her, sniffed Craig's hand, and gave it a single lick. He then stood still and allowed Craig to scratch his muzzle.

Tears rushed to Megan's eyes, though she wasn't sure if they were from seeing the unexpected softness in Craig, the growing trust in Sledge, or both. She was trying to blink the tears away when Craig stood up and noticed.

"Hey." He planted a kiss on her forehead and brushed her cheek dry with the side of his thumb. "You okay?"

She nodded. "Just touched."

"If I knew that was all it took, I wouldn't have messed with the flowers."

A laugh bubbled out as he scooped up the daffodils, offering them to her.

"Thanks." She took them, letting Sledge have a whiff. They had uneven stems and no packaging whatsoever. "Did you pick these yourself?"

Craig winked. "I figured you wouldn't want something store-bought in case it wasn't sustainably grown and certified by the Rainforest Alliance."

"So instead you robbed some old lady's garden of spring flowers?"

"No, I risked life and limb stopping on the side of the highway to pilfer them off an exit ramp."

"Wow, I didn't see that one coming." She giggled, picturing him in his nicely pressed dress shirt and pants meandering the sloping hillside of an exit ramp to pluck daffodils.

"Well, thank goodness you're okay."

She pulled the keys from her pocket and made a step toward the door. "I'd better get Sledge inside. And since these are black-market flowers, I'll get them in water."

He stopped her, locking an arm around her waist. His free hand slipped into the back of her hair and he leaned in, drawing her lower lip between his teeth. Then his mouth parted and he kissed her slowly, like he had all night and nothing else to do. "I missed the hell out of you," he said when he pulled away. "It's been a long week. Unfortunately, it'll be a bit longer till we can really have some time. I'm due to pick up the kids in about twenty minutes. I think I told you I have them this weekend."

"You did." She nuzzled her head against him and inhaled, savoring his smell the same way she did the moist, wet wind that preceded thunderstorms.

With Paul or the couple of guys who'd come before him, she hadn't had these whole-body stirrings. Hadn't felt that losing them would be like losing the ability to breathe.

Craig smoothed a hand over her back and drew her closer. Her belly pressed deep into the space between his groin and hip, bringing her thoughts back to the baby. Would he surprise her like this, the flowers and the gentle way he treated Sledge, when she told him she was pregnant? Or would it be their unraveling?

Despite the warmth radiating off him, goose bumps pocked her neck and arms. Shifting the flowers and leash to one hand, she locked her arms around him like a vise. She was probably smashing pollen into the back of his shirt, but she didn't care. Sledge shifted in place beside her, unsettled.

"Hey, you okay?" Craig asked, pulling back to look at her.

She shook her head and swallowed, her throat parched and scratchy. *Tell him and get it over with. A few days isn't going to change anything.*

It was there on the tip of her tongue. She even opened her mouth to form the words, but she couldn't force herself to do it. What if keeping this baby meant losing him?

"Whatever it is, it's going to be okay," he said. "Because of me, we jumped into this fast. I made some mistakes, but it doesn't mean I regret a single second we've been together."

When she kept quiet, he continued. "That time away from you got me thinking. We went from being friends to a committed relationship we were hiding from the world…even if it was unintentional. We got so deep so fast, it felt like I had to keep you apart from the rest of my life to keep everything afloat. I didn't want Sophie and Reese to know, not this soon. But that didn't make it right. My baggage isn't an excuse not to treat you the way you deserve to be treated. And you deserve the best. So no more hiding this or avoiding the world or whatever it is we've been doing."

An unexpected panic was setting in. She could picture her life playing out as if it were that simple. They'd go on dates. She'd start telling more people than Ashley. She'd face Sophie and Reese as more than just someone who works at a shelter.

It could be well and fine and even spectacular if she wasn't five weeks pregnant.

If.

"So," he continued, "I can't believe I'm saying this, but how about nixing the sleepovers for a while—spectacular as they've been—and going on a few honest-to-God dates? We could start Sunday afternoon. I take the kids back around two. If it's okay with you, I thought I'd wait until we had a date or two to actually tell them. In case they ask what it is we do together." He grinned at the last part and brushed his thumb over her lower lip.

A mountain of anxiety pressed in from all directions. "I don't…I don't know."

"I've got ten years on you, Megan, and one thing I've learned is that sometimes it's okay not to know."

If.

If she could have one wish, would it be to wish the baby away and head down this path that could be so simple and easy and natural?

And then his words sank in. *Sometimes it's okay not to know.* Right now, more than ever in her life, the unknowns were pressing in with hyper-gravitational force. The path Craig was talking about, romantic and wonderful as it sounded, felt impossible considering her reality.

She had no idea what was ahead. Maybe they could make it past this. Maybe they couldn't. Time and nothing else would tell. There was only one thing she knew—and knew with great clarity.

She'd never wish this baby away.

Chapter 21

STACKED IN A TOWERING PILE OR SPREAD ACROSS HER BED, her borrowed collection of pregnancy books was overwhelming. She'd only wanted to take a few, but Ashley had insisted on lending her all of them. Prior to diving headfirst into this, Megan had had no idea how much there was to know about bringing a baby into the world.

When Ashley was pregnant, it had seemed fun and exciting. But now that it was happening to her, it was such a different story. Her breasts were incredibly sore. And there was the nausea. All week, it had come on with zero warning. Mornings were the worst. Carbs helped a bit, but certain things set it off every time she encountered them. Stinky trash cans for one. And the smell of fresh crap when it wafted through the kennels' doors. She'd heaved into her office trash can twice last week and once more this morning, a Saturday morning no less, and the main room had been chock-full of people. If this continued, Patrick would pick up on it for sure.

Knowing the best way to deal with the changes morphing her body was to understand them, Megan was determined to get through as many pages tonight as she could. She'd started the week attempting to tackle the books page by page, one at a time. She'd gotten restless the more she read and started picking and choosing which ones to skim, depending on her mood. From what she

could control to what she couldn't, the seemingly endless list of potential disasters was unsettling at best. Soft
cheeses and deli meats were a danger, and cleaning out
the cat litter seemed akin to strolling through a war zone.

It still amazed her how something so natural was
fraught with risk at every turn. How so many people got
over their fears and intentionally determined to bring
life into this world was unfathomable. Developmental
risks. Genetic disorders. Birthing complications. And
that was just getting to day one.

The more she read, the more worried she grew about
telling Craig.

Not wanting to think about anything heavy, she chose
one of the lighter books—one that did a great job of
making the humiliating humorous—and settled into a
pile of pillows and blankets to read. Within seconds,
Moxie and Max were by her side, purring and kneading
her thighs.

She made it through thirty or so pages when she
started dozing off. She fought it for a few pages but
eventually gave in with the lamp still on.

Blinking in confusion sometime later, she sat upright,
attempting to surface from a deep sleep. A kink from the
way she'd fallen asleep was locking up her neck. She
was doing her best to massage it out when her cell phone
beeped, indicating a missed call.

So that's what woke me up. Standing, and feeling her
stomach lurch, she reached for her phone. She blinked
at the name on the screen. Sophie. On a Saturday night.
What was she doing calling at nearly one in the morning?

She dialed the number, clearing her throat and rubbing the sleep from her eyes.

"Thanks for calling back," Sophie said without saying hello. She was crying, clearly, and sniffling.

Alarm rocked through Megan's body. "What's wrong, Sophie?"

"Nothing. It's, um... Can you pick me up?"

"Uh..." Megan shook her head, thoughts racing. "Are you with your mom or dad?"

"I'm at this girl's house...from my school. I can't call my parents. Not about this."

Megan dug through her nightstand drawer for paper and a pencil and wrote down the address. Promising she'd be there as soon as possible, she hung up, chugged a glass of water and took a box of crackers to nibble on in the car, grabbed her keys and purse, and headed for the door.

Using her phone for navigation, she left the familiar streets of Webster and was soon in the heart of Ladue. The house her phone led her to was sprawling and probably cost more than all the condos on her street put together. As she slowed to a stop, she spotted Sophie off to the side by the driveway.

She hung by the curb, sucking on her lower lip, a bag slung over her shoulders. The headlights shot beams of light on her face. Her eyes were swollen and her cheeks tearstained. Letting the ignition idle, Megan stepped out and headed over.

"Oh, shit, Soph," she said, hugging her tightly. "You okay?"

Sophie sobbed into Megan's arms before sucking in a ragged breath and releasing it in a snort-laugh. "Yeah, I'm okay. Thanks for coming. I would've died if I had to call my parents."

Megan glanced toward the house. Accent lanterns lit the yard, and soft lamplight filled several of the rooms. Not a soul was visible anywhere. "Are your friend's parents here?"

Sophie shook her head. "Can we go? I want out of here."

Megan let out a controlled breath. Nothing in *Volunteer 101* or *How to Deal with Your Boyfriend's Kids* covered this. "So do you want me to take you home?"

"No way. I can't face either of them right now. What if we went to your place for a bit?"

Megan chewed her lip. "What if they call for you?"

"This was supposed to be a spend-the-night. I've got my phone. They don't need to know anything else."

With reservation the size of an elephant swelling in her belly, Megan headed over to her passenger door and pulled it open. "Yeah, Soph, let's go."

They drove in silence as Sophie cried, brushing away silent tears and sniffling. Then, as they made it to Webster, Sophie abruptly burst out with "I *hate* who I am."

Megan blinked, taking note of the girl's word choice. She treaded forward hesitantly. "You mean the part of you with a giant heart who loves animals and who's doing an awesome job at the shelter? Or the part who's kind to her little brother even when he's pissing her off? Or the part that's kicking butt in school? I'm confused. What part do you hate?"

"You don't get it. Grown-ups never get it."

Megan flipped on her blinker and turned down a dark, empty street. "Actually, I think I might, but I was trying to make a point."

"What point?"

"That what you *hate* isn't you. It's that other people don't get you. Or don't like you or appreciate you. And you aren't alone there. I'm pretty sure that's just human nature."

Sophie dragged her hand under her nose and stared at her. "But how do you change it? How do you make other people stop hating you?"

"You want the truth?" Megan shot her a quick glance and smiled sympathetically.

"Yeah," she said. "The truth."

"The truth is you can't. Not without losing yourself. And believe me when I tell you that you're too awesome to lose yourself."

"So what, I'm just supposed to deal with my friends hating me?"

"Can I ask you something, Soph? Do you think they're real friends if they act in a way that makes you think they hate you?"

"No," she said after a long pause. "I don't."

"I know when adults tell kids these things, you think we've lost touch with reality, but our reality changes as we grow. When you're my age, you'll get that it isn't worth trying to be friends with assholes. Pardon my French."

Sophie laughed, then sniffed. "I wish I could grow up now."

"Well, it happens quicker than you might think. Just hang on to what makes you happy. And whatever happened tonight—whatever it was—you're worth more than that."

"I feel so dirty, you know?" Sophie said, brushing away fresh tears.

Megan's throat plummeted into her stomach. She tried to keep her voice light. "Were there boys there?"

From the corner of her eye, she saw Sophie bite her lip. "Promise you won't say anything to my parents?"

"I won't tell them. But, Sophie, depending on what happened in there, you may have to. Even if it's the hardest thing you've done."

"I can't," she said. "I told them there'd just be girls there. That's how it was going to be, but some of the really popular girls came and they invited the boys. Trisha's sister was supposed to keep an eye on everything, but she spent the whole night upstairs with her boyfriend."

Megan pulled into her driveway and turned off the ignition but sat in place waiting for Sophie to continue. *Please, God, don't let anything really bad have happened to Sophie.*

"I know they're not my friends, not even Trisha. I always knew. They make me do things to stay in the group. Things I don't want to do." Her tears started flowing again. "I didn't want to be a part of it, but I was scared to say no."

No, not that. Please no. "Oh, Sophie."

"It's not what you think. I didn't do *that*. But I did go into this closet with Miles when it was my turn." Sophie shook her head hard, and her hair bounced over her shoulders wildly. "I tried to do what he wanted me to do, but it was so gross I threw up. Right on a stack of magazines. Everybody made fun of me. I grabbed my stuff and ran out, and nobody came after me. None of them even *cared*."

Megan pulled Sophie into a tight hug. She smelled like a mix of soda and popcorn and overly sweet perfume. "Oh,

Soph, I'm so sorry. So very, very sorry." What Megan needed to do was help get Sophie's mind off this terrible night. "Let's get you inside. You can take a shower, and I'll make you something to eat. And while you eat, I'll fill you in on all the great adoptions we've had this week. You won't believe some of them. Remember meeting Mrs. Sherman? The lady with ten cats? She did some research and found out that two of the cats she's adopted over the last couple years are actually mother and daughter, though nobody had any idea."

Sophie swiped away a few fresh tears. "Really? That's cool."

"Yeah," Megan said as they stepped out of her car and headed inside. "That's the thing about the shelter. There's always a story or two to remind you that the world's more connected than you first think."

Chapter 22

IT TOOK CRAIG A FEW SECONDS TO ORIENT HIMSELF IN THE darkened room. At first, he only knew it wasn't the stiff queen bed in his apartment that he'd grown accustomed to sleeping in. It was the slight body pressed against him and the sinewy arm draped across his stomach that helped him remember. He'd fallen asleep in Reese's room. They were lying sandwiched in Reese's twin bed, using Reese's iPad to skim baseball stats. That was at ten thirty. Now it felt like the middle of the night.

Extracting himself from Reese's rarely felt embrace, Craig managed to slide out without waking him. The iPad, which had become tangled in their legs, thudded to the floor.

He found the doorknob in the darkness as the doorbell rang, reminding him that something had jerked him from a deep sleep. He shuffled out of the room, shutting the door behind him. A glance at the clock on the stove revealed it was nearly two in the morning.

Bracing himself, he cracked the front door. The person on the other side attempted to shove in immediately, vanquishing his grogginess. He drew an arm back reflexively before the intruder's voice pierced the darkness.

"Why didn't you answer your phone? I called a dozen times on my way here." Jillian pushed past him into the hallway of his apartment. "It's Sophie. She left the party. We've got to get Reese and go get her. I'm not leaving him here alone."

"What do you mean *left the party*?" Craig headed for kitchen and flipped a switch, wincing at the bright light. "With whom?"

"I haven't a clue. She's not answering her phone." In the glaring light, Jillian looked exceptionally pale. Exhaustion and fear lined her nearly flawless skin. She kept moving, crossing the small apartment, and barging through Reese's closed door.

Swiping crusts of sleep from his eyes, Craig followed her. As she coaxed Reese awake, he tried to get her to make sense of what was happening. "If she's not answering, how do you know she left? Did Trisha's parents call you? If you were tracking her phone, it could have been stolen, or a friend could have taken it home accidentally. You know she's lost phones before. It isn't like Sophie to leave a friend's house without telling us."

"If you would've answered the phone, I could have told you all this," Jillian said, facing him once Reese groggily sat up. "I woke up with a bad feeling, and I called Soph. When she didn't answer, I went online and checked that app we installed. It shows she's at a house in Webster. Then I called Trisha's parents. They'd been out all night and just gotten home. Last minute, they left their sixteen-year-old in charge of the party! I ended up talking to Trisha. She wouldn't own up to it at first, but finally, she said Sophie texted an hour ago that she'd gone home with another friend. And no one questioned it!" Her pitch rose at the last words, and she wrung her hands wildly. "I would've gone alone, but I don't know what I'm facing here."

Seeing she was on the verge of hysteria, Craig scooped Reese into his arms, blanket and all, and headed for the kitchen. "We can get to Webster in ten minutes. Grab my shoes from the hall closet, will you?" He could drive barefoot for now, and he didn't need to bother changing clothes since he had fallen asleep in lounge pants and a Henley. Shifting Reese in his arms, he swiped his wallet and keys from a tray in the kitchen.

"Dad, I'm awake. I can walk."

Refusing to waste time, Craig kept Reese locked in a vise grip till he reached the car. He hadn't carried Reese in years, and the solid weight of his son surprised him. He was growing up fast. So was Sophie, for that matter, if she was hopping rebelliously from one party to the next. Only that didn't sound like Sophie.

They buckled in, and Craig swept out of the parking lot fast enough that the tires squealed.

"What's up with Soph?" Reese asked from the back-seat, yawning out the first half of his words. "Were there not enough arts and crafts so she ditched and went to another party?"

Sarcasm—his son wore it better than the blanket he was snuggling.

"Reese, please." Jillian's tone was strained.

Craig glanced her way as he zipped through the streets toward a part of town he was getting to know fairly well. He'd seen that look of complete exhaustion before. Losing Andrew had changed her, as it had changed them all, but with Jillian, it was different. She was attempting to carve out a world with zero unpredictability.

Not surprisingly, it wasn't working for her. Newbie teens weren't predictable. Neither were ex-husbands who unexpectedly fell asleep in their son's bed and left their cells muted in the other room. Sons learning to live without twin brothers weren't too cooperative either.

Jillian hadn't always been the woman whose refrigerator contents were placed with precision organization. Who, every day, worked out two hours, did yoga for one, and checked in with her therapist at least once.

Back when they were newlyweds, they'd had a joint business trip to New York. On a whim, they'd taken a few days off when the meetings were over and flown to Paris because she'd had a lifelong dream of making out on a bench in view of the Eiffel Tower. She'd been over five months pregnant with Sophie then, radiant and glowing and always wearing a smile.

Remembering that woman, the one he fell in love with, his heart ached for all the loss they'd endured. He merged onto the highway and squeezed Jillian's hand reassuringly.

No one spoke until he pulled off the interstate. Reese's soft, even breathing showed he'd fallen back to sleep. Sleeping like a log was the one normal boy thing Reese did.

"Where to?" Craig asked, locking both hands on the steering wheel as he headed into Webster, a part of St. Louis he'd grown to associate exclusively with Megan since both the shelter and her condo were in the heart of it. Jillian directed him down Big Bend Boulevard, past the turnoff to the shelter, stately churches, and the university.

When she instructed him to turn down the same street that led in three more turns to Megan's, his heart sank. He pulled to the side of the deserted road and came to a stop.

"Let me see your phone."

"I can get us there fine. Let's not waste time."

Sighing, he held out his hand. "Jillian, I think I know where she is."

If it were possible, she seemed to grow even paler in the dim dashboard light as she surrendered her phone. Sure enough, with a few swipes of his finger, the map led him to Megan's cul-de-sac and her condo.

Turning off the navigation, he passed Jillian back her phone. "I don't know why she's there, but I know where she is. She's with Megan Anderson. From the shelter," he added unnecessarily.

"I know who Megan is, Craig. She's not with her. She's at a house. I saw it on Google Live View."

"Megan isn't at the shelter."

The ensuing silence lay between them like a lead blanket, Reese's rhythmic breathing the only thing to penetrate it. Jillian folded her arms across her chest as Craig pulled back into the lane and navigated the streets without need for a map. He could tell her he'd come here once with the kids to see Tyson and his brother. And even though it would be the truth, the idea of it felt like a lie on his tongue.

Megan's home, and the way to it, were intimately familiar to him now. Waking up in her bedroom no longer caused that feeling of disorientation he'd experienced in Reese's room a bit ago. And while he hadn't shared any of this with his ex-wife over the last few months—or anyone for that matter—he wouldn't try to make it look like they weren't.

He could feel the storm growing in Jillian. His body reacted to it automatically, the surface of his skin hypercharged as if it were conducting a strong current. Like always, the stiller she grew, the more obvious Jillian's discomfort was. No fidgeting, no huffing, no drumming of an ankle. Just silence and control. He debated whether there was anything he could say. She wasn't one to fight publicly, so he wasn't worried about her making a scene in front of Megan.

Besides, he'd done nothing wrong. It was true he'd met Megan way before he'd planned on meeting anyone. But his marriage was over. Emotionally for a long time, contractually for less, but over still.

When he turned down Megan's quiet cul-de-sac, Jillian cleared her throat. "So Sophie knows. Does Reese?"

She knew. And she wasn't going to make him explain. "Neither of them knows anything."

"Then why is Sophie with her?"

"I don't know, but I suspect something happened at that party and she wasn't ready to face us. Volunteering with Megan as Soph does, they've developed their own relationship."

He pulled into the driveway but left the ignition running. Reese slept on, undisturbed.

Craig unbuckled and opened his door but paused when Jillian didn't move.

"I knew it at Sophie's party." Her tone was even and low but accusatory. "I knew it from the way you two avoided each other. You gave that money to her shelter, and she wouldn't look at you. And then there was the fact that you gave an animal shelter money in the first place. You always choose children's charities."

"I won't defend my decisions, Jillian. I don't have to. But I'll tell you this. Our relationship started after—"

Unfolding her arms, she held up a hand. "That's the beauty of divorce. I don't need details." She unbuckled and opened her door. He could see her chin starting to wobble. "But I'll tell you this. Whatever girlfriend-daughter bonding's going on inside that house, it ends tonight."

She popped out of the car but left her door open wide. He knew it wasn't that she'd forgotten but that she wanted to be able to hear Reese if he woke up and called for her. But he was ten, he'd been here before, and he was Reese. He wouldn't call out for his mom if he woke up. He'd get out and come inside.

Jogging around the front of the car to catch up, Craig closed his hand over Jillian's elbow. "I get you're pissed. Keep in mind the kids don't know. And Megan doesn't deserve to feel any wrath over this either."

Jillian's chin was wobbling harder, but she didn't look close to tears otherwise. "Your relationships aren't my concern. My concern is why my daughter left a party in the middle of the night and came to another adult's house. That's my *only* concern."

Craig paused in front of the door, wishing he'd taken the time to swipe his cell off his nightstand before leaving. For Megan's sake, a phone call would be so much less of a shock than opening her door at two in the morning to find him and his ex-wife hovering there. Light was pouring out of the windows from cracks in the curtains, so at least she and Sophie were awake.

It took Megan a minute to get to the door. It cracked open, and she peeked tentatively around it. She made eye contact with Jillian first, and her eyes widened only slightly. "Hey."

Whatever she'd stepped up to do with Sophie in the

middle of night, Craig felt a rush of gratitude toward her. She pulled the door open the rest of the way. She was barefoot and dressed in low-rise yoga pants and a dark-pink cami, her hair a mussed mess, all of which called to him even amid this commotion.

"So, um, Sophie's here. Obviously you know, or you wouldn't be here in the middle of the night. She's in the shower," Megan said, shutting the door behind them. She looked more shaken than she sounded. "Did she call you?"

"She didn't. She's not answering her calls," Craig said. Jillian stepped into the foyer after him, scanning the condo, taking everything in. "We have that find-my-phone app. It led us here."

"Oh." Megan's cheeks flamed scarlet, but she motioned them toward the living room. "I was making a quesadilla for her. Let me make sure the stove's off."

Craig wondered if any of the color in Megan's cheeks was due to how Jillian was standing in the exact spot in the foyer where they'd first had sex. Likely she wasn't thinking about that. Likely she was just panicked that she'd been caught harboring Sophie for whatever reason he'd yet to learn.

When this was over, he'd make it up to Megan.

"What happened at the party? What made her want to leave and come here? Before she gets out of the shower, I'd like to know what she told you." Jillian's words cut through the room, though they were spoken without any strong inflection. She strode to the living room and pivoted to face them, her arms still folded across her chest.

Megan paused halfway to the kitchen. She turned, tucking a mass of hair behind her ear. "I can understand you want answers, and I hope you can understand that I owe her my confidence." Clearly catching one of Jillian's brows disappearing into her forehead and her cheeks drawing sharply inward in response, Megan continued. "She's okay. She isn't hurt, other than emotionally. But she needed to get away from that party, and she wasn't ready to face you. Either of you. She called me and asked me to pick her up, and I did. We haven't been here that long. Less than half an hour."

Jillian released a breath of air like steam from a kettle. "If there was bullying or anything close to it, I'd like to know."

"I understand, but I think Sophie needs to be the one to answer that." She rubbed one thumb into the other palm. Her shoulders were lined with tension. "I don't know if I did the right thing by agreeing to pick her up, but I do know betraying her confidence right now is the last thing she needs."

"Jillian," Craig said in as benevolent a voice possible, "it can't hurt to wait a few minutes longer to figure this out. The truth is that Sophie didn't call us. Either of us."

Jillian said nothing and shifted her weight to one side, working the heel of her ballet flat in small circles around the ankle that always troubled her. She pursed her lips and finally shook her head, her inner turmoil barely contained.

Craig's heart went out to both of them. To Megan, along with a hell of a lot of admiration, for holding her ground against Jillian's everyone-listens-to-me face. To Jillian for maintaining her composure after everything she'd learned tonight. And underneath all of that, a rippling current of concern was growing for his daughter.

He wasn't ready for his little girl to be swept into teen drama. He knew those years were ahead and closing in, but she was still such a kid. An innocent, impossibly kind kid.

From inside Megan's bedroom, a door pulled open. With intimate familiarity, Craig knew it was the door to the master bathroom by the way it caught on the frame, skidded, and then pulled open freely. If his tools weren't in storage, he'd have brought a shim to fix it.

There was the padding of bare feet and a pause. Before Sophie rounded the corner of the bedroom door, he had just enough time to wonder if she'd be wearing a towel on her head—if she'd been comfortable enough here to wash her hair—when her voice penetrated the small condo.

"Oh my God, Megan. Does this mean you're pregnant?"

Craig's ears buzzed instantly. He gripped the top of an armchair as the words reverberated through his head. Then Sophie, floppy towel on her head, looking down at a book rather than up at them, rounded the corner.

His vision tightened as if he was looking through binoculars as he scanned the book cover in his daughter's hands. A pregnancy book, one Jillian read years ago.

Then Sophie looked up and saw her parents standing twenty feet away. "Fuck."

The word barely registered over the buzzing in his ears. He'd never heard her say it before. He wouldn't have believed she had it in her. Her hands flew to her mouth. The book tumbled to the floor, and her towel turban slipped sideways.

Jillian was first to break the stupor holding the room. Crossing at lightning pace, she picked up the abandoned book and tucked it on the side of her body farthest from Sophie. As if doing so could make Sophie unsee it. He glanced at Megan, who'd gone from bright red to ghostly pale in a few seconds. If he'd been harboring hope she'd blow it off with a wave of her hand and give a plausible excuse, it faded.

"I'm sorry," Sophie pleaded. "Moxie was on your bed and I went to pick her up and I saw all the lumps under the covers. I didn't know—"

"It's okay. Those books aren't mine. A friend of mine lent them to me." Megan had told him weeks ago she was a pathetic liar, that she couldn't bluff to save her life. Before now, he'd never seen her try.

If someone had predicted he'd learn something this powerful, this life-altering, with the three women he cared about most all in the same room, he wouldn't have believed it.

What was worse, he wasn't the only one to put it together. Jillian's under-the-tongue whisper penetrated the room like a scream. "Jesus, Craig, you didn't."

———※———

The smoke alarm piercing through her home from the charred quesadilla was a bizarre relief. For the minute or two Megan dealt with the smoky fiasco in her kitchen, she wouldn't have to look any of them in the eye. She wished fleetingly the three people standing in her living room would think it was a real fire and run out, never to be seen again.

Her hands shook wildly as she yanked the pan off the burner and used tongs to transfer the blackened tortilla-cheese brick into the sink and douse it until it was waterlogged and no longer smoldering. The smell of burned flour mixed with savory, melted cheese made her stomach lurch.

Refusing to look at her guests, Megan heard Jillian's mumbled accusation replaying like a broken record in her head until the smoke cleared enough that the alarm silenced. Somehow Jillian had worked out the depth of Sophie's ill-timed proclamation. It seemed impossible though. Craig would have said if he'd shared anything about their relationship with his ex-wife.

If only she hadn't thought those books were safely hidden under her bedcovers. If only she'd thought of a better hiding place while Sophie was in the shower. If only she had told Craig the news on any of the last several chances she had.

Though she wouldn't risk a glance toward the living room, the silence filling it grated on her nerves. Finally, as she shut off the faucet, Craig cleared his throat.

"Sophie, it's late. We should get you home." He was crossing the room as he spoke. Megan could tell that much without looking.

"How'd you know I was here? My phone?"

"Yes, and we're going to want answers." It was Jillian, and she'd become nasal. To Megan's horror, she realized Craig's ex was crying—silently, but crying nevertheless.

Unable to keep turned away any longer, she watched Jillian use her thumb to swipe her cheek dry. Craig was returning from the back of the room. He'd opened the sliding-glass patio door to clear the cloud of smoke clinging to the ceiling. Sophie looked back and forth between her parents, twisting the wet towel in her hands like a rope. Had she heard her mother's quiet accusation? Megan prayed she hadn't. Or if she had, that it didn't register.

"Sorry I came here without calling." Sophie glanced Megan's way a second and shrugged her shoulders apologetically. "Megan helped me work something out. But I'd rather talk about it later."

Jillian had set the book upside down on Megan's side table. "Reese is asleep in the car. Let's get you home. You guys are with me the rest of the night. Your dad can bring your stuff in the morning."

"Yeah, but can you give me a second first? I'll be right out." Sophie gnawed her lip, waiting for a reply.

Megan made eye contact with Craig for the first time since Sophie had made her declaration. His jaw was clenched, and the muscles lining his neck and shoulders rippled with tension. What on earth could she say? Nothing, that's what.

Jillian answered for both of them, telling Sophie in that nasal tone to gather her things and be out in a minute. She headed out without so much as a glance Megan's way, and under the circumstances, Megan couldn't blame her.

Craig paused by the door, rapping on the frame with his palm. "Megan, I'll, uh, I'll be in touch."

She knew she couldn't answer him without crying, so she nodded. Her hands wouldn't stop shaking. Worse, the trembling was climbing up her arms, and now her chin seemed to have a mind of its own. Fearing they'd notice, she locked her hands behind her back.

"It's a mess," he added, hovering in the doorway under Sophie's curious gaze. "But it doesn't mean we can't figure it out."

As close to crying as she could get without tears sliding down her cheeks, Megan forced herself to hold it together for Sophie's sake. Finally, he was gone, the door was shut, and it was just her and Sophie.

"That got weird," Sophie said, wadding her towel into a ball. "Sorry if I embarrassed you."

Megan forced a shrug and kept her hands locked under the waistband at the back of her pants.

Sophie opened her mouth, blushed scarlet, then shut it without saying anything. After another second or two of hesitation, she said, "So did you tell them anything about what happened?"

"No," Megan said, feeling the tears retreat a bit at the change of topic. "But I do think you should. Maybe not tonight, but when you're ready. If you need reinforcements, I'm here, awkward as it might be." She held her hands out for the towel. "I'll take that. You should grab your bag and get moving."

Sophie tossed her the towel, then stepped forward and hugged her, smashing the wet towel against her chest. "You're the best, Megan."

She dashed into the bathroom, grabbed her overnight bag, thanked Megan again, and headed out to join her parents. The door was barely closed before Megan sank to the floor, covering her face in shaky hands.

Chapter 23

BY FIVE IN THE MORNING, MEGAN WAS RESIGNED TO THE fact that sleep would be as elusive as the end of a rainbow. The few hours before Sophie called were all she would get. She made a pot of herbal tea—quitting caffeine was underway—threw on some clothes, and headed out the door for work. Hopefully, getting busy would keep her thoughts from circling into oblivion.

She hadn't even made it a few blocks when she started recounting her mistakes. She'd made two big ones that tortured her. If she could undo just one of them, the disaster in her apartment—and what she feared it would lead to—could've been so different. She could've told Craig Friday night when she met him in the parking lot. She was in a good space. She should've gathered the courage and told him.

But he was in a hurry, and the time hadn't seemed right. The second mistake was not hiding those books better. Just a little more caution on her part, and she could've told Craig in the way he deserved to be told. Not throw it at him in front of his daughter and ex-wife.

How she'd ever find the courage to see him again, she didn't know. He'd texted an hour after leaving, asking if she was awake. She didn't answer. She wasn't ready to face him. She shuddered at the thought. It was Craig's look as he hovered by the door that haunted her. Tense. Tired. Resigned. Beaten.

She was still trying to erase that look from her mind when she pulled into the empty shelter parking lot. The unusual stillness that greeted her when she stepped through the door at such an early hour was as welcoming as the familiar din of barks, yips, and howls that would fill the air later in the day. However, she suspected that even when the building grew noisy, Sophie's sharp declaration would replay over and over again in her head. Those few words had exploded through her home like an air bag triggering.

She cursed herself for looking at Jillian first, not Craig. Because whatever happened in the future, she'd missed the opportunity to see the look on his face the exact moment he learned he'd created another child. Maybe it was better she hadn't though, in case it was disappointment or rage or something she wouldn't want to remember.

Instead, burned into her retinas was the look on Jillian's face, eyebrows drawing sharply upward and lips pressing flat. And her gaze darting to her ex-husband.

The truth was there'd be no doing anything today aside from reliving those life-altering seconds and worrying herself sick with fear over their repercussions. What was this going to do to those kids? Would anyone tell Reese? Would Sophie hate her? Hate her dad? And what about Craig? Would he hate her for not telling him when she should have?

She was a complete mess. A complete pregnant, worthless mess. Truth was, she'd likely be better off getting away from the shelter today altogether. A strenuous hike would settle her nerves, but thunderstorms were expected to roll in. Long drives usually worked too. She was mulling over places to go when Patrick walked in at three minutes to eight—allowing the precise amount of time to hang his jacket and put his usual ham-and-salami sandwich in the fridge.

Chance trotted over to greet him. Patrick sank to a squat and pulled a treat from one of the pockets of his cargo pants. He had the habit of only buying pants with eight pockets. Each pocket held something important to him. Megan could see the outline of his trusted Swiss Army knife in one and his mini flashlight in another.

"I thought of you last night when the Cards came from behind like that and won in the bottom of the tenth inning."

The smile that appeared on Patrick's face as Chance chomped his treat and wagged his tail in unison grew wider. "It was a good win. That happened last year six games out from the end of the season, only then we ended with four runs and we were playing the Cubs."

Patrick seemed have a limitless ability to commit three things to memory: shelter facts, baseball stats, and chess moves. Megan had never met anyone who could outdo him in memory recall in any of those areas and doubted she ever would.

This morning, Patrick's solid sense of self was even more soothing than her cup of tea had been. A bit of consistency to count on when her world was in upheaval. The fact that he felt good about this season's lineup, despite what the critics had to say, was immensely reassuring. She suspected deep down that this had less to do with baseball and more to do with all the daunting single-mother stats rolling around her head all morning.

Good things happened despite worrywarts and naysayers. This thought brought her mom to mind. Her mom was the only one she knew who actually used those two outdated words in conversation anymore.

Her I-don't-care-if-it's-in-style-or-not mom.

Right away, Megan knew where she needed to go today. Sooner or later, she was going to have to tell her mom, and it might as well be now. And the relief of getting out of town today of all days would just about negate the stress she typically felt going home.

Once the idea took hold, there was no getting around it. After the baseball talk wound around to animal talk and an update of all that needed to be done today, Patrick headed into the back.

Megan spent a half hour going through paperwork, making sure she was setting Patrick and Kelsey up for success with the shelter left in their hands for a short while. Tomorrow was Monday, and for the first time in months, she had two days off in a row. She was going to go for it and head home to Springfield.

It was a three-and-a-half-hour drive. She'd done the trip there and back in one day often enough, fueled on the ride home by the decade-long grudge she'd been holding against her mom. But Megan suspected this time would be different. She'd need the extra few days for several reasons. She was exhausted starting the trip. Her sleepless hours were already making her eyelids feel like they were coated in sandpaper. Trying to drive back tonight might even be dangerous. And then there was the news she was bringing with her. It wasn't just going to come out in casual conversation. She'd need time with her mom alone, once Tyler and Tess had gone to bed, and Rick too for that matter.

And then there was Craig. She knew he'd want to

see her, even though his hands had to be more than full with Jillian and the kids and the aftermath of last night's party. But she needed time. She didn't want to face him today. What if he asked her to have an abortion?

She wouldn't. Not a chance. But if he did, *if* he asked her to, things between them would never be the same.

And she wasn't ready to lose him.

It seemed easier to put him off entirely for a few days. To get herself together before facing him. She couldn't fathom what he thought of all this. The truth was, she didn't want to try.

Megan couldn't rewind the clock. But she could get her crap together and figure out her next steps. And, almost surprisingly, going home to Springfield felt like the right place to do it.

After a quick trip home to pack and make sure the cats were well fed, Megan was just about to merge onto the interstate for Springfield when it struck her she'd forgotten something. Actually, not something, but someone. Checking her mirrors to make sure it was safe, she whipped a U-turn and headed back to work.

Bringing Sledge along wasn't against shelter protocol. Reliable volunteers could choose to foster animals they couldn't find homes for. Megan had gotten Moxie and Max that way. Since they had feline immunosuppressive virus, they couldn't stay in the shelter without the risk of infecting other cats. She brought them home with the idea of eventually placing them elsewhere. But they'd snuck into her heart, and a month into fostering, she made their adoption official.

Only she couldn't do that with Sledge. He was a ninety-pound German shepherd. Her landlord didn't allow dogs, and Megan didn't have the money to move. If she could, she would though.

Sledge was phenomenally well trained, and she could swear he wanted to start trusting people again, signs that he'd had someone in his life who'd cared about him a lot.

And all of this was working together to have her falling for him big time. After a few days of all-on bonding, letting him go to someone else was going to be a lot harder. But bringing him along on the trip home felt like the right decision. He'd be welcome company for the quiet drive—and even more welcome company in the home she always felt like she was invading when she visited. And with both her mother and stepfather being dog lovers, she knew she'd hear no objection.

So, another twenty minutes of readying his supplies later, she was back at the same spot, merging onto the interstate toward Springfield. Only this time, she had a canine companion filling her backseat and leaning forward every so often to pant in her ear and lick her neck.

She plugged in the auxiliary cord to her iPod, set her playlist on random, and settled in for the drive. She was an hour into it and listening to "Heartbreak Warfare" while thinking of Craig when the storm that had been building on the horizon met her with a burst of force.

Rain and wind pummeled the windshield. Sledge whined as she shifted to the right lane and locked her hands at ten and two. Her phone rang at the same time that a burst of wind threatened to shove her off the highway. Ignoring the call, she focused on the only spot of highway she could see—fifty feet right in front of her—and hoped a freeway exit and gas station were near.

During a break in the wind, she flipped over her phone to see the missed call was from Craig. He'd left a voice mail. When the storm was over, she'd call him, though the idea of doing so made her heart flutter a little too reminiscently of morning sickness.

The worst of the storm and the gas station arrived at the same time. She parked by a pump and sat in her car under a covered awning, waiting it out as the world around her shook and blew. She willed herself to pick up the phone and call Craig. Or at least listen to his voice mail. Maybe he was telling her he loved her and it was going to be okay.

Or maybe he was demanding they meet so he could give her ultimatums about the baby.

When the skies were clearing and the rain was down to an easy drizzle, she grabbed her phone and hopped out. Sledge, who shoved out from the backseat a bit awkwardly, seemed relieved to be out of the car. His tail wagged a dozen times before he started eyeing the world around him. After starting the pump, Megan wrapped the leash tight and headed to a strip of bright-green grass at the side of the gas station.

"This is it," she said to Sledge as she dialed her voice mail. "The moment of truth. What are you betting?"

Sledge glanced her way for a split second but turned his attention back to a semi that was pulling in. Megan was dodging a puddle and hopping over the curb onto the grass when he bolted sideways, jarring the phone from her hand.

And straight into a puddle.

"Crap!" She dove for it, but her heart sank. The puddle was deep, and her phone was completely immersed. In the back of her mind, she heard Patrick telling her she needed a waterproof case like his. She worked in a shelter full of hoses, water bowls, and excited animals. And she heard herself telling him she'd never lost a phone to water damage.

The images on the screen were already going haywire. She turned it off immediately and dabbed it dry with her shirt while Sledge peed a forever pee. When he was finished, she ran him to the car, shut him in, and headed into the gas station for the supplies she'd heard could help. A ziplock bag of uncooked rice. Unfortunately, she wouldn't know if it did for a few days.

She was a bit surprised that the small shop actually had rice. She grabbed a box of dog treats as she passed, paid, and returned to the car.

"Well," she said, ripping open the box and letting Sledge's powerful tongue swipe treats from her fingers, "I guess it wasn't the moment of truth after all."

Craig's unease showed in the burned toast, runny eggs, and coffeepot he ran first with only water. He'd never wish his kids away, but when Sophie had talked Jillian into letting them stay with him as originally planned, it would've been better if he'd objected and picked them up later today.

Or if they'd at least slept in. He hadn't remembered to close the curtains, and they were up with the sun at seven. He'd been awake till five. Finally determining that Megan wasn't going to answer his texts, he'd fallen asleep on the couch after pacing a line through the living room carpet.

Now it wasn't the lack of sleep unnerving him, but being powerless. Megan was pregnant. She hadn't confirmed it, but she had to be.

With his child.

Sophie, thank God, hadn't brought it up again. The fiasco of last night's party probably helped get it off her mind. He could tell from her downward glances whenever they discussed it that whatever had really happened there wasn't something she was ready to share yet. And this morning he wasn't in the space to push for more either.

Added to that, Jillian was a mess. At least as much of a mess as she'd allow herself to be. Few people aside from him, her therapist, and possibly Sophie would have any clue about the storm brewing inside her—not of anger, but of fear.

And possibly sorrow.

She hadn't voiced this to him, though she'd voiced more than enough after he'd gotten the kids to bed and answered her call. She'd never admit that any part of her would consider moving on in that way without Andrew. Still, Craig suspected the sorrow was there, flowing under her surface.

He'd never considered moving on in that way either.

But now, that reality was staring him in the face, and he suspected that, of the tumult of emotions churning inside him, a nervous, buzzing excitement and the quiet whisper of hope were part of them.

If only Megan would've answered her phone while the kids were eating their subpar breakfast. It was the one chance he had to step away. Last night had been so unexpected, so bizarre, that he needed to know what she was thinking.

She hadn't told him the truth, and he understood. He forgave her for not having the courage.

If the kids hadn't come home with him, he'd have driven over to her place—regardless of whether she was asleep—banged on the door till she answered, and just held her.

He needed it as much as he suspected she did. He knew his insides wouldn't quiet until he held her long enough that her Meganness sank in and calmed him.

Swiping his phone off the counter, he typed into it with shaky fingers. He made as many typos as progress, but finally got it right.

> With the kids but thinking of you. How are you holding up?

He wouldn't ask for more details till he saw her in person. He'd head to the shelter late this afternoon after he took the kids back to Jillian. He could keep it together that long at least.

Chapter 24

TYLER AND TESS WERE IN THE FRONT YARD DESTROYING A circle of grass with two sturdy sticks and the garden hose when Megan neared the house. Neither her mom nor Rick were anywhere in sight, but at eleven and nine, the kids didn't need constant supervision any longer.

However, Megan suspected her mom wouldn't be happy about the Frisbee-wide hole they'd dug in the yard. Or the mud their hands and feet were caked in.

Unseen, she slowed the car to a crawl and surveyed the house and surrounding acres. It was a ranch house, older but nicely kept and well situated on four rolling acres. Not only was there a nice pond out back, but also a white-fenced pasture and two plump miniature ponies that her mom had rescued from an older woman in town who'd had no idea how to care for them. Her mom hadn't either, but they'd tamed down and become somewhat friendly over the two years they'd been here. And most importantly, they remained stubborn enough not to take abuse from Tyler and Tess, who good-heartedly dished out more than they should.

Megan's heart twisted as she looked over the place. It was quaint and homey and inviting. And though she'd lived there for more than three years before going to college, it had never felt like home. Her home—the one they sold a year and half after losing her dad and moving here—was seven and a half miles away.

Often she'd head there first. The people who bought it were rumored to be recluses, and Megan always felt like the police would be called if she lingered out front too long. In winter, the house was fairly visible from the road. Rather than being situated like this one on a perfect little knoll, it was tucked at an angle into a wooded hillside.

In spring, it would be harder to see, but she'd still be able to pick out her bedroom window and see if the tire swing was still hanging on the big oak out back.

The detached garage where her dad had spent his free time restoring classic cars could be seen all year long. There was a rolling pang in Megan's heart, reminding her of a rag being twisted to get all the water out, whenever she saw it.

But today she was exhausted and didn't have the energy to see it. She'd swing by on her way out tomorrow and, like always, contemplate pulling in the driveway long enough to run up and throw open the side garage door to see if she could catch wind of her father's spirit.

But on top of a sleepless night, a long drive, and a hell of a lot of stress, that energy wasn't something she could summon right now.

Tyler and Tess spotted her car, dropping the hose and running to the edge of the yard to greet her. She pulled in the driveway and killed the ignition.

"Hey, guys. Hold it there," she said, warding off mud-covered hugs. "Let's get back to that hose and wash off those hands and arms before I see how much stronger your hugs have gotten."

They raced to the hose, waving her along. "Mom didn't tell us you were coming," Tess said, grinning and revealing two missing bottom teeth as she rinsed her hands. The mud fell off in easy sheets.

"That's because it's a surprise. Just like those new teeth you lost."

"And the dog in your car." Tyler jutted his chin toward Sledge, who was eyeing them from the backseat. "Did you get a dog?"

"Right now he belongs to the shelter, but I brought him along for the ride. I thought he could use some time off leash to run around. Now that you're clean, I'll introduce you. But how about you turn the hose off before you flood the yard any more."

"Will he chase ducklings? The Easter Bunny brought us five." Tessa's forehead knotted in concern as they returned to the car.

"You know, he might, so we'll have to be careful. And you guys are going to have to treat him like you do all the dogs when you come to the shelter. And you can't try to ride him like you do those little ponies. I know they're about the same size."

Tyler and Tess rolled their eyes in unison. "We know."

Sledge hopped out and tentatively licked Tessa's nose as she burrowed her fingers in his fur. Tyler was next—then, fifty feet away, the front door opened. Her mother, a twenty-year-older version of Megan, stood in the threshold with her painting shirt on, holding their excited corgi back with her bare foot.

"You won't believe this, but I had a dream last night that you came home. Call Rick if you don't believe me. He's fishing with the boys." Her mom twisted her head, checking out the impressively sized shepherd in her driveway. "Is he friendly with other dogs?"

"I think so, but we should introduce them on the leash. Believe it or not, Shorty's got more spunk than Sledge."

As Megan suspected, Sledge's tail disappeared between his back legs when Shorty approached, acting considerably taller than his twelve inches.

Her mom hugged her tight, holding on longer than Megan wanted her to. "You sleeping well?" she asked when she pulled away. She kept her hand locked around Megan's elbow.

"Well enough."

"Not well enough, I'm thinking. Those dark circles are back. I'd ask what wind blew you here, but any wind that blows you here is good enough for me. Come on, let's get you and that giant dog of yours inside."

Megan agreed and followed her mother in, half dragged by the kids. While Sledge went to town sniffing everything in sight, trailed closely by the corgi, Megan let herself get absorbed in Tyler and Tess's world of artwork and school projects and new toys. Thanks to their unending enthusiasm, she forgot her inner turmoil for the first time since the doorbell rang last night. In doing so, she relaxed and fatigue swept in.

Fortunately, she was able to keep her attention locked on the kids for the next few hours and, as a result, held off the onslaught of questions she knew would eventually come from her mom.

Except for one.

"Why would someone who works your hours want to quit caffeine?"

Megan kept her eyes glued to Tyler's Lego tower as she cursed the casual comment that slipped out about quitting caffeine after her mom picked up on the yawns and brought her a cup of coffee.

"It's a headache trigger, or so I've heard." It was a play on words, not a lie.

"So you're getting headaches? You haven't said."

They talked twice a week, Wednesday nights and Sundays. Megan mostly kept to shelter news. She'd told her mother about Craig only as a donor and someone who'd joined the board. She hadn't wanted her mom's relationship advice because she knew it would probably ring true. Like warning her about the risks of having constant, mind-blowing, uncommitted sex with a man fresh out of divorce.

She and Craig had done a lot more than that, of course. Hours upon hours of talking, back rubs, long walks, candlelight dinners, a bit of cooking together, and a few movies. But it had always been at Megan's house, and eventually, it had always led to sex.

And now she was five weeks pregnant.

Her mom hovered over Megan, the mug of steaming coffee held out as she sat in the middle of the floor alongside Sledge, Shorty, Tyler, and Tess, and surrounded by Legos, as if Megan might change her mind and take it. "How often?" her mom added, referring to the headaches.

"They're nothing to call home about," Megan replied. She searched for a change of topic and ended up spotting the clock on the mantel. "I didn't know it was almost five. I need to call the shelter and check in. I dropped my phone in water earlier, and I've been incommunicado all day."

"Go for it."

Megan grabbed the home phone and headed down the hall toward the bedrooms as she dialed. She was glad when Kelsey picked up. She'd get more valuable information with less effort than from Patrick or Fidel, and the favor she needed to ask was one she'd only trust Kelsey with.

The day there had been a good one, it turned out. No surrenders and three adoptions. One dog and two cats. A good day for a small shelter.

"That's great," Megan said when Kelsey finished. "Really awesome. Hey, I was wondering if you could do me a favor before you leave."

"Sure," Kelsey said, her voice muffled as she slammed a cabinet door, reminding Megan of their never-ending workload. "What?"

"I was wondering if you'd email Craig Williams for me. He's in our system contacts."

"Yeah. What for?"

"We had some business to take care of. We were supposed to meet tomorrow. Can you email him that I'm here at my mom's and I'm sorry to cancel, but I'll call him when I get back? And mention my dead phone, will you? Just in case he tries calling."

"Sure. Got it."

There was a knot in her stomach and a little voice screaming this was a cowardly way of putting Craig off another day. She should use her mom's phone and call him herself. Not send a spineless email through Kelsey. Sighing, Megan promised herself she'd do it later. Right now, she simply didn't have the energy.

—⁓—

Disappointment settled in Craig's stomach as he pulled in the shelter lot at twenty minutes after five and found it empty. He'd just come from Megan's house after dropping the kids off with Jillian. He'd driven the most direct route here and hadn't passed her.

For the first time since they started seeing each other, her phone had been off all day and she hadn't replied to his message or texts. He reassured himself that with their chaotic night, she must have forgotten to charge her phone. And now she was probably running a few errands before heading home.

He scoped the grocery store on the way back to her house but didn't see her car. Exhausted as he was, he pulled into her driveway, rolled down his windows, and closed his eyes. He dozed off easily, too easily.

When he woke up, the sun was setting. Dew was lining the interior of his car and covering his clothes, and his neck was stiff and kinked. And Megan was nowhere to be seen. Groggy and with his frustration rising, Craig pulled out his phone. No texts or missed calls from her.

He scanned his email and felt a flutter of hope when he glimpsed the shelter's name embedded in an email address. It melted away when he saw the sender was Kelsey. Still, he clicked on it, discounting the dozen other emails in his inbox waiting for him.

He read the message four times, his stomach sinking lower each time.

Mr. Williams,

Megan apologizes, but she has business to take care of and has gone to her mom's in

Springfield. She will not be able to meet with you tomorrow.

Pawsitively wishing you the best.
Kelsey

Dropping his phone, Craig stumbled out of the car and sucked in a breath. *Dear God, Megan, what the hell are you up to?*

———

It was a bit like Chinese water torture, lying beside Tess till she fell asleep without doing so herself. Tess's room used to be Megan's before she left for college. Tess had moved into it from the one she'd shared with Tyler when she was four. The combined familiarity and foreignness was enough to keep Megan's weighted eyelids open. The walls were a different color and the bedspread was new, but the furniture and view from under the covers were the same.

Lying in this old bed, she didn't feel so far from the troubled, resentful teen who'd lain awake late, learning to live without her father and watching her mother have such an easy time of it. Everything this stirred up kept her awake until Tess's breathing was even and soft.

Lifting her sister's small hand carefully off her stomach, Megan rolled out and tiptoed across the room. She needed to call Craig and have the conversation she'd been avoiding. Whatever his reaction was, waiting it out any longer wasn't going to change it. In fact, it might only make things worse.

But she also needed to talk to her mom. As she

tiptoed out of the room and down the hall, she saw her mom cuddled on the couch reading the latest copy of *Good Housekeeping* by soft lamplight. Hearing Megan approach, she set the magazine down and twisted to face her.

Sorry, Craig. My mom wins by proximity.

All day, she'd kept the reality of why she'd come pushed at bay. Now it flooded her. She was pregnant and, as of this moment, had absolutely no idea if she'd receive support—emotional or otherwise—from the father.

Now nothing was keeping this heartfelt conversation at bay. The kids were asleep. Rick, who had the early shift at the plastic fabrication plant where he was foreman, had gone to bed with them.

"So I turned on the kettle. Would you like some tea?" her mom asked.

"That'd be great." Megan collapsed onto the love seat, twisted sideways, and kicked up her feet. She tucked a throw pillow over her stomach, creating a barrier between the world and the life taking form in her belly.

"Chamomile, I take it?"

"Sounds great."

Her mom shuffled into the kitchen in fuzzy slippers and came back a few minutes later with a tray of steaming mugs of tea and a plate of shortbread cookies.

Megan swiped a cookie and nibbled on the edges, gathering her courage.

"So…" Her mom settled into the corner of the long couch, leaning against the arm and tucking her feet under her.

So? Her mom wouldn't be winning any awards as

a conversation starter. But the truth was, quite a few so's were boiling beneath Megan's surface. The one that slipped out first wasn't the one she expected.

"Did you love my dad? Ever?"

Great, Megan. Bravo. Don't just throw it out there. Add an insult while you're at it.

Her mom's eyebrows arched in surprise. She leaned forward for one of the mugs, held it to her lips, and blew gently. After taking a tentative sip, she shot Megan a direct look.

"After all the stories you've heard over the years of the crazy things we did together, the wild ride of our teen years, of eloping and starting a life together, you still don't know the answer to that question?"

"Then why was it so easy for you to get over him?"

The only hint of her mom's discomfort was the sudden stiffness in her back and shoulders. "I'm glad you're finally ready to clear the air. I've attempted to broach this with you a dozen times since you started college, but you'd never have it."

"Well, maybe I figured out *not* talking about it won't make it go away."

"Then let's talk. I've nothing to hide." Her mom rested the mug on the arm of the sofa and rolled her neck, an obvious effort to keep in control. "You're a woman now. And you were a teen when your father died."

"Thirteen, mom. I was thirteen."

Her mom held up a finger. "You asked, so let me talk. I know how old you were. But you were one of those kids who grew up before your time. And that started before your father died. Now, you asked if I loved him. The answer is yes. Absolutely. I know you've heard those stories of us being sixteen and head over heels for each other. And how after four years of dating, we rushed to the altar because I was pregnant. We didn't keep that a secret from you." She went quiet for a moment, then added, "The answer to your question is yes. I loved your dad a great deal."

Megan choked back a mouthful of too-hot tea and tried not to wince. Tried to keep her whirlpool of emotions in check.

Her mom sat forward on the couch. "It's your second question that's troubling you though, isn't it? Why I moved on so much faster than you wanted me to."

Megan's lungs threatened to close up. She'd held it in so long. Too long. "Yes. It bothers me. It's always bothered me."

Her mom brushed one finger under her nose and sniffed. "No one's going to tell you it isn't fair, holding a grudge. He was your father, and I knew before he died he was everything to you. He always was. But, Megan, now that you're older, maybe it'll be easier for you to understand. There's a difference between a father and a husband."

"What? You can only have one father, but husbands come cheap?" It was mean and hurtful, but she didn't try to pull it back.

"I understand that some cuts run deep, but let's do our best to stay civil, shall we?"

"I just want to know why it was so easy for you to forget him."

Her mother sniffed again and yanked a tissue from the box on the side table. "That's simpler than you think. It wasn't. The flaw you fear that's at the surface of all

this isn't in him. It's in me. I loved your dad, Megan.
And I've never gotten over him. I still talk to him when
I'm alone and the house is quiet. He was my best friend
at a defining point in my life. We fought sometimes—
okay, a lot—and life wasn't perfect. There was never
any money. But I loved him. And now, filling up his
place, there's Rick. And he's a fabulous man. Don't
think he isn't. If you judged them on a goodness scale,
he'd probably outweigh your father.

"Everyone says you and I are so alike," she continued, "with our looks and our love for animals, but we
aren't. You have that independence of your dad's. He'd
go off into that garage and get lost in his cars or head
off on a weekend trip with his buddies and not think
about me. You're the same. You ran off the first chance
you got, and you never came home. You're director of a
shelter, and you have that perfect little house. You don't
need a man to define you. To make you whole.

"But whether or not either of us likes it, I do. I'd like
to think I've matured, but the truth is, if Rick left me or,
God forbid, something happened to him, I'd probably
let someone else in before I should all over again. Don't
think I didn't hear the rumors around town when Rick
and I married. But a year of being alone was an eternity
for me. The six months we dated was all the time I
could handle."

Her mom rubbed a palm over her face. "But that's
my fault. Not your father's. Not Rick's. When your dad
and I were married, when we were dating even, if I was
away from him for even a day, I didn't feel complete.
And I get that's not a good thing. I read self-help books.
But it's who I am. It's my weakness."

Her mom paused to swallow some tea while Megan considered their life after her dad died in a new light.

"So," her mom continued, "I found myself thirty-three years old and a widow. And every day was a jail sentence. Then along came Rick, offering me love and safety." She stopped and swallowed hard, swiping a stray tear from her cheek. "Only guess what? He's a good man, Megan."

"I know that, Mom. I always knew that."

"At first he was a distraction. A drain cover hiding a deep hole. But time changed that. He wanted kids and right away. And so did I. With your dad, it was always waiting for the right time to add to our trio until it seemed that time had come and gone. And then it went from the three of us to the two of us. And I knew that unless I changed something, one day it would just be me."

Megan felt her jaw gape open. All the thousands of hours of mulling it over, and she'd never thought of what happened in that light.

"When Rick came into the picture, I knew he'd be a good father. He'd be one to you now, if you'd let him. But you, you're just like your dad. You don't let anyone in without a battle. And, someday, when you fall in love the way I did with your dad, back when the world seemed small and simple, you're going to love so ferociously it'll scare the hell out of you. And we both know your ex-fiancé, Paul, wasn't it. Paul was choosing a path that couldn't creep in and tear out your soul."

Megan pulled at the corners of the pillow she'd cradled on her lap. So much of what was said surprised her. What she hadn't understood about her mother. What her mother understood about her. It was true too. With Paul, she'd never had the feeling that if she opened the door a little more, everything she was could be swallowed up. Paul was a life planned out, simple and predictable. Only not quite right for either of them.

And now there was Craig. Being with him was like treading impossibly deep water. Too risky to let herself go. If she let him in all the way, it could be best thing in the world. But there were no guarantees.

Now that she was pregnant, everything was even more precarious. She had no idea what to do. Suddenly it felt like the best person in the world to give her advice was the one person she'd been resisting advice from for years.

And she was sitting right across from her.

"Thanks," she said, cuddling the pillow tighter. "Some of that wasn't easy for you to say, I'm sure. But it helps me."

"Is that why you came today? For a bit of clarity?"

She swallowed hard. "I'm pregnant."

Her mom choked on her spit. She opened her mouth, closed it, and shook her head.

Megan chugged half her tea while it sank in.

"The caffeine. Those dark circles. Oh God, tell me it wasn't Paul."

"It wasn't Paul."

"I didn't… I didn't think you were seeing anyone."

"I didn't want to tell you because he's exactly the person you were just talking about. At least there's a possibility he could be. On my end anyway."

Her mom shook her head again. She half stood up, then sat back down, resting her elbows on her knees and cupping her hands together. "Wow. I'm shaking. Wow." She leaned forward, pressing her forehead into her knees a minute. "Well, the night's young. I'm all ears, Megan. I'm going to be a grandma, and I'm freaking out a bit, but I'm all ears."

Megan pulled in a deep breath. The only way to tell this story was to start from the beginning.

Chapter 25

CRAIG CURSED HIMSELF FOR WASTING SO MUCH TIME. HE'D been here hours earlier. If he'd thought of it then, he could've taken action sooner and not have been stuck in this tormented state till nearly dawn.

Using the light of his phone, he scanned the pots lining Megan's back patio. There were five altogether of varying sizes, filled with a combination of spring flowers and herbs. It'd been late winter and they'd been empty when she'd pointed them out.

He squatted down in the dark and tilted back the first, the robust scents of oregano and sage filling his nose. No key. He found success on the third pot. Snatching it, he killed the light of his phone and navigated by moonlight around Megan's side of the condo to the front door.

The key was damp and rusted along the edge. He worried it wouldn't work. He slipped it in and held his breath. Relief flooded him when, after a bit of cajoling, the door swung open.

He flipped on the light in the foyer and grimaced as his eyes adjusted to the bright light. Moxie trotted into view and paused in the middle of the living room to stretch. Max was curled on the coach, one front leg tight over his face as if he didn't want to be disturbed. Craig joined Moxie, kneeling down to scratch her chin as he debated where Megan might keep an address book. He'd never seen it but knew she had one. He remembered lying in her bed, stroking her smooth skin, and teasing her that she preferred a physical calendar to a virtual one.

She confessed that rather than printing labels, she used an old address book when it came to Christmas cards. She would put on one of her favorite Christmas movies and write them all by hand. He'd mocked her for being so young and still being old school, but at the same time he appreciated it. Like he did almost everything else about her.

He stood up, and Moxie circled his feet, rubbing her face on his pants. He reminded himself he wasn't an intruder. Megan had pointed out the key and told him more than once that if he ever needed to, he could make himself at home.

And he couldn't think of a time when he might need to more than right now.

Since she didn't have a desk or an obvious work area, it took opening a few drawers before he found the address book in the end table drawer next to the sofa. He carried it to the kitchen and flipped it open on the counter. Moxie hopped up alongside him, purring and rubbing against his hands as he flipped the pages.

There were three bowls full of food on the floor and two of water, rather than the usual one each. Going out of town was simpler when you had cats than it was with dogs. When Moxie started biting at the pages of the address book, Craig picked her up, placed her in front of a bowl, and shook it. Obediently she started to eat.

He returned to the book without the distraction of an affection-starved cat, hoping Megan's mom's name would pop out to him if it wasn't recorded as simply

Mom. He'd heard her say her stepfather's name a few times, but he couldn't recall it offhand. He was looking for phone numbers in and around Springfield, but she had other family and friends there too. He couldn't just make calls until he got lucky. Especially not at quarter to four in the morning.

If he could narrow it down to a few names, he could write the numbers down and call from work closer to six thirty or seven. Late enough not to be too much of a disturbance, but early enough to stop her from making a huge mistake, if that's indeed what she was doing.

He flipped through the book, pausing on a few that seemed plausible, before finding what he was looking for under *M*. *Mom and Rick Mueller*, she'd written. The birthdays of Tyler and Tess were scribbled in the corner. He'd seen their pictures and had committed their names to memory. Like he was hoping, there was a home phone and cells for both Megan's mom and Rick.

Just below, calling to him with unexpected urgency, was their address. Two innocent lines that could lead him straight to a house in Springfield.

And to Megan.

An alarm blaring in another part of the house roused Megan from an impossibly deep sleep. The pale yellow of early morning filtered into the room through thin linen curtains. A blanket of fog hung over her, impeding thought. She blinked and brushed her hand against the plush couch. She was on her back, crunched up against the back of it. She was still on the love seat, a throw blanket covering her.

She pushed up and attempted to swing her legs to the floor, but they wouldn't obey. She winced, realizing how deeply asleep they were. Getting the blood flowing was going to be painful.

Standing was precarious at first, her legs were so numb, but they held her. Shuffling to the wall for support, she began bending and flexing as shards of pain danced down her legs.

Sledge, who was sprawled across the full-length sofa, hopped down and stretched. "I don't know how you ended up with the big couch. That absolutely wasn't fair." He yawned in response, then dropped to the floor and rolled onto his back, his tail thumping the wood. Shorty, the corgi, was nowhere in sight. He tended to stick to her mom like glue.

Megan struggled to remember when she'd fallen asleep. She and her mom had talked an hour or longer, but she didn't remember the conversation ending. She must have dozed off midsentence.

Considering the bomb she'd dropped, her mom had been understanding, even helpful. It'd been a tad humiliating to admit how she'd avoided Craig and had no idea how he was taking the news.

It didn't take her mom's raised eyebrows to realize she wasn't exactly being a thoughtful lover.

From down the hallway, her mom's door swung open and Megan heard her shuffling across to the kids' rooms. Not wanting to get caught up in the getting-ready-for-school chaos, Megan swiped the cell—her mom's—that'd been abandoned on the coffee table.

It was seven o'clock. Typically Craig was at work by now. "Come on, boy," she said, heading for the front door.

The leash was hung next to it. Megan started to clip it to Sledge's collar but hesitated. He'd been out last night before Tyler and Tess went to bed. They'd let him off the leash, and he'd stuck by Megan's side like glue. She dug her fingers into the thick fur on top of his neck and scratched. "How'd my buddy like to try being off leash again?"

Sledge followed her outside obediently and paused by the edge of the porch. As the cool morning air swept over her skin and into her clothes, it occurred to her that she hadn't taken the time to use the bathroom herself. Now that she was thinking about it, holding it was going to be a pain if Sledge took his time.

She was debating cajoling him back inside for a minute when he pricked his ears and cocked his head.

"What is it, boy?" Megan was reaching for his collar as if she had all the time in the world when he bolted off at a full sprint around the side of the house.

Please say he won't go far. To her horror, the direction he was running sank in. He was beelining toward the pond out back. The pond where, very likely, Tyler and Tess's spritely ducklings were returning after hunkering down somewhere for the night.

She clutched the leash but tossed the phone into a rocking chair and broke into a sprint. She was barefoot and in pajamas—lounge pants, an old T-shirt, and no bra.

She scaled the white wooden fence with relative ease, fueled by adrenaline, and did her best to sprint across the pasture, even though it was much more painful than the manicured yard. Stiff blades of grass and rock pricked her feet with each step.

A hundred feet away, Sledge was barking and

circling the pond. There was a scatter of commotion along the water's edge. Flapping wings and the honking of angry mallards.

Please don't let him grab the babies. Her stomach lurched as she neared. Sledge was plunging into the water in pursuit of Tyler and Tess's five down-covered ducklings and the three older mallards that had stuck around last winter. They'd formed a tight circle and their wings flapped wildly as they raced toward the center. Clouds of feathers filled the air.

But Sledge was still barking, which mercifully meant he had nothing in his mouth. He was leaping and bouncing along the edge of the water, but not moving in deep enough to swim.

"Sledge!" With all the commotion—the barking, honking, and flapping of wings—she knew she couldn't get his attention. Not knowing what else to do, she skated down the bank and jumped in after him.

He lurched sideways while she was in midair. Megan, who was hoping to get her arms around him, fell face-first into the water. She bolted up, spitting out a mouthful and spluttering.

Her antics seemed to spur Sledge on. He barked louder and lunged deeper into the water, starting to dog paddle while Megan looked at him in dismay.

Then a shrill, commanding whistle pierced the commotion, yanking Sledge's attention from the ducks. He whirled a hundred and eighty degrees and dashed out of the pond, up the bank, and out of sight.

Are you kidding? All I had to do was whistle? From her spot in the water, she couldn't see anything. All she knew was that she was grateful to whoever had come to the rescue, thinking to whistle with that kind of authority.

Mucky water dripped down her forehead and hair. The smell of pond water was terrible on a good day.

She stumbled out of the water and up the muddy bank, soaked and shivering.

Then stopped in her tracks as she rounded the top.

Every one of her senses seemed to buzz with the impossibility of it, but Craig was standing in the middle of the pasture clipping a leash—the leash she must have dropped while running—to Sledge's collar while Sledge sat obediently at his side, panting and wagging his tail. *Oh my God, he's here.*

That whistle of his had gotten the miniature ponies' attention too. They were trotting over with their ears flat back to check out Sledge, who was every bit as big as they were and who'd invaded their pasture.

But all that paled in comparison to the fact that Craig was here. Fifty feet away. Dressed in tan slacks and a light-blue oxford. Ready for a day at the office. Which was exactly where, not even two minutes ago, she'd placed him as she imagined their conversation playing out.

Only he was here in Springfield. Standing in the middle of her mom's pasture after securing an over-excited Sledge, a task she'd have thought impossible considering his general lack of animal magnetism. And he was being circled by two angry miniature ponies, one who looked about to bite, the other who looked about to kick.

She wanted to laugh, to cry, to run away and hide, to run straight at him and throw herself—her soaked, stinky self—into his arms. She wanted to sink to her knees in relief. Whatever was about to happen, it was all about to play out here and now. Emotion coursed through her like a busy day at the raceway.

And of all the wants and desires coursing through her, to her horror, the one that won out was hunching over and hurling up everything in her stomach. There wasn't much inside, but it didn't matter. She dry heaved until she saw red. When she was finished, her stomach was knotted into a tight ball, she was shivering, and Craig was standing beside her, looking concerned.

Their eyes met, and he smiled apologetically. *Oh my God, he's here. He's right fricking here.* Up close, he didn't look as sharp and put together as he had from far away. There were dark circles under his eyes, and he hadn't shaved in a couple of days. He looked more exhausted than she'd ever seen him.

"I'd say 'good morning', but you might think I'm being flippant with the *good* part, considering the color and smell of that water dripping down your face and arms." He brushed the tips of his fingers over her bare arm, which was covered in goose bumps.

Megan wiped her mouth on the back of her arm. They hadn't even said hello, and he was making jokes like his showing up here was perfectly normal.

She shook her head and forced her numb legs not to buckle underneath her. "You aren't funny." It wasn't just Craig and Sledge who'd come to her side. The ponies had followed and were circling angrily. "And neither are these ponies. If you haven't noticed, they're in attack mode."

She postured as menacingly as she could, attempting to shoe them away. Sledge whined and tucked his tail as he surveyed the closest pony. Its ears were flat against its head, and its teeth were bared.

Craig's here, and instead of talking this out, there's going to be a miniature pony/German shepherd show-down. "Run out of the gate with him, will you? It's Sledge they're mad at, not you."

Craig frowned as the darker, fuzzier pony swiveled its hind end around and aimed a double-hoofed kick in Sledge's direction. Thankfully it missed by a foot. "Isn't Sledge the predator here? I thought horses were vegetarians."

"I'm not sure this is the best time to discuss animal behavior." Megan smacked her hands together and shooed them off as Craig finagled a whining Sledge through the gate to safety. She followed them out backward, warding off ponies that would make great offensive linemen.

In the commotion, she slammed into Craig, who'd turned to see if she needed help. "Your clothes. I'm sorry."

So swiftly she didn't realize it was happening, she was enfolded in his embrace. It was anything but a typical hug, the way he enveloped her, enclosing her in his arms and disintegrating the space between them. He didn't speak or move. The warmth of his body radiated through her soaked clothes, warming her as he became wetter and wetter.

Sledge cowered by their legs, whining at the ponies stamping their hooves and swishing their tails.

Craig didn't move or relax his embrace. It took her a minute to realize he was trembling. Not shivering from the cold, but trembling from the inside out. Craig, the man who never let people in and never lost control.

"I'm sorry," she blurted out. "For everything." She pulled back enough to look at him. "For a week, I don't think I've done anything but make mistakes."

"It's okay." He ran his thumb along her chin. "Megan, I thought…I was afraid you came here because you'd made the decision to have an abortion. I was sitting in my car, trying not to doze off as I waited for seven o'clock to knock on the door. Then I opened my eyes, and there you were, tearing across the yard to stop Sledge from getting to those ducks, and God help me, I couldn't help laughing. You get it—what I learned when we lost Andrew. You get how precious life is. Whatever brought you here in such a hurry, I knew when I saw you plunge into that pond in your pajamas that you wouldn't make that sort of decision without at least telling me."

A shiver ran up her spine. Now, if her mind wasn't playing tricks on her, the worst of her fears was dissolving like the water dripping off her clothes to the ground. Craig was here and holding her and revealing that his strongest fears weren't so very different from her own. All along, whether she resisted it or not, it had felt like an incredible force helped pull them together. And no matter what happened in the future, over moments that were the most beautiful she'd known, they'd created a life. And that life would be as precious to him as it would to her.

Maybe there were still a million little reasons to be afraid, and maybe there was a mountain of obstacles they needed to overcome. But the biggest one, the one she'd been terrified of—that his reaction could lead to her falling out of love with him—was anything but the truth.

Before she could voice her thoughts, the sliding glass

door at the back of the house opened and Tyler and Tess tumbled out, laughing and talking over each other and racing their way. As if emboldened by the new commotion, Sledge barked and dropped into a play bow at the closest pony, who was still baring his teeth on the other side of the fence.

Megan slipped the leash from Craig's fingers and pressed the back of his hand to her lips. "Come on, you can meet the kids and my mom, and then I need to get in the shower and wash off this smell or I'm going to puke. Again. And we'll see what you look like in Rick's clothes, unless you brought along something to change into."

Chapter 26

"So this still feels surreal. Like everything could dissolve and your coming here not have happened."

From across the table, Craig stretched out his legs, locking his ankles around hers. "Doesn't the fact that I'm in a restaurant wearing dress shoes and a pair of tight, three-inches-too-short exercise pants help ground this in reality?"

Megan giggled. "I never would've guessed Rick was so much smaller than you." In the nearly four months she'd known him, she'd never seen Craig look anything but put together. Rick's one-size-too-small, short-sleeved Nike shirt wasn't bad, but it stretched over Craig's biceps, chest, and back, highlighting muscle tone like he was showing off. From the waist down though, the combination of too-small Adidas pants and shiny leather shoes made it obvious some sort of mishap had occurred.

But the mom-and-pop coffee shop they'd come to was on the outskirts of town and as good a place as any not to be judged. It was equal parts country diner and wannabe hip barista bar. The modern coffee bar on the side of the restaurant was accented with stainless-steel lighting, slate counters, and contemporary stools. Honey-colored oak tables and booths filled the rest of the place. The walls were dotted with antiques: a giant wooden fork and spoon, old photos of the town, and metal plaques advertising everything from Coca-Cola to Route 66, Borax detergent, and Uncle Sam.

Margo's Cup, it was called. Megan had been coming here since she was a kid, but a change in management was causing the clash of styles. The parents were retiring, and their trendy daughter was taking over. The quality of the food had only improved though, and from what her mom had shared, customers weren't complaining.

Megan was still cradling her mug of hot tea when the server came, carrying blackberry waffles for her and an omelet for Craig. She found it sweet when, even though he shifted in his seat, he kept his ankles locked around hers.

He was on his second cup of coffee and looking a bit less fatigued, but the dark circles wouldn't go away until he had some decent sleep.

"I'm sorry," she said again. "For what I put you through."

He shrugged as he sliced into his omelet. "I've gotten to meet your family. And I'm going to get a tour of your hometown. It's working out fine."

They hadn't talked about the baby with any significance. Megan sensed he was too exhausted. And there was so much to weed through. Where they stood in their relationship. How they'd created a life, and how nothing was ever going to be the same. How he'd fit Sophie and Reese and Jillian into this changing world of his.

And all of these topics needed a relaxed mind that hadn't been deprived of sleep for nearly two full nights. But he wasn't angry with how she'd handled things, and he wasn't holding blame. He was attentive with Tyler and Tess, polite with her mom, and after the kids got on the bus, he let her drive him here even though he looked a bit ridiculous.

And all of this piled together made one thing very clear. She loved him. And not a questionable bit. She loved him a the-world-is-a-deep-scary-chasm bit. And she was fairly certain he loved her the same way.

Only it was too big of a feeling, and the idea of voicing it when so much still needed to be decided seemed precarious. She was pregnant, and they had a long row of adult decisions to make.

She needed to keep a layer of bubble wrap around her heart while they discussed logistics. Confiding how much she cared wouldn't help matters.

She nibbled on a slice of bacon and remembered his comment from what felt like years ago, though it was only just over a week. He was committed. He had been before either of them knew she was pregnant. It was enough. She'd hold on to that, and it would get her through what was ahead.

They finished eating, and Craig had a third cup of coffee—black.

"If you're too tired, we can go back to my mom's and you can take a nap. I can show you around later."

"No, I'll get another cup to go, and we're not stopping till I've seen it all. You spent your first eighteen years here, and there are a lot of big moments in those years. I want to see it all. The long-winded 'Grandpa's had too much to drink and is rambling on and on' tour." He winked as the server returned with his card.

Megan laughed. "Just so you know, the long version will be sweet and sad and pathetic and a tad humiliating. But we might as well start now. My dad and I ate here on

Saturday mornings at least once a month. But that sleek coffee bar wasn't here. The old counter was from the fifties. The stool seats were cracked and wobbly when they swiveled, and my dad never got mad when I wouldn't stop swiveling."

She smiled and shook her head. "One day, a boy from my school who was here with his dad got yelled at for swiveling. He was this kid who had everything. The right clothes, any toy you could think of, and always the latest Game Boy. But he didn't have a dad who let him swivel, and I never forgot it when I saw him."

Craig's lips turned up into a half smile as he slipped his credit card back into his wallet. "I would very much like to have known your father. He sounds like a man who got it right the first time around."

Megan swallowed hard and reminded herself of the protective wrap she'd placed around her heart today to get through all this. Craig had lost a child. If he'd ever been a dad to snap first and regret it later, he'd never be it again. They both had had a powerful brush with the impermanence of life. And with it, understood how giant some of the small things could be.

"He was," she said, rubbing her thumb over Craig's wrist. His skin was warm and inviting. "Maybe that's the gift they're given, those people who don't get to stay here as long as the rest of us. Maybe they have an easier time getting it right."

⌇

It took two hours and a few unnecessary loops around town, taking into account a lack of planning, but she showed him everything. Her elementary school and the half-moon climber out back where she'd knocked out a permanent front tooth. He enjoyed the story of how a group of teachers sorted through mulch chips to find it while she held a towel to her bleeding gum. Her principal was the one who found it. She dropped it in a carton of milk, and Megan's parents came and rushed her to the dentist. Afterward, she could only eat soft foods for a week.

She showed him her junior high and the narrow door at the back where she and Ashley slipped out at a dance with a couple of wild boys and they'd both had their first kisses. From there they went to her high school and the garden where she escaped at lunch to be alone in the weeks and months after her dad's death. Seeing it, it seemed natural to head to her old home first, then the graveyard where her father was buried alongside his grandparents, people she'd never known.

After that, she wanted to lighten things up. She drove twenty minutes out of town to an old hangout at the railroad bridge that spanned the James River, a spot where fall bonfires had been legendary and she'd laughed even after it seemed she might never laugh again.

It was only when they were walking underneath the rusted bridge that she remembered how one afternoon, a month or so after her dad died, she'd clambered across to the middle and jumped into the river. It was fifty feet above water and hurt like hell, but she'd been unscathed. A long list of kids had done it before her, as had a long list after. Most were fine. One hadn't been though. A local boy who everyone said was always down on his luck. He dove and hit his head on a rock under the water. He slipped from life into legend and kids, being kids, still jumped. They talked about him and jumped anyway.

Life was funny like that, brushing against death, but moving along like the James River—in a hurry at times, impossibly slow at others.

After the bridge, to keep the bubble wrap in place, she stuck to skating rinks and burger joints, treehouses and lemonade stands.

"There's one more place," she said when the fourth cup of coffee seemed to be wearing off and the first yawn of the tour escaped him. "But I'm not sure I should go there with my lover—literally and figuratively."

They'd passed the road twice and she'd considered it, but not turned down it. Her first serious boyfriend had been in college. Here in her hometown, she'd had sex only once. The guy, her first, wasn't worth making the tour but for the single fact that he'd been her first.

Craig's hand was resting on her thigh. He stroked it with his thumb. "Where's that?"

Her cheeks grew warm as she broached the topic. "I told you my first serious boyfriend was in college."

He cocked an eyebrow but waited for her to continue.

"There was someone before him. I wouldn't exactly call him a boyfriend. We had the same group of extended friends, but we never dated. We just…um, you know… hooked up once."

"And you want me to meet him?" His voice took on the slight tone of incredibility.

"No. Heavens no. The where in this case is a bit more notable than the who. I thought I'd drive by and point it out." She cleared her throat. "If it won't offend you, that is."

He chuckled. "By all means, let's see it."

"It's kind of pathetic, I guess. I was a senior and getting ready to go away to college. And I didn't want to start a virgin, if you want the truth. Looking back, it seems ridiculous to surrender what could have been a big moment over a stigma, but it's what I did. And you wanted to see everything."

They were outside of town in the farmlands. She drove down a winding road with green fields and cows and big circular bales of hay. Craig was quiet, taking it in.

"Maybe a bit too predictably, it was senior prom. One of my friends lived on a farm. After prom, we came back here for a bonfire. Her parents didn't care if we drank, as long as we didn't leave."

Letting the car roll to a stop, she pointed to a farmhouse on her right. "Her name is Trish, and her family lives there. At least I think they still do. The bonfire was to the left out in that field."

"You had sex for the first time in a field?"

Megan giggled. "No, I wasn't that drunk." She twisted and pointed to the other side of the road. "Me and this guy, Trish's boyfriend's cousin, we skipped out and ended up in that old barn across the way."

The barn was big and ancient and faded red with a sagging roof. The doors were pulled open wide, and a couple of goats milled around the outside nibbling on grass.

Craig was quiet for so long that she turned to look at him. He was scoping out the road, not the barn. He reached forward and flipped on the hazards.

"Pull to the shoulder, will you? There's no way we're not checking that out."

"Are you kidding? You can't just walk across a field

in the middle of the day and into someone's barn. It's called trespassing." She glanced at the house a hundred yards away. It looked quiet enough, but still. They could have an attack dog or a gun. This was a farm in the middle of the country. Odds were that they had a rifle at the ready.

"Then pull up a few hundred feet. We'll enter from the other side. They won't see us from the house. Besides, we don't look like we're here to steal something."

"You're forgetting you're dressed like you might be a bit crazy."

He winked and hopped out. "Good thing you aren't," he said before closing the door.

Heart hammering in her chest, Megan pulled forward out of sight of the house and off to the shoulder. The road was largely deserted, but she hid her purse under the seat, took her keys, and locked the doors. She jogged down the road to meet Craig, laughing and shaking her head.

"This is insane," she said. "Some parts of the tour were supposed to be roadside only."

"I don't remember agreeing to anything of the sort." He scaled the fence and offered his hand. Without the adrenaline of early this morning, clambering over the fence was a bit more awkward. As she swung over, he closed his hands on her hips, sending a different sort of rush up her spine.

They made it to the barn without seeming to alert anyone or anything aside from the goats. They bleated and trotted inside after them, nipping at Craig's too-tight pants.

"It's no Ritz," she said as he sidestepped the goats and scoped out the old building.

Sunlight poured in from cracks in the wood, the door-ways on both sides, and the open loft windows. It was a big barn with half a dozen empty stalls, an old tractor, and a few plows. The gentle breeze that swept through it carried a fresh, earthy smell.

"It could be worse," Craig said. "Much worse. At least it's got an ambiance to it. My first time was in a storage closet in a friend's basement at a party. It was dark and tight and reeked of mold."

"It's hard to picture you as a teenager." She scratched one of the goats behind the ears. When it tried to eat her shirt, she gave it a firm no and stepped back.

"What makes you think I wasn't in my twenties?"

She laughed. "Not possible. Well, maybe if you dressed like this every day."

"I was more awkward back then than you might guess. I'm fairly certain a delayed loss of virginity was entirely possible, had it not been for a bit of luck." He stepped close and folded his arms as he surveyed the barn. "So, my dear Megan, are you going to reveal where this infraction occurred?"

"Um, no. But I'll give you three guesses."

"Three, huh? I don't think I'll need them. How about I take you there, and if I'm right… Well, we'll see."

She couldn't help but wonder what the odds were that the sudden energy building between them would result in an impromptu romp in the hay. But this tour had already shed her defenses. Doing that would tear down the last of them. "I'm not sure that's such a good idea. Just Friday, you said you wanted to nix sleepovers."

"I did, didn't I? I believe I was clearer headed then." He finished scanning the barn and pointed to the hayloft that stretched over the back half. Before she knew it, he was scaling the built-in ladder leading to it. Then he disappeared over the top.

It was quiet for a full minute before his voice trailed down from above. "I'm right, aren't I?"

"Yes, but it doesn't mean—" She stopped short. From the direction of the house, a door slammed and a dog barked.

Craig appeared at the edge, searching out the loft window. "You aren't going to like this, but the farmer seems to be headed this way. And a dog, but it looks pretty benign. If Sledge were here, he could take it easily if he needed to. Though after seeing that encounter with those ponies, maybe not. So do you want me to come down there and talk to him, or do you want to climb up here and wait it out?"

Without processing it, she was scurrying up the ladder. She was breathless and shaking when she reached the top. Craig took her hand and pulled her over the ledge. She rolled over on the straw-littered wooden floor and bit her lip, tense.

"Let's move back farther in case he needs hay." Craig led her around the towering stacks of bales.

"I'm not meant for a life of crime. My whole body's shaking," she whispered.

He pulled two bales down from one of the lower stacks, creating seats out of sight from the main loft. Down below, the goats bleated and the dog let out a single yip.

She sank down and locked her shaky knees together. The farmer was inside. She heard him sniffling. Craig scooped up her hands and pressed his lips against one palm, then the other. "Look at the bright side," he whispered. "It'll be something amusing we can tell the baby one day."

Megan's heart slammed against her rib cage. Craig had said *one day* and *we* and *baby* in the same sentence.

For the full two hours of the tour, their focus had been on her life when she was a kid and a teenager. Their relationship and her pregnancy felt like a conversation being saved for another time, another day. And earlier, at breakfast, he asked her a few simple things like if she'd been feeling sick, how many weeks she was, and if she was sleeping okay. They'd talked about Sophie and how she was feeling after the party and brushed the surface of how Jillian was taking things. But nothing deeper. He was so exhausted that she didn't think he had it in him.

But now, this comment was different. It referred to staying power. Like there was no question as to whether or not they had it.

He shifted on his bale and pulled her in to his chest. His arms wrapped around her, and his lips pressed into her hair. He whispered in her ear. "I could pick your smell out of a thousand other people. Blindfolded."

A playful reply about pond water and the hint of bleach that never seemed to leave her fingers was on the tip of her tongue, but she swallowed it back. It was a defensive trick her mother had pointed out, the way she used humor to keep people at bay. Instead she brushed her lips against his.

It was a soft, quiet kiss that carried on along with the bleating of the goats and clanking of metal down below. He placed the palm of one hand flat against her stomach.

Over the baby. She was reminded of the small things she'd seen over the months between him and Sophie and Reese. Little things that added up to make him a phenomenal father.

A rush swept over her. It was like standing at the top of Niagara Falls. If she let herself, if she took a leap and trusted, she could be swallowed up by all he could be to her. By all they could be together.

If she trusted herself to do it.

On the main floor of the barn there was an abrupt slam. Seconds later, the tractor revved to life, filling the barn with the sound of its loud engine.

Craig dropped his embrace and wrapped one hand around hers. "I know this caused you a scare. I'm sorry." She could barely hear him over the tractor. "Let's give him a minute to get out of sight, and we'll get out of here."

She shook her head and stood up, positioning herself directly in front of him as the tractor chugged out of the barn. "I think another ten minutes will be fine."

She was wearing a button-down shirt, half-open, and a cami. She slipped them off and tossed them onto the empty bale, but left her bra in place. She wanted his attention another moment. She had things she wanted to say. If she could gather the nerve.

Instead of talking, she took an easier route. She kicked off her sandals and tugged down her jeans a bit less gracefully than she'd have liked, then climbed onto his lap. He was quiet, eyeing her but not moving.

Doubt crept in. If it wasn't for the growing bulge in his already tight pants, she'd probably duck and run. Finding herself drawn in by the proximity she'd been missing, she ran her lips over his neck and nipped at his chin.

He pulled back abruptly and closed his hands over her temples. "Are you doing this because you think I want you to or because *you* want to? Because it was crazy of me to expect it. Here. Now. We absolutely don't have to."

This was it. Time to call a spade a spade. Her throat went dry, and her fingers shook. Vulnerability didn't have to be a weakness, her mom had said. It could be one step in a remarkable journey.

She swallowed hard. "This is me letting you in. I love you. More than I knew was possible. And we're going to have a baby while we still have so much to work out. And that scares the hell out of me. And I'm sure you too. But whatever happens in a world of tomorrows, none of that can make me love you any less today." She pressed her lips together. She wanted him to interrupt, to say something. Anything. But he was staring at her with a look that was just a touch incredulous.

"So," she continued, "in answer to your question, yes. I just stripped out of my clothes because I want to, not because I feel I have to."

His answering kiss was desperate. He kept one hand in her hair and locked the other behind her back, drawing her against him. When he'd kissed her so long that she was breathless, he pulled away and brushed his lips over her forehead, cheek, and temple.

His lips brushed against her ear when he spoke. "Megan Anderson, in that world of tomorrows, I'm going to make damn sure I don't do anything to make you love me any less than you do today."

Chapter 27

FIVE WEEKS, TWO DAYS, AND TWENTY-SIX EXTRAORDINARY dates later, Craig parked his car in front of the shelter. He paused to admire the new sign that had gone up last week. It made him proud that his favorite graphic artist at his company had come up with the new logo and everyone at the shelter had loved it. The words *High Grove Animal Shelter* were in purple, and the profiles of a dog and cat were adjacent to them in green.

The trim around the front windows had been painted purple to match, giving the brick building a splash of brightness and color. Purple and green pots filled with bright flowers welcomed visitors on either side of the entryway.

Next up, the inside was going to get a facelift. The last of the revisions were underway. The plan called for the walls and ceilings to get fresh coats of paint. The dated counters and most of the office furniture would be replaced as well. The biggest changes would be in the kennels. Several runs were being expanded for the larger dogs, and the smaller ones were going to get ramps and raised beds. Automatic water bowls were being installed. And last but not least, the back half of the empty lot behind the building was being fenced into a private dog park with agility equipment that had Sophie bubbling over with excitement to see in use.

He headed inside and found Megan was on the phone

in her office. He knew right away that something was upsetting her. Her cheeks were flushed, and she was clenching her jaw between sentences.

He forced down the urge to butt in and see if he could help. She was more than capable of fighting her own battles. He sank to the top of her desk as she disputed a cost increase with the shelter's dog chow supplier. Trina hopped down from the top filing cabinet and crawled onto his lap, purring so loudly that he could feel the vibrations traveling from her three paws to his thighs. He scratched her chin and waited.

After a few minutes of bargaining, Megan's shoulders and jaw relaxed. She reached for a pen and scratched six hundred dollars off the invoice in front of her.

When she hung up, she rose from her chair and met him halfway for a kiss. She didn't look out the door first any longer. A few weeks ago, she'd told the staff they were dating.

"What are you doing here?" She paused for another kiss. "I thought you had a busy day."

"Never too busy for some time with you. And congratulations on that successful bargaining." He dropped his voice to a whisper, sweeping a lose strand of hair behind her ear. "Though I'm not sure the stress you're under is good for the baby."

Megan's pregnancy was still something she hadn't revealed. She intended to give it another month, then tell everyone.

She sank back to her chair, slid it directly in front of him, and closed her hands around his calves. "I'm working on it. Promise. So what's up? Because I can tell something is."

He cocked an eyebrow and did his best to feign innocence. She could see right through him. "Why do you say that?"

"Because if you were a cat like Trina, I'd put money down that you just ate a mouse." She sat back and tapped him on the knee. "And you just left my house a few hours ago. You didn't say anything about coming by today."

"I was in the area and thought I'd stop by."

"Um, nope, something's up. I can tell. Did you land a big new client or something?"

"No, not even close." He laughed. "I'm just in a good mood."

She leaned forward to rest her arms atop his thighs after Trina hopped to the floor and headed out into the main room. "Nope. Something's up. You've got guilty written all over you."

"I think your changing hormones are causing you to imagine things. It's a fabulous summer day, and I'm dating an incredible woman. I'm happy. That's all."

"Fine then, don't tell me. Do you have time at least to take me to an early lunch? I'm starving."

He brushed his thumb over her cheek. "I'd love to."

To Craig's amusement, she flushed bright pink as Kelsey stuck her head around the frame of her door and found them seated so intimately. Kelsey returned it with a deep flush of her own. "Hey, guys. Wes's on line one for you, Megan." She ducked out before Megan thanked her.

Megan reached over Craig to pick up the phone. Seeing that he was close to blowing it, he reached for his cell and scrolled through his email while she took the call. Her brows furrowed into tight peaks as she listened to Wes.

"You aren't kidding, are you?" She rolled her chair backward and sat up straight. "Whenever I take Bernie's calls, you read me the riot act and warn me about insurance and whatnot. You tell me that bit about how people bring animals to us, not the other way around."

She was silent a few minutes as she listened. Begrudgingly, she consented and took down an address. When she hung up, she groaned.

"What's Wes got you up to?" Craig slipped his phone into his pocket, wishing he'd taken a drama class in college as he attempted to plaster on a look of mock concern.

"Animal control, it seems. He wants me to go to someone's house—some divorcing woman his son met online—and pick up her surrender. It's here in Webster though, and I know the street. It's just a few blocks from my place."

"Why doesn't he do it himself?"

"In case you hadn't noticed, Wes hardly does anything himself anymore." She stood up and tucked the address into her pocket. "Think I can have a rain check on lunch?"

"Not a chance." Craig stood up from the desk. "If you're getting pulled into an Internet dating-ring dog-custody battle, I'm going to be there to back you up."

"Ha. Let me grab a crate. Who knows what shape the dog will be in. And I'll drive. We can't stink up your BMW."

Kelsey passed by as they stepped out of her office. "There are two crates up front still. They're new. Someone donated them earlier."

"That was easy," Craig said. He hadn't thought about her heading into the kennels for a crate and how that would have given her the opportunity to realize what was missing back there. *Who* was missing. "Want the bigger one? I'll toss it in back."

"Sure," she said, swiping a leash off a hook before heading outside.

"Nice day." He popped the crate into the trunk and settled into the passenger seat. She flipped the ignition and offered him a smile that made him feel as if he'd made it home.

After a few minutes, she turned down the street matching the address she'd been given. She frowned as she scoped the historic homes, stately yards, and tree-lined streets.

He knew what she was thinking but asked anyway. "What's the matter?"

"You've walked this street with me before, remember? It has most of my favorite houses in Webster." She pulled to a stop in front of the one matching the address Wes had given her and clicked her tongue. "This was one of my favorites. How sad. I guess someday I'll stop assuming some people should be immune to such things as not being responsible for their pets."

"It's a shame. Where's the dog? Around back?"

"No, Wes said it was inside but that no one's home and there'd be a key under the mat."

Craig attempted his best *I'm skeptical* face and stepped to the curb. "Make sure you knock, at least. This whole thing is bizarre."

They headed up the stone path that led to the spacious colonial brick two-story.

As Wes promised, the key was under the mat. Craig knew it would be since he'd put it there himself. After getting no response to knocking, Megan slipped the key in the lock. Craig busied himself looking in a window where a small gray spider had taken up residence on the brick rim.

She swung open the door tentatively. "Wes was right. It's empty."

He walked in behind her and watched her scan the room. The house was clean and barren but inviting. Light poured in through tall windows, highlighting rich hardwood floors and a stunning old mantel around the fireplace.

There was no dog in sight. Craig had expected that too, since he'd shut him in one of the upstairs bedrooms. The one the old owners had used as a nursery and seemed the most fitting for the occasion.

Megan frowned. "I wonder where it is."

As soon as she spoke, a baritone woof resounded from the top floor.

He did his best to feign innocence a minute or two longer. "I've got money down on upstairs. How about you?"

She headed for the wide staircase, and he followed. She stopped in her tracks when she spotted the rose petals strewn every few steps. "This is weird." She turned to him as if in confirmation. "Don't you—" Her lips parted, and suspicion lit her features. "This is you, isn't it?"

He shoved his hands in his pockets and fiddled with the dog treats hidden in them. "What is me?"

He watched her reconsidering her thoughts. It was

a big assumption, connecting him with this big, empty home and the petals strewn up the steps.

"If for some reason you're behind this, I'll…"

He felt the half smile breaking out despite his best attempt at restraint. "You'll what?"

Her jaw tightened, then relaxed. "You're not funny. You're hardly ever funny when you think you are."

"Right now, I'm feeling perfectly serious. What do you make of that?"

"Craig. Please. Can't you just tell me what's going on?"

He pulled her in for a quick kiss and smoothed his thumb across her cheek. "Can't you follow the trail?"

Begrudgingly, she broke into a smile as another *woof* resounded through the upper floor. "Okay, I can do that."

He took up the rear, following her up the stairs. He watched her hand trailing along the curved banister. The house fit her perfectly. He'd known it would.

At the top, the trail of petals continued down the hall to a closed door where a whining dog waited.

"Do I open it?"

"If you'd like."

She swung it open, and Sledge bounded out, his purple-pink tongue lolling and tail wagging.

"Sledge." She spent a second or two taking everything in. Sledge bounding around her. Him not able to suppress a chuckle. The lone table in the center of an empty but picturesque nursery.

The walls were a soft, creamy yellow. A thick chair rail and white bead board covered the lower half. At the back of the room, a bay window seat flanked by white curtains overlooked the backyard.

When she didn't move past the doorway, he guided her to the table in the center.

Rather than looking at the jewelry box centered on top, he whistled softly to Sledge. The excited dog lurched to the side of the table as they'd practiced and sat at attention.

Craig slid the ribbon off the table and into Sledge's view. It was attached to a spring trap that would pop open the box when tugged hard enough. Perhaps this part was a bit overkill, but when he'd planned it out with Sophie, she'd insisted Sledge have an actual part rather than be an innocent bystander.

As he'd done with Sophie dozens of times in practice, Sledge carefully mouthed the ribbon and backed up. On the second tug, the lid popped open. The box was secured to the table or it would have been yanked off, something they'd realized early on in practice.

"Good boy." Craig surrendered all his treats at once.

Megan shook her head, wiping tears from her face. "I wouldn't have believed any of this if you told me." She reached out with shaky fingers to pick up the lone ring inside. It was pewter, imperfectly round, and had a blue agate stone welded into the center.

"If you don't want me to get the wrong impression, I think you need to say something." She returned it to the box and pressed her hands against her temples.

He picked it up and sank to one knee, winking. "It's just now occurring to me what a hard act to follow Sledge is going to be. Even worse, I had something all thought out, but in the pressure of the moment, words have fled."

Fresh tears were building on her lower lids, glistening in the light. "Then maybe you should wing it."

He slid the ring as far as it would go on his pinkie, then placed his hands firmly on her hips. "All right. My dear Megan, as you know, my track record of happy, successful marriages isn't anything to write home about, but I was wondering if you might be interested?"

She burst into laughter and pulled him to his feet. "No you don't. On your feet. That can't be the proposal that follows all this."

He let her slide the ring off his finger and hold it up in the sunlight. "It's god-awful, isn't it?"

"No, I love it. It just looks handmade. Very."

"Well, knowing you, I thought you'd want some sort of fair-trade-certified diamond. Since I didn't want to give you any reason to protest, I went to an art studio downtown and made one until you can choose a suitable replacement."

"You made this." She bit her lip. "You made me a ring. Now that's romantic. You know I'll never want another one."

"Is that a yes?" Taking it, he slipped it onto her finger and pressed his lips to her palm.

"Craig, you must be knee-deep in a midlife crisis. You've only been divorced half a year. Besides Sophie and Reese—"

"Are dealing with all this very well. Sophie worked for two hours last night teaching Sledge that trick. We had to ask Kelsey to sneak him out after the shelter closed."

"You mean you told them all of this without telling me first?"

"I needed to make sure they liked the house. I knew how partial you were to it, since you gawked at it every time we passed by on a walk."

Her face went pale, and she grabbed his forearm as if to steady herself. "You…you *bought* this house?"

He cupped his hands around her elbows. "I should have thought about a chair."

"I'm okay." She waved him off. When he could see the color coming back to her cheeks, he consented and let go. "I didn't even know this house was on the market."

"It wasn't. I had an agent approach half a dozen home-owners of homes you'd pointed out around here. As it turned out, this family was more than ready to get out. They were sinking in debt and about to face foreclosure. My offer came at the right time and the right price."

"This is crazy." She stepped back and dragged her fingers through her hair. "You bought this house. *You bought it.*"

"I was hoping you'd find it romantic. If you don't like it, we never have to move in."

She crossed the room and sank to the wide window seat. Sledge joined her, whining as he peered out the window. The backyard was private and flat. A few old trees towered over the back of the house, shading the yard. Craig loved the quaintness of it, envisioned pass-ing hours in it with Reese and Sophie and eventually the new baby.

"You okay?" She'd lost some of the color she'd regained.

She nodded and reached for his hand, pulling him to the seat beside her. She planted soft kisses on his cheeks, chin, and lips. "Promise you'll never change who you are for me."

"I promise, but it doesn't mean I won't do it for me. I love you, Megan. And loving you has brought me back from a dark place. If you'd consider spending the rest of your life with me, I promise you won't regret it."

"I know I won't."

He kissed her a bit too long and had to force his attention back on the moment. "It won't be perfect. You know the baggage I'm coming with. You've seen my temper and know I'm a recovering workaholic. Sophie and Reese won't be a cakewalk, especially in their teens. And their mother, Jillian, will always be in my life. You were on board with my asking her to come back to work for the company. She agreed, by the way. She could use the distraction, and by the time the baby arrives, I'll have someone there I trust. It'll free me up to be here. With you. I know it all adds up to a complicated mess, but I promise I'll make it worth your while. I want you, Megan. For the rest of my life, I want you."

Her eyes lit with happiness, but she clicked her tongue. "So about this house. Have you checked the closets?"

He shook his head. "I'm not following."

"For all that baggage you're coming with. Does it have enough storage?"

A hearty laugh escaped him. "Can I take that as a yes?"

She arched her back and let out an exaggerated breath. "Well, your proposal was a bit weak, but the ring and the house are better than I could've dreamed of. And Sledge... I hope his being here means he's part of the package. And I might be saying this last bit as a hint in case that wasn't your idea."

He scratched Sledge on the shoulder. "I wouldn't dream of separating you two. And you're right about that proposal. You deserve something better than my asking you to jump aboard the crazy bus." He stood up and pulled her to her feet. When he dropped to one knee again, she didn't protest. "It's coming back to me now."

He tugged the ring off her finger and held it up.

"Megan Anderson, protector of those who cannot speak for themselves and shamer of those who fail to act rightly, I'm madly in love with you. From your passion for life and your dedication to making the world a better place, to your eclectic taste in wine and the way you make a mess of your hair when you're deep in thought, I love everything about you. The idea of bringing a child into this world with you is exhilarating. I want you in my life every day for the rest of it. And I want to be a part of yours the very same way. So what I'd like to know is, will you marry me?"

She said nothing in reply. She closed her eyes, her face a mask of concentration.

"What is it?"

She held up a finger. "I'm trying to remember it. Every word. Something tells me you may never be this romantic again."

He stood up and drew her close, kissing her fully on the lips. When he pulled away, he cupped her face in his hands. "Never underestimate a man who's been given a second chance at happiness."

"It actually doesn't matter if you aren't. I'll take you just the way you are. Exactly the way you are. That impossible humor of yours. Your somewhat irritating ability to get so much done in one day. That metabolism that's like four times mine. And Sophie and Reese, I love them. I'll take as much of them as they'll let me. As for Jillian, well, I'm getting over my fear of her a bit more every time I see her. And Sledge. Of course I'll take him too."

"That's good," Craig said, leaning in to kiss her again. "That's very good."

Whether it was because he heard his name or because he was picking up on the excitement in the air, Sledge plopped to the floor and rolled onto his back, wiggling back and forth. He let out a long, exaggerated whine-growl and his tongue flopped sideways, his lips curling back in a smile.

Like he was in perfect agreement that nothing could make his world any better than the people he'd be sharing it with.

Shelter Facts

While the animals and people featured in *A New Leash on Love* are fictional, the amazing devotion of shelter workers across the United States is not. More than ever before, shelter adoption is becoming a popular, feel-good way to find your next pet.

Here are some shelter facts you may not know:

- Thanks to animal advocacy groups and education, more people are turning to shelters to find their pets than ever before. It's estimated that four million animals each year get a chance at a forever home thanks to the more than three thousand U.S. shelters.
- Pets adopted from shelters are most often health screened, vaccinated, microchipped, and spayed or neutered. Plus, adoption fees are a fraction of the cost of purchasing these services independently.
- The average age of animals entering shelters is a still-very-playful eighteen months.
- Today, the rate of euthanasia of dogs and cats in shelters is just 10 percent of what it was in 1970.
- In the United States, 20 to 30 percent of adoptable pets in shelters are believed to be purebred. Have a breed you love? Chances are there are rescue groups dedicated to this breed that you can connect with online.

Have a happy story to share about your adopted pet? Email me at authordebbieburns@yahoo.com. Your successful, positive stories of pet adoption can inspire others to consider adopting homeless pets. And, to read on in the Rescue Me series, sign up for my newsletter. You'll receive updates on the release of the second book in the Rescue Me series.

A Sky Full of Stars

THERE WAS A GIRL IN OWEN SHAUGHNESSY'S CLASS.

A. Girl.

Okay, a woman. And she wasn't a scientist and she wasn't awkward. She was…pretty. Beautiful, actually. Though he had no idea if she was awkward or not. She had walked into the lecture hall minutes ago, and there were only five minutes left in his talk, so…why was she here? Maybe she was the girlfriend of one of his students?

Looking around the room, he ruled that out. He seemed to be the only one taking note of her presence. He chanced another glance her way, and she smiled. He felt a nervous flutter in the region of his belly, and as he continued to look at her, her smile grew.

And now Owen felt like he was going to throw up.

He immediately forced his gaze away and looked at the notes in front of him. "Next time we'll be discussing dust trails and dust tails, which represent large and small dust particles, respectively. Please refer to your syllabus for the required reading material." Lifting his head, Owen scanned the large lecture hall and noted the almost universally bored expressions staring back at him.

Except for her. She was still smiling.

He cleared his throat before adding, "Class dismissed."

There was a collective sigh of relief in the room as everyone stood and began collecting their belongings. As the students began to file past him, Owen did his best to keep his eyes down and not react to the words he was hearing.

Geek. Nerd. Weird. Awkward.

Yeah, Owen not only heard the words being murmured but knew they were being used to describe him. It was even worse considering the students in the room were all interested in the same subject he was—astronomy. So even in a group of his peers, he was still the odd man out. He shrugged. He'd learned not to let the hurtful words land—to fester—but sometimes they stung a little.

Okay, a lot.

Packing up his satchel, he kept his head down as the class of two hundred students made their way out. Or escaped. Maybe that was the better word for it. He didn't make eye contact with any of them—he simply went about his task of collecting his papers and belongings so the next instructor could come in and set up on time. He was nothing if not polite and conscientious.

His phone beeped to indicate a new text, and he couldn't help but smile when he pulled out his phone and saw it was from his twin brother, Riley.

Skype. Tonight. 8 your time.

Refusing to acknowledge how once again he and his brother were in sync with one another—Riley loved to say it was because they were twins—Owen was at the very least grateful for the timing. There were just times when he needed to talk to someone—or, more specifically, Riley—and there he was.

And the more he commented on it, the more Riley would go on about twin telepathy.

It was ridiculous.

As a man of science, there was no way Owen could accept the phenomenon as fact. Coincidence? Yes. Fact? No. His phone beeped again with a second text from Riley.

Whatever you're stressing about, we'll discuss.

He read the text and chuckled. "Nope," he murmured. "It was just a coincidence."

The last of the students exited the lecture hall as he slipped the phone back into his satchel, and Owen relished the silence. This was how he preferred things— quiet. Peaceful. He enjoyed his solitude, and if it were at all possible, he'd stick to speaking at strictly a few select conferences and then spend the rest of the day doing research and mapping the night sky.

"Excuse me," a soft, feminine voice said.

His entire body froze, and he felt his mouth go dry. Looking up, Owen saw her. Up close, she was even more beautiful. Long blond hair, cornflower-blue eyes, and a smile that lit up her entire face. And that light was shining directly at him.

She wore a long, gauzy skirt with a white tank top.

There was a large portfolio case hanging over her shoulder, along with the sweater she'd obviously chosen to do without in the too-warm classroom, and multiple bangle bracelets on her arm.

Gypsy.

No. That wasn't the right word. Gypsies were more of the dark-haired variety and wore a lot of makeup. This woman was too soft and delicate and feminine to meet that description.

Nymph.

Yes. That was definitely more fitting, and if he were the kind of man who believed there were such things, that's what he would have categorized her as.

He couldn't form a single word.

Her expression turned slightly curious. "Hi. Um... Dr. Shaughnessy?"

She was looking for him? Seriously? Swallowing hard, Owen tried to speak—he really did—but all he could do was nod.

The easy smile was back. Her hand fluttered up to her chest as she let out a sigh of relief. "I'm so sorry for showing up so close to the end of your class. It was inconsiderate of me. I meant to be here earlier. Well, I was supposed to be here for the entire lecture, but I lost track of time talking to Mr. Kennedy." She looked at him as if expecting him to know who she was talking about. "He's the head of the art department," she clarified.

Again, all he could do was nod. He cleared his throat too, but it didn't help.

"Anyway, I'm supposed to meet my uncle here— Howard Shields. He suggested I come and listen to you speak. He thinks very highly of you and thought I'd enjoy your lecture."

Seriously? Howard Shields thought someone would *enjoy* hearing him talk about meteor showers? That wasn't the normal reaction Owen received from his talks. Informative? Educational? Yes. Enjoyable? Never.

Not sure how he should respond, he offered her a small smile and felt a flush cover him from the tips of his toes to the roots of his hair. She was probably regretting listening to her uncle. As it was, she was looking at him expectantly.

"Anyway," she said, her voice still pleasant and friendly, "Uncle Howard talks about you all the time, and when he told me you were in Chicago guest lecturing, I knew I had to come and meet you. My uncle really respects your work."

Owen finally met her gaze head-on because her words struck him. It was no secret that Owen looked up to Howard—he'd been a mentor to Owen for as long as he could remember—but to hear it wasn't all one-sided? Well, it meant the world to him.

Most people in his field looked at Owen a little oddly. It wasn't because he didn't know what he was talking about or that he wasn't respected; it was because of his social skills. Or lack thereof. It seemed to overshadow all of his fieldwork, research, and teachings. He was more well-known for being painfully shy than anything else. He was filled with a sense of relief—and pride—to know that Howard had said something nice about him.

And now he also knew he was going to have to speak.

"Um...thank you," he said softly, feeling like his

mouth was full of marbles. When he saw her smile broaden, it made him want to smile too.

So he did.

But he had a feeling it wasn't nearly as bright or as at ease as hers.

"Ah, there you are!" They both turned and saw Howard walk into the room, his white lab coat flowing slightly behind him. "I was on my way here and was sidetracked talking with Dr. Lauria about the waiting list for the telescope." He shook his head. "Students are up in arms over the lack of availability."

Owen nodded but remained silent.

"I see you've met my niece, Brooke," Howard said before leaning over and kissing her on the cheek.

"We haven't been formally introduced," she said shyly, turning back to Owen.

"Well, let's rectify that," Howard said, grinning. "Owen Shaughnessy, I'd like you to meet my niece, Brooke Matthews. Brooke, this is Dr. Owen Shaughnessy."

Her smile looked so genuine as she held out her hand to Owen. "Feel free to make fun," she said.

Owen looked at her oddly. "Fun?"

Her head tilted slightly. "Yeah…you know. Because of my name."

Now he was confused. "I'm sorry," he said nervously, "is there something funny about the name *Brooke*?"

Howard laughed out loud and clapped Owen on the shoulder again as he shook his head. "Don't mind him, Brookie. He doesn't get pop culture references."

Pop culture references? Owen looked back and forth between the two of them for some sort of explanation. Then he realized Brooke's hand was still outstretched, waiting for him to take it. Quickly wiping his palm on his slacks, he took her hand in his and gave it a brief shake. He murmured an apology and averted his gaze before stepping back.

Tucking her hair behind her ear, she nodded. "My parents named me after Brooke Matthews, the model." When he still didn't react, she added, "She's also an actress." Still nothing. Looking at her uncle, she shrugged and let out a nervous chuckle. "Well, anyway…um, Uncle Howard, I'm afraid I was late to Dr. Shaughnessy's class."

Howard placed an arm around her and hugged her. "I knew pointing you in the direction of the art department was going to be a problem." He chuckled and turned to Owen. "Brooke is an artist and looking to either intern here at the university or maybe get a lead on a gallery where she can work and perhaps get her paintings looked at." He smiled lovingly at her. "She teaches painting classes during the summer semester at the community college, but she's far too talented to keep doing it."

"Uncle Howard," she said shyly.

"What? It's true!"

Owen still couldn't quite figure out why Brooke was here or why Howard had thought she should come to hear him lecture. He was just about to voice the question when Howard looked at him.

"Brooke's specialty is painting the night sky."

For a moment, Owen wasn't sure how to respond.

Brooke blushed and then looked at Owen to explain. "I know most people would say the night sky is simply dark—or black—with some stars, but I don't see it that way. I see the way the stars reflect off one another and how it causes different hues in the sky." She gave a small shrug. "Most of the time my work is a little more… Well, it's not abstract, but it's more whimsical than a true portrait."

"Don't just tell him about it," Howard suggested. "You have your portfolio with you. Why don't you show him?"

"Oh!" Brooke turned and took the leather case from her shoulder and laid it on the desk in front of her.

Owen watched in fascination as she worked, noting her slender arms and the music that came from her wrists as her bracelets gently clattered together. Her long hair fell over one shoulder, and it was almost impossible to take his eyes off her.

"I hope we're not keeping you, Owen," Howard said, stepping closer. "I probably should have asked you earlier about your schedule before we both sort of bombarded you like this."

He shook his head. "I…I don't have anything else scheduled for this afternoon. I had planned on heading back to the hotel and doing some reading before dinner. I'll talk with Riley later." Howard and Owen had known each other for so long that he didn't need to specify anything regarding his family—Howard knew all about them.

"How's he doing? Is he back in the studio yet?"

"Not yet. He didn't want to do another solo project, but getting the band back together isn't going as smoothly as he'd hoped."

Hands in his pockets, Howard nodded. "That's too bad. Still…I'm sure the time off is enjoyable. How is Savannah doing?"

Owen smiled at the mention of his sister-in-law.

"She's doing well. She found an agent, and she's submitting proposals for a book she's been working on."

"Wonderful! Is it based on her work interviewing rock stars?"

Beside them, Brooke straightened and gasped.

"Are you okay, my dear?" Howard asked.

But Brooke was looking directly at Owen. "You're Riley Shaughnessy's brother," she said. It wasn't a question but a simple statement of fact.

A weary sigh was Owen's immediate response. This was how it normally went—not that it happened very often. At least not to him. But he heard from his other brothers what usually occurred when a woman found out they were related to Riley. And it wasn't as if Owen knew Brooke or was involved with her, but he braced himself for the disappointment of knowing that from this point on, she was probably only going to want to talk about his famous brother.

And for the first time in a long time—possibly since high school—he resented his twin.

Might as well get it over with.

Clearing his throat, Owen nodded. "Um…yes. Riley's my brother."

Brooke nodded, her smile just as sweet as it had been since she walked into the lecture hall. "How fascinating! I mean, I think it is, anyway, to see such diversity in a family."

And here it comes, he thought.

"You're both so talented but in such different occupations. Your parents must be incredibly proud of you both!" Then she turned and straightened her pictures.

Wait…that was it? She wasn't going to obsess or go

on and on about how talented Riley was or how much she loved his latest song?

"So let me ask you," she began as she turned to face him, and Owen braced himself again. Now she was going to do it. Now she was going to gush. "What colors do you see when you look up at the night sky? Do you just see black, or do you see different shades of blue?"

He stared at Brooke.

Hard.

And his jaw was quite possibly on the floor.

"Owen?" Howard asked, stepping forward. "Are you all right?"

"Oh…um. Yes. Yes. You were going to show me your paintings," he said nervously, and he stepped forward to take a look.

And was rendered speechless.

Not that it was hard to do—Owen was already a man of few words—but the canvases Brooke had strewn across the desk were nothing like he was expecting.

The colors were bold and bright, and made with large brushstrokes. He thought of Van Gogh's painting *The Starry Night* and admired how she had layered the paint.

He stepped closer to the desk, picked up the closest painting, and studied it. This one was darker—it portrayed gravitational waves—and Brooke had managed to capture all of the light and the colors, and make it feel as if you could reach into the painting and touch the stars. It was brilliant. It was compelling. It was… He put it down and picked up the next one. A shooting star. It was a little more whimsical than the previous one, but the colors were just as vibrant, and looking at it made Owen feel as if he were looking through his telescope and watching the stars fly across the night sky.

"So what do you…?"

He placed the painting down—ignoring Brooke's attempt at a question—and picked up the third painting. This was the one that reminded him of Van Gogh. This had depth, texture. Owen wasn't in the least bit artistic, but he knew what he was looking at was amazing. Gently he ran his hand over the canvas, taking in the feel of the paint, and was mesmerized. How many times had he wished he could reach out and touch the sky, to feel the heat of a star and study its contours? And standing here now, that was exactly what he felt he was doing. Unable to help himself, he looked at Brooke with wonder. "This is…amazing." And then he wanted to curse himself because that description didn't do her work justice.

And yet she looked pleased.

Relieved.

Her hand fluttered up over her chest as she let out a happy sigh. "Thank you. I know they're all different. I'm trying to find the style that calls to me the most and reflects how I'm feeling, but they all do. It sort of depends on the night. Does that make sense?"

Owen had no idea if it did or it didn't—he certainly had never tried this medium, so who was he to judge? But he was still confused. What did her artwork have to do with him? And again, as if reading his mind, Howard spoke.

"Brooke's favorite subject is nature—particularly the night sky and sunsets, that sort of thing. She's been talking about wanting to go out to the desert and paint, and I immediately thought of you and the Nevada project."

It still didn't make sense to him. "The Nevada project?" Owen parroted. "But…that's to watch the meteor shower, and it's for students and undergrads. I…I don't understand."

Beside them, Brooke cleared her throat and began collecting her paintings. "I should probably let the two of you talk," she murmured. "I thought it was already—"

Howard cut her off. "I meant to discuss this with Owen sooner, but our schedules haven't quite matched up. You don't need to leave, Brooke. It's good that you're here and we can go over it together."

Nodding, she continued to put her things away and then stood back silently while her uncle explained his idea.

"I fully support Brooke's work and her desire to experience different places to paint. But her heading off to the desert alone just isn't practical or safe. Her mother has some…issues, and Brooke is willing to respect them for the moment. So she needs to go with a group."

Nodding in agreement, Owen offered a suggestion. "Perhaps she could find painters interested in doing the same thing. Make it an artist's retreat." That was a thing, wasn't it?

"I want you to hear me out, Owen. I have a proposition for you."

Dread sank like a lead weight in his belly.

Acknowledgments

A handful of years ago, before I joined the writing community, I took my first stab at drafting this story. Thankfully, as I honed my novel-writing skills in workshops and at conferences, these characters kept inviting me back into revision-land. Finally, I had a shareable manuscript. That was when the big improvements began. As they say, it takes a village…and this village has my gratitude.

I'd like to first thank the amazing publishing team at Sourcebooks Casablanca who helped my long-held dream become a reality. This includes my talented editor, Deb Werksman, who fell in love with this project and offered the encouragement and insight needed to make it stronger, as well as her supportive team including Susie Benton, Laura Costello, and Emily Chiarelli, and my amazing publicist, Stefani Sloma.

My heartfelt gratitude goes to my wonderful rescue-dog-loving agent, Jess Watterson, for believing in me and in this manuscript, and to Amanda Heger for her invaluable advice, encouragement, and support. Thanks to Sandy Thal for beta reading more versions of this story than there were fingers on one hand, and to my dear friends, who are too many to name individually, but who've read my stories and who've been cheerleaders throughout this journey.

And of course my deepest appreciation goes to my

family. To my mom and dad for their unlimited support. To Eldar for being the first person to believe in me when I said I wanted to write a book. And last, but never least, to my kids, Emily and Ryan, who could have found reason to doubt this dream over the years and never did. When it comes to a matchup between "the odds" and the little voice inside you, never forget which one to listen to.

About the Author

Debbie Burns resides in St. Louis, Missouri. *A New Leash on Love* is her first contemporary romance and has been a finalist in multiple contests. Her writing commendations include first-place awards for short stories, flash fiction, and longer selections from the Missouri RWA and the Missouri Writers' Guild. You can find her on Twitter @_debbieburns, on Facebook at www.facebook.com/authordebbieburns, and at her website, www.authordebbieburns.com.